Hunting

NoK

Hunting

NoK

Shaun W. Curry

Contact author on:

talk2shaunc@gmail.com

follow on twitter @shaunwcurry

This book is dedicated to my partner Audrey who put up with my fixated obsessions, gave me support, confidence, a plethora of great ideas and who made sure I didn't get 'hangry' by feeding me when I forgot to eat.

I would also like to thank to Philip and Harry who are a rare breed indeed … honest friends.

A special thanks goes to Frances who, when my command of English reached its limit, took this work to the next level.

All your input was greatly valued.

Morality is for those who can afford it.

Prologue

For what it's worth

The moral question

Illegal drugs account for around 750,000 deaths a year. Some of these are direct deaths, from overdose, and others indirect deaths through illness or related activities like murder. Rough estimates indicate that, around 150,000 die from overdoses, another 500,000 die from related illness and a possible 100,000 die from drug related murders.

Shocking, isn't it?

But how does the damage done by illegal drugs compare to the ills inflicted by the state legislated drug of choice, alcohol.

Alcohol is responsible for around 3,000,000 deaths per year. This represents about 5.3% of all deaths and 13.5% of deaths in the 20 – 39 age bracket. Alcohol is a causal factor in over 200 diseases, and in total is responsible for around 5.1% of the global burden of disease.

These basic figures don't even take into consideration alcohol related injuries, violence, associated mental health problems.

So how about one for the road before you mount your moral high horse and ride off into the sunset.

Outrage

How you view the risk posed by illegal drugs as opposed to the risk caused by alcohol all depends on how you view risk; obvious, perhaps not. Risk is a factor of likelihood and severity; the more likely it is something will happen coupled with the severity of the potential outcome constitutes the risk. When people consider drugs, however, the likelihood and severity equation subtly changes. Risk no longer becomes a factor of likelihood and severity; it becomes a factor of severity and outrage.

Outrage is at its most apparent in the arena of politics. The public love it, it's a real vote winner. Dead is an absolute state, whether the cause is drugs or alcohol, it cannot get any more severe. When then did you last see a politician stand up and make an impassioned speech about fighting a 'war' on the dealers in alcohol when a 19-year-old chokes on their own vomit? When did you last see the front page of a newspaper taken up with someone dying of cirrhosis of the liver after a lifetime of alcohol abuse? But have one pretty girl die of dehydration because she was dancing too much after taking ecstasy … now that's front-page news, that's outrageous!

We should all know by now the damage to society caused by alcohol, but would you back it being banned? Well of course not, because you're a moderate user, a responsible social drinker. Why should the minority who can't control themselves spoil the pleasure of millions of people like you? Who wants to live in a nanny state?

Regardless of the damage it does to society, it seems the hard reality is this, banning alcohol is by far more socially outrageous than dying from it.

Morals are up to you, this is the business

End of year accounts

Illicit drugs global GDP:	$1 trillion
Global economic burden of illicit drugs:	$300 - 500 billion *
Alcohol global GDP:	$1.4 trillion
Global economic burden of alcohol:	$400 - 700 billion

*see 'The war' to account for 100 billion of this figure.

The trade in illegal drugs constitutes around 1.2% of all global trade. The majority of illicit profits are absorbed directly into the legitimate economy. It has been speculated that during the global depression of 2008 the liquid capital from laundered drug money became an essential factor in interbank loans which rescued many businesses from collapse.

The drugs trade, like any other business, is subject to market forces, it balances demand and supply with risk and reward. And in the economy of recreational escapism demand is high, supply relatively easy, risk acceptable and rewards phenomenal. Faced with this economic environment is it any wonder business is booming.

The war

The War on Drugs costs an estimated $100 billion a year. For an investment of this magnitude, the powers that be need to show they're delivering a return on investment in order to justify their existence. Battle victories are well publicised, headlines such as *"heroin with a street value of $2,000,000 seized and a ring of four hardened drugs barons arrested,"* makes for reassuring reading. In reality this press coverage is little more than a publicity stunt designed to combat public fear and mask the futility of the enterprise. The actual seizure rate for illegal drugs is around 1%. For serious importers and exporters, the war on drugs is regarded as nothing more than an unofficial tax. And at a rate of 1% any businessman would be happy to carry on trading.

Also consider the estimated recovery value of $2,000,000 - how do they know? The mark up on heroin is anywhere between 1,300% and 2,300%. It all depends on how many times it is cut, how many hands it passes through before it gets to the end user. And of course, let's not to forget which part of the country you sell it in. The retail value being vastly different if sold in Knightsbridge as opposed to Jaywick.

The average law enforcement officer has no more idea how much the mark up is on the drugs they confiscate any more than the average production line worker knows how much it costs to build the cars they assemble. And as for the hardened criminals, well they may be criminals and they may be hard, but they are rarely the brains of the operation.

When dealing with serious importers and exporters of recreational pharmaceuticals you will never find a zip sealed plastic bags behind a cistern. You will never detect residue on a rolled-up bank note stuffed in the back pocket and you will never find unaccounted for money under the bed.

Authorities may know who's behind the scenes pulling the strings, but they can rarely prove it. Most businessmen do clean business. You will never have heard of them, and they will never see the inside of a court let alone a prison cell.

The authorities may win the occasional skirmish on drugs, but the war will always be lost!

The art of the deal

There are two main types of transaction, regular supply with a trusted source and established trade routes, good solid bread and butter income. Then, if the pot's sweet enough, there is the one-off hit. Both business models carry their own unique risk profile.

With regular supply the risks are largely front loaded. It's in the setup, establishing relationships and building infrastructure. Once the groundwork is done, business moves into safer water. You know where your product's coming from, who it's coming from, the quality is assured, and the route is lubricated.

Everything can be accounted for, even down to factoring in stock loss due to intervention by the authorities.

The one-off deal is a far riskier business, lots of unknown factors who, what, where, when? Lots of questions with only partial answers. As a rule, people who proffer a sweet one-off deal can't be trusted. If they have enough merchandise at a bargain price to tempt you, then they will have rarely come into possession of it honestly. But if you have the heart for it a lot of money can be made picking one-off fruits.

Whether it's the setting up of steady business or a one-off hit, deals are all about minimising risk. Conducting transactions are nothing like films would have you believe. I'm sure everyone is familiar with cliché, the heads of two organisations meet in an abandoned warehouse, each side with half a dozen heavily armed henchmen, drugs in one car, money in the other.

This never happens. More people, more chance of a security breach, equals more chance of being caught. And seriously, why would the top man be there? Is any intelligent businessman going to put himself in a position where he could be either killed or get life in prison?

At the risky ends of business, the set ups and the one-offs, personnel is kept to a minimum, ideally one highly trusted, highly skilled operative.

That's where I come in.

Alex Whyte

I

Bangkok today

Just call me Jerry

The air was heavy with a cacophony of aromas. The smell of sweating vegetation, sizzling street food and unwashed bodies, underwritten with the soft base note of an inefficient sewage system. Lacing all of this together was the thin silver ribbon of jasmine. Alex loved jasmine. It seemed to be the perfume that stitched this country together; from the Golden Temple to the throbbing night club, from the 7 - 11 to the lowest 2am streetwalker. Jasmine, dew sweet and seductive. It was the smell he fell in love with seven years ago when he first stepped out of the sterile world of an air-conditioned taxi and onto the glistening streets of Bangkok. The whole effect of this olfactory noise should have been nauseating, but Alex revelled in it. He imagined that this was what it must be like to have synaesthesia. It filled his senses, he no longer just smelt it, he tasted it, he heard it, he could almost see it. He stopped for a moment closed his eyes and took a deep breath. It took him back, back to a time, a time when … STOP!

'No time for that now, no time for a trip down memory lane,' he pulled back from this indulgence to bring himself into the moment, 'Now is the time for Now! Nostalgia is the grave of those dead in the present' and Alex needed to focus on the present.

He cut on through the heavy humid air, which held him in the firm grip of its left hand, while its watery right hand ran over every inch of his body. It had only been an hour since he last showered, but already, he felt like he needed to do so again. He stopped thirty metres from the hotel and watched. The garish red, green and blue of the nearby neon signs reflected in puddles at his feet, still fresh and fulsome from the recent down pour. They advertised everything from cheap children's clothing, to a *"very good massage by professional lady or a beautiful young man"*. All around was animated. Children sold flowers to leather faced ex pats sitting with girls thirty years their junior, some girls feigning interest, whilst others barely concealed the distain they felt for their preying company. Stall holders plied their wares - tee-shirts, silks, watches, sunglasses - tee-shirts, silks, watches, sunglasses - tee-shirts … the stalls seemed to repeat themselves in an endless variation on a theme. Like the ever-repeating backgrounds in a cartoon chase scene *"same, same but different"* as the local saying went.

Alex examined closely the hotel across the street, 'The Grand Plaza Hotel'. Back in the U.K. he was deeply suspicious of hotels that called themselves 'The Grand' or 'The Royal'. It

2

always reminded him of the imposing Edwardian mausoleums lining the seafront of Great Yarmouth. Their names bellowing unashamedly to the world of the luxury they provided for the affluent clientele they once entertained. Built for a time when gentle folk promenaded to escape the miasma of the city and take the restorative ozone of the coast. But now barely whispering adequate through peeling paint and threadbare carpets.

Here, in a city like this the nomenclature 'Grand' had no such baggage. Developed Bangkok was too young, too brash for that. Here 'Grand' meant grand and that was modern, well-polished steel, solar controlled glass and a nod to colonialisms with a porter in a red frock coat and deadman top hat. Attire that may have been practical outside The Strand in London in January. But here in Thailand it just looked uncomfortably hot.

Alex had been watching this place for five days now and everything was as it had always been … good. The carriers had arrived about half an hour ago. A little heavy handed, three of them, but not unmanageable for him. Their whole demeanour had been too obvious he thought, more in the shop window than in the shop. This boded well for him. He still wondered what Korean's were doing trading in Thailand. Most Asian countries had the death penalty for drugs trafficking; operating in these geographical areas was a specialism that few had the stomach for. Why would they

3

have come out of their own country to trade? Unnecessary movement only increased risk. Alex had traded with Korean's before, but always in Korea.

In his initial conversations he had touched upon this with his contact. The vagueness of the answers had led Alex to the conclusion that their change of country had not been by choice. The whole set up reeked of lucky amateurs peddling stolen goods for which they only knew a fraction of their true value.

At that moment, a yellow meter cab pulled up. A mound of nicotine-stained fat wound down the window. Alex remembered reading somewhere that experts were reassessing the range of normal body mass index for Asians, as generally they carried a higher proportion of body fat than westerners. This driver's mass skewed the mean for half a dozen of his fellow countrymen.

'Taxi meter, Mr,' slobbered the mound.

The grubby steering wheel cut into his gut where it had left a dirty line across his once blue shirt. He craned his neck, if a dewlap of fat below the chin could be described as a neck, to look out of the window.

'No, no taxi,' …

Alex pulled himself up, *'shit! Not English, not on this job'*, on this job he was German.

'Where you go?' the fat man came back.

4

His blubbery, purple veined lips seemed to move independently of the words, like in some cheap spaghetti western. Purple lips, heart condition. You could take this guy out with a fright, it would be quite a kind end, unlike some of the ways Alex had finished jobs.

'Ilch brauche kein Taxi,' Alex replied.

He had been studying German for only nine months but already he had become pretty fluent. In Germany no one would be fooled by his accent, but here, in Thailand, as long as they thought it was some Scandinavian country it didn't really matter. It was details such as these that would confuse the trail of any investigation to come.

Alex discovered that he had an unexpected talent for learning languages and over the last seven years he had become fluent in five and picked up the rudiments of several more. In that time this talent had served him well, as foreigners invariably believed they could talk freely in front of the English safe in the knowledge that they were linguistically lazy.

German or English the fat driver was not to be turned away so easily.

'Today all taxi half price, today government day, you Norwegian, Norsk?'

Norwegian, not bad close enough, however, the devil is in the detail.

'Nein auf Deutsh … German,' Alex clarified.

Jabba pressed on.

'You want lady?'

A thin string of clear saliva escaped from the corner of his wet mouth as he pulled a stained well-thumbed picture post-card out of his back pocket. The manoeuvre was a sight to behold and seemed to require some considerable physical exertion. Beads of sweat formed on his temples and ran down to his dewlap. The card was an advert for some fun-filled massage parlour with a picture of various girls rubbing each other with foam. Alex had seen a thousand pictures like this. They were the same from the top to the bottom of the country. Same girls same settings, just the address in the bottom right-hand corner changed. Alex thought there must be a factory somewhere churning these out $24 - 7$, supplying every whore house, taxi driver and bar in Thailand.

'I get you good deal, pretty lady, or if you like Kathoey, you choose, I help you find,' persisted the mound with a lecherous smile.

This man had wasted too much time. Alex made a few err and ah noises, as if searching his limited vocabulary for the right English words to put into play. Then leaning forward, thrusting his face through the open window found the universal phrase instantly decipherable in every language on earth …

'FUCK OFF!' he proffered with the appropriately accentuated vowels.

It was immediately clear the message had got through. Offended that his offer to be the official guide for a 'good time' had been so rudely rejected Jabba babbled something in Thai, wound up his window and pulled off; only to pull up less than twenty metres away where he started the same conversation with another faceless farang. Although Alex only managed to catch one or two words of his parting tirade, he knew he had not been wished a good night.

It was time for Alex to move. He had been standing watching for longer than was necessary and he didn't want to attract any more attention. Taking his life into his own hands he dodged the traffic and crossed the street to the hotel entrance. As he did, he pulled his mobile from his inside pocket and started a one-sided conversation in German with the dead handset. He had learned enough of the language to talk about oil and getting engineers for a new asset. Nobody bothered a man on his phone. A man on a phone looked like he belonged and a man talking business was important. A phone could also obscure one side of a face without looking suspicious and Alex knew which side the security camera was on. He trotted up the few marble steps to the large glass doors. The overly hot porter opened the door for him with a deferential smile and a nod.

'Danke schön,' said Alex in passing.

He strode across the expansive reception, his leather soled brogues tapping their way across the white marble. The décor was no-taste Nouveau riche. Too much gold and too much glass with a large feature fountain in the shape of a fish sitting smack in the middle foyer. The lobby was open plan, with sitting areas and waiter service, typical for this type of hotel. Several casually smart men sat with coffee and computers pushing various pieces of paper between them. It was all very beige. Alex's 'uniform' of chino trousers, brown brogues, open checked shirt and light linen jacket blended in perfectly with the general profile of the clientele. And the case in his hand could easily be carrying a seismic survey of a potential oil reserve or the figures from some latest market transaction.

A young couple checking in momentarily caught his attention. They didn't look like guest material for a hotel like this, young surfing types in their early twenties. The girl wore a vest and baggy tie dye trousers, a head scarf held back long auburn hair that had not seen a brush for several weeks. The boy had blond shoulder length hair with cargo shorts and an evolution of man tee-shirt, charting the progression from ape to diver. He was short and slim with almost feminine features. Their baggage consisted of two back packs that looked older than their combined age. The girl was beautiful, very beautiful. Her light green vest was wet with sweat that had yet to be dried by the air-conditioning. It was tight and showed every serpentine curve of her perfectly formed body. She stood at reception and with her arms above her head drying herself in front of the fan on the counter. As she did her top rode up leaving a six-inch gap of flawless skin at the base of her spine. Peeking out of the top of her baggy trousers Alex could see the beginnings of a tattoo. The girl was attracting quite a lot of discrete middle-aged attention. As diversionary tactics go, she could not have been better. With her to look at Alex was virtually invisible.

He made his way to the elevator and pressed the button, with the second knuckle of his left-hand index finger, minimising trace evidence. As he did, he caught sight of himself in the smoked bronze mirrored doors. The Alex Whyte that looked back was a very different Alex Whyte to the one of seven years ago when he'd made his first trip to this city. His once lean 6ft 2' figure was at least fifty or sixty pounds heavier. Most of it was useful and carried across the shoulders but there was just enough spare weight to fill out his cheeks and bring a roundness to the jaw line that was never there in the angular features of his youth. It was Viv who had taught him the value of carrying a bit of weight. Alex could hear his words now delivered in his own indomitable style.

"What's the use of being able to run, even fuckin' Linford, 'what's his name' Bolt can't outrun a bullet. Fighting with the

9

fists is a mugs game son, a lot of it can be avoided just by looking the part. But if your back's against the wall, there's no substitute for a bit of weight."

Alex studied himself as he waited for the elevator to arrive. His distinctive red hair was heavily streaked with grey and shaved into stage six male pattern baldness. A four-week beard masked his chin. Coupled with a pair of gold rimmed spectacles the whole effect added at least fifteen years to his age. His newly receding hairline had further exposed the thin silvery line of a scar that cut high up on his head and ran down to just above his right eye where it terminated in a sharp right angle. Even though he had spent twenty minutes trying to cover it up with foundation he could still make it out. He remembered the night the skin had peeled back like a flap to reveal the white dome of his skull beneath. Without makeup the scar was livid purple which became tight and throbbed in the cold. It was a memento he'd picked up on his third job and was a potent visual reminder never to feel pity for anyone, ever! Viv said it had been a cheap lesson … Viv said a lot of things.

The lift arrived, the doors opened, and he stepped into the muzak of Akker Bilk played on the pan pipes, 'Strangers on the Shore', well why not, he thought. Luck was on his side, no one came out and no one got in with him. He pressed the button for the ninth floor and closed his eyes to envisage what could be waiting for him. During his fighting days he had come to understand the power of visualisation. Start with the end in mind and then project multiple paths to your destination. Walk down each of them in detail. Know the terrain, always have an entry and exit point. These people were lucky amateurs of that he was sure, he had suspected that from the very first telephone conversation. They were selling 800,000 GBP wholesale for 250,000 USD. With that sort of transaction, it's all about economies of scale. You have to have a warehouse full of product and be in an established relationship in order to offer those sorts of bargain basement prices. Then there was the set up "How do you want to play it?" they had asked. If you produce on that scale, you don't ask the buyer how they want to play it, you tell them your game plan. No one had specified how they wanted the currency, "we want dollars" was all they had said; no indication of denominations, new, used, non-consecutive numbers, nothing. And there was never any mention of transfers through a legitimate front company. The last clue was the place of exchange. This hotel was flash, just too flash. In places like this the staff are paid to be attentive, to follow you around, to take care of your every need, in short to notice you. When you have delicate business to do, the last thing you want is to be is noticed. Middle of the road was always best, always do normal and middle of the road. But still that

11

amount of potential fine grade was a lot of luck, so Alex was not going to underestimate the opposition. It was his job to end their lucky streak tonight.

He considered his targets, three men, two younger and an older 'little Napoleon'. One of the younger men was heavy set, the other tall and edgy looking. They were the muscle, no doubt hired for visual impact, but probably knew little about the trade. Then there was the holder of the goods, old and flabby. His over inflated attitude writing cheques that Alex doubted his ability could cash.

The numbers clicked above his head, illuminated in Times New Roman. His hand tightened around the handle of the case at his side which contained $250,000 in well circulated currency. He had no immediate intentions of parting with it that night, but sometimes if the odds were bad, too bad, he actually had to pay. Alex had always lived by the old Samurai adage *"A fool can die any day"*. The number one objective of any transaction was to come back alive, and Alex always ensured he stacked the odds heavily in his favour. 90% of the time both the merchandise and the money came back. This secured a double cut for him, a percentage of the street value of the goods and a percentage of the returned capital.

As he stood counting the ascending numbers the anticipation of what was to come began to make his senses tingle. This was pre-engagement excitement. Excitement was good as it prepared the body for action, but if not controlled right it carried the danger of overwhelming the mind with a wave of adrenaline. The fourth floor clicked by, and Alex focused on centering himself. He could afford the luxury of unfettered excitement once the job was complete.

The number nine pinged and the doors slid open. The corridor ahead was painted ivory with ash flooring edged in ebony. Geometric up-lighting cast angular shadows across the walls. The style was trying, but just failing, to evoke the style of Art deco. Not bad, but totally destroyed by large works of inoffensive art hung at regular intervals between the bedroom doors. The mistake was one of cultural knowledge. Chat Noir, Toulouse Lautrec, Renoir and Degas, about two or three generations too early, not the sort of thing that should adorn the walls of a 20's, 30's deco purist.

He walked down the corridor the tingling he felt inside now replaced with a focused calm. He found his inner fighter and had to live it until the curtain fell on this deal. He stood outside the door, room 936, slowly closed his eyes and had one final run through of several possible scenarios. When the time came, he wouldn't have the luxury of thought, his actions must guide themselves. 5 deepen breath, 4 muscles relax, 3 centre the moment, 2 mind clear, 1 knock!

The door opened. It was the stockier of the two bodyguards. Short black hair, about twenty-seven, thirty maybe. His angular face, which had a surprisingly child-like countenance, was held up by a big bull neck. Beneath the cheap Tarentinoesque suit, Alex could see a deep broad chest which narrowed to a tight waist. His hands were thick and vascular with calloused, distended knuckles. Although he was a good six inches shorter than Alex, he must have been of a comparable weight and there didn't seem to be a lot of excess baggage. He had to go first and quickly. He held Alex's eye just long enough to feel uncomfortable before, without a word, stepping aside and motioning him into the room. As the door closed behind him Alex quickly scanned his surroundings. Twin beds, table, chair, TV cabinet. Functional, simple and spacious, plenty of room for someone to get behind him. He somehow needed to keep the Bull in front of him, can't have a man this size at his back. The other hired hand was in his early twenties, he stood with his back to the voile veiled window. The diffused light from outside providing him with a warm neon halo. Although he was taller than the Bull, he was much thinner, with deep set eyes and sallow sunken cheeks. He was visibly nervous. His breathing was irregular, shallow and the forefinger of his left hand was desperately trying to rub the skin from his thumb. His eyes darted all over Alex never finding a resting point, but looking like they weren't actually taking anything in. This man was as tight as a bowstring, twitchy. Alex knew that nervousness could be more

14

dangerous than power. Power usually had direction; fear can shoot off anywhere … Still on balance Alex thought it best to stick to the game plan unless circumstances dictate otherwise, the Bull would go first! Both men wore identical suits. On the Bowstring, however, it looked more like the suit was wearing him. There must have been a two for one offer that day, but there was only one size available, and that size wasn't his.

Alex's contact, a Mr 'just call me Jerry' as he had insisted on being addressed, sat in a chair on the opposite side of the bed. He was a waxen faced man in his late fifties. He had the sort of pallor that shouted sick to the bone and although his frame was slight, no more than 120 pounds, he had flaccid features and a double chin. Dark, heavy bags hung under his brow shadowed eyes. Incubating on the right-hand side of his face was a mole the size of a broad bean, livid and purple, brown. It sprouted a dozen or so course black hairs, none of them under six inches long. The ability to grow hairs from this one spot was in vivid contrast to the rest of his face that appeared as though it had never had the need of a razor. He sat with his legs crossed and his head cocked to one side. Slowly and deliberately, he smoked a cigarette. It was an affected pose and it looked like he had rehearsed this scene many times to create the 'right' impression.

15

On the bed opposite was a purple and black holdall. It was the only baggage in the room and the only one Alex had observed them bringing with them. This must be the product. Alex decided to position his back to the wall with the bag and all the players in the game in front of him. Contrary to popular belief, when in a confined space facing the door in order to run should there be trouble was rarely a viable option. The split second it took to open a door was ample time for anyone to close in on you.

Just Jerry spoke first breaking the momentary silence.

'Ah Mr Zimmerman, eventually a face to the voice. Please,' he gestured towards the corner of the bed for Alex to sit.

'And you would be Mr Jerry I take it,' said Alex, more by way of a statement than a question.

He kept up the faint hint of the German accent that Just Jerry had been used to in their set up calls. Although Alex had no immediate intention of letting these men leave the room alive, you never knew, things could change quickly. He offered his hand in greeting. The thought of actually touching the homunculus didn't exactly fill Alex with warmth. As he extended his hand to take Just Jerry's the Bull swiftly stepped forward and grabbed him round the sides. He brought his hands up sharply under Alex's armpits. Was this an assault? He prepared to fight. Just Jerry's words, however, were quick to quell the situation.

'Mr Zimmerman please, please no need for alarm, there is no harm meant here, Park,' he indicated to the Bull, 'simply needs to know none of us are in danger.'

Alex stopped his mental preparation and lifted his arms. The Bull proceeded with a cursory search. He patted his hands over Alex's shoulders, made a sweep down his sides and then spun him around to pat down his upper back. He finished with a firm cupping of Alex's testicles accompanied by an eye to eye thousand-mile stare. This last bit was obviously for effect, but who knows, Alex thought, he might just be a lonely and misunderstood boy. The examination was less than superficial, no waist band check, no legs, no lower back. One thing was for sure the Bull had never worked in security. Lack of training was a mistake that would cost him dear.

'I hope you understand Mr Zimmerman, the precautions are nothing personal. I do not know you.' said Just Jerry, as though this joke of a search had eradicated any threat Alex might pose.

'Of course, I'm sure you understand, I don't know you either,' Alex replied as he motioned to the Bull to lift his arms.

The Bull didn't move.

'I trust you are going to afford me the same caution,' Alex went on, 'you read such bad things in the papers these days.'

The Bull remained motionless.

17

Eventually Just Jerry interjected to break the tension. He spoke to Park in Korean.

'Let him Park, you can do what you want to him later.'

How many westerners understand Korean? Alex did, but he made no indication he had understood the exchange. So, it was later when they expected to make a move. What did they have in mind, put a tail on him, follow him down a back lane and Robert's your aunt Fanny's live-in lover! Alex would be put down as just another tourist who lost his way on the wrong side of town. Alternatively, were they going to do it here, in the room, once they had established he had the money?

'Up's a daisy big boy.'

Alex lifted the Bull's arms out to the side and proceeded with a thorough frisking. He was clean, chances were, they were planning to settle things outside the room. This was good now he could execute a pre-emptive strike. Alex ended his search by stopping his hand just over the Bull's crotch. The Bull's eyes never flinched.

'I wasn't thinking of bothering to search there, but if you want me too?' Alex smiled, Park didn't.

Park addressed Just Jerry in Korean.

'I'm doing this one right!'

Just Jerry subtly nodded and then speaking to Alex said,

'So now are we all satisfied we are safe Mr Zimmerman?'

'What about you and him?' said Alex looking to Just Jerry and the thin Bowstring.

With an air of reluctant indulgence, they undid their jackets and lifted their arms. Both were clean.

'Now shall we do business?' asked Just Jerry with an indignant sigh.

The Bull snatched the case from Alex's hand and threw it on the bed nearest the door. Clicking it open, he began to pull out bundles of notes thumbing through each one without actually counting. Despite not taking a full inventory he seemed to be happy with what he saw and gave Just Jerry the thumbs up.

'If you're good, is that mine?' asked Alex nodding to the purple and black holdall on the bed nearest to the twitching Bowstring.

The young man pushed the bag towards him and nodded. Alex opened it and pulled out one of the packages. Freezer bags tied at the top, seriously, it was not even well wrapped. Reaching into the inside pocket of his jacket he took out his chemical testing kit. One of the best tools in the trader's arsenal. For only $59.99 it could save you millions or even save your life. God bless some of the more liberal states of America, got to keep your junkies safe.

The kit was designed to stop the ever-increasing wave of OD deaths. The cultural myth is that people go on an all-night

19

bender and end up having one line too many or jacking up just that bit extra to take them higher. The other story is that their fix has been cut with some toxic substances such as rat poison. Truth is, it's rarely any of these scenarios that lead to an OD death. Take the size of the dose, any seasoned junky knows what it takes to get them where they want to be, and once you're at the top you can't really get any higher. It is true the body develops a certain amount of tolerance, but not enough to double a dose. Now there are dirty dealers out there who will pollute your fix with rat poison, but as for cutting, most drugs are cut with relatively benign bulking substances like talc or chalk. No dealer, who wants to keep their customers, leaves a string of dead bodies in their wake, that's just not good for business. What mostly kills is purity. One batch cut a few times providing that familiar high as compared to another batch passed down almost uncut: same dose but several grades purer. That's the high that will take you all the way to heaven.

Alex undid the top of one of the bags and harvested a spatula of the creamy powder and dropped it into the plastic test tube of liquid. He gave it a light shake. It turned a rich coffee colour. Comparing it to a colour chart he could see that it was almost 90% pure, more than he expected, a very pleasant surprise.

'Are you happy Mr Zimmerman?' enquired Just Jerry.

'More than happy Mr Jerry,' replied Alex.

'Then we have completed our business.'

Jerry gestured towards the door as if dismissing Alex from the room.

Alex sealed up the blue freezer bag and dropped it back into the backpack along with his chemical kit. Placing the bag behind him, he stood with his back to the wall and the three men in front of him. The twitching Bowstring to his left, Mr Just Jerry still sitting at the table in front of him and the Bull who had come round to the corner of the bed to his right ... perfect!

'Do you do this full time then?' Alex said.

Just Jerry's pug face wrinkled.

'Pardon?'

'This, do you do this full time, deal drugs and such?'

'I think what I do full time is not a concern of yours,' said Just Jerry dismissively

'Only trying to be friendly, get to know the people I am doing business with.'

'I think this is all the business we will be doing.'

At this Just Jerry turned his head away as if to indicate disengagement from the pleasantries.

'I didn't always do this you know,' Alex continued

'Really!'

There was an air of irritation beginning to enter Just Jerry's voice.

Alex disregarded it.

'Do you know what I used to be?'

Just Jerry shrugged his narrow shoulders and took another deliberate drag of his cigarette. The smoke lingered on his lips before curling round the greasy lock of thinning hair hanging over his pallid forehead. A forehead which was now flushed dappled red.

Alex went on watching every micro motion.

'I used to be a carpenter. I don't do it as a profession now though, this pretty much takes up all of my time, but I still like to keep my hand in, you know make the occasional thing out of wood … Our Lord used to be a carpenter you know.'

Just Jerry's eyes narrowed as he pulled his head back.

'Our lord?' he snorted.

'You know Jesus' Alex chirped.

Just Jerry curled his lip.

'He's not my lord Mr Zimmerman.'

The Bull was now starting to clench his gnarled fists. His blood was up and the veins on the back of his hand grew thick and blue. The Bowstring in the window was stretched so tight the colour drained from his face bleaching his gaunt features.

'Wood doesn't always get the full respect it deserves. When you cut down a tree, you're killing a living thing. A life that could be hundreds of years old. That deserves respect. The things you make from that life deserve respect,' Alex mused.

Silence hung in the air. Just Jerry was the first to make the verbal move.

'Mr Zimmerman I am not a Buddhist I don't give a fuck about the life of a tree.'

The first physical move was seconds away Alex slowed time and played the sequence of moves in his head.

One … The Bull, maximum damage two moves, watch him fall, leave him.

Two … The Bowstring, close the distance, three moves, time consuming but doable.

Three … Just Jerry, jammed in by the table, as he was, Alex knew he wouldn't have time to escape.

Alex continued.

'Do you know the best thing about wood is its depth, the movement of the grain, the patina, it keeps its life even when felled.'

Just Jerry looked up under his deep-set yellow eyes. Grinding his cigarette into the ash tray and licking his tight lips he said,

'Park, show him where the door is, we all have what we want.'

The Bull reached out to grab the skin on the back of Alex's arm, a painful move he knew worked well when escorting drunks from twenty-dollar strip clubs. As he closed in, Alex

23

slowly reached behind him as if to straighten his shirt but instead ripped out a four-inch wooden blade which he had carved to fit undetectably in the curve of his lower back. Before his hand could reach Alex's arm, the blade was buried deep in the side of his neck just behind his windpipe. A cocktail of shock, pain, anger and terror came over the Bull's face. Alex went to yank the knife forward to sever the oesophagus in preparation for his next move on the Bowstring. But something stopped him. The Bull's broad hand was wrapped around Alex's wrist preventing the knife from moving. He was staring at Alex with more life than he wanted to see at this stage. The Bull's other hand was now trying to reach for Alex's throat. This delay in the plan was enough time for the Bowstring to make his move. He dived in taking Alex's back, frantically fumbling to get him in a strangle hold. This was not good. Now Alex had a man at his front and his back. One had to go and quickly. Alex sharply brought his knee up and made a crunching contact with the Bull's genitals. No matter how big the man, this was always an irresistible distraction. He was relieved to know that the Bull was no exception. His grip slackened as the pain hit him, it was enough to create an opportunity. Alex pulled the blade forward and the Bull's singing career was over. It had all happened in the blink of an eye and before his second assailant could get anything more than a schoolboy head lock Alex

24

caught him with a reverse elbow to the temple. Then twisting 180 degrees Alex turned and plunged the knife into his chest, driving through his rib cage and into his heart. The young man slumped to the floor dead, the kindest kill of the two. The Bull stood for only a moment then toppled backwards hitting his head against the wall with a sickening crack. He sat bolt upright on the floor, a wet guttural sound coming from the maw that was now his neck. He attempted to inhale then to cough but could do neither. His eyes rolled back, his lips tried to mouth something, but no sound emerged other than a weak splutter. He committed himself horizontally to the carpet, still staring at Alex.

All this had taken at least four seconds longer than Alex had projected. Quickly he tried to regain his bearings and his game plan. He turned to Just Jerry. To Alex's utter astonishment he had not moved an inch. He sat his eyes fixed and dilated, his face ashen, his body limp. Alex could see from his olive-coloured trousers that he had urinated himself. Alex made his way round the low table and took his flaccid head in his hands, his fingers pressed tightly into his loose, soft skin.

'Mr Zimmerman … please!'

Just Jerry's voice was thin and feeble. Alex pressed one finger to his lips to quiet him and stared into his face. He looked like a well beaten pug, his eyes bulging and shot through. A tear escaped the corner of his eye and ran over the back of Alex's hand. Just Jerry's breath fluttered.

'You know it's a pity you weren't a Buddhist,' said Alex.

Not for the first time that night, but most certainly for the last time ever, Jerry looked confused.

'Sorry,' he stuttered.

'Well, you might have been coming back!'

With that, Alex deftly jerked his head back and to the side. He heard the definitive crunch he was looking for.

The deal was over, eight minutes since first entry. He looked at Just Jerry in front of him, slumped in the chair. Then he looked to the Bull and the young Bowstring. In the early days Alex never fully understood his feelings at these moments. In the midst of death, he saw only beauty in the bodies. At first it used to disturb him. He began to think there might be a danger of him doing this sort of thing just for the hell of it. But with deep reflection he began to understand the root of his feelings. In death there was no guilt, no sin, no evil, all past wrong doings were purged in an instant. Although Alex was not a religious man, he imagined that this was what it was like to give absolution, the satisfaction a priest felt to bring peace to a troubled mind. These people were now forgiven and deserved no more punishment, all that was left was the beauty of their newfound innocence.

2

Pattaya, Thailand, seven years previously

Boring

On the fringe of Pattaya, Alex sat in a quiet side room of the Wat Nong Yai temple. He sat with his legs crossed and eyes shut. A breeze brushed his cheek, and he felt the lazy flick of his red hair tease his eye lid. He sat cradled in the sweet smell of jasmine. To the right he could hear a little bird quietly chittering in its cage. The hot sun massaged his back, but the cooler breeze balanced the temperature, creating a perfect harmony. Behind him, were the muffled voices of tourists slowly gliding their way through the golden pillars and sumptuously decorated rooms. An ancient saffron draped monk sat on a raised platform in front of him silently watching him meditate. The scene was peace, Alex was peace. This external image, however, revealed nothing of the scene playing out in his head.

On Alex's mental film the colour was washed out, the sound was mute, and emotion was absent. He had created this oasis of peace for rationalisation not for emotional indulgence. In his head Alex was reviewing the fights of the previous evening. Each attack, each counter, every knee, fist and elbow deconstructed in slow motion and from every angle. In the first five fights he had clearly seen his opponents weaknesses. He had found a way into their minds. He had read the pattern of the fight and broke the strategy of their game. But that last fight had followed too hard upon, his senses had been dulled. He had found it hard to see the structure of the match or to fathom the mind of the opposition. Emptiness of mind and instinct need to coexist with thought and strategy in order to fight with intelligence. The previous bouts had been hard but manageable. That last round, however, was 95% instinct leaving him little head space to develop a strategy. He pieced together what fragments of the final fight he could remember, systematically trying to correct the mistakes he recognised. But there were bits missing and those were the bits wherein his defeat lay. He had gone as far as he could. The next step would be back in the UK reviewing the fight with Graham. He knew Graham would spot the mistakes he missed. He also knew what Graham's first observation would be … *'six fights in two days, that was your biggest mistake'*. Alex was well aware of this but that was the schedule, that's what he had signed up

28

for. As high-ranking fighters from the previous year, Decha Puntasrima and Yod Rak Sakda had got an automatic by through to the final and the semi-final. This, in itself, was not unusual. But as a farang, no matter what your credentials were, you had to battle your way through the entire bill. This ensured that any foreigner even to make to the quarter final had to have undertaken a minimum of four consecutive fights. It was then that they faced the seasoned champions in their first bouts of the night, fresh and sharp. Thai's liked Thai champions. It was good for moral, good for publicity and good for business. And the Kraduk Khaeng tournament was structured in such a way as to almost guarantee it was a Thai that was victorious.

Kradūkkhǎng literally translated as 'hard bones', a Thai idiom that essentially meant somebody who was hard to kill. In its early days, the tournament was little more than a local match between different Muay Thai stables to settle who had the best trainers. Very quickly it began to gain a reputation as a competition where real fighters went to test their mettle. Rules were few and even by the standards of Thai boxing the fighting was merciless. As its reputation grew so did its following. With an increase in profile, it was not long before it attracted the attention of foreign fighters. With growing recognition audiences grew, venues grew and advertising injected cash, an element of commercialism had entered the competition. With the introduction of foreign fighters, however, also came the danger of Thais being forced out of their own game. It was this that led to the rules of the competition being heavily weighted against non-national entrants. Even at the application stage very few foreign fighters were accepted. It was frequently said that the criteria for acceptance to the competition was based on the fact that you would put up a good fight, but not too good of a fight. It was corrupt, everyone knew it was corrupt, but this never stopped people flocking from every dojo in the world to try their hand. In fact, it was the very nature of the corruption, the stacking of the odds against you that was the essence of the attraction. If you won at the Kradūkkhæ̌ng you were a force to be reckoned with.

Such was the bias against foreign dominance in the seventeen years since the competition was founded, only one non-Thai had won it. This was the legendary Jeroen Jansen, The Beast of Amsterdam. He held the title for one year until at the next championship the organisers revoked the bi rule and then threw the entire country at him. Outside of The Beast only two other people had made it to the finals. Now Alex had made it three. He should have been proud, it was a hell of an achievement, but still he was no Jeroen Jansen. He really needed to sit and review his performance with Graham.

Alex had been trained by Graham for the last ten years after he progressed from his last Shifu. Although Graham's core disciple was Wing Chung, he possessed a broad knowledge of multiple martial arts from conventional boxing to BJJ. He was also an expert in Suntukan or dirty boxing. This had made him the perfect coach to prepare Alex for the Kradūkkhǽng, where rules were merely a whisper of suggestions. Graham himself had applied for the tournament eight years in a row but had never received an invite. When he became aware that age was starting to take its toll on his reaction and recovery time, he ploughed his energies into Alex. In Alex, Graham recognised a great talent for the 'art' of combat. When the invite came after Alex's second application it was a surprise to both men. In the nine months they then had to prepare Graham had been merciless in Alex's training in order to steel him for the ordeal ahead. The bitter disappointment came in the final week when a family bereavement robbed Graham of his chance to go with Alex. He'd left Alex at the airport with the simple, but supportive words *"Do your best."*

Alex's train of thought was nagged by a dull throb from a cut beneath his right eye and two of his ribs pricked him as he deepened his breath. The pains were afterglow of a blindingly fast hook to the head and vicious knee to the side. Apart from the lessons he had learned, these pains would be the only trophies for his endeavours. There was no second place at the

Kradūkkʰǽng, no cups, badges, belts or titles for the runners up in this competition. The only prize for those who didn't win was the recognition of a handful of people who knew what it took to compete. But for some that was like gold.

The pain refocused his attention on the world around him. He heard the old monk in front of him shift position. He heard a child outside cry and a Japanese tourist ask someone to take their photograph. He heard a footstep behind him and then a familiar voice cut in.

'Fuck me this is boring.'

With an introduction like that it could only be Richie. Everyone had a good friend who was not good, Richie was Alex's. He had known Richie for fifteen years ever since, at the age of eleven, he'd moved to Alex's school. On the surface of it, the boys were chalk and cheese. Alex was given to introversion and Richie loved an audience. Alex was comfortable with silence, to Richie silence was abhorrent. Despite this the two boys struck an enduring friendship. Perhaps there was an underlying recognition that in a strange way they both felt like outsiders, each, however, dealing with it in polar opposite ways. It was never said but they both knew it and in that knowledge they both looked out for each other.

Richie didn't fight, Richie never fought anything, least of all impulse and temptation. Everything for Richie was a twice in a lifetime opportunity. If you didn't like it the first time, try it

32

again as you might have done it wrong was his philosophy. It was this zest for life that made him irresistible and, sometimes in equal measure, irritating to be around. Things happened when you were with Richie, things you might not always want to happen, but things you'd never forget. It was Richie who had been able to step into the empty seat left by Graham.

'Are you not finished with that Karma shit yet!' he said.

Alex slowly opened his eyes, the colour of the world flooded in. The old monk sat silently on his platform; his face remained impassive.

'Come on mate show a bit of respect,' said Alex nodding towards the seated priest.

'What?' said Richie.

Respect in this setting meaning little to him.

'This is a temple.'

Shrugging off Alex's concern Richie replied,

'So?'

'So!'

Alex beckoned Richie's ear to his mouth and whispered.

'Keep the fucking language down.'

Richie smiled as Alex raised an eyebrow. Alex stood and bowed to the priest. Still the old man's face showed no sign of acknowledgement but as he met Alex's eye, he raised his chin. It was an almost imperceptible gesture, but the message was clear … come. Alex approached the platform. The man was old there was no doubt, but his age was hard to determine. His face was not weathered with care, his forehead showed no furrows, and his eyes were wrinkled only with kindness. The priest held out his hand and took Alex by the wrist gently drawing it to him. The old man's hands were stained with liver spots. He reached behind him and produced an intricately platted yellow and orange bracelet and tied it round Alex's wrist. He closed his eyes and cupped Alex's hand in his. In almost a whisper he mumbled a blessing. Finishing with a dignified bow he set Alex's hand free and returned to his motionless neutrality. Alex pressed his hands together, backed away two steps and bowed, before turning to leave. As he left the room, he dropped a couple of notes into the donation box. Richie followed him out into the bright mid-day sun and back into the throng of tourists. The presence of all these people was now even more conspicuous after their curious absence from the retreat in which Alex had just been sitting. Richie spoke.

'How much did you just drop into that donation box?'

'400 baht.'

'400 baht! Fuck me that must be about, about, well….it must be over … over, well that's a lot mate,' he said giving up on the calculation.

Alex helped out, knowing mental maths was never Richie's strong point.

'It's about eight pounds.'

'Eight quid, seriously!'

Richie grabbed Alex's wrist and examined the thin yellow, orange bracelet.

'Eight quid, for that, I could pick one of those up in any tourist tat shop for 20p. In fact, they're free at some of the guest houses, they leave them on your pillow.'

'It was a donation mate, it's for good luck,' Alex countered.

'Good luck, the only one getting lucky in here is that old shyster selling a 20p piece of string for eight quid,' he said tutting.

Alex undid the platted bracelet and gestured to Richie to give him his wrist. 'Here,' he said tying it on, 'this might remind you that somewhere in there you have a soul.'

'I only have one soul mate and that's my arsehole, which if weighed against all this philosophy stuff I think you'll find is far more practical. But thanks for the expensive piece of string anyway,' replied Richie giving Alex an affectionate dig in the shoulder.

'Now,' he continued, 'shouldn't we be getting back to the hotel, we've only got three hours to get ready before we hit the town and although it'll only take ten minutes to make me look good, you might need a lot more work.'

Alex stopped.

'But I wanted to go to the zoo this afternoon.'

35

'Are you for real!' said Richie, his voice rising at least two octaves.

'Yes, they've got a crocodile farm and you can hold an Orangutan.'

'Lizards and monkeys! You can see those on telly mate. Listen tomorrow we fly down to Phuket and then off island hopping. But today we're in Pattaya, the female hospitality capital of Thailand, so you and me my friend are going to sample some of this town's real wildlife and none of it is going to have a David Attenborough voice over.'

3

Lamp: Rococo

'You're not leaving, are you?'

Aat lay naked on the bed, the white linen sheets tangled around him. Aat was Thai, about fifty-five years old, but with the body of a man at least twenty years his junior, toned and well trained. The fan in the ceiling sent waves of cool air to caress his skin, but still he shone with bloom of post coital sweat. Nok stood on one leg by the side of the bed slipping on her panties. It was mid-day and shafts of white gold cut through the blinds creating alternate bands of light and shade over the room and the two figures. Only the occasional intrusion of a distant tuk tuk or dog bark broke the intimacy. The room was cheap and serviceable, with a faint hint of damp.

'I have to get to work, I have a lot to do,' said Nok.

Her ham strings tightened as she steadied herself on two feet again. Her skin was flawless, the colour of honey lotus blossom. Honey was the all-encompassing adjective for this girl. Everything about her was sweet, her colour, her perfume,

37

her taste. She held herself erect by the side of the bed her long blue-black hair shining in the banded light that ran over her svelte form. A wisp of her hair lay over the front of her shoulder and licked the side of her breast.

Aat reached out to her beckoning gently.

'I still have a lot I want to do.'

'Are you not tired?'

She slipped a short one-piece dress, white with a large yellow and red orchid print, over her head. It slid independently down to her thighs. The dress, like Aat, not wanting to leave an inch of her body untouched. It consumed her like a hungry lover.

'You said only short time. You had business,' she said.

'But we have time enough for just one more, come.'

He caught hold of the hem of her dress and gently tugged her towards him. Nok swayed looking down on him. Aat could smell the fresh mingling of their essence. It was a reminder of the fruits just eaten and an entrée for the fruits to come. She sat on the side of the bed and stared towards the window.

'You do not tire?' she said looking into his expectant face.

'How could I tire with you?'

Aat pulled her closer.

Nok had slipped the powder into his drink over an hour ago. It should have been taking effect, but Aat still looked as fresh as ever. Damn Kiet, this was going to mess everything up. He said the stuff he gave her would knock out a horse in two minutes. He was a cheap bastard! It was not him who was now faced with this situation, it was her. She was acutely aware time was running out. There was only half an hour before Aat's meeting, and she wanted to be long gone by then. The way she saw it she faced two options, walk away now and leave without what she came for or adapt the plan. Whatever her choice she needed to act quickly. Her hand took hold of the shaft of the lamp by the side of the bed. Suggestively she stroked its length. It was ornate with gold scrolls and a heavy onyx base, trying to look regency rococo, but looking exactly like what it was, tasteless seventies tat. Nok ran her delicate hand over Aat's face closing his eyes.

'Shh close your eyes and I will give you something to last you a long time,' she whispered.

Aat gave a satisfied moan and smiled. He reclined back on the bed his penis throbbing with anticipation. Just as his eyes closed and he settled his body she snatched up the lamp and brought a heavy blow down on the side of his head. Nok's frame was slight, but she put every pound she had behind the swing. His head bounced four inches off the pillow with the force of the blow. Aat's eyes were now open but instead of, pain or surprise they raged with the clarity of a predator. She went to deal a second blow, but it was too late. Aat grabbed her wrist with a grip so fierce the lamp fell from her hand and

39

dropped to the floor. He attempted to get to his knees, his head spun, and the room flashed with lights. He couldn't get his balance. She tried to pull away, but his hold was too strong. As she pulled back, he lunged forward, they both tumbled to the floor, his body landing on top of her. Nok struggled to free herself from under him, but he was at least half as big as her again. She gasped for breath. To her relief Aat now seemed to be suffering from the blow to the head and the effect of the drug. She could see he was finding it hard to focus but he kept going. His left hand clawed its way up the side of her body ripping her dress while his right forearm pinned her neck to the floor. Soon both of his hands encompassed her delegate throat and started to squeeze. Frantically she flailed under him, but he was too heavy and too strong. The sides of her vision began to fade to black. Seconds before she lapsed into unconsciousness, she felt the onyx base of the fallen lamp with her hand. She brought it up and struck out. It was a fraction of the force of the first blow, but it landed true. Aat was tough but not that tough. His arms gave way, and his torso came crashing down on her almost knocking the last weak breath from her lungs. He lay twitching and she could feel his shallow breath on the side of her cheek. He was actually snoring.

 She lay for several seconds trying to catch her breath, but his weight was starting to press the air out of her. Wriggling and

40

squirming she managed to grapple her way from under him. This had not gone to plan.

Quickly she got to her feet and checked herself over. Apart from a sore throat she had suffered no permanent harm. Looking over her clothes there didn't seem to be any blood. The blow to the side of Aat's head had been severe, but it had crushed the skin more than cut it. The rip to her dress would go unnoticed and there was no need for her to clean up. She believed she knew exactly where 'it' was and prayed that the information she had been given by Kiet was right. She went to the corner of the room to a veneered chest of drawers and dragged it to one side. Lifting up the corner of a fusty blue carpet she exposed a loose floorboard. 'Please let it be here' she thought. Loosening the board, she found what she was looking for, a large brown paper package. Tearing open the paper what she saw was the cliché of every gangster film she had ever seen. There were five large and two small blocks of beige coloured powder wrapped in translucent cling film. Each block was tightly bound and brick hard. Whoever wrapped it was determined that not even one gram of the precious cargo would escape. The total weight must have been around six or seven kilos. In terms of value, how many nights with a man did this represent. She had no idea, but it was probably more nights than she had left to give in her entire life. Lifting out the

41

package she crossed the room and with trembling hands stuffed it into her backpack.

Nok took one last look at Aat lying naked and unconscious on the floor. He had been far gentler with her than she had expected. Men like this were usually greedy. Sex was rarely about pleasure and more about power for them. He had not been like that at all. He was a considerate lover that seemed to put her pleasure at the forefront of his intentions. Bending over his body she could see his eyes lightly flickering under his lids as though he were dreaming. She never enjoyed sex, but there was something about this man that could make a woman feel safe and at least that was a feeling … Pity.

She kissed her hand and gently touched him on the side of the head. The wound from the lamp was now swollen and turning scarlet, black as the blood pooled under the skin. Pin-prick droplets were starting to ooze through the pores. This, however, was not the time for sentiment. Standing upright and smoothing out her hair she flung the backpack over her shoulder and made for the door. It was then there was a knock.

She froze literally mid step, her foot hovering an inch above the floor. The knock came again, three short raps, two in rapid succession, a pause, then another. She stood glued to the spot staring at the door. The noise of her own heartbeat sounded like thunder in her ears. The knock came again, rap,

rap ... rap. How long would this person keep knocking? How long would Aat stay unconscious? As if to answer one of those questions Aat began to stir. He gave a weak cough followed by a splutter and made a feeble attempt to prop himself up on his elbow. Adrenalin rushed through her body, and she was gripped by fear. Rather than risk what was on the other side of the door she needed to gain a few more seconds to gather her thoughts. Before Aat could get any leverage and get back to his feet, she once again snatched up the table lamp and hit him. He slumped back down with a thud. Then came the voice from behind the door.

'Aat, it's Dermot, you in there?'

Nok knew accents and this one was Irish. She made no reply.

'Look I'm sorry I'm early but there's been a bit of a rescheduling,' the voice explained.

Still Nok made no reply, perhaps he would go away. This didn't happen and the voice came again.

'Listen, I know there's someone in there, I heard you. Come on mate don't mess around, open the door,' the voice had a persistent edge.

Quickly Nok decided the best course of action might be bluff. The table lamp was the closest thing to a weapon Nok had and it had already served her well. Picking it up and concealing it behind her back she crossed to the door and tentatively

43

opened it a few inches. Outside stood a short slim man in his mid-thirties with close cropped hair and a well-groomed goatee. He was carrying a green sports bag. He had an overall gentle appearance, which was incongruous with his harsh Belfast brogue.

'I'm here to see Aat, tell him it's Dermot,' he said.

Nok decided that feigning ignorance might be the best approach and she answered.

'Chạn mì kĥêācı khuṇ, sorry English no.'

This didn't seem to deter him and like every other British person abroad he tried to make himself understood by speaking louder.

'Aat, get Aat, I'm Dermot, you get Aat, understand.'

As he spoke, he tried to see round the crack in the door, but Nok closed it a little further. Then as he looked her up and down, he saw something that caught his eye. Nok's assault on Aat had not been as bloodless as she first thought. A minute spatter had caught her on the left cheek. As the Irishman took a pause to process the situation Nok took the opportunity to end the conversation.

'English no, Lā k̀xn, ka,' she said closing the door.

Nok stood behind the door listening intently. She could hear no sound but could almost sense the presence of the man still outside. Then from behind her she heard the sound of a phone ringing. Her eyes darted to the bedside table. On it lay

44

a mobile happily vibrating and playing the Soft Meadow ring tone. She stared at the phone willing it to stop … and then the door crashed open. In walked the Irishman holding up his mobile. Illuminated on the screen it said *'calling Aat'*. Instantly he saw the body of Aat on the floor.

'Now lady, I know who that is,' he said nodding towards the unconscious body of Aat, 'The question is, who the feck are you?'

Before she could even think, once again Nok lashed out with the table lamp. It met its target with a violence that jarred her arm. The Irishman staggered and fell, his head smacking the corner of the bed frame. This time there was no ensuing fight, he just lay there, deathly still, his eyes wide open. What it lacked in style this lamp made up for in its usefulness as a weapon. Years of subsistence living had taught her to be a keen opportunist and instinctively she snatched up the man's green sports bag and pulled back the zip. She didn't expect what she saw. Toiletries, pens, a book, a shirt, even underwear perhaps, but what she was met with took her breath away, money and lots of it. This wasn't the time or the place to count it, but it was more than enough to buy her out of the pitiful existence she knew. Heart pounding, she fled the room.

Life in the street was going on as normal. Girls cried out to passing trade to attract business, food sizzled, and tourists

45

haggled mercilessly for a penny they would never miss. It was the same as yesterday and it would be the same tomorrow. Inside, however, Nok was churning up. Detached from the world it felt like there was an invisible barrier between her and everything that was going on around her. This cocoon made even breathing difficult.

There were questions racing through her head. Stealing the drugs was planned for, but there had been no mention of this other man. If Kiet never mentioned him, chances were, he probably didn't know he was going to be there. And if he didn't know he was going to be there it was unlikely he knew about the money. Right from the start Kiet's only interest lay in the drugs. If this was the case, then potentially the money was hers to keep. Her immediate instinct was to run and run now. Drop the drugs, take the money and forget about her deal with Kiet. On the other hand, what would be the consequences of running? She was pretty sure Kiet was a nobody, and this was the only big idea he'd had in his life. But what if he was a nobody who worked for a somebody. Would they come looking for her? Would running put a target on her back, then what? It could get messy. After some deliberation she decided it was best to stick to the original plan. Hand over the drugs and take her payment. This would conclude her end of the bargain with Kiet, and she would have fulfilled everything that had been asked of her. If later on further information about the missing money came to light by that time she would be long gone. In Thailand with this amount of money it would be easy for her to disappear.

Reaching into the side pocket of her shoulder bag she pulled out her mobile. Pressing three on the speed dial she waited. Kiet answered his reply was abrupt.

'Well?'

'I have it,'

'Any problems?'

'No,'

'Good. Meet me at the Shark Club at ten, bring it with you.'

'Bring it to the club?'

'Yes, is there a problem?'

Nok paused, the Shark Club would be very busy at that time of night. It hardly seemed an appropriate place to be handing over a bag of drugs in exchange for a large amount of money. Thai law was harsh on drugs, and she didn't like the idea of carrying a potential death sentence into the centre of town. Kiet's voice broke her thoughts.

'Is there a problem?' he repeated.

She hesitated.

'I said is there a problem. Are you fucking deaf?'

Nok put on a front.

'No, no problem,' she replied. 'Will you bring the money?'

She heard a snort of derisive laughter.

47

'Just be there and just bring it.'

The line went dead.

4

The Archbishop of Canterbury

Alex lay on the bed dressed only in his shorts thumbing through the Lonely Planet guide. The patio doors of the balcony were fully open letting in the bustle of the lane below. The air outside was heavy and sluggish. The air-conditioning hummed in the background and meeting no resistance from the outside atmosphere, the thin voile at the window billowed outwards. Richie stood naked in front of the mirror combing his eyebrows. Despite being only 140lbs and almost 6ft tall Richie still managed to look podgy round the waist. Alex put this down to his diet of alcohol, pizzas, coffee and chocolate in that order. To Richie a body was something to be enjoyed and his represented an experiential feast. To him this was beautiful. The room was bland white, but the conversation was colourful. It had returned to the 400 Baht donation Alex had made for the bracelet at the Wat Nong Yai temple. Richie had his opinion.

'Look all I am saying is that it's all those people out there running around working sixteen hours a day who allow those baldy bastards to sit on their lazy arses; no wonder they live to 175 or whatever it is. They've never had to do a day's work in their lives.'

Alex lowered the book. It was no good trying to read when Richie wanted a discussion.

'They work in other ways mate,' he countered.

'Like how? Thinking about work and telling other people not to do it? Even the street walkers make donations to them. You know what that makes those monks don't you, cock sucker's by proxy!'

Richie drew Alex in, he always did. He may not have been the most eloquent of men, but there was always a core to his opinions worth exploration.

'Not everything can be measured in money. You can't weigh a philosophy on scales. A philosophy gives structure, values to live by, that's all I'm saying. You might not be able to sell it in a bag, but it has a value.'

Richie had Alex on the line now.

'Yes, but the only reason they have the time to sit and think about these things, to offer peace and love and whatever else, is because they don't have to live in the real world. Listen, you saw that place today, hilltop setting, middle of nowhere, no cars, little streams, 'bons-what's-it' trees. Anyone can be serene if they don't have to pay a mortgage, live in a shit hole and work till their back breaks just to eat. Come on that's an easy gig to sit in the lap of luxury watching other people working their fingers to the bone to keep you. Then adding insult to injury by telling them to let go of their worldly possessions. Seriously you buy that shit?'

Despite his presentation style Richie always thought about things and had a strong sense of injustice. It sounded like this was something that had got to him. Alex could see where he was coming from.

'I'll give you that,' said Alex, 'in that respect it's a bit like John Lennon I suppose, 'Imagine no possessions' well he would have to, wouldn't he. But really these guys are more like the Archbishop of Canterbury.'

Richie turned from the mirror, not the full-frontal Alex wanted, but after sharing many rooms and tents with Richie he was used to it now.

'Ah! but you see the archbishop has a real job,' said Richie thinking he had made an important distinction.

'Doing what?'

'Well, I don't know, funerals, marriages, helping little old ladies.'

'Does he do anything for you?' pushed back Alex.

'No but I'm not a God botherer mate.'

'So why do you pay his wages?'

'I don't,' said Richie raising his eyebrows.

Alex saw the chink in the armour.

'Who do you think does?'

Richie shrugged his shoulders.

'I don't know, the Pope?'

'I'll tell you where his wages come from, taxes mate, Muslims, Hindus, Jews, you, me we're all paying, through taxes, the Archbishop of Canterbury's 80k a year, his free house and gold frocks come out of your pocket, whether you like it or not.'

Richie stopped preening for a moment and furrowed his brow, this was something new to him, something he'd never considered. Alex went on.

'So, who's the worst? You might want to call these monks scroungers, but at least all the money they get is given freely as donations. People give it to them because they want to; not like the Archbishop of Canterbury, who just takes money off you, and you don't have a choice. If monks are scroungers, what does that make him, a mugger?'

Richie went quiet, he turned the issue round in his head several times before he formulated his retort.

'You make a fair point, but I put it to you, in a court of law you don't prove your innocence by proving the guilt of others. All those twats are as bad as each other in my book,' he said by way of a summing up.

With that he returned to the mirror preening his various bodily hairs. Alex returned to the Lonely Planet, its pictures being far preferable to the sight of Richie in front of him.

'You know, it says in here that we can get a boat from Phuket to the Phi Phi islands and that's where they filmed The Beach,' said Alex as a complete non sequitur to the last subject.

'Well, I am sure you can find the place where Leonardo DiCaprio sat and wank over it mate. But tonight, we storm the bars of Pattaya, and you my friend are in need of some serious relief.'

Richie spun from the mirror and stood with his hands on his hips legs astride.

'Now how do I look?'

'How much money you got.' said Alex.

'Shit loads'

'Then you're going to look beautiful mate!'

5

Sun Wukong

Aat stood in front of the desk. His head was still pounding from the blows he'd received earlier that afternoon and his vision was still vague at the edges. He'd managed to get to a local hospital where, at his own request, a purely cursory examination had established there was "probably no permanent damage". That was a doctor's opinion of his current medical condition, but the day was still young. He might have walked away from this afternoon, but it was yet to be seen whether he would walk away from this room. He touched the temporary dressing on the side of his head and his eye winced more out of expectation than pain.

This was the office and town pied-à-terre of Chai Son, his friend, his brother, his adoptive son, his boss. The apartment sat atop his main town club. Any apartment of Chai Son's spelled minimalist. The floor was bare Daeng wood polished like burnished copper. In bright sunlight it had a dizzying effect as if you were standing on a mirror. The two sofas were sharp black-and-white designed totally with form over function and there were no cushions to ease the body from the precise angles. In front of this was a genuine Isamu Noguchi table. Aat knew this as he was with Chai Son when he bought it. At the time he couldn't believe how something that looked so cheap could be so expensive. Part of the room was taken up with a small gym area, a mat, kettle bells, two bags and a muk yan jong, wooden dummy, something which Chai Son would strike for hours on end until the nerves in his fist, forearms and shins were beaten into submission. The only nod of indulgence was a 70-inch LCD TV which took up a large proportion of the back wall. Chai Son, however, never watched TV, his only frivolity was video games always of a puzzle nature, which he played without sound and invariably on his own. The desk in front of which Aat stood was constructed of three plain panels of black granite, on the corner of the desk was the only ornament in the room, a large bronze figure of the monkey king Sun Wukong, leaping from the swirls of his flying cloud, his staff in hand ready for battle. It had been a gift from Aat for Chai Son's 21st birthday. The nose of the monkey king was a mellow gold contrast to the rest of the statue's rich dark patina. It showed the years of Chia Son's appreciative hands stroking its muzzle in deep thought.

55

When Chai Son was a boy Aat used to sit him on his knee and tell him stories of Sun Wukong and his journey to India with the priest Xuanzang to retrieve the Buddhist sutras. Chai Son would sit enthralled. Looking up at Aat he would demand story after story of the monkey king's feats of strength and how he had conquered demons of many guises, splitting them in two with his magic staff. After some time, the stories of the legend ran out, but Aat told and retold the quests, embellishing the tales with his own additions. No matter how many times he told the same story it was always greedily received by his little audience. Would the sight of Sun Wukong evoke the same memories in Chai Son as it did in Aat? After all they had shared together would he be treated like any other employee?

At the age of eight Chai Son had fallen into the river near their village and nearly drowned. One of the women pulled him from the water and brought him semi-conscious to Aat. As Aat held him in his arms the little body started to twitch into life and as Chai Son opened his eyes he looked up and in a low voice said …

'I cannot die.'

At first Aat thought it the confused words of a traumatised child. But later Chai Son told him of his vision in which it was revealed to him that no man would ever put an end to his life. It was this vision, this deep unshakable belief, that was the foundation of Chai Son's rise. He was never overtly reckless but his conviction that no man could harm him gave him a supreme confidence that did not invite others to question it. He approached every situation in the absolute knowledge that he would be the one to walk away.

Aat had been by Chai Son's side for almost thirty years when his first wife took him in as an orphan of little more than three years old. No man had been closer to Chai Son than Aat. Later when his wife died Aat, and the boy were left on their own. Aat had always been on the fringes of crime, a hand-to-mouth criminal. But with the restraining factor of his wife gone, his brief forays into crime developed into a full-time occupation. Over the following years Aat had taught Chai Son every cheap hustle, scam and double deal he knew. Chai Son had been a voracious learner and it was not long before the pupil surpassed the master. It was only when Chai Son started directing the business that what was formally a subsistence living grew into a structured empire. With Aat by his side Chai Son became one of the most feared and respected Cha Pho bosses in the country. His influence stretched from the borders of Burma in the North and West to Laos and Cambodia in the East down to Malaysia in the South. The two men had a deep, rich history but Aat knew that even thirty years might not be enough collateral to offset what had happened.

Aat knew all business depended on reputation and reputations were made by examples. It was Aat who had brought Chai Son into this business, it was Aat who taught him the rules. It was Aat who had provided the role model and it was now time for Aat to face the consequences of his tutelage.

Chai Son stood behind his desk facing the window. The lights outside making him appear almost translucent. In clothes, his form was almost gracile, narrow at the hip and sharp at the shoulder. But it was a grave mistake to think that there was anything effeminate about him. Aat knew only too well Chai Son's MO for dealing with internal failures; he had witnessed it first-hand many times, trial by combat. At first the organisation thought this approach was madness and in the early days Chai Son had a number of challenges to his authority. There had been attempted coups and nibbling of profits by would be's who thought they were in a position to best him. Each of them in turn had faced Chai Son. To Aat's reckoning, none of them had lived past three minutes. After a while, the legend of Chai Son's invincible immortality took root. Challenges and scepticism were replaced by unquestionable respect and loyalty.

Aat studied Chai Son's form. In his darker moments he often wondered whether this time would ever come and if it did, could he beat him. In his present state, who knows? He had certainly seen bigger, more confident men crushed by Chai

Son. But perhaps he was asking himself the wrong question. Perhaps the question was, if it came down to it, and Aat could win, would he want to win. The question may not be could Chai Son do it to him, but could he do it to Chai Son?

Chai Son turned and looked at Aat, his black eyes staring right through him. To those that didn't know him Chai Son's feline features never showed emotion. No matter what the situation his expression was neutral. But Aat knew him better and the micro inflections he detected were those of a deep sadness. Aat held his gaze for only a second before turning his eyes to the floor. As it was with his expression Chai Son's tone was neutral.

'You disappoint me,' he said in almost a whisper.

'I'm sorry.'

It seemed futile, but it was all Aat had to offer. Chai Son closed his eyes to the apology and continued.

'There is enough corruption in this country without you paying towards it.'

Chai Son always had a strange moral compass that Aat never fully understood. He knew the whole history of this man, the people he had killed and had ordered killed. He knew the vast fortune he had amassed on the back of drug trafficking. He had seen Chai Son torture people for information and for punishment. This was not a man who would be going to heaven. Despite all of this Chai Son never pushed drugs in his own country. All of his stock was produced in vast fields in the north and his large workforce well cared for in terms of living wages, health and education. Even though he could have doubled his profits he never ran prostitutes or allowed them in any of his clubs. He never ran protection schemes or allowed them in any area under his control and he never recruited young and vulnerable boys to do his dirty work, as was the way of many in his line of business. If anyone died at the hands of Chai Son, it was guaranteed they were part of the game. If anyone worked for Chai Son, they did so with a full understanding of what they had signed up for.

No one knew exactly how much, but each year Chai Son donated millions of Baht to legitimate rural development schemes and without his patronage many remote villages would have been without proper water or sanitation. Chai Son was proud of the traditions and moral codes which had built his country. The West, he saw as a corruption. He saw the fat old men taking advantage of young girls with nothing to sell but their bodies. He saw loud brash ways of the West, the way it thought money could buy respect. He decided early on that Western arrogance and greed was something he could exploit. So, he took their money and shipped them drugs. As he had once said to Aat, "Let their homelands fester in filth, let their families cry over lost children and the money they pay for this 'privilege' will make our country stronger. So, as they shrink, so shall we grow."

Chai Son stared hard at Aat. He needed information.

'What do you know of her?'

'She was a girl from the street,' Aat answered honestly.

'Her name?'

'Nok, I have a photograph.'

Aat reached into his pocket and produced his mobile, opening up the photo folder and tapping on the picture of Nok he handed it to Chai Son. Chai Son examined it closely.

'And is this what you commit adultery for?' he said with an indifference to the beauty of the girl.

All he saw in this image was quarry to be hunted down. Aat said nothing.

'Where did you find her?'

'In The Double Beat, but she was an independent,' replied Aat.

'The Double Beat is run by Billy the Kat; he has keen eyes.'

Lost in thought Chai Son ran his hand over Sun Wukong. He stroked its gold worn muzzle and closed his eyes. The silence in the room turned into a tangible pall which defied interruption, the still air threatening to choke the life out of words before they could be uttered. Aat knew the moment had come when his mistake had to be paid for. It was Aat who eventually broke the tension.

61

'Lek and I have been having problems, I just needed to …'

He knew this was a pathetic excuse, but he felt his betrayal needed some context. Chai Son raised his hand and stopped him.

'My friend, I am not looking for excuses,' he had used the words my friend, 'you have been in business a long time, sometimes the filth of the street is hard to wash clean. Take Lek up north, repair between you what has been damaged, you will be provided for as once you provided for me.'

It was not the relief that he would live that lifted Aat's heart, but the knowledge that there was still a bond between them. That Chai Son had remembered the same lost boy he had taken in all those years ago. The boy who hung on his words and shared his stories still remained and valued the love he carried for him. A passing tear formed in the corner of Aat's eye, it may have been this, or the blurring of his vision from the injury to his head, but he believed for the first time in many years he saw a warmth in Chai Son's face.

Once Aat had left the room Chai Son got down to the business of damage limitation and recovery. This could not have happened on a worse transaction. The stolen shipment had been scheduled for a new client, who had been referred on the recommendation of a regular buyer. A mistake like this was a blow to his professional standing and his pride. The situation had potential to inject distrust and cast uncertainty upon further transactions. This needed to be dealt with swiftly, decisively and with spectacle.

Chai Son always researched new clients. Information had indicated that this British contact was on the assent and the seed of business had the potential to grow. He had heard that, if crossed, this Englishman could be erratic, unpredictable. Intelligence indicated that there were stabilising influences within his organisation. He would capitalise on these factors to preserve peace. In the event of conflict, Chai Son was safe in the knowledge he had more than adequate resources to obliterate any offence. However, he deeply disliked dealing with clients this way as it made for an unstable marketplace.

Chai Son knew that with each passing moment the chances of getting back what was lost, diminished rapidly. He had eyes and ears all over the town, it was time to turn them on and to give them focus. He picked up Aat's phone from the table and dialled for Billy the Kat. Billy the Kat made your business his business. If you were not known by Billy, you were not worth knowing. By rights, the amount of information Billy had at his disposal should have gotten him killed years ago. But Billy was smart. His mouth was tight, and he only had one outlet for all the dirty secrets of the town and that was Chai Son. Chai Son protected loyal, valuable assets.

Billy answered in his usual street persona with faux American affectations.

'Hey, Aat, how's it hanging with my man in a suit?'

Chai Son was there to talk business, not pass pleasantries. He corrected the mistaken identity.

'Aat's phone, Chai Son speaking. I'm sending you a picture. I want everything you can find on this girl. I understand she has been operating in your bar.'

Billy's tone changed from informal to business like efficiency.

'Certainly, Chai Son forgive my initial mistake.'

Pulling up the image of Nok, Chai Son forwarded it to Billy. There was a moment's pause before the image popped up.

'Have you seen her?' asked Chai Son when he heard the ping of the picture arrive.

Billy opened it up and studied the face.

'She was in here last night with Aat, but she doesn't work here, I don't have her name.'

'She goes by the name of Nok. This much I know, but I need you to give me more,' pressed Chai Son.

'She was a random, probably an independent. I may not know her, but she was in here twice last week with Kiet and that's a man we both know,' expanded Billy.

Chai Son had an encyclopaedic knowledge of even the lowliest of his organisation. 'Kiet, do we not use him for small running, am I right?'

'That's the man,' confirmed Billy.

'Well, let us hope he has not run too far. Billy it is time to put your name to the test be a Kat and bring me a rat.'

6

Four in a row

Thai street bars are like fractals, the same shapes within the same shapes, within the same shapes. Sometimes it was hard to see where one bar ended and the other began. Each bar had the same drinks, the same games and the same girls. Even the talk was the same, 'Hello handsome man, Where you from? What's your name? How old are you?' But for those who were merely visitors to this adult playground everything was different and new.

Richie sat staring at the Connect 4 board in front of him. If anyone had told him just two weeks earlier that he would have been sitting at a bar, in Thailand with a beautiful girl playing Connect 4 for money, he would have laughed in their face. Yet here he was. He held the blue chip in his hand and hovered over the left of centre slot. Through the holes in the board, he could see the girl's firm sun kissed breasts, misted with a fine film of sweat. They were fighting to get out of a restraining camouflage vest. Bizarrely enough he was starting to see them as a distraction. After losing six games in a row, and 600 baht into the bargain, he was determined to salvage some dignity and a small percentage of his money by winning at least one game. He watched her face as she rested her chin on her hand, smiling playfully and nibbling her little finger. He hesitated, then dropped the chip. It slid down the slot and landed with a decisive clack at the bottom. Quick as a striking cobra, with no discernible thought, the girl made her counter move ... Clack!

'I win!' she jeered.

Richie's brow furrowed and his eyes darted round the board, red, red, red, blue, red, blue, blue, red, red ...

'Where?' he demanded incredulously.

'There I win four in a row, and you lose again.'

She pointed to a diagonal of four reds she had just created.

'Loser, loser!'

She made a little L with the forefinger and thumb of her right hand and held it to her forehead in rhythm with the loser chant.

'You own me 100 baht and a lady drink.'

'Fucking hell not again!' said Richie taking a deep draught from his bottle of Singha.

Alex watched with amusement his friend's seventh humiliation in a row.

'How much has playing that game cost you now?' he asked.

'That's 700 baht and seven drinks mate,' replied Richie.

He thumbed for the money in his pocket as the expectant girl held out her hand awaiting her winnings. Alex shook his head.

'These girls play every day twelve hours a day. Did you seriously think you were going to take money off them?'

'It's only a kid's game how hard can it be?' said Richie handing over the cash.

'Too hard for you obviously,' replied Alex with a smirk.

'You know I could have had a short time in a hotel room for the money I've just lost playing this,' said Richie looking disproportionately upset at his defeat.

Alex smiled, he marvelled at the way Richie seemed to be able to equate most things to sex and money. He was a natural for the bars in this country.

'Well, I need to take a short time out back, but out of necessity not for recreation,' said Alex.

'What?' said Richie contemplating another wager.

'I'm going for a piss, be back in a bit.'

Leaving the bar, Alex exited the arena of Richie's humiliation. He pushed his way through the pulsating crowd and headed for the bathroom housed at the back of the complex. Ever the optimist, Richie started on game eight.

Kiet stood with his back against the wall. His whole style was a confusion of American rap, Japanese cyber punk and grunge biker, all on a ten-dollar budget. His entire body vibrated with perpetual ticks. Even at rest his eyes never landed on anything for more than two seconds. He was thin and wiry. Self-inflicted denim blue tattoos jostled for position with veins as thick as pencils up and down his knotted arms. Kiet was a dirty job 'bellhop'. He had been working for Chai Son for almost two years. More accurately he had been working for someone, who was working for someone, who worked for Chai Son for the last two years. He fetched, he carried, he picked things ups, he put things down. He passed on low level information and if a fall had to be taken and time had to be done, no doubt it would be done by Kiet.

At first, he harboured big ideas. His ambition was to be sitting at the head table within a year. This was something Hollywood had led him to believe was perfectly achievable. The fresh talent off the street has a chance meeting with the Don and within two and a half hours he controls the entire organisation. Kiet's ambitions, however, bore little resemblance to his abilities. The reality of his situation had been very different. In the last two years he had never even met Chai Son. The closest he had been was standing once or twice outside of Chai Son's club watching him step from the door to his car and back again. The harder Kiet seemed to try, the harder it seemed for him to be taken seriously. He started to become acutely aware of his position within the hierarchy of this organisation. Kiet was at the bottom and was unlikely to be afforded the opportunity to rise any higher. With this personal insight came no Zen like contentment, only a festering resentment.

One quality he possessed in droves, if it could be called a quality, was the lack of loyalty. This made his name 'Kiet', somewhat of a misnomer, Kiet, in Thai, meaning honour. He lived his life like an urban fox, always on the lookout for an opportunity to take what he could when he could. It was never more than crumbs from the table, nothing that would ever be seriously missed, but it boosted not only his income, but also his ego. It made him feel as though he were smarter than the system. Crumbs from the rich man's table, however, rarely sated an appetite like Kiet's. As time passed, they only left him feeling more hungry and more dissatisfied. It was then he started to think that if his talents weren't obvious to his current employer, they may be appreciated by another.

He had heard of the growing Croatian influence in parts of Pattaya. Kiet saw them as a progressive opportunity. They had no moral objection to dealing in prostitution or street drugs, areas in which Chai Son had little interest. He also knew that Chai Son had discretely shut down a few Croatian operations when he thought they would stray into his territory or offend his sensibilities. Perhaps these people would be interested in what he could offer. Subtlety was never Kiet's strong point. By way of an introduction, he simply walked into a club he knew to be under Croatian influence and conspicuously announced who he worked for. It was a risky strategy, but it seemed to pay off. Within days he was taking a pay packet. His job was easy, any information that came through him went to them. Times, dates, people, contacts, they wanted to know exactly how Chai Son conducted business. Trouble was, although Kiet had told them this was something he could do, in reality he had little idea how Chai Son's real business worked, any information of consequence was never entrusted to him. After several weeks in his role of 'spy' it was becoming obvious to him that his new employers were growing tired of listening to an errand boy's list. Kiet needed to provide them with something of real worth before they decided he no longer warranted the effort.

Over the ensuing weeks Kiet made sure that he was in every dark corner he could find. He listened quietly at locked doors and looked in through shuttered windows. After putting himself about eighteen hours a day, eventually he picked up something that could be of interest. For some months there had been backroom rumours in the system that Aat had troubles at home and had become estranged from his wife. This, however, was no more than idle gossip. The domestic affairs of Chai Son's right-hand man were of little commercial value. But then he learned of a transaction which was going to be made by Aat personally, a transaction he thought of as substantial. Knitting together these two pieces of disparate information Kiet had formulated a crude plan. He had identified a weakness and had conceived an opportunity to exploit it.

His new employers seemed pleased with this information and his idea was incentivised by a large bonus if he could deliver what he promised. Finding a suitable girl would be the last piece of his sordid jigsaw.

Luck seemed to be smiling on Kiet at last. He found the ideal candidate working the street. She was truly beautiful, with a face that radiated innocence. The proposition he put to her fell on fertile ears. He saw in her only what he saw in himself greed and amorality, perfect traits for what he wanted her to do. He possessed no human empathy to be able to detect her desperation. To him she was simply the perfect honey pot. She would get the last pieces of vital information and, coward that he was, he would let her recover the goods. Essentially, she would take all the risks and he would reap all the benefits. The whole plan had been formulated around nothing more than speculation.

Would Aat go for this girl, would she get the information he needed, would she be able to retrieve the goods. Luck, however, had played right into Kiet's hands. The phone call he had received from the girl earlier that evening confirmed that everything had fallen into place. His seedy plan had worked. All that remained was for him to get his hands on the merchandise. His darting eyes caught sight of Nok weaving her way through the crowd of night revellers. She approached carrying no bag and wearing only a thin dress. As she drew close Kiet got straight to the point.

'Where the fuck is it?'

His voice was rough, like the crunching of gravel under foot.

Nok was well acquainted with displays of aggression, Kiet's manner didn't intimidate her, and she shot back.

'Give me my money first.'

'I'm not standing in a bar with 100,000 baht in my back pocket. You give me my stuff and I'll make sure you get your money,' he said.

In reality Kiet had no intention of paying Nok for anything. He had managed to secure the 100,000 baht as an upfront investment from his new employer. But true to his nature, this was something he thought he could clip for himself. Nok was not buying this *give me what you have now, money later* line. She had endured considerable danger. Although this had reaped her an unexpected windfall, she had nearly been strangled for her efforts. She wanted what had been promised to her. She turned his own words against him.

'Well, I'm not walking in a bar with seven kilos of heroin, you give me my money and I'll make sure you get your stuff,' she said.

Kiet's duplicity was something she'd been expecting. His whole manner had indicated that he was a treacherous weasel. Kiet didn't like his own tactics reflected back and he stepped up the heat.

'Don't be talking about that in here you dumb whore. Now you fuck off and get what I want, bring it here as agreed and then I might think about paying you.'

As far as Nok was concerned it was his fault they were in an inappropriate place to do an exchange and she felt he needed to be reminded of that.

'Dumb whore! I'm not the one who chose the most public place possible to do the exchange? I'm not walking round with a death sentence in a bag any more than I need to. You give me my money and I'll tell you where the stuff is. I don't want it, but after what I went through to get it, I want paying for it.'

This was too much for Kiet. This little slut was not going to upset his plan. He was counting on this last piece of this puzzle to fall into place tonight. On the strength of this he had already made promises he was duty bound to fulfil. If he failed at this stage who knows what the consequences would be. Kiet shot out a wiry forearm and caught Nok by the throat, forcing her up against the wall. His fingers bit into her flesh.

'I want what's mine!' he hissed.

Despite the pain Nok kept her features as passive as possible. Sucking in the air she spat in his face with as much force as she could muster. Kiet's jaw tightened and through clenched teeth he said,

'This is going to get fucking ugly for you!'

At this, Kiet let loose a punch that caught Nok square in the mouth whipping her head backwards and smashing it against the wall. This was followed by a second blow that caught her high on the temple nearly knocking her unconscious. Her legs bucked beneath her. She would have fallen to the floor, but Kiet was much stronger than his slight frame disclosed. He held her in place by the throat. He was about to go for the third punch when Alex turned the corner on his way to the bathroom. Alex just managed to catch the advancing fist.

'You're not doing that again,' Alex said restraining his arm.

Kiet spun round. Loosening his grip, Nok slid to the ground. He may have been thin, but what he lacked in weight he made up for in viciousness.

'What, what did you say white boy, this is none of your fucking business, now fuck off!'

It was not Alex's style to brawl in bars with strangers. But he was not going to stand by and watch a passive girl beaten by a street monkey like this. When people were brutalising women, it was everybody's business.

'This is my business,' he said still holding on to Kiet's arm.

The two men stared at each other. Then with a surprising turn of speed Kiet wrenched his arm free. His hand darted behind his back, and he produced a twelve-centimetre butterfly knife from the band of his trousers. With a flourish, the blade was point on in Alex's face. Alex had watched the opening of the knife. It had been reasonably efficient. This move had obviously been practiced. Alex was now observing the posture of the aggressor. Kiet was standing square on, the knife held out in front of him with an outstretched arm. This was an overt threat gesture from a man who wants to intimidate, but doesn't know how to, or necessarily want to use his weapon. Even so Alex knew blindly thrust knives kill, and the skill of the person avoiding a blade has to be far greater than that of the person wielding it. Alex took in the scene and marked Kiet's position. He cast his eyes down and held his arms to the side of his head in surrender.

'Ok, ok I'm sor …'

The word sorry was never finished. Attacks on the off the beat were always more effective. Instantly, Alex's arm swung round Kiet's locking it at the elbow, preventing him thrusting or moving the knife. At the same time Alex stepped through and tipping Kiet over his leg threw him to the ground. In a fraction of a second, he twisted Kiet's wrist. The pain forced his fingers to open, and the knife clattered to the floor. Alex kicked it away. Kiet screamed, he felt as though his wrist would break and his arm would be torn from its socket. It was only a brief moment of pain as Alex's foot caught him point on behind the ear knocking him senseless. The whole episode had taken less than three seconds, but the altercation had been witnessed. A bar girl came running over. Bar girls had a keen eye for trouble and were quick to quell any situation that might threaten trade. Diffusing alpha males and displacing violence was their business.

'Hey, hey mister no fighting here!'

4ft 9 of angry nineteen-year-old looked up at Alex. He held up his hands to placate her and said the first thing that came into his head.

'I wasn't fighting. He fell over drunk.'

It was a pathetic lie, and he didn't even know why he'd said it. The girl wasn't having any of it.

'He no fall over drunk, I saw you, you hit him, you no fight in here,' she berated.

Alex thought it best to tell the truth.

'Look this guy was beating her up,'

He gestured to Nok, still with her back against the wall and a smear of blood staining her bottom lip.

'He pulled a knife on me.'

The girl looked around.

'Where knife, I don't see knife, I see you hit him, you want fight you fight somewhere else, you no fighting here,' she said slapping him on the chest.

Alex scanned the area. He hoped to pick up the weapon to show he wasn't lying, but he must have kicked it harder than he thought. It was nowhere to be seen. He was on holiday, the last thing he wanted was trouble or involvement with the police. Rather than stay and argue the point he thought discretion might be the better part of valour.

'Ok, ok I'm sorry I'm leaving.'

He turned to Nok, who was still stunned. He held her by the arm. Even at this slight touch her skin was the finest he had ever felt.

'Are you coming with me?' he said supporting her.

Nok nodded her head and the two of them made their way through the bar and back to the place where Richie was sitting smoking. He had obviously given up on the Connect 4 and was now making eyes at a striking looking lady at the other side of the bar. She was panther-like, square jawed with high cheekbones, tall, lithe and muscular. Alex pulled up with Nok behind him and attempted to wrest Richie's attention away from the woman.

'Listen I think it might be a good time to leave,' Alex said with some urgency.

Richie turned and seeing Nok on Alex's arm broke into a wide grin.

'Fucking hell mate, you're quick. You don't move on much but when you do it's quality.'

Alex brushed the comment away.

'Look there's been a bit of bother, it might be good if we leave.'

Trouble never seemed to faze Richie, in fact he always thought it was an excellent spectators sport. Besides Alex had a prize and he had his eyes on a prize of his own. He pulled Alex's ear to his mouth. He wasn't ready to leave.

'Look mate this place is just starting to get interesting.'

He nodded in the direction of the huntress. She smiled back holding up her drink with a sculpted hand.

'Listen you have some fun; I'm just starting to make mine.'

Alex followed Richie's eye across the bar. She certainly was something very different to all the other girls.

'Seriously Richie, I just think ...'

Richie cut him short and patted him on the arm.

'Seriously, you go off, enjoy, get a couple of hours in with, what's her name here and I'll see you back at the hotel.'

Alex knew the man lying on the floor at the back of the bar had not seen him and Richie together. No friends had come to the man's rescue, so probability was, he was alone. Alex concluded that leaving Richie by himself was unlikely to put

79

him in danger. Besides, he really wanted to spend time with this girl and find out more about her. Alex conceded.

'Ok look I'll see you back at the hotel and don't do anything I wouldn't do ok?'

It was parting advice that he knew Richie had no intention of following, but he made it anyway. Not taking his eyes off the girl across the bar Richie said under his breath.

'Believe me mate I'm going to do a lot of things you wouldn't do.

7

My cock

The smell of wood stain and varnish filtered up from the workshop below. The walls of the room were half panel oak above which hung William Morris floral print wallpaper. The furniture was French Restoration, reflecting the classic influences of the earlier Greek and Egyptian periods. Light streamed in through four large Georgian windows set into the front wall and looking out onto the street below. The flood of light mellowed the dark theme, giving a warm sepia glow to what could have been an oppressive room.

This was the upper rooms of City Antiques; the main office of Vivian Brownsword, known to everyone as Viv. Viv had an almost encyclopaedic knowledge of all things relating to crime and the perpetrators of crime. If you could take a PhD in thuggery, then Viv would be 'The' professor emeritus at Cambridge. Viv, however, was a practical man and never understood the purpose of knowledge unless it was put to good use. Ever since he was a child all he wanted to be in life was a gangster. Now at the age of 47 he was a fully paid-up member of the underworld fraternity. His tight grip extended over the entire North of England, and he had favourable relationships with most of the other significant players in the country. If you bought hash, needed steroids to boost your ego, put your money in a slot machine, received a short-term loan, needed 'insurance' or simply required money to be collected quickly and without 'fuss', Viv Brownsword was the man.

It had always intrigued him that Al Capone's business card introduced himself as a *'used furniture dealer'*. Wanting to improve on Al's business model Viv had the idea of buying cheap second-hand furniture and pretending to sell it on as high-end antiques. Then, with a little creative accountancy, it would be possible to launder money gained in ways that the law would not look upon favourably. Al, however, must have known something that Viv did not because right from the start he had found it extremely difficult to filter money through City Antiques. Buying furniture was time consuming, it was difficult to manufacture customers and the shop simply didn't have the capacity to launder sufficient amounts. As a result, 99.9% of his illegitimate income streams still filtered through his extensive network of gaming machines. Despite City Antiques clearly being unfit for its intended purpose, Viv kept it running.

Over the years, from a venture to launder money, it had morphed into what was now a reasonably respectable antiques shop. Even so the shop barely broke even and if objectively weighing profit against effort he would have probably closed it down long ago. In reality the shop was a whimsy, Viv's vanity project. He felt it gave him an air of sophistication. And it acted as a useful talking point on the occasions when he had to mix with people on the other side of the legal fence.

Viv was behind his desk barking down the phone. The call was long distance. Archie sat opposite watching the conversation unfold. It was not going well. Carl stood to attention watching light bouncing off the motes of dust which hung in the air, his hands clasped behind his back, the classic pose of a man in the dock. Despite living in Newcastle for over thirty-five years Viv had never lost his cockney accent and when he lost his temper, which was frequent, it became even more pronounced.

'I don't give a tuppeny fuck for your loss mate, if you can't keep hold of your powder that's got fuck all to do with me? What I do know is that I've got a fuckin' man in hospital and two-hundred grand of my money, my fuckin' money is …'

Archie cut him short before he could finish his sentence.

'Vivian open land line mate,' he reminded him.

Only Archie called Vivian, Vivian, and that was only when he need to grab his attention. To everyone else Vivian was Viv.

Viv and Archie had known each other a long time, ever since Viv's parents relocated up north when he was twelve. Viv had been slight as a child, which was hard to believe looking at the bulk he had acquired over the ensuing years. His then, lack of stature had not affected Viv's ability to intimidate. Right from the outset he'd never let being an outsider or being outnumbered become a disadvantage. In fact, in many ways Viv made his 'otherness' work for him. Most of the kids in the school thought his dad was an East End gangster who used to work for the Krays. Viv neither confirmed nor denied these rumours. And as Archie was the only person ever to visit Viv at home, no one ever met his parents in order to dispel the myth. Only Archie really knew the rumours were not true, but he never told. In reality Viv's dad was a self-employed accounts manager who had sold his modest house in SW15 to buy a very large house in NE34 so his wife could be near her aging parents. Given his middle-class respectable upbringing it was hard to see where Viv's penchant for violence and crime came from. This question would undoubtedly require a much deeper delve into the nature verses nurture debate.

 Archie and Viv had hit it off almost from day one when, in a fight, Viv had bitten off more than he could chew taking on three older boys. It was Archie who had come to his defence. The two boys had still not been a match for their larger assailants, but the experience forged an instant bond. Even as boys they unconsciously understood that they filled gaps for each other. Viv had a talent for violence and intimidation. He had a personality people wanted follow. His edge of danger mixed with a rough charm was a heady social aphrodisiac. If left unrestrained, however, Viv's violent outbursts had a tendency to be indiscriminate, and his need to be recognised could lead to self-destructive behaviour.

Archie on the other hand had a talent for strategy. He could spot opportunity; he understood caution and recognised the right time to exercise force and the right time to exercise diplomacy. On this basis their relationship had developed. Viv was the force to be reckoned with, leading the troops, first over the wall to storm the castle, Archie making the battle plan and negotiating the terms of surrender. It was not just a relationship of business; it gave both men the brother they never had. Although it was never said one didn't really function without the other, they both knew it.

Taking Archie's reminder, Viv resumed his telephone conversation but this time in slightly more guarded terms.

'Are you telling me that someone's made off with my shipment of hand-crafted furniture?'

It was a thin disguise after what he had just said but it was good enough. From the opposite chair Archie gave him the thumbs up. When he was in a temper Viv's words had to be tactfully directed. With a reassurance his analogy was appropriate Viv continued.

'Too fuckin' right you'll find out what happened,' there was a pause, it was unclear whether Viv was listening or simply winding up for his next barrage, 'well forgive me if I've lost confidence in your, 'on the life of my dear, sweet, grey-haired mother guarantee.' I'll make you a guarantee son. By tomorrow I'm going to be standing in front of you and you better have a fuck site more answers than I'm getting now.'

With that he slammed down the receiver. It hit the phone so hard it nearly split in two.

'Cunt!'

Viv had signed off.

Carl, who up until this point showed a remarkable lack of interest in the conversation, decided that now was the time to show concern.

'Something wrong Boss?' he ventured.

Carl had been with Viv for five years. He was only twenty-four but was as large as a gable end. His eyes were heavy lidded, his words slurred and even at his young age most of his hair had gone. He cut a shambling figure and gave the appearance more of a man in his mid-forties. Viv kept Carl around because he didn't think too much, armies needed people like Carl. Carl's were the bread and butter of the front line and this one was Viv's number one debt collector and bringer of retribution. He had no moral limitations with regards to how his work was done. Carl didn't think too much and was excellent at following orders, as long as those orders were clear. He never asked why or what for, he just did. He was also puppy dog loyal, which was a rare commodity. When he received no immediate reply, Carl repeated,

'Something wrong Boss?'

Viv slowly looked up from behind the desk and his eyes met Carl's.

'What did you say?'

Viv's words were slow and deliberate. Archie had seen this look before, the calm before the storm.

'You just sounded upset like, something wrong?' Carl said with an air of sympathy.

Viv started to wind up for his reply.

'Something wrong, something wrong, are you for fuckin' real! Where the fuck have you been for the last ten minutes. Sometimes I wonder what goes on in that thick fuckin' head of yours. Fuck all I suspect. I'll tell you what's wrong you fuckin' moron, two-hundred grand gone, Dermot in some fuckin' ting tong hospital and can't even remember his name, bent fuckin' chinkies that's what's wrong. I should have my head examined. Too fuckin' soft that's my trouble, my mum always said I was too trusting.'

Carl nodded his head in sage like agreement and then offered his pearl of wisdom.

'Aye Boss you got to be hard in this game like.'

Viv's eyes widened, was this Carl offering him advice. He thought he would clarify.

'What!'

Carl stumbled on.

'You know, hard, like, you know, when you show weakness and that. That's when the dogs move in, like, isn't it?'

This was an opinion not asked for and not appreciated. When Viv wanted opinions, he usually beat them out of people.

'Are you deliberately trying to wind me up?'

He made it sound like an actual question rather than a statement. Carl's tone was one of genuine surprise.

'No Boss, I'm just saying if you haven't got an edge, like, that's when people take advantage. You know man, you know, if I believed people when they said they didn't have the money whe …'

Advice from Carl was the final insult to the injury. It was time to put an end to this conversation.

'Fuckin' edge, edge, I'll show you edge. One more word out of you and I'll cut your fuckin' ears off, is that edge enough for ya.'

Carl looked like a hurt child.

'Boss I was only trying to …'

Carl's sentence was never finished it was cut short by a Caithness glass paperweight that sat on the corner of Viv's desk catching him just above the left eye. An instant later Viv was on his feet and landed heavy slap to the side of Carl's head. Viv thrust his finger into Carl's face.

'When I want your advice I will fuckin' ask for it, do you understand? I pay you to tell you what to do, don't you never tell me how to run my business, never tell me how to think, do you understand, you fuckin' retard.'

Although Viv was a big man Carl was a lot bigger and seemed to have an unlimited capacity for soaking up pain. The impact of the paperweight and the ensuing slap made little change to his passive, albeit slightly confused expression. Despite not fully understanding the offence he had caused it was obvious Viv was not happy and Carl apologised with a deep sincerity. Archie let Viv get a few moments of rage out of him before stepping in. Coming up behind Viv he put his hand on his shoulder and in a voice that seemed too quiet to be heard over the emotions of the situation said.

'Vivian, Vivian he doesn't understand, you know that. The problem's not in the room mate. We need to talk.'

Archie's voice always seemed to get through to Viv even under the most difficult circumstances. The assault stopped;

89

Viv took himself out of Carl's face. Archie took charge of the diplomacy.

'Carl are you alright mate?' he said soothingly.

Carl replied as though he had just been caught in a light shower of rain.

'I'm ok Archie, sorry and all that like. Is the Boss ok?'

Archie put his arm round Carl's broad shoulders and led him towards the door.

'He's alright, mate it's just the stress of management can be hard sometimes. You understand?'

He knew Carl wouldn't understand, but he felt he had to give some explanation. Carl nodded his enormous head in empathy of leadership pressures. Archie opened the door for him.

'Now Carl, what I would like you to do is go and make us all a nice cup of tea, then you can have the rest of the week off, how does that sound?'

Carl's face opened up in a broad smile.

'Really?'

'Really mate, you've been working hard lately, you deserve it.' Archie said patting him on the back.

Once Carl had left the room, Archie knew they had to get down to business. The situation that faced him now was far more difficult to diffuse than a few misplaced words by Carl. Viv summed up what was in front of them.

'£200,000 of my money.   Who the fuck does he think he's doing business with, some fuckin' Mickey Mouse part timer who shits his pants when things go wrong? If this cunt thinks I'm just going to sit back and wait for the phone to ring he's got another thought coming.'

Viv ranted more to himself than to Archie.

Viv had been a little cagey about the exact details of this deal right from the start. He was evasive regarding how he'd made the business contact and as for the £200,000, this bit of detail was new to Archie. Moving forward Archie thought it best to know just what had gone missing.

'Listen Viv £200,000. I thought we agreed a test shipment of a hundred grand and then take it from there?'

Archie rubbed his temple; they'd had this conversation before. He had nothing against expansion in principle, but he was aware that there was a fine line between expansion and explosion. Right now, however, it was clear that this was a line of enquiry Viv did not want to go down.

'Ok, ok, I know, I know what we agreed. But it's you that keeps banging on about scales and economy and all that. You're the one that says let the numbers speak for themselves. 40% return on 100k, sixty percent return on 200K. That's maths!'

Viv never said sorry, but Archie could tell by his tone that he was contrite. Viv reflected on the wisdom of his decision.

'I should have fuckin' known it. My mum always said you couldn't trust these people, not after what they did during the war.'

Archie knew that this was a lot of money to recover and not a task that Viv would be happy to leave in the hands of others. But he didn't quite understand the reference to the war. He sought to clear up his confusion.

'Sorry Viv, the war?'

Viv looked as though Archie had forgotten the date of the battle of Hastings, so he clarified.

'The war, you know, the second world war, escape from the river Kwai and all that.'

'The River Kwai was the Japanese,' Archie corrected.

Viv waived his hand dismissing what he saw as pedantry. 'Well Japanese, Chinese they're all the fuckin' same.'

Archie knew that in his dealings with people Viv was blind to race, creed, religion and sexuality. But when Viv lost his temper, this was sometimes hard to tell.

'That's a bit casually racist; these people are Thai's mate' Archie interjected.

Viv ignored Archie's concerns regarding political correctness and continued with the misguided self-satisfaction of someone who believes they have made their point.

'Exactly and that's what I fuckin' mean in'it. Get us two tickets to Hong Kong now, tonight!'

Archie had seen this temporary confusion before, Viv's thoughts would clear once the adrenaline rush had passed.

'Don't you mean Bangkok Viv?'

'Bangkok, Hong Kok, my cock, just get two fuckin' tickets we're going.'

8

Michelin Star

The night air was still and heavy, the side street narrow and dark. The only light came from the windows of the close-set low-level apartments on either side, casting pale watery shadows onto the wet pavement. Here and there an occasional rat was caught in the jaundice glow. A blanket of silence hung over every surface, a jarring juxtaposition to the visceral bass music of the night life that could only be half a mile away. The whole atmosphere was one of neglect, peeling paint and crumbling plaster. This was where the bar girls and street walkers lived, the people who fuelled the whole crazy sex and alcohol machine that was Pattaya. Quiet by night, as they were all working, quiet by day, as they were all sleeping. In any other city property this close to the centre of everything would be prime real estate, affordable only to those in the upper income bracket. But not here, prosperity and poverty lived cheek by jowl in an uneasy alliance.

The girl walking next to Alex didn't speak and had not done so since they left the bar. She had been walking in silence by his side for fifteen minutes. She moved with a grace and determination he had never seen in another woman and every time a rare soft breeze teased her midnight hair, he caught the thin note of sweet jasmine. This girl was truly beautiful. She raised the back of her hand to her mouth. Alex saw her face contort as she touched the split on her lower lip where the thug in the bar had caught her with a punch. Her tongue flicked out to catch a thin trickle of blood.

Awkwardly Alex broke the silence.

'You alright?'

She nodded.

'How's your mouth?'

She made no reply.

'You speak English?' he asked.

'I speak English very well,'

Her accent had an American flavour with a breathy melody.

Alex was never what anybody would describe as a 'chat up merchant'. One liners and free flow witticisms were not his stock in trade. Richie was the man for that. Sometimes Alex would cringe at Richie's opening lines with women and sometimes so would the lady who was the target of his affections that night. Richie though, had always treated rejection and acceptance with the same cavalier attitude and his style suited him. It was not Alex's style. He may not have been 'silver tongued', but Alex had always found it easy to talk to women. With this girl it was different. He found himself fumbling to say anything outside of the functional. Eventually all he could think to say was,

'So, what was all that about in the bar?'

Her reply came in one word.

'Nothing,'

Alex tried again, 'Boyfriend trouble?'

Again, one word,

'No,'

'Pimp?'

He knew the moment he said it, it was the wrong question. She stopped dead in her tracks and turned her probing black eyes on him.

'What?'

Words fell from Alex's mouth in no particular order.

'Err, look sorry, I meant ... it was just that, I mean the bar, you know and ... and err, look I just thought that ...'

Her eyes burned, but her attitude was cool and controlled, her words measured but cutting.

'You just thought. And what did you think?'

'Look I'm sorry, I didn't mean to say, but the club and....'

'You farang are all the same. Little Thai girls are fairground rides for you. Pay your money and ride the rollercoaster.

96

With your shrivelled dicks and fat wallets, you think everything has a price,' she hit back.

Alex had witnessed the dynamic she was talking of in just about every bar he had visited in this town. He even recognised elements of this attitude in Richie, but that was not him. She had to know this; he was different.

'Listen please, I know what I said, but that's, that's not what I think, that's not who I am.'

'Oh yes, you're different, not same, same but different, but really different, right! Fuck you, I don't need your money or your help. Go find yourself a whore to rescue hero.'

Turning her face from his she strode off into the night. Alex watched her panther like curves disappear into the darkness and round the corner. It must have only been five seconds, but he couldn't bear to let her out of his sight. He ran after her. As he rounded the end of the street, she was only two or three metres ahead. She heard him approach and turned.

'Don't follow me,' she snapped.

Alex held up his hands to show he meant no harm.

'Look, please, I've offended you and I'm truly, truly sorry. I've only been here a week, I came for a competition, and this is only really the first night I've had out, but I've already been offered twenty massages, ten long times and fifteen short times. In every bar I've been into it's "handsome man, where you from, what you do, you like Thai lady." And what is it

97

with guys offering to make me a suit every time I pass a shop. It's all just a bit confusing. Please, I am really sorry, I'm not trying to pick you up, honest. You just looked in trouble and I only wanted to help.'

His words came out like a stream of consciousness. He paused for breath; her dark eyes were studying him intently. He had her attention.

'Listen I've not eaten for hours. I'm very hungry. Please let me buy you something as a way of saying sorry. Eat with me … Please'

Watching closely his body language, his awkward stuttering apologies, his open face, filled with, not lust, but deep desire, she considered his offer. Although young she had had many years of experience reading people. She knew when they were lying, which was most of the time, she knew when they were telling the truth, which was rarely, and she knew when they were genuine. This man seemed genuine. Genuine people were easy. As she looked at him, she began to think his fortuitous arrival could be just what she needed to take the heat out of her current predicament and the seeds of a crude plan began to germinate in her mind.

'Ok,' she said.

Five minutes later they were sitting in a street food bar. Despite being nearly one o'clock in the morning the place was full. Steam and the aroma of spices filled the air. Lemon grass, galangal, sweet basil, garlic and coriander, knitted together with the ubiquitous fish sauce and sharpened with a murmur of lime chilli to tingle the taste buds. A film of sweat covered the two diminutive middle-aged women who frantically worked the five roaring woks, all of them big enough to take a bath in. Their sinewy forearms mottled with burns from the years of exposure to spitting oil and charcoal sparks. Patrons sat at plastic tables, on plastic patio chairs, shovelling rice from cheap plastic bowls or sipping soup through plastic straws out of plastic bags all under the glare of sodium orange light. The furniture and fittings may have been plastic, but the fare was far from it. Although the establishment may never win a Michelin Star, the food was the best Alex had tasted since he arrived.

As they began to eat, they chatted, and Alex found himself settling into her company. His words came in an order he recognised, and the lump had moved from his throat. Nok, which he learned was his companions name and apparently meant bird, had let him choose the whole meal. He hadn't understood much of the menu, so he'd opted for the predictable, but safe, green curry and Pad Thai, with two Singha beer. During the course of the conversation Alex noticed a subtle change in Nok's accent. In the back lane when she was angry it was precise with more than a touch of American influence. Now it seemed softer, rounder more, melodic, more … Thai. He hailed an effete boy waiting the tables.

'Another Singha, please,' and then to Nok 'what would you like?'

'Singha good,'

'Two Singha please,' ordered Alex.

The young boy scurried off. Her passiveness during the meal was very different to the fire he saw in her earlier. Was this cultural? Was this the male female dynamic? He chanced the question.

'Do Thai girls choose anything?'

Nok met his gaze full on and her eyes probed every inflection of his face. She recognised this look, could it be time to draw him in. Her voice deepened.

'We choose some things,' she said holding his gaze.

Alex returned her stare as long as he could before breaking to find an uncomfortable interest in the table between his elbows. He had never had anyone look at him like that, to strip him naked and to see the longings and vulnerability that lay within. Nok knew she was taking control, but how could she use this to her advantage? She needed a plan. Nok held the silence for a beat too long, before subtly shifting gear.

'What you doing in Thailand, holiday?' she asked.

'In part,' Alex replied.

'In part?'

He illuminated the question.

'It's a holiday now but I came here for the Muay Thai.'

'You like to watch the Muay Thai?'

'More than watch.'

Alex lifted his hands in a guard and feigned a right elbow cross. Nok raised her eyebrows.

'You like to fight, you any good?'

She knew a lot of people came to Thailand for the Muay Thai, most were posers.

'Not quite good enough I'm afraid got through to the final of the Kraduk Khaeng but lost in the final to a Thai guy from Chantanubri.'

He touched the fine cut below his right eye. Alex had always been lucky when it came to cuts, his face rarely showed signs of damage. Thick skin Graham called it, thick skin and a tight-fitting brain, hard to cut, hard to knock out.

'You fight in the Kradūkkhǎeng?'

She sounded genuinely impressed. Alex nodded. Nok had heard of the Hard Bones Tournament. She knew well what it took for a foreigner to even get a place on the invite list, never mind get through to the final. Was this a good thing or a bad thing for her tentative plan? She decided that it was a good thing, it could give Alex some credibility as a street player. She reached out and gently stroked the wound under his eye and made a mock *"aww"*.

101

'I don't like the fighting, flattens men's noses, Thai men noses already flat. You have a good nose, don't flatten it.'

The touch of her fingers on his face was exquisite.

'What about you?' Alex enquired, 'what are you doing here?'

The story she told was a familiar one for her and tripped easily from her tongue.   There were slight variations depending on the circumstances, but essentially everyone got a version of this story as an introduction.   She had other versions but for now this one would work.

'Five week ago, I come from my village after my father die. My mother have no money for me and my sister, so I come to here, long way for job. I met Kiet when I was collecting chair on beach. He helped me with somewhere to live and was very kind … but …' she paused for effect.

Alex interjected.

'Kiet, Was that the guy in the bar?'

Nok nodded and swallowed as if suppressing her emotions, then carried on.

'Then he started to tell me he wanted me to work in other ways, to pay him back for what he had done for me.   He brought two men back to my room, they had a camera. They wanted,' her voice wavered and tailed off. 'I managed to hit one and run away. Tonight, I try to tell him I don't want to see him anymore, but he says I owe him.'

Although he had never been before Alex had read about how things worked here. Prostitution was so open and free. On the surface it appeared as though the girls were empowered to pick and choose as they saw fit. It was easy to believe that what went on was a victimless transaction. But for every bar girl that thought she could tout the bloom of her youth to the highest bidder in order to make 'easy money', there were countless others like Nok, forced into it through poverty and oppression. These girls were caught in a downward spiral that would chew them up and vomit them out in ten years' time, ravaged and penniless.

'What are you going to do now?' Alex said.

'I think I will go back home, it quieter up north, not like here.'

'Do you live up north? I've heard it's very beautiful, I really wanted to do some exploring while I was here, but I fly to Phuket tomorrow, and I have to be home in a week.'

This piece of information was valuable to Nok. This man's intention of not being in the country too long might be useful.

'How about tonight?' Alex ventured.

'All my things are in the apartment, I'm afraid to go back and get them but I need them. Then I will find somewhere just for tonight. I can leave tomorrow.'

As she spoke, she allowed a pool of tears to gather in her eye. It had the desired effect. Alex couldn't let this girl go, to

103

turn her back into the night at the mercy of people like Kiet was abhorrent to him. He found himself blurting out.

'Why don't I come with you back to your apartment. We can pick up your stuff; I don't think he'll be much trouble if he's there and then.' Alex hesitated; his voice nearly broke, but he managed to continue. 'Then, if you want, you could stay with me for the night.'

She reached across the table and placed her palm on his cheek.

'I hope you'd ask,' she said and kissed him gently.

They were now nearly twenty minutes away from the street cafés and deep into the impoverished part of town. In a heavily tourist area this was a place in which a foreigner was still an alien species and hardly seen. This was a part of town that was the underbelly of the underbelly, where you found the people that supplied unsavoury services to the people who supplied unsavoury services. Here rooms could be rented by the hour with sheets at an extra cost. Despite this, Alex felt an easy lightness of being. Nok had taken his arm and rested her head on his shoulder all the way there. As they walked and chatted, Nok was actually beginning to find Alex's company restful. The years of having her heart hardened towards men began to melt away. His interest in her and the light touch of his questions were putting her at ease. Her normally guarded approach to men was softening. Despite

104

herself she began to open up about her background, injecting more truths than she was normally comfortable with. She spoke of her childhood near the town of Thung Na about 500 kilometres north. She described her little village of no more than eight traditional houses about five kilometres outside of town on the banks of the river Ping. She recalled her family home, the balcony overlooking the river, and remembered a time when she was young, she and her sister had stuck shells round the front door and painted them in bright colours. She told how, in her family's more affluent days, her father had owned a farm. He worked the land, and her mother tended the chickens and the pigs. She related how the government had forced the purchase of their farmland for development paying them only a fraction of what it was worth. Then she told how her father, in a desperate attempt to care for his family, had invested what little he'd got for the land in a business that crashed, leaving them to subsist day to day. Nok even began to shed a tear as she recounted how the strain of the situation had taken such toll on her father's health, he eventually died of a heart attack at the young age of forty-five.

As Nok spoke she spun together reality and fantasy. Tragic though this story was she wished it were true. She labelled this story a simple fiction to pull at the heart strings of a gullible farang. The psychological truth was far harsher. The real function of this story was to construct an alternative

105

reality to protect her from the inner torments that came from years of sexual abuse and domestic violence. A combination that had beat her childhood out of existence. Alex knew none of this, all he knew was that the more she spoke the more he wanted to care of her.

Eventually they stopped outside a yawning hole of a doorway in a concrete slab of a building. This was brutalist architecture at its most brutal. Beyond the doorway a dark enclosed stairway disappeared into midnight black.

'This is it,' she said, 'this is my apartment.'

It didn't look like any apartment Alex had ever seen. It was more like an abandoned sweatshop. She made to enter the building. Alex stopped her.

'What if he's there?'

'I don't think so.'

'I'll come with you, just in case,' he said taking hold of her arm.

'No!' she pushed him back with surprising force, 'he will not be here. Trust me, I know he will not be here. Please wait for me, I will not be long.'

With that she gently kissed him and left him in the street as she ascended the stairs into the blackness. Outside Alex stood alone. Without the sweet jasmine fragrance of Nok at his side the acrid tastes of the gutter started to assail his nostrils. He watched a lizard with half a tail climb the wall and

106

somewhere in the distance two cats fought like lions. Although it was twenty-seven degrees, he folded his arms around himself to keep warm. A two-stroke scooter passed the end of the road. He heard it pull up just out of sight, but no one appeared. Three floors up he noticed a faint light flicker on a windowpane.

Inside Nok flicked on the table lamp. This was no real living space, just a functioning drop off / pick up, crossroads of a room barely functional with little in the way of comfort. Dragging a battered vinyl chair with her, she went straight to the shower room. Her heart was thumping like a hammer against her chest. Pulling the chair close to the wall she stepped up and prised a section of tiling away to reveal a recessed area behind. She let out a sigh of relief. The tension in her began to relax. It was still there. She pulled down the kit bag she had stashed earlier and took it into the main room throwing it on to the dirty unmade bed. A cloud of dust rose in the yellow lamp light releasing a stale smell of mould. She unzipped the main compartment to check the contents. Money and drugs untouched. Quickly she resealed the bag and slung it over her shoulder. The strap bit into her skin. She flicked off the lamp and stood in the doorway gazing into the darkness of the room. It was unfortunate to make Alex a casualty of her situation. But she knew what she needed to do to survive.

9

Where are you?

Kiet had only been unconscious for a few moments, but when he came round, he was no longer in the club. He was lying on a walkway outside, overlooking the sea. His head throbbed from the beating he had just received. If dying was something he was going to do someone didn't want it happening in the club and had dumped him. His mind was foggy. What had just happened? As the mist shifted, it started to become clear to him. He had been double crossed. What were the chances of a fighter like that turning up? It was obvious the bitch had got herself a bodyguard, or an accomplice or something. Whatever the setup, one thing was certain, this was going to mean trouble.

He darted back into the club and pushing his way through the throng looked for any sign of Nok or the man. There was none, no doubt they had left almost the second he'd hit the ground. God knows where they would be now. He walked into the street. The crowds milled up and down highlighted by the garish glow of neon. It was a typical night on Walking Street, the party central of Pattaya. Not knowing where to start, he made a search of the local clubs and bars. It was as he had initially feared, nothing. He checked his watch; he had been due to drop off the drugs over two hours ago. He knew those waiting for him would start to get impatient. Over the past few weeks, he had begun to develop an uneasy feeling that his new Croatian employers were becoming bored with him, and he believed this was his last chance to impress before … before what? But this was not his fault, they couldn't blame him for this. He didn't know the girl would pull this last-minute stunt. He didn't know she was working with someone behind his back. As these thoughts raced through his mind, his mobile rang. He looked at the number. This was the call he had been expecting. But how to handle it? It was no good running. Perhaps if he explained the situation, they could help him find what he'd lost. He answered the call and was met with three words.

'Where are you?'

He fumbled for his answer, knowing what might ride on it.

'Err, there's been a problem, the girl didn't bring the stuff to the club as I told her. I was going to get it off her, but she had a man with her.'

He seized on the opportunity to paint a better picture of the situation for himself.

'Two men actually, sort of bodyguards, big bastards. I pulled a knife on one of them and cut him bad, I was going to finish him off but the other took me down from behind.'

The voice was unimpressed and cold.

'Come in, now!'

The tone gave little away, but Kiet didn't like it, perhaps he could still fix this.

'Listen this isn't my fault. I was nearly killed tonight working for you. Give me a couple of hours I can sort this out. I'll have that fucking girl trussed up with her throat slit and the stuff on your table by tomorrow morning. I guarantee.'

There was a long pause before the reply.

'Kiet, your time is up. It is what it is now.'

The line went dead.

10

Honey tinged with sweet lemon

Alex's body pushed Nok's against the wall of his hotel room. Her firm breasts had little give, they pressed hard against his chest. This was the ripeness of youth at its fullest. He ran his fingers through her blue-black hair, it felt like Charmeuse silk. Her tongue flicked teasingly in and out of his mouth and he felt the gentle scratch from the fresh cut on her bottom lip on his. His hand explored her leg making tentative excursions to her inner thigh. Slowly he caressed the moistness of her crotch on the back of his hand. He was breathing heavily, his body was awash with adrenalin and excitement, which made his legs quiver and the breath catch in his chest. His heart was pounding as though he had run a marathon and he heard the rush of blood in his ears. He had never been so excited.

In situations such as this Nok usually played a role she thought men wanted. She had learned long ago that the slow subtle close of an eye, the glimpse of a tongue, a wetted lip and the flutter of breath on a cheek was far more powerful than a volume of talk about how big a man was, how long he could last and how deep he was going. But there was something about this man's lean well sculpted body and his passion, physical, but respectful, that was beginning to awake sexual feelings in her. Feelings she had not had for a long time.

Alex gently turned her back to him and pulled her buttocks towards him. He brushed his palm over her flat stomach, her skin was dry with no trace of sweat. Sweat was something which had been Alex's constant companion since he arrived. God she was so hot. Catching his hand on the ring in her navel, he made his way to her panty line. He felt the delicate lace that adorned the waistline and slipped his hand inside. This was the first time he had been with an Asian girl and just everything about them was more feminine to him. He touched the top of her pubic hair. It was, short, straight and as soft as the hair on her head. One of Nok's hands was behind him drawing him in tight. With her other hand she pulled her panties just a little further down. She radiated sweetness. Alex became self-conscious that the night had been long, and he may not be so fresh. He nibbled her ear and whispered, 'Would you like to take a shower with me?' Nok's delicate hand slithered serpent like over the top of his hand and crept inside her panties. It overtook the tips of his fingers and plunged between her legs. He could feel her making rhythmic

112

circular motions. She let out a low, almost inaudible, moan of pleasure. Slowly she withdrew her hand and raised it over her shoulder to Alex's mouth, running it over his lips and down to his chin. Alex licked, it was sticky and tasted like honey tinged with lemon. She arched her back and pushed her head back until her mouth was close to his ear and in a low breathless voice said,

'Would you rather taste me or soap?'

11

Jomtien Beach, Pattaya

Men without fathers

Petar Horváth hung up the phone, sat back in his chair and ran his fingers through his tightly curled hair. The information he had just received needed some thought. He stared at the chess board in front of him. It was fruit wood and ebony check, set in a briarwood frame with a teak and mother of pearl chevron border. The pieces were hand carved white and black stained Ivory in a neo-gothic style. It dated back to 1888 and was given as a present from a grateful 'client'. The game he was plotting was a replay of the classic 1907 Rotlewi vs Rubinstein match. It was nearing its end. Rotlewi was on the brink of resigning in the face of an imminent and inescapable checkmate with Rf3 Bxf3, Qxf3 Rxh2. Petar reached out his thick finger and laid it on top of the white king. He rocked it back and forth twice before toppling it on its side. Like the move on Rotlewi, this phone call had come as a surprise.

Petar was Croatian born and bred. Croatia's turbulent past had transformed the country into a land of limitless possibilities for those who knew how to spot a weakness and exploit an opportunity. The aftermath of the war had left many power voids, and, within any system, nature abhors a vacuum. The vacuum that followed the conflict was quickly filled by men of enterprise, men who knew how to seize advantages and didn't care on which side of the law those advantages lay. War furnishes people with a lot of skills, many of which become redundant in civilian life. Petar had risen to where he was by recognising how to effectively apply the skills he had learned in war to crime. He knew violence and he had a calculating mind. The combination of the two had enabled him to build a vast and varied business empire. He controlled protection, prostitution, drugs, property, people trafficking, night clubs and the removal of difficult people, to name but a few of his income streams. This had provided him with all of the trappings of wealth, respect, multiple houses, boats, cars, fine art and women. The bitter irony was that, despite these societal markers of success, there was a void inside him that would never be filled, no matter how many possessions he had or how much money he accumulated. His life was reduced to one dimension when in October 1991 his wife and three children were among the seventy people massacred by the Yugoslav People's Army in his home village of Lovas. Petar was in the south fighting at the time, and it was three weeks before he found out. He watched them dig the bodies out of a mass grave on TV. This was the last time he was ever to cry. He never returned to his home village. The bitter emptiness this left inside Petar began to fill with power, perhaps as a desperate attempt to take control in a world which held no meaning for him and in which he felt so utterly impotent.

He had built up his empire mapping out his every move and counter move like a game of chess, the only thing for which he still had any vestiges of, what could be called, passion. The tactics of the game informed all of his business dealings. Business, like chess, was war. Petar knew there were five main types of chess player the same types which could be found in any walk of life.

There were the Passive Players, risk averse and who won't even sacrifice a pawn if it feels remotely unsafe.

There were the Gamblers, for them it is the lure of the risk, it's not just 'The' game, but any game that attracts them.

There are the Perfectionists contemplating for hours over one move, trying to play the ideal game, a game which never exists.

Then there are the Strategists who plan out the whole structure of play from the opening pawn to the mating nets, all before they sit at the table.

Finally, there were Attacking Maniacs, men who are out to kill, win big or lose big, men without fathers as Petar called them.

The key to success in chess, as in any field, was the ability to climb inside the mind of your opponent. Understand what type of person they were, establish their strategy and adapt your style accordingly.

For the last fourteen months Petar had held controlling interests in a number of clubs in Pattaya. These served as a nice side-line in prostitution and money laundering, good bread and butter. Petar liked Thailand and spent all his winter months there. Essentially this branch of his business paid for his villa overlooking Jomtien Beach and his catamaran. Petar was beginning to come of a mind that Thailand was a country in which he could take up permanent residence. A country free from the physical reminders of war.

In a bid to expand his local base he had tried several times to move into the profitable heroin trade. All attempts at establishing this new line of business, however, had come to nothing. He was unable to find any local providers, no one would move on the street for him, and even fledgling operations seemed to quickly close down. Only recently two of his men had disappeared without a trace. It was clear that there was a monopoly in the area. Only ever in hushed tones, the same name kept appearing in front of him, Chai Son. The whole region seemed to be beholding to Chai Son in one way or another. No matter who or how hard Petar pushed, no one was willing to cross Chai Son.

If he were to take power, he needed to know more about the man who was standing in his way. Chai Son, however, was a difficult man to get information on. If any questions were asked, they were met with stock answers of philanthropist, entrepreneur and property developer. Any further probing quickly closed down the line of enquiry. Control of the Chai Son public image was flawless. The way the man conducted business, how he thought, who he really was, was an enigma to Petar and Petar didn't like puzzles he couldn't solve. For him it was not so much the desire to control the whole of the region that began to eat at him, but the fact that he was being prevented from doing so by someone he didn't understand. Someone was out manoeuvring him and that he could not abide.

When, therefore, he received news of an unlikely character entering one of his clubs liberally using Chai Son's name as a badge of honour, it came within his circle of interest. Further enquiries had established the man as Kiet, a minor runner within Chai Son's organisation. Petar gave orders to cultivate him, to gather intelligence. Even at the lowest level it always paid to have eyes in the camp of the opposition. Kiet was easily turned, young greedy men with blind ambition always were. As Kiet began to pass information it started to become clear that he had vastly overplayed his hand. Petar was not expecting information from the high table. But he was expecting something that would satisfy his professional curiosity, something that would be of value, something that would give him an insight into the internal workings of Chai Son's business structure … and his mind. But no, as time went on all Kiet seemed to be privy to was fetching and carrying of day-to-day supplies and the passing on of mundane information. Petar was just on the verge of terminating this arrangement 'permanently' when Kiet came with something that was of interest. A time, a place and shipment of goods and to Kiet's credit he had even come up with a half decent plan on how to get his hands on it. The move, like any other, had its risks, but if anything were to go wrong Kiet would be the fall guy, he would be easy to dispose of so erasing any connection to Petar's organisation.

In monetary terms this was small beer, six or seven kilos of heroin with a wholesale value of a little under two million kuna. The real opportunity for him was to pull the tail of the tiger and to see how it reacted. What would Chai Son do when his security was compromised and his authority undermined. This opening gambit may provide valuable information as to his internal security responses. That was the plan, but now the game had changed.

The phone call he had just taken revealed that Kiet had successfully executed the first part of the plan and separated the product from its owner but had failed miserably in the second part of the plan, delivering that product to its new home. Somewhere along the line, more people had become involved. With more people came more chance of tracing things directly back to him. At this stage of his reconnoitre he did not want full-on conflict. His desire had been to create a splash and observe the ripple, not to start a war.

The game had changed, so too must the tactics. Kiet and anyone associated with him needed to be taken off the board, quickly. It was important that whoever he appointed to deal with this situation needed to be efficient, self-directed and loyal. Most of all they needed to be new to this scene. No one who was a known associate of Petar in Thailand. Chess was a game where every piece had an integral role to play, and the front line was led by pawns. If managed and supported right, these pieces, of limited manoeuvrability, could become very powerful indeed. It was now time to open with, not one, but two pawns. Not strictly within the rules of the game, but you could stretch a metaphor too far. He knew exactly who to send, two men with a limited area of speciality, but two men who did what they did very, very well. In Croatia, these men had been to the opposite side of the board with Petar several times and this made them incredibly useful. It was time to send for Nikola and Viktor.

Nikola and Viktor or the Twin Peaks, as they were 'affectionately' known. The two men were alike in every respect. They were the same height, they dressed the same, they were both bald and neither man said more than ten words a day and if they could get away with less, they would. They looked in every aspect, fruit of the same womb, two of the same seed. Truth was Viktor was four years older than Nikola and they had only known each other for nine years. In that time, they had formed a nuclear bond, drawn together by their mutual inability to fundamentally understand or build relationships with others. However, even the most disturbed minds suffer in isolation. Together the two men could sit in comfortable silence and share their common confusion regarding members of the human race without feeling utterly on their own. Did they keep each other sane, or did they just keep each other company? It was hard to tell.

Nikola and Viktor, a combined mass of 650lb with no more than ten percent body fat equally divided between them. Individually the two men were a force to be reckoned with. But the secret to the Nikola plus Viktor equation was that they were never divided, NEVER!

In his heart Petar feared them, although he never let this show. It was not good management to be afraid of the hired help. Fear was weakness and, in Petar's game, you rarely got a second chance to show a weakness. Nikola and Viktor were men without feeling and Petar knew first-hand what such men were capable of. He had seen this emptiness of morality before, in the war. Men like these fought for neither politics, principles nor profit. The violence of the situation was reward in itself. General life offered little pleasure.

Croatia was a place where the ostentatious showing of wealth was not considered crass. Others under Petar's employment lived a comfortable life, openly enjoying their fiscal status with cars, women, houses and designer clothes. Petar knew exactly the state of Nikola and Viktor's finances, he was their sole employer, and they were far from poor, though by looking at their lifestyle you would never have guessed it. They shared a two-bedroom apartment in a run-down, bohemian, part of town. They dressed as if from a charity shop and had one battered Ford Mondeo between them. They had no family that he knew of, hardly ever drank, never took drugs and never socialised. Apart from buying copious amounts of chicken and rice, he had no idea where the money went.

Nikola and Viktor for their part feared no one and no thing and cared not whether people feared them. Fear, hate, love, it was all the same. The taxonomy of people was simple, they were tasks or tools, one or the other. People's emotional state was of no consequence.

Petar reached for his mobile, took a deep breath and dialled. Less than three hours later Nikola and Viktor were standing at Zagreb Airport, passports in hand bound for Bangkok.

12

Cobra Arms Freedom .380

Kiet spent the rest of the night crawling around every rat hole and dive he knew searching for Nok and this new man. His phone rang frequently. It was always the same number. He ignored it, only delaying what he knew would be the inevitable confrontation. His night's work turned up nothing. In the early hours he made his way back to his apartment but was too scared to go inside just in case there was somebody waiting for him. He stood outside for over an hour pacing up and down, watching the door and looking up at the window. He saw no one. As the sun started to chase the night he decided to risk returning. There was something that he needed to pick up if he were to keep himself safe. Tentatively he crept up the grotty stairs to his one room flat.

He stood outside the door and listened intently, nothing, no movement, nothing. He knocked on the door and listened, ready to flee should there be the slightest sound, but still nothing. He put the key in the lock and entered. It was just as he left it. Inside was sparsely furnished and he made straight for the chest of drawers in the corner. Yanking open the top drawer, until it nearly came fully out, he thrust his hand inside. His fingers closed over the butt of his gun. This was to be his bodyguard. It was a Cobra Arms Freedom .380, one of the cheapest handguns on the market. It was almost the first thing he had purchased when he started as a lackey for Chai Son. He had never used it in a 'professional' sense, but he found that occasionally waving it about on a personal level, gave him a modicum of the reputation he aspired to. He dropped out the magazine, despite its seven round capacity there were only four inside. He had only ever bought twenty rounds when he first picked up the gun, sixteen of which he'd unloaded in the forest shooting at bottles and a passing bird. He never hit any of them. The number of rounds in the gun were of no consequence and it didn't matter that he would find it difficult to shoot anything more than five metres away. Kiet knew that when he stuck it in that farang's mouth he would comply with anything. This new man might be good with his hands, but victory doesn't always go to the one with the fastest fists. He inserted the magazine back into the receiver. His optimism of ever catching up with Nok and this man was beginning to wane, but if he did, he would make them pay.

Behind him the door to the apartment stood ajar. In his haste to turn himself around he had not shut it. The door swung silently open. In the dimly lit shadows stood Billy the Kat who, despite the gloom of the room, still had on his shades. Style had always taken precedence over practicality for Billy. He was flanked by two larger younger men.

'Every rat eventually returns to its hole I see,' Billy drawled in his faux American street slang.

Kiet spun round. The sound of Billy's voice punched him in the stomach with the force of a heavyweight boxer. It was all he could do to prevent himself from spontaneously vomiting. The two younger men were strangers to Kiet, but he knew Billy and he knew Billy knew Chai Son. He was Chai Son's eyes and ears on the street, that's what made him so useful when it came to finding people.

'Going Somewhere Kiet my man?' Billy enquired with a smile.

The dim light briefly caught his gold incisor.

Kiet's arm shot up and he pointed the gun at the three men framed in the doorway. He shook from head to foot and had an almost uncontrollable desire to urinate. His whole attitude was at odds with the words he heard coming out of his mouth.

'Fuck off, take one more step and I'll shoot you in the fucking face,' he spat.

Billy himself was not a violent man, he'd never beaten, tortured or shot anyone. But he had arranged for a lot of this to be done on Chai Son's behalf and had supervised much of it to make sure it was done right. Guns held little fear for Billy, after all being frightened would not be cool.

'Woah, woah Kiet cool your heels my man. What have I done to deserve a welcome like this?' His tone was relaxed and easy.

Kiet had assumed the worst, that somehow, they knew what he had done. Perhaps he was wrong. There followed a brief moment of uncomfortable silence.

'Billy,' he stuttered, 'I, I didn't expect … I thought you were …'

'Thought I was who Kiet man?'

Billy's tone was still soothing. Kiet slowly lowered his gun.

'Sorry Billy, I thought you were someone else.'

'Now I would hate to be that someone else,' Billy replied with a straight lipped, tight smile.

'What do you want Billy?' Kiet asked tentatively.

'As you know, I know people who know people. That's why people who are in the know, know to use me to find people, if you follow. And tonight, I'm looking for someone you might know.'

'Who, who are you looking for?'

Kiet struggled to keep his voice level and not to quaver.

Billy continued.

'We're looking for a girl, 5ft 5, long black hair, slim, about twenty-two or twenty-five years old, very attractive, I think you might know her.'

'I know a lot of girls and that could be ninety-nine percent of the female population round here. You will have to be more specific Billy.'

Kiet was pleased at his seemingly nonchalant attempt at wit.

Billy drew his phone from his pocket, tapped in the code and pulled up the picture of Nok that Chai Son had sent him. He pointed the screen towards Kiet.

'This more specific for you?' he said showing him the photograph.

Kiet knew who it was going to be even before the light from the screen hit his face, Nok! Kiet's mind raced. He could salvage this situation; he knew he could. He made an overly elaborate effort to show the internal workings of a mind searching for recognition. Eventually he said,

'Yes, yes you know I think I do know her, yes.'

'Do you want to tell me who she is?' Billy probed.

Kiet waved his hand as though dismissing the acquaintance as inconsequential.

'I, I think they called her Kanda or Kanya or something, she was just a girl off the street. I think she was quietly trying to pick up business in the Double Beat.'

Billy pushed further.

'What sort of business?'

While Billy talked the two large youths either side of him never moved and never took their eyes of Kiet's gun which now hung impotently by his side. They looked relaxed, but alert.

'You know the usual,' Kiet replied.

'And what would be the *usual*?'

Kiet started to detect an edge creeping into Billy's voice. He was keen for this gentle interrogation to end.

'Come on Billy you know, she was just a slut, a Sopheṇī, a girl off the street, looking to pick up a guy. Fuck me Billy we live in whore central. She came in, I saw her milling around, I asked her which bar she was with, she tried to pretend she was just in for a drink and then she left … That's all I know Billy … honest!'

A tangible silence gripped the air. It wrapped its fingers round Kiet's throat, he felt like it was choking the breath out of him. It may have only lasted five seconds, but it was twenty heartbeats for Kiet. Billy's eyes stared out invisibly from behind his dark glasses. Billy lazily broke his blind stare.

'Shit my man, I was hoping you knew where we could find her. Well, it's going to be a long day for Billy and the boys. Looks like we're going to have to hit the street.'

Billy's easy manner had returned and Kiet thought he looked genuinely disappointed at his lack of leads. He felt his heart returning from his throat to his chest. Billy turned to go followed by the two young men. As they were leaving the man to Billy's left turned and spoke.

'Do you mind if I use the bathroom before I go?'

Kiet was so glad it was all over; he wasn't about to refuse.

'Yes,' he said, 'it's the door just behind me.'

The young man made his way across the room. Kiet kept his eyes firmly on Billy, who now seemed to be leaving to wait outside. Lightly brushing by him on his way to the bathroom the young man left Kiet's peripheral vision. The second he was out of his line of site, Kiet felt sharp crack on the back of his neck followed by a searing light of orange pain passing through his head. In the distance he heard his gun, or was it his body, fall to the floor with a dull thud. The next second, he lapsed into unconsciousness. The intense orange light faded. All was black.

13

Kathoey

Light streamed in through the half open balcony doors. The warm morning breeze playfully flicked the pearlescent voile throwing dancing, translucent shadows over the tiled floor. Alex always preferred to sleep with a window or a door open. He liked the movement of real air, not the artificial atmosphere created by air-conditioning. He lay on the bed under a thin cotton sheet, Nok's perfect form moulded to his. It was only 10.00am, but it was already hot. A thin layer of sweat had formed between them. Their bodies moved frictionless against each other. Nok moved like a graceful cat in his arms, she seemed to undulate from the top to the bottom of her body. The tiny changes in pressure against his skin were exquisite.

Alex stroked her blue, black raven hair. His mind was torn between the perfection of the moment and the reality to come.

He had never met anyone like this before. He'd never felt so at one, so utterly willing to give himself over to another. Reality, however, told him that he didn't know anything about this girl, other than the brief history she had shared with him in the small hours of the night. In his rational mind he knew that relationships between Thai girls and western men were fraught with emotional danger. They tended to be asymmetric couplings, the girl looking to be cared for which, in her world, meant financial security for her and her family, the western man looking for love and fidelity. Love, however, is a secondary consideration in an environment of crippling poverty. Alex had heard stories of how this dynamic could create a downward spiral of mistrust and misunderstanding. The western man looking for reassurance that his partner was not just with him for his money withholds funds to test her loyalty. The Thai girl feeling insecure and uncared for becomes ever more distant. The process of disintegration was exponential. Although he didn't want to acknowledge it, there was a thread in his brain that told him this could be a bar girl. He would take her out, they would have some fun, they would exchange emails and he would return home. At first messages would start with how much he was missed and how much she loved him. Then, after several weeks, there would be a problem. She would ask for rent money, or possibly even the airfare so she could visit him, a visit which would be cancelled at the last minute due to the death of a relative or some such excuse. He knew that bar girls could have several men sending them money in this way. Each man sitting in his respective country, Norway, Germany, Holland, Britain, all thinking that she was keeping herself out of the bars and patiently waiting for them and them alone to return. Feelings and thoughts fought a silent battle inside him. Nok stirred, she raised her head from his chest and looked up at him with half closed eyes.

'Morning,' she said in a faraway voice.

Her soft lips kissed his chest. He felt her gentle breath on his nipple.

'Morning,' said Alex caressing her cheek and holding it in his hand. 'What now?' was all he could think to say.

'We eat, I'm hungry,' she said languidly.

'No with us, what happens with us?'

Nok pushed herself up on one elbow and looked into his eyes. She studied him for a few moments. His breath was uneven, his cheeks were flushed, and his pupils dilated. He seemed to be worried at the prospect of what she was about to say. She felt a deep pang of guilt inside her, she knew exactly how this was going to play out. Alex's gentle, naive kindness had taken her by surprise. This was something she had never had before, feelings for a man. She drove the emotions deep inside; it was too late to change the plan. Her future and the future of her sister depended on it.

'I must leave here today, it's no good here anymore, not safe,' she said bowing her head. At least this was a truth.

'Where will you go?' Alex asked.

'Back to my village.'

'Are you going to travel back up north to Thung Na to stay with your family and your sister?' Alex asked, remembering what she had told him when they were walking together in the street.

Nok paused, although she didn't show it, she was angry at her slip. The ease of Alex's company had led her to give away too much personal information. Her conversation was never what men wanted her for and farang rarely remembered anything they were told. Most men struggled to remember her name for more than five minutes.

Not finding a plausible way to backtrack she said,

'Yes, I go to see my sister. I have missed her very much,' keen to move the conversation away from herself she posed her own question, 'What about you, what you do?'

'Richie and I had tickets to fly down to Phuket today, spend our last week or so seeing a couple of the islands.' He paused hesitant to test the water of her intentions 'Look if you need any money, you know, just to help, just to get up to Thung Na, I don't have much, but I could …'

Nok put her finger to his lips.

'Shh, you are sweet, but I don't want your money, I have enough for what I need to do.'

Alex felt a rush of relief. She was not after money. Perhaps this girl was different. Her hand slipped under the light sheet and snaked its way over his stomach and down to the top of his crotch. Her fingers lightly brushed the tip of his penis as her thumb massaged his inner thigh. He could feel himself stirring to her touch.

Just then the bedroom door burst open. It was Richie in the full assault of his morning energy.

'Well, well, look who got lucky, but I know who got luckier,' he boomed as he bounded into the room.

Behind him in the doorway stood the square jawed predator Richie had been eyeing the previous evening. She was a good three or four inches taller than him and her large breasts were incongruous to her lean hard body, which clearly showed a six-pack peeking out beneath the straining crop top.

'Come on mate hands off your cock and on to your socks,' said Richie flopping himself on the corner of the bed and slapping Alex hard on the chest.

Alex rolled over on his side and groaned. No matter what happened the night before no matter how drunk, no matter how late the party, Richie always grabbed the morning with both hands and throttled the life out of it. It was one thing

135

that Alex loved about him, but it was also the one thing that could get right on his fucking nerves. Nok seemed to take the intrusion in her stride. Slowly and modestly, she drew the sheet across her body, the white linen doing little to conceal her perfect curves. The profile offering a tantalising promise of what was beneath.

'Now, who's for breakfast, I'm starving, I know Pan's starving,' Richie said waving his hand at his newly acquired partner, 'are you starving … err?'

He gestured for an introduction to Nok.

Nok propped herself up on the pillows.

'Nok, and you're Richie,' she said filling the gap in his knowledge.

'My reputation goes before me Nok, I bet he never stopped talking about me all night,' he beamed.

'He mentioned you once or twice,' she said with a smile playing in her eyes.

'Well then you'll know that I'm man of appetites and right now that appetite is saying breakfast … and lots of it. How's about all eating together on the balcony? What do you think mate, four-some breakfast on the balcony?'

Alex swung his legs out of bed, morning Richie was a force to be reckoned with. He slipped his boxers on and stood stretching to greet the day. Richie was now rooting around on the table against the wall. Eventually, under a discarded tee-shirt, he found what he was looking for, the room service menu. He beckoned Pan over. She was lounging on the spare bed. Pan slinked over with deadly grace, like a lion stalking a mouse. Richie wrapped his arm round her waist; God it was hard.

'Listen darling why don't you and Nok get to know each other by ordering breakfast while I have a word with my friend here. Order anything you want, make it a lot and if a beer or two was to fall on the tray I wouldn't be offended.'

He presented her with the menu.

Alex shook his head.

'It's just after 10.00,' he protested.

'Exactly less than fourteen hours left in the day, so no time to waste.'

Richie was on form today.

Outside on the balcony life below was beginning to stir into action. Pattaya was a party town, so the slow pace of the mornings were far removed from the one hundred miles an hour night life. A smell of warm waffles wafted up from a street food stall ushered in by the sea breeze from the shore, which was only half a block away. The light was a brilliant golden blue. Rubbing sleep from his eyes Alex blinked himself to full wakefulness. Richie was feverous with excitement, he needed to share his story.

137

'Jesus, mate, what a night, I mean really, what a night. You won't believe what she can do. I mean you'd need at least three women to compete with her. I've never ... well, five times, five! It was, seriously mate, you just wouldn't believe, unbelievable.'

Words fell from his mouth in a stream of consciousness. It was obvious Richie was finding the experience hard to articulate.

Alex smiled.

'Well, you two made enough noise about it. I must have heard you at it again about 08.00 this morning.'

'That was only the fourth time mate we did it again after that,' he said with obvious pride.

Alex thought this would be a good time to mix his metaphors by seizing the bull by its horns and address the elephant in the room.

'Listen Richie, I'm not trying to be funny or anything, but are you sure she's ... well,' he struggled to tactfully broach the subject.

Richie's eyebrows knitted.

'Sure she's what?'

'Well that she's a ...,' feeling his way carefully, 'a she!'

Inside the room Nok was studying the menu from her bed while Pan sat at the mirror brushing her long aubergine hair. She flicked her head. In the strong sunlight her hair split into a

138

cascade of rich wine and shards of deep cobalt with shadows of midnight. The muscles of her back were prominent through her vest. A Thai music channel played quietly on the TV. She hummed along with the tune and then she spoke. Her voice was deep and sultry.

'I haven't seen you on Walking Street before, are you on Soi Seven?' she asked Nok.

'I don't work in Pattaya, I do other business,' said Nok evasively. She quickly changed the subject. 'What would you like to eat?'

Pan drawled out her order.

'Get something with noodles and chicken and eggs and some pancakes and a fish and some orange juice, something like that.'

Nok picked up the phone and started to dial.

'How was your night?' she asked.

'He suck good cock good?'

Nok knew there were no prizes for guessing the gender of Pan.

Out on the balcony Richie had dropped his bombshell.

'What do you mean you're not coming?' exclaimed Alex.

Richie held up his hands in passive defence.

'I didn't say I wasn't coming, I just said I wanted to spend another couple of days here that's all.'

Alex thought they had already been through this before they left home.

'Look when we came out here you were the one who said let's stick together.'

Richie tried to pour oil on the water.

'We can, why don't you stay here too, with 'what's-her-name' in there.'

'She's leaving today,' said Alex, 'then what am I supposed to do, hang around with you and she hulk in there? Anyway, we've flights booked.'

'We can book some more. They were only thirty quid.'

'That's not the point,' said Alex.

Richie was sorry to do this to him. But from his perspective there were still a few more days attraction in Pattaya.

'Listen mate, I'm sorry, I didn't know Pan was going to pop up did I. Look why don't you fly down to Phuket today as planned. You can go see that temple or big Buddha thing or whatever it is you want to see. I'll come down in two days. Then we can still get the same ferry to Phi Phi Don. Everyone's a winner.'

Alex looked straight down to the pavement below and sighed. Richie continued.

'Come on mate, it's all good. I would only be a pain in the arse. Temples bore me shitless you know that. Besides, you wouldn't believe the filthy things I still have left to do with her.'

140

Alex shook his head and smiled.

'You're a dirty bastard Richie.'

Back in the room Nok was out of bed and had locked herself in the bathroom. Pan had been so wrapped up looking at herself in the mirror she'd paid no attention to Nok taking a cling film wrapped package from her bag which she had stored at the bottom of the sliding doors wardrobe the night before. She had also taken Alex's backpack with her. Inside the bathroom Nok paused and stared hard at herself in the mirror. Did she really want to do this? Alex had shown her nothing but kindness. But then at this stage, what were her options? She could leave town as planned, but then she knew that Kiet, and probably anyone he worked for, would most likely look for her and her alone. The coincidence of Alex turning up when he did and doing what he did was just too 'fortunate' an event to ignore. If this happenchance were coupled with a false trail, it would be a powerful diversion. A tactic that might paint her as an insignificant character, someone not worth bothering with. She knew, however, what the laying of a false trail would mean for Alex. If her plan worked, Alex would become the primary target for anyone looking for the drugs or the money. This would put him at the mercy of the scum of the street and the Thai judicial system. And she knew mercy from either would be in short supply.

She thought of her sister Gia. She thought of the abject misery of her family home. She thought of how, for almost two years, she had sold her dignity, her very soul to try to make enough money to lift them both out of a situation neither of them had created or deserved. Her mind cast back to the night she'd fled the house vowing to come back and collect Gia when she had made good. In the ensuing two years things had not gone exactly how Nok had foreseen. But regardless of the path she'd taken to get here Nok now had more money than she had ever dreamed of. Not just enough for her and Gia to get by but enough to set them up for life. Enough to wash them clean of the stench from the past. Driving these thoughts to the forefront of her mind, she steeled herself for what she was about to do. Her heart was heavy, but she had to frame Alex as any other cheap farang, simply out for what he could take and nothing more.

Picking up Alex's backpack she began to pick at the lining. Working quickly, she made an incision in the padded back panel. She pulled out a section of the stuffing and placed it in the bin next to the sink. She then took the package of caramel powder and stuffed it into the space she had created. Before she did so she split the package and rubbed a little of the fine dust into the porous webbing. It wasn't a lot, but it was enough for any dog to detect from a hundred metres away. She needed to ensure that Alex was detected at the airport

142

before he flew. To maintain a casual air, she chatted to Pan through the door. Pan was still singing along to the music channel on TV. It was a song about unrequited love, where an overweight hero is spurned by a pretty girl who is infatuated with the college jock. It had not yet reached the part where the girl discovers the jock is a jerk and Mr Cuddly has hidden depths. Nok actually liked this one.

'What did he do when he found you were kathoey?' Nok shouted through to Pan.

Pan's voice resonated through the door.

'Not kathoey, Phûhȳing, woman and he not mind.'

As Pan spoke her eyes never left her reflection.

'Really?'

Nok thought Richie didn't look the type. She thought the size of his ego might have been hiding some deep-seated male insecurity which would be threatened by a 'girl' like Pan.

'No, he not mind, after six bottle of Singha not many men mind.'

Pan knew the workings of men, well she would, wouldn't she?

'He doesn't seem to mind this morning and the Singha has worn off,' Nok called back through the door.

'Men like Phûhȳing praphet, better than a woman. We know what men like and we can do everything a real woman can and more. Yes, men like Phûhȳing, men like Pan,' she said with the confidence of experience.

143

Nok took the complementary sewing kit from the side of the sink and began to stitch up the tear she had made in the backpack, sealing in the package. It wasn't a tidy job, but she'd made sure it wouldn't be noticed. Outside the bathroom Pan continued to sing along with the TV. Nok was just finishing up when there was a knock at the door. It was Alex.

'Breakfast's here,' he called.

In a panic she fished through his backpack and pulled out a tee-shirt. Slipping it over her head she opened the door and handed him the bag.

'I hope you don't mind I stole one of your tee-shirts, it smell of you. I hope you don't mind,' she said as apologetically as she could.

Alex wouldn't have minded if she'd had his entire wardrobe on.

'Of course not,' he reassured and kissed her on the cheek, 'it's yours.'

Tentatively he raised the subject of what would happen later.

'Look it's just an idea, but would you like to spend a few days in Phuket with me? Richie's going to stay here with Pan until Thursday before he comes down, so I'll be on my own. We could spend some time together before you head off to Thung Na to see your sister.'

Again, her stomach sank, why did he have to remember details about her sister, about her hometown. She consoled herself in the belief that, if he suspected she had set him up and disclosed this information, it was highly unlikely that the Thai authorities would believe him. Thai prisons were littered with farang who *'just happened to meet someone in a bar'*. They would be far more concerned with making an example of a foreigner who thought they could flaunt Thailand's drug laws than tracking down a phantom bar girl. And as for Kiet and any of his potential associates, by the time they got any information out of Alex her and Gia would be far away with new lives and new identities.

She sensitively turned down his offer.

'I would love to spend time with you, but my sister needs me. I need to be with my family. Family is very important to Thai people, please do not make me feel sad about it,' she touched her hand to the side of his cheek. 'Buddha says it's not how hard we hold on but how deeply we let go. Now let's enjoy breakfast, you have a plane to catch later.'

The rest of the day passed quietly watching television with a few drinks, eating and chatting. Richie eventually calmed down around one o'clock in the afternoon when the late night caught up with him and all four of them lapsed into an afternoon nap. Around four o'clock Alex packed the last of his things and called a taxi to take him to the airport. Richie promised to meet up with him in two days' time and Nok walked him to his taxi. It was a short goodbye. As the taxi

145

driver struggled to lift Alex's luggage into the boot, Alex asked one more time if Nok would change her mind and join him. She was resolute to see her sister as soon as possible, but left him with the promise that, once she was settled, she would call him. They parted with the gentle kiss of a long affectionate marriage, not one steeped in the first heat of lust.

Nok watched and waved until the taxi turned the corner. It was time for her to move. She hailed the very next yellow taxi meter, slung her bag on the back seat and hopped in.

'Chon Buri, railway station,' she instructed.

It was a short ride and when she arrived the station was throbbing with life. Pattaya Station has the highest daily footfall of all the stations on the Ban Phlu Ta Luand Main Line. Leaving from here she would be impossible to trace. She bought herself a first-class ticket through to Thung Na. With only twenty minutes to kill she stocked up on a few provisions for the journey. It was going to be a long ride, she wouldn't be arriving until late in the evening and she didn't want to rely on train food, which could be of variable quality.

Once she was safely ensconced in her private compartment, she pulled out her phone and dialled Kiet's number. The phone rang several times before it was answered. She was expecting to hear his abrasive voice, but instead was met with a long silence. When eventually Kiet spoke, his voice sounded far away, weak and wet.

146

'Where are you, you fffucking bitch.'

His words were slurred, and he was having problems with his f's. He must have been drunk. The diversion was set, all she needed to do now was put the wheels in motion. She spoke slowly and carefully covering her mouth with her hand to deaden the noise of the train.

'Listen did you really think that Alex turning up at the club was a coincidence? That's what you get for trying to fuck me over. Well, I hope you're happy because all your dirty drugs will be leaving with him from Bangkok Airport tonight and it's too late to stop him you cheap bastard.'

Not waiting for Kiet's reply she hung up.

She had spelt it out as plainly as she could and only hoped it didn't sound too contrived. However, Kiet was stupid, and she didn't want to leave any doubt. More than likely Kiet and any help he could muster would now spend their time looking for Alex. A white man who didn't know he had a target on his back, not hiding, should be easy to find. Especially after he was picked up at the airport with a quantity of heroin on him. Thai's liked to publicise when they caught foreigners trafficking in their country. There was always extensive coverage in the press and on TV. Live footage of petty criminals in squalid prisons cells uncontrollably sobbing after it has been made clear they could be facing the death sentence was a good deterrent. This tactic had a certain effectiveness, but there were always some who thought they could beat the system. If Kiet was really serious about finding what he had lost, he would undoubtedly check traffic at the airport. Nok had done her best to ensure that trail would lead to Alex.

Following his impending arrest Alex would probably end up in Bang Kwang prison or, as it was affectionately known, 'The Bangkok Hilton'. With luck on her side Bang Kwang would spell the end of the hunt. Any drugs or money would now be in the hands of the authorities and beyond reach. Any discrepancy on amounts would undoubtedly be put down to the corrupt system skimming off the top for itself.

Nok sat back in her carriage and sighed. She was finding it hard to reconcile her feelings. On one hand she was elated at the prospect of seeing her sister and the life they would have in front of them with her newfound wealth. On the other, there was a deep sadness that this future was going to be bought with a decent man's life.

She closed her eyes in the hope that sleep would ease her mind.

14

Blood's hard to get out of carpet

Chai Son perched on the corner of the desk in the back office of his modest club the Double-Beat. Despite the heat outside, the office was cool. A single lamp lit the room casting foreboding shadows over the gaudy decor. Kiet sat zip-tie bound to a chair in front of him. Chai Son took the phone from Kiet's ear where he was holding it and looked at the display, it read 'Nok, duration eleven seconds'. It had been on loudspeaker; Chai Son had heard every word. Slowly he lifted Kiet's head, which hung limp on his chest. He looked into the bloody mess that was once his face. His nose was beaten flat, his right cheekbone was shattered, his lip was split exposing his gums where his teeth once were.

'You still persist you don't know this girl,' Chai Son said, 'shall we start again?'

Many aspects of Kiet were shallow, but his profound cowardness and greed knew no depths. It was fear and greed that had kept his mouth shut for the last few hours. It was a fear of what Chai Son would do to him if he found out he double crossed him coupled with a blind optimism that he could still get away with it, find the drugs and ingratiate himself with the Croatians. In light of the phone call Kiet had just taken it would be difficult for him to plead ignorance any longer. He started to talk. Always the opportunist the story that spilled from his mouth was a version of events that had little connection to reality but might just cast him in a favourable light. He told how Nok, whom he still maintained he barely knew, had approached him and tried to sell him some drugs. He told how he thought he would show Chai Son how useful he could be by buying them for him and giving them as a present. He spluttered how the girl tried to double cross him, tried to steal his money and how he and Nok had argued at the Shark Club. It was then her farang bodyguard had turned up. Kiet protested that he had no idea why Billy's men had picked him up, why he was being treated like this. If only Chai Son would give him another few hours, he was sure he could find Nok and this farang and make things right. To Kiet's credit the story was creative, but altogether it was less credible than a tabloid horoscope.

Chai Son let the drivel flow over him. He stared into the far distance digesting the information. Billy the Kat sat silently on a battered leather sofa concealed in a deep shadow. Coiled

150

around him was Jade. Billy was not an attractive man, but he seemed to have something women liked. People said it was his own night club. This undoubtedly helped, but Billy also had the added advantage of a bucket full of ostentatious charm. Jade was the living mirror that reflected Billy's inner appeal. In the same way you couldn't buy charm, as a Thai, you couldn't buy green eyes. Jade's eyes were emerald gems housed in a unique setting. She was not conventionally beautiful. A more apt adjective would have been striking. She compelled attention. Billy loved that people stared at Jade and Jade loved to be stared at with Billy. It was a perfectly symmetrical relationship of egotism. Together they had passively watched Kiet's ordeal unfold before of them. The gathering silence of the room was punctuated only by the pathetic sounds of Kiet breathing. Chai Son was contemplating his next move. The information he had received from Kiet and what he had just learned from the phone call needed to be tackled on two levels. Eventually Chai Son spoke, addressing Billy direct.

'Billy, go over to the Shark Club, now. Find out if what Kiet said about this altercation is true. Talk to everyone, look through the CCTV. I want you to go on the streets and find everything you can about this Nok and this man Alex. When you have something call me.'

Chai Son turned to leave.

151

'What about him?' said Billy nodding to the wreckage tied to the chair.

'Throw him in a car and have him sent to my office. I have a meeting with my foreign investors. He will be a good example of how we deal with treachery,' then he added as an afterthought, 'Billy, you might want to put some plastic sheeting in the boot, blood's hard to get out of the carpet.'

Chai Son mulled over the information he had received from the girl's phone call. It troubled him; it just did not feel right. She gave too much away. No one moved drugs through the airport other than rank amateurs. If this Alex tried to do this, especially with nearly seven kilos, chances were, he would be caught. If he wasn't caught, then Chai Son wanted to know exactly who he was and where he was going. He needed someone who was able to gain access to flight itineraries and could deal with the Thai authorities if need be. He knew just the man for the job, James McNulty. James was Chai Son's legal right-hand. He knew every corrupt official, police officer, judge and government representative in the country. If this Alex ended up in the system James could find him. James could retrieve him.

Chai Son opened up his phone and dialled his number.

15

Stirling Moss

The taxi ride from Pattaya to Bangkok airport was 140km, but it took well under two hours. This was remarkable considering that, due to heavy traffic, nearly half of the time was taken up doing the last 10km into the city. Alex's driver, who bore an uncanny resemblance to Dobby the house elf, constantly kept referring to himself as Stirling Moss, whom he obviously thought of as a kindred spirit. The ride was white knuckle and physically uncomfortable. This was due to the fact that Lucky, which Alex came to know was his drivers' actual name, seemed to find more interest leaning over the back seat talking, than he did looking at the road ahead and insisted on having the air conditioning switched to just above absolute zero. Despite Alex's many protestations that 'he really wasn't in that much of a hurry' Lucky thought speed was doing him a favour. Though Alex failed to see how putting his life at risk by erratically overtaking, undertaking and never leaving more than two feet between him and the car in front was a favourable thing to do. Alex could not help thinking the name Lucky was either apt or ironic.

 Eventually they reached, what Alex thought was, the departure terminal. But looking at the sign above the doors he was actually being dropped at arrivals. He decided to say nothing. Lucky had managed to get up to almost 80kph just overtaking the line of traffic queuing for a spot to park, so exiting the car took precedence over the accuracy of the drop off. There must have been something different under the bonnet than the standard 1.2L of this aging Opel Astra, as it seemed to be able to go from zero to insane in the blink of an eye. Lucky jerked the car into the tightest spot available, ousting the car which had clearly stopped to reverse into it. Lucky jumped from the car and there followed a tirade of verbal jousting and hand waving. This was out of character to the usual reserved nature of Thai's when it came to public displays of emotion. His rival for the parking spot bested, Lucky bounded back to the car all smiles. Alex opened the trunk to retrieve his backpacks, but Lucky insisted he got them out for him. He had the same trouble getting them out as he did when he put them in. They were obviously too heavy for him, and he struggled to drag them to the curb side. Despite his better judgment concerning rewarding bad behaviour Alex found himself tipping 100 baht. A million couldn't have got a

154

better response. Lucky vigorously shook his hand and even jotted down his telephone number. He told Alex that if he were ever in Thailand again, he would be his personal driver and would take him anywhere, any time at a very special rate, only for friends. Alex politely took his number with absolutely no intention of ever seeing him again. This time Alex had managed to get out of the car alive, next time might be stretching the odds too far. Lucky hopped back in the car happy in the knowledge of another satisfied customer. In his mind Alex was now an advocate who would spread the word about the fastest, most reliable, taxi driver in Thailand. The car swung into the drop off lane announcing its departure with a blast of the horn which, to Alex's amusement, was the Dixie tune made famous by the General Lee on the American TV show The Dukes of Hazard. Lucky's hand waved enthusiastically from the window as he cut up several cars before he'd even left the drop off area, which was technically the pickup lane.

Alex watched Lucky leave expecting to see carnage before the car got onto the main road, but no carnage was forthcoming. Lucky remained lucky for another day. He picked up his backpacks strapping one to his chest and throwing the other over his shoulder. Making his way over to the departure gates he fumbled in the front pocket of his day-bag looking for his booking form and passport. Wrapped in

155

his search he had his head down when he joined the queue waiting to go through the initial security check, the first x-ray machine and the metal detector. Many airports now operated this two-tier screening system, implemented following the 9/11 attacks. Alex threw his large backpack from his shoulder onto the conveyor belt and took his day bag off his chest, dropping it in a tray along with his mobile and iPad. He made his way through the metal detector to wait for his belongings at the other end.

Scanning round the airport he took in the vast variety of travellers. Bangkok airport was a true melting pot. Armani suits stood in the executive queues while two metres away stood fat men in vests with tattoos of bulldogs on the backs of their bald heads. Immersed in the colour of the scene, he didn't notice the x-ray machine operator stop and rewind on his backpack. The man behind the machine examined the image carefully, a faint orange outline floated on top of the contents of the bag. On his screen the man adjusted the contrast filters. To the operator's trained eye there was an outline of something unusual. Before letting the bag proceed through the tunnel, he made a call on his radio.

Alex's day bag emerged from the rubber flaps of the tunnel and skidded down the conveyor rollers. He lifted it off the platform and was going to make a grab for his large backpack as it closely followed, but he was intercepted by the guard.

'Routinesuche,' said the guard.

Alex recognised this as German, but that was as far as his understanding went. Shaking his head, he replied,

'Sorry English.'

The man came back with a remarkably good English accent.

'Routine check, is this your bag?'

'Yes, this is mine,' said Alex thinking nothing of it.

'Did you pack his yourself?' the guard enquired.

'Yes,' Alex replied.

He had been through airports many times and like most people he was used to random checks, he knew the format.

'Are you on your own?' asked the man lifting up his bag.

'Yes,' Alex had never been asked than one before.

'Stand over here please,' the guard guided him to the side of the baggage trough and out of the main flow of the exiting traffic. 'Wait one moment.'

Almost immediately the words left his mouth two further guards emerged from the general airport throng, one with a dog, the other carrying an M16 assault rifle clutched to his chest, barrel pointing to the floor, an extended index finger covering the trigger.

Alex had been stopped before, but never with dogs and guns. He knitted his brow.

'Is there a problem here?'

The guard carrying the rifle was quick to respond.

'You stand to the side, do not move, do not speak!'

'But …'

This was the only word Alex got out before the guard with the rifle shot back.

'Do not speak!'

Alex stood quietly. This guard didn't look like the sort of man who told you anything more than once. During this time, the x-ray machine operator had emptied Alex's backpack and was rifling through the contents and inspecting the bag. He didn't seem to find what he was looking for. But then he placed the bag on the floor and the guard with the dog moved in. The dog sniffed enthusiastically round the bag its tail wagging with excitement. It was particularly interested in the padded webbing on the back of the pack. Then in the middle of its vigorous sniffing it abruptly sat in front of its handler. It shuffled and let out a thin whine. It's handler was particularly happy with the dog's performance and lavished it with praise as well as handing out a treat. The guard with the M16 glared at Alex. He had intense black eyes bisected by a ravine-like furrow. His face was gaunt and deeply pock marked. He looked like a vintage straight razor, well used but still deadly sharp.

The x-ray guard picked up the bag and producing a folding knife he cut a hole in the lining of the backpack. Fishing around inside he pulled out a cellophane wrapped slab of brownish powder. Without saying a word, he held it up and showed it to the two airport police. Popping the package back in the backpack he handed it to the man with the dog. Alex was dumbfounded, he couldn't take in what he'd witnessed. He made a feeble attempt to protest.

'Look I've no idea wh ...'

He was cut abruptly short by the razor faced guard.

'You turn around, hands behind you.'

'Look what's all this about?' Alex stammered.

'Turn around, hands behind back, last time!' The razor guard ordered.

This time the barrel of his weapon was raised to the horizontal. He looked poised to point it directly at Alex. This was not the UK and Alex was wise enough to know that in this country "last time" probably meant last time. Trembling he turned his back and placed his hands behind him. The next thing he knew a pair of ridged speedcuffs were slapped tightly on his wrists and his arms were wrenched halfway up his back. The jolt almost sent him stumbling to the floor. He let out a cry of surprise. Alex was marched through the airport. The razor with the rifle had now slung it over his back. He had one hand on the handcuffs and one on the back of Alex's head gripping a handful of hair. He was keeping Alex permanently off balance so that he had to skip along on his toes to avoid falling over. All Alex could see was the shiny floor immediately in front of his feet, but he could still hear the, not so quiet, whispers of the people as he passed.

'Looks like he's up shit creek.' … 'I wouldn't want to be in his shoes.' … 'No sweetheart the man has probably lost something, and the guards are trying to help him find it.' … 'People never learn.' … 'Fucking hell, you wouldn't want to mess with them.'

The comments were as varied as the accents.

While he walked, Alex could hear the dog handler relaying information to someone via his earpiece. After five humiliating minutes they arrived at a reinforced door, discretely concealed down a quiet utility corridor. The guard with the dog swiped his security pass and typed in a six-digit number. The door clicked open. There was a smell of fresh paint and new carpet. In front of him was a corridor with a row of windowpanes on the left looking onto two, sparsely furnished and under populated offices. People watched screens showing selected CCTV footage of the airport, answered telephones and worked on computers. Alex was stopped at a heavy-duty door on the right. This door was opened with a lock and key. Inside the room it was not overly intimidating. There was a table with four padded chairs, two each side, a large TV screen on the wall and a water fountain in the corner. The room lacked the windows of the other offices. The razor guard with the black, dead eyes pushed him into the chair with the

160

command 'SIT!'. Alex knew it was futile to resist or ask questions and he passively obeyed. The guards left slamming the door behind them. Alex heard the key turn in the lock. Sitting alone with his hands cuffed behind his back, the silence of the room started to become oppressive.

16

Spilt milk

The wood splintered into needle like shards. Not just the lock gave but the whole door came crashing in. Part of the frame clung desperately to the hinges.   Nikola and Victor stood silhouetted in the doorway. To be more precise Nikola took up the entire width of the door and Victor stood behind him. Only fifteen hours after their phone call from Petar Nikola and Viktor landed at Bangkok airport. Taking no rest, they hired a car and drove straight to Pattaya. It had not taken them long to find Kiet's grubby little room.   Like most wannabes Kiet thought he would make a name for himself by being conspicuous.   Everybody knew what he looked like, and everybody knew where he lived. Although this gave him some kudos with the low life on the street, for real players it just made him easy to find.   There was no end of people who could tell you where Kiet lived and if they thought you were going to do him harm many would have driven you to the door themselves.

The two men crunched their way over the fallen door and stood surveying the room. On the surface empty. Despite the apartment being only two rooms and having a total area of no more than six by six metres they still searched for personnel. During the war in their home country, they knew how adept people were at hiding. Doorways were always the most dangerous. When entering a room people's focus was exclusively on what was in front of them. If you didn't properly secure the entrance, you could find yourself with the enemy at your back. Viktor learned this lesson the hard way clearing a house in Srebrenica. He was Blue2, securing bedroom 1. As the last man entered the house a trapdoor opened in the floor just inside the threshold. The first indication of this was when white hot bullets came spitting from behind them. Two operatives were killed and one left paralysed. Victor himself took a hit to the leg before he located the direction of fire and put two rounds into the man's head. Today, as always now, he stamped on the floor in the doorway. Concrete, little chance of anyone being beneath them here.

Nikola crossed to the bed lifting it from the floor with one hand and flinging the stained sheet across the room with the other. Viktor made his way to the bathroom. There was a

163

stained panelled bath, a pedestal sink and a toilet. He pushed his fingers into the cheap plastic panelling on the side of the bath until … crack, he had a hand hold. He ripped it open. Taking a flashlight from his pocket he shone it into the fusty darkness, nothing. Meanwhile in the main room Nikola had crossed to the chest of drawers in the corner and started rifling through them, again nothing. Just then he noticed a familiar stain on the carpet next to the leg of the drawers. He bent to one knee and rubbed it with this thick finger. He held it close to his eye. It was a rusty brown colour and still slightly damp, blood. There was a pooling under the furniture, then a smear in the direction of the door. He closely examined the threadbare carpet. Viewed from ground level the knap showed two faint furrows. A body had lain on the floor for a short time, been hoisted to its feet and then dragged out of the room. As Viktor came out of the bathroom Nikola held up his hand rubbing the sticky brown blood between his thumb and forefinger. Viktor looked at the stain and his eyes followed the same route to the door. Someone had got to their quarry before them.

Just then they stopped. There was the unmistakable slap of a flip flop on the stairs leading to the apartment. Despite their size Nikola and Viktor moved noiselessly across the room and stood like sentinels either side of the felled door. The footsteps reached the top of the stair and paused. Whoever it was had obviously seen the door had been kicked open. Viktor and Nikola's breath was even and shallow. The steps moved tentatively towards the gaping hole where the door once was. There was no sound of a weapon being cocked and the pace of breathing indicated fear. Just as the footsteps reached the mouth of the door Nikola sprang from the room. One hand shot to the throat of the incomer while the other demobilised the arm. Viktor followed a nanosecond later and disabled the other arm. There was a clatter as a bag of groceries fell to the floor, several tins bounced down the stairs and a carton of milk burst open on the floor. Their target let out a strangled grunt as the two men smashed the body into the opposite wall of the corridor. Nikola pressed his massive head up to the face of his prey. It was a boy, a young fresh-faced boy, no more than fifteen years old. Nikola's vice like grip did not slacken one bit. He knew that boys could kill just as well as men.

He spoke two words, quiet and calm.

'Where Kiet?'

The boy was now crying and struggling for breath. Nikola noticed that his feet were physically off the ground. He lowered him to the floor and repeated.

'Where Kiet?'

The boy was trying to talk but was finding it hard due to the fingers crushing his throat. Nikola loosened his grip and compensated for it by almost snapping the boy's wrist.

'Kiet?' he repeated.

The boy spoke, his effeminate voice strangled due to the restriction of his windpipe.

'Dî pord xỳā thả̉r̃ay c̄han,' he spluttered.

'English!'

Once again Nikola's hand tightened round his throat as though he could throttle English out of him.

'Please don't hurt me, I don't know, I don't know,' was all the distressed boy could say.

His lips were starting to turn purple, and Nikola could see that he had burst a blood vessel in his left eye. Nikola's face remained impassive. He tightened his grip even more on the boy's throat and then just before the moment of blackout released it again. This was an art form he excelled at. His voice came slow and measured.

'Where Kiet? English,'

The boy's voice was weak. 'Billy, Phūd khuy kạb Billy.'

Nikola's grip tightened for a second, then eased again.

'English!'

'Billy, Billy,' he gasped.

Nikola released his grip a little more. The boy coughed and painfully sucked in air.

'I don't know, I don't know a thing, please Billy, Billy said I live here now. Kiet gone. Please, please, that all I know.'

'Where Billy?' Nikola's demanded.

'The Double Beat, Billy own Double Beat club. He nearly always there,' the boy cried.

Nikola pressed his face in closer taking up the entire field of the boy's vision.

'Where this?'

'Soi, soi 7 Double Beat, he always there.'

Nikola looked to Viktor. People would tell you almost anything under extreme pressure. Normally they would keep a prisoner until they could verify the veracity of what had been said. This was a luxury they couldn't afford in this situation. Dragging a boy round town would be too much of a liability. Both men said nothing, there was an understanding of what needed to be done.

The boy's feet left the floor once again and his head was driven backwards into the wall. There was a crunch of bone and his limbs hung loose. Nikola carried the pathetic body into the room and laid it gently on the bed. The two men left for the Double-Beat.

17

Have you seen this before?

Alex had no way of telling how long he had been sitting. All he knew was that it felt like hours. Outside, eyes watched him through the close circuit camera as a forensic examination was made of his luggage and his passport details were checked. Eventually, just as Alex thought he would fall asleep through sheer mental exhaustion, he heard a key turn in the lock. An incredibly slight man entered with an even slighter woman. Both were impeccably neat with crisp white short-sleeved shirts and dun trousers. The woman carried Alex's backpack, which she placed on the side of the table. Crossing over to the wall, she opened up a locked panel to reveal a stacked recording system. She pushed a button, waited a second, then said something in Thai. The gentleman made a short verbal contribution, and they took their seats opposite Alex. They said nothing and neither did Alex. The gentleman unfastened a file in front of him, scanned a few notes, then spoke.

'Good evening, my name is Jao Benjawan, and this is my colleague Maladee Prapass, we are from the airport security team. Could you confirm your name and date of birth please?'

His voice was soft, calming, almost soporific. Alex thought he would try to seek an explanation for what was happening to him.

'Listen I don't know what all this is about. I'm sure you've made a mistake, but if you tell me what it is I've supposed to have done then …'

He was quietly and politely interrupted.

'We will come to that, but first I need to confirm some details. Please, your name and date of birth?' continued Mr Benjawan.

Alex dutifully answered. This was followed by confirmation of his UK address, his previous residence and his future destination in Thailand. As he spoke Mr Benjawan quietly nodded looking down his list while Ms Prapass took notes. Mr Benjawan spoke again.

'And could you tell me your purpose in visiting Thailand?'

Before Alex could think of how it would sound, he said,

'To fight.'

The woman stopped her note taking and Mr Benjawan looked up from his file.

'To fight?' he repeated.

Alex's answer needed further explanation.

169

'No, look not like that, I came to fight in the Hard Bones tournament, the Kraduk Khaeng. I came for that, but I also came to do some tourism, to see the country, visit the temples, the beaches.'

Mr Benjawan quietly whispered something to Ms Prapass, and she duly wrote it down. They did not seem impressed. The only word exchanged between them Alex understood was Muay Thai.

'Now Mr Whyte could you confirm to me that this is your bag,' Mr Benjawan said pointing to Alex's backpack at the end of the table.

'I think so,' said Alex.

Mr Benjawan sought a definite answer.

'Is that a yes or a no?'

Alex answered more affirmatively.

'Yes, yes, it is.'

There then followed a series of rapid closed question. It was obvious they were only after one-word answers.

'And can I confirm that you packed this bag yourself?'

'Yes,'

'Did anyone interfere with this bag after you packed it?'

'No,'

'Have you been asked to carry anything or are you carrying anything for anyone else?'

It was beginning to dawn on Alex where this trail of questions was leading and a cold bead of sweat ran down his side, it made him shiver.

'No,'

'Is there anything you want to tell me about the contents of this bag?'

Alex swallowed hard.

'No,'

'Have you seen this before?'

At this question Ms Prapass produced a sealed plastic bag which contained a tightly wrapped slab of caramel coloured powder.

Alex's voice faltered.

'No,'

'No?'

Alex corrected himself.

'Well only at the x-ray machine.'

'Do you know what it is?' asked Mr Benjawan.

There was a long pause. Alex knew what he feared it was, but he didn't want to say it aloud. His answer was tentative …

'Drugs?'

'Could you tell me how these came to be concealed in your backpack?'

Alex's mind raced and the more it raced the more it shut down. His words spilled out in a nonsensical cascade.

'I swear to god, I've never, those are never, I don't do drugs. That, that, I've never seen that before in my life, I have no idea how that got there, I'm just, I mean, I don't know, I'm just on holiday. You can't be serious, someone must have, it must have been someone. Please you've got to believe, this is not me, I'm …'

Mr Benjawan held up his hand and left it hanging in the air until Alex stopped to draw breath. 'Mr Whyte please, I have all I need for now, please excuse us.' The two officers closed their notes. Ms Prapass picked up Alex's bag and crossed over to the recording equipment. Both her and Mr Benjawan verbally signed off. She stopped the tape and relocked the panel. With only a "Wait please." From Mr Benjawan they both left the room and locked the door behind them.

They had both been working this position for many years and had heard every excuse under the sun, everything from *"Someone said they would kill my family if I didn't carry it for them, to 'it's like a medicine and I need it."* But by far the most common excuse was *"I've never seen it before.'* They'd seen people, cry, faint, vomit and get so violent that it took several guards, pepper spray and a taser to subdue them. They had seen young men, old men, women and even children in pushchairs in this room.

The people, the reactions, the excuses varied, but the central fact always remained the same; they were carrying drugs and

172

carrying drugs was a black and white issue in Thailand. The whole interview had taken no more than fifteen minutes. It wasn't up to Mr Benjawan or Ms Prapass to establish guilt or innocence. Their job was to gather basic information and confirm drugs were being carried.

Once again Alex sat alone in silence. He was soon to be someone else's problem.

18

I spy with my electronic eye

Billy knew every bar and club owner in town and every bar and club owner knew Billy. After, in a carpet friendly manner, he had loaded Kiet in a car and dispatched him to Chai Son's office, Billy made his way to the Shark Club. He went straight to the back office to speak to Dang. Dang had been running the club for eleven years. If there was information to be had she would have it. Dang was not her real name, she was actually named Hathai, Hathai meaning heart, as her father said, she was the heart of the family. Dang, however, was a name she had gone by nearly all her life. The nickname was earned due to the fact that ever since she was a child, she wore nothing but red, Dang meant red. When she was young it was Lek Dang, Little Red, now it was just Dang. Billy gently knocked on the door and not waiting for an answer, let himself in.

'Hey Red my main girl, how does the world hang with you this fine day?' he beamed.

Dang looked up from the computer screen where she was trawling over the monthly accounts strategically and creatively massaging the figures.

'Hey Billy, now here's a pleasure I don't get too often. Come in, come in,' she said as she gestured to the black leather swivel chair in front of her desk.

Dang and Billy went back many years. In the drunken hours of the night, they had often been friends with benefits, but the very things that made them similar were also the very things which kept them apart. In terms of a deeper relationship, they had always been and would always be a *'nothing better to do'* fill in for each other. Something they both knew and something they were both happy with. Billy sank into the chair.

'So, lady how's business?'

'Good enough to keep a poor woman in modest dresses. But given that I haven't seen you for over a month, I suspect it's not my business you came to talk about, tell me what's your business?' she said arching an eyebrow.

Billy smiled, Dang always had a way of cutting through his bullshit.

'Red lady, you always did cut to the chase. Thing is, I need a bit of background. Last night in the club there was a disturbance, it would benefit me and my friends greatly if we could find out who the main players were.'

'Billy disturbances are part of the game; you need to be more specific.'

'This was between a Thai and a farang and there was a girl involved. Now if you've caught something on that shiny new CCTV of yours, I would be very interested to see it.'

Billy did his best pleading face.

'You seem to be very knowledgeable about my security systems, I only had it fitted two weeks ago,' she said, looking at Billy from the corner of her eye.

Billy gave a chuckle.

'Red you know I have eyes and ears everywhere, but for now I need to see what you've spied on your little electronic eye.'

Dang closed down her accounts and tapped into the previous night's footage. It had been a relatively quiet night and it didn't take long to find the incident in question. The grainy footage confirmed what Billy had already been told. There was Kiet and the girl and right after Kiet had hit the girl, the farang had stepped in and laid Kiet out. Kiet may only have been sixty kilos in a wet shirt, but he was armed. Billy couldn't help thinking that this new man showed some pretty efficient moves when confronted with a knife. Just as the man's face turned to the camera Billy asked Dang to freeze the scene.

'Now that was the disturbance I was talking about. I know this man,' Billy said tapping on the image of Kiet 'but what I need to know is who are these two, the girl and the farang,' he said pointing to Alex and Nok. 'can you shine your light on them for me?'

Dang moved closer to the screen looking at the grey image.

'Billy I'm good, but not that good, those are random to me.'

Billy knew Dang wouldn't hold anything from him, if she knew them, she would say so. He took out his mobile and snapped the image on the screen. Tracking Alex and Nok through the club on the other cameras, he saw Alex lead the girl up to the bar. Alex then stopped to talk to another man playing Connect 4 with a bar girl. Probably losing money Billy thought. He asked Dang to freeze the screen again.

'So, Red what about this one?' he said pointing to the Connect 4 victim.

Dang shook her head.

'I don't know him either, but I do know who he left with last night.'

'And who would that be?' asked Billy.

'He took Pan with him. Want me to ring her?'

Billy showed a full set of pearly whites, studded with gold.

'You find her Red and you've found my sweet spot … again.'

One phone call later and Billy had the information he needed. Within fifteen minutes Billy was standing in the reception of

177

the Nana Apartments Hotel. The grainy screenshots and a few baht to the right person were enough to get copies of both Richie's and Alex's passports, copies made when they checked in. The receptionist told him that Alex had checked out, but that Richie was still in room 427 and would be in there for the next two days. Billy had struck it lucky finding information on the two men. But he was yet to get a decent break finding information on Nok. He spent the next few hours calling round his contacts but failed to turn up anything. No one had any useful information other than a few possible sightings. Billy figured she must have been new to the area and working independently from the bars or any protection ring.

After he had exhausted all his possible leads, Billy called Chai Son to appraise him of his findings. He was apologetic about his lack of information on the girl, but sent over the CCTV screenshots from the club, copies of Alex's and Richie's passports and the address of the hotel in which Richie could still found.

Happy with his work Billy returned to the Double Beat.

19

Masturbate!

The airport didn't have the facilities to securely detain people for extended periods of time. Less than an hour after his interview, having had only one glass of water and, despite several requests, no phone call, Alex was escorted from the interview room by two uniformed guards. This time he didn't have to do the humiliating march through the terminal suffering the stares and comments of other travellers. He was ushered down a backstage corridor to a port resembling a goods entrance.

Outside the main building they were greeted by two officers of the Thai Royal Police, one with a clipboard and side arm the other holding a Remington 870 Express shotgun. They stood next to a van with heavily blacked out windows along the side. Emblazoned on one of the panels, both in Thai and in English, were the words 'Prisoner Transportation'. Information was exchanged and duly noted by both parties. The officer holding

179

the clipboard then popped his notes onto the passenger seat, took control of Alex's handcuffs and marched him to the double doors at the back of the van. He was closely followed by the officer carrying the shotgun. His escort's words were calm and robotic.

'When I will take off these handcuffs. You will not move; your hands will stay behind back. You will sit in van with hands behind back. You will then be secured. You will not speak. Nod your head to agree.'

Alex nodded his head. The officer unlocked the back of the van and opened one of the doors. Inside was a reinforced steel cage, which he unlocked. A nauseating smell of stale sweat spilled out. The van had bench seats down each side with a bar running underneath. There were already three other people inside. Seated to the left were two Thai men dressed in vests, flip flops and shorts, their wiry bodies crawling with faded denim tattoos. Opposite them sat a thick-set Nordic looking man with skin cropped blond hair wearing a Konkwista 88 tee-shirt. From the shadows of the van the unlikely bedfellows squinted at him in silence. Alex was told to sit to the right. His hands were freed from his cuffs and immediately shackled between his legs to the bar running beneath the seat. The cage was closed, and the rear door slammed shut. The change of air pressure cuffed his ears making the whole atmosphere oppressively claustrophobic.

His chest tightened and he felt as though he could physically see his heart beating beneath his tee-shirt. The van set off for its destination, as to where that was, Alex didn't have a clue. During this whole ordeal he had been offered no information. The line of questioning from airport security was directed only to confirm the very basic facts, his identity and ownership of the bag. Their next consideration seemed to be to get him off their hands as quickly as possible. The suddenness with which the situation was thrust upon him had deadened his senses. All he could think was nobody knew where he was, he had no one to help him.

The first part of the journey was quiet. This silence was briefly punctuated only once by the sounds of early nightlife winding its self-up for action. Someone slapped a hand on the side of the van which was followed by a short cheer. The hollow metallic thud made Alex start. They must have been passing through a town. After only ten minutes the sounds of life were replaced by the melodic drone of an open road. Inside the van the journey had proceeded without talk. His fellow passengers exchanged neither looks nor words. Then one of the Thai men spoke to the other and they shared a smile. Alex didn't understand what had been said but by the way the man inclined his head he was obviously referring to the large Viking. Sitting next to him.

The big man glowered his best intimidating look; one he had practiced for some time. He had honed it to instil fear.

'What?' he barked.

The two men said nothing. The younger man stared at the floor, but the older one met the Viking's eye with an unflinching gaze. The big man spoke again his accent was heavy Polish.

'What the fuck you looking at, skinny gimp!'

The man shook his head and turned to his friend.

'I will slit his throat, cut out his kidneys and feed them to dogs.'

The threat had been made in Thai and the large man's lack of understanding infuriated him.

'What was that? What the fuck did you say? Say that in English you skinny fucking monkey.'

The younger man answered on his behalf.

'He speaks no English. He is sorry if he upset you, he hopes we can be brothers in misfortune.'

He had not really said this to keep the peace, but more for his own amusement.

The Viking was not to know this, so the placatory words took some of the heat out of the situation, thought he was not ready to embrace his new kin just yet. He felt as though he needed to issue a final warning by way of a full stop.

'He had better be sorry. He needs to keep his fucking eyes to himself,' he said by way of closure.

The older man smiled and nodded. Once the silence had been broken the Viking reached out for a kindred spirit in Alex.

'Do you speak English?'

Alex didn't want to speak at all, but he thought it prudent to answer. He kept it as brief as possible.

'Yes,'

'They are not brothers, we are brothers, you and me. We share white brotherhood. If we are not brothers, our pure race will die. When the time comes you need to take your side,' he said making his racial allegiances abundantly clear.

Alex could never understand a mentality such as this. This concept, of a pure race, was an anathema to him. On the surface of it he himself couldn't have looked more Aryan. He was tall, pale skinned, red haired and had china blue eyes, yet he knew his grandmother was Yemeni. This was only going back two generations. Going back further about sixteen million people are probably related to Genghis Khan. What did it actually mean to be pure blooded? He was sure if he looked into this man's family tree, he wouldn't have to go back too far to find what his self-imposed racial brother would have thought of as 'inferior blood'. Why would people like this choose to travel Alex thought. Why would they surround themselves with a people and a culture that they had nothing but distain for? Alex had always thought of travel as expansive. It was enriching to experience the cultures of others. This man obviously only left his country to seek out targets of hate.

Unfortunately, Alex's silence seemed to be taken for agreement and he was subject to a ten-minute lecture on the importance of white unity and the need to be ready when the inevitable race war started. He didn't feel this was the time to start an educational outreach programme, so he sat passively contributing nothing, either by look or word. In between sentences he managed to make eye contact with the Thais opposite and discreetly raised his eyebrows and shook his head. He hoped this small gesture was enough to distance himself from the man sitting next to him and convey he shared no part in his views. Eventually, not finding the audience he was looking for, the large man ran out of steam and a welcome silence returned. After about forty-five minutes the van slowed and pulled to a halt. Alex heard the drivers exchange words with someone outside. There was a sound of a gate opening, a short drive, then engine went dead. They had arrived at their destination, Bang Kwang Prison.

Bang Kwang, known locally as the 'Big Tiger' as, like a tiger, it devoured its victims without mercy. With over six thousand inmates its speciality was long-term, high security prisoners. It also contained Thailand's primary death row for men. Bang

Kwang was internationally notorious for its harsh conditions and brutal regimes. Its population contained a disproportionate number of foreign prisoners. With severe penalties and a sluggish judicial system detainees could spend months in Bang Kwang without ever seeing the inside of a court room. Inmates ran the prison to their own internal set of codes with little interference from the wardens. They were largely autonomous. The guards job was to simply stop them spilling out on to the street. Suicide rates were high, murders were not uncommon.

The doors of the van opened, and its passengers were ordered to shuffle to the back. One by one they were unchained from the seat and immediately chained again when they exited. The next step for this chain gang was to be 'processed'. Inside the main building each man had his details confirmed and fingerprints and photograph taken. Alex asked for a phone call, but it was met with a short. "Process first, phone call later."

After the preliminary administration, Alex was led to a side room where a guard sat looking supremely bored. He couldn't help noticing that this guard was wearing latex gloves. The request came as one word.

'Strip,'

By the disinterested tone of the man's voice, this was a conveyor belt procedure for him. Alex paused, perhaps for a second too long, the word was repeated. Only this time with the whip of authority.

'STRIP!'

Alex began to remove his clothes. It seemed futile to try and hold on to any vestige of dignity under these circumstances. The guard with the latex gloves approached him carrying a tick sheet fastened to a clip board. He started at the top of the sheet and worked his way down. With each new examination he ticked another box off his sheet.

'Run your fingers through your hair,' … Tick.

'Show me behind your ears,' … Tick.

'Open your mouth,' … Tick.

'Lift up your arms,' … Tick.

'Stand with your legs apart and lift up your testicles,' … Tick.

'Pull back your foreskin,' … Tick.

'Lift up the soles of your feet,' … Tick.

'Turn around, bend over and spread your buttocks,'

Alex was expecting and dreading this one. There was the shine of a torch but nothing more. He gave a small sigh for a small mercy …

Tick!

Once the humiliating ritual was over, Alex was led, still naked, down a bare corridor lit by a flickering florescent light. He was dragged to a halt beside a caged window with a grated serving hatch. The man behind the hatch looked him up and down, then disappeared into the back of the room. He returned with a folded parcel of clothes, one terracotta short sleeved shirt, one pair of white boxers, one pair of terracotta trousers with an elasticated waist, one pair of black canvases slip on shoes, one pair of white cotton socks. Alex was uncuffed and told to dress. As he did the man behind the window handed over something that rattled through the hatch. It was a set of leg cuffs. Alex was shackled around each ankle as the guards on either side of him held him firmly by the arms. He was then escorted down a maze of narrow corridors and through several security doors until he came to a large wide gallery paved with red tiles. Alex was surprised how well he could walk in the leg irons. He had been expecting the range of movement to be like what he had seen in American chain gang films, where all that was possible was a shuffle. But these chains allowed a fairly normal gait. Despite the relative ease of walking, it was obvious that any form of running would be impossible.

The red paved hallway was furnished on both sides by a row of communal cells. It was now late in the evening. Despite the hour a dozen or more inmates clung to the bars of their cages to see the new 'guests'. It would appear watching new arrivals was what passed for entertainment. There were none of the expected shouts or jeers. Instead, there was an even more intimidating silence. When he'd entered the room, Alex saw

187

that his fellow travellers, who had been with him in the van, were already present and standing in a row. He was placed at the end and told to wait. No one spoke. After what seemed like an eternity, which in reality was only minutes, the security door at the bottom of the compound was opened and a tall, corpulent man walked in. He was dressed in the same light khaki uniform as the other guards, except his epilates sported considerably more gold and his chest was emblazoned with several impressive rows of medal ribbons. He crossed the space between them slowly and purposefully. Stopping three feet away he looked up and down the row of men then beckoned to one of the guards who handed him several sheets of paper. Quickly he glanced over them then lifted his head and spoke. His voice was surprisingly high for such a portly man. His address was in Thai, delivered in sharp staccato sentences. After each sentence, the guard to his left translated into English.

'My name is Narong Saeueng, I am the head guard. You will address me and all other guards as Sir at all times. Any infringement of the prison rules or any challenge to our authority will be met with swift and severe punishment. Due to the nature of your offences, you will be held here up until and during any forthcoming trial. You have a right to contact legal representation, in due course you will be allowed to make a phone call. The quality of your life here depends upon your behaviour. You will show respect at all times. Do you understand my words?'

There was a moments silence which was too long to be 'respectful'. The question was repeated almost immediately.

'Do you understand my words, you will all answer yes!'

Both Alex and the two Thai men answered yes in their respective languages. The Polish Viking, however, remained conspicuously mute. He was approached by the translator. The guard stood looking up into the big man's face. The Viking was a good six inches taller than him and drew himself up to his full height in an, ill thought out, gesture of intimidation. This posturing didn't faze the guard one bit. His voice was steady.

'You speak English, you will answer yes, you will show respect,' he said looking up.

The Viking's mouth began to curl into a sneer. He would never show those teeth again. In a nano second the guard had drawn his baton and smashed it across his face. The action was so swift the Viking didn't even have time to flinch. There was a cracking of bone and he fell to his knees with a muffled cry of pain. Splintered teeth and blood spattered the floor in front of him. Out of shock anger he cried out.

'Wanker!'

This was a word the Head Guard was not familiar with. It was, however, clearly understood by the translator, who dutifully obliged by filling in the gap in his vocabulary. This was a challenge that could not be tolerated. Authority needed to be maintained. The Head Guard issued his orders through the translator.

'Get to your feet.'

The Viking didn't move. He remained kneeling, cupping his mouth in his hand, blood running through his fingers. The question was repeated only this time the guard tapped his baton under his chin and lifted his head until he made eye contact. His voice was flat, monotone.

'Get to your feet.'

The big man stood, but this time his head hung low. The guard continued to translate.

'Take down your trousers.'

The Viking looked confused by the request and made no move to comply. The baton flashed once more this time catching him on his fleshy upper of his thigh. The pain was searing.

The order was repeated.

'Take down your trousers!'

The Viking obeyed, unfastening the cord on his waistband his trousers fell to his ankles.

'And your shorts,' ordered the guard.

The Viking hesitated. The guard raised his baton once more. This time he didn't have to strike, the threat was enough to ensure compliance. The big man took down his boxers and stood naked from the waist down. Despite the temperature being over twenty-five degrees, he shivered.

'Now,' said the guard, 'masturbate!'

The drama had brought a growing crowd of inmates to the bars of their cells. They watched the unfolding street theatre in silence. This was the highlight of the evening. The surreal nature of the request had paralysed the Viking and he had to be given a gentle reminder of what he had been ordered to do. The guard bounced his baton off the Viking's testicles.

'Masturbate.'

Fearing what might happen next, the Viking took his penis in his hand. The effect of his body being awash with adrenalin meant there was not much to get hold of. Still, he rubbed his flaccid member. His lame effort didn't satisfy the guard.

'Faster!' he shouted.

The Viking sped up, but no amount of stimulation was going to coax an erection out of this situation. The instruction came again,

'Faster,'

and again,

'Faster,'

and again,

'Faster,'

The pain, the fear and the ritualistic humiliation was too much. As he stood there in the middle of the room, blood dripping from his open mouth, masturbating in full view of more than a dozen people he began to sob. The guard translated his superior's words once more.

'It is now you that are the wanker,' he said with a satisfied grin.

Alex felt a deep despair. How long was he going to be in this hell hole?

20

The Kit Kat Kaboom

Viktor and Nikola parked their car on the sea front at the bottom of Soi 7 and made their way up to the Double Beat. Kiet had gone missing, and Billy was the only name they had to work with as a lead. Next to walking Street, Soi 7 was the party central of Pattaya. The road was narrow and flanked on each side by open front bars, each one with its own character, but each very much alike, *'Same, same but different'*.

When in full swing Soi 7 appeared as one organic mass, one business blended into another, and crowds ebbed and flowed like a flock of starlings. It was still young in the evening, life on the street had not yet warmed up. Each bar had no more than half a dozen patrons, who were the last of the 'day tourists'.

Even at this early hour two men walking down Soi 7 would be regularly accosted on each side by girls trying to attract business into their bars. But there were no such approaches to Viktor and Nikola. There was something about the way they walked, not fast but purposeful, eyes fixed ahead with no distractions, something that said, 'Keep away!' Even the way they dressed said they were not here for fun. Shorts and vests were the standard attire in 30 degrees of heat, not thick sweatpants and pilot jackets. They were only approached once on their short journey. An enthusiastic Iranian gentleman, with an open shirt and gold chain stepped out the doorway of a tailor's shop and attempted to greet Viktor like an old friend. His smile beamed from ear to ear as he blocked their path.

'Hello, my good friend, now you look like a gentleman who could benefit from a suit. A big man needs a big suit, I can do a big suit for a small price.'

He took Viktor's hand and began to shake it vigorously using, what he believed was, a grip to be respected. Viktor took his handshake passively and looked curiously at the man in front of him. The man babbled on with his sales pitch.

'How about you come into my shop and look at my material. I can measure you, but I might have to get two tape measures, yes?' he said believing he was building rapport through flattery.

Viktor tensed the muscles in his right arm and the overly exuberant shaking instantly stopped. Slowly Viktor started to tighten his grip. At first the man gave out a nervous chuckle.

'Oh, my friend that is a good hold you have!'

Then the pressure increased. The man began to squirm with pain.

'Please, please my friend,' he pleaded.

194

Viktor paid no heed and sharply increased the squeeze. Abruptly there was a crunch of bone. The man dropped to his knees sobbing and nursing his crushed hand. Viktor walked away leaving him in his wake. Nikola looked to Viktor and said,

'Child!'

Viktor's eyes never moved. A smile of amusement played on his lips. Neither man looked back.

The Double Beat was not like the other street bars. It was more of a hybrid night club. The two men walked in through the double doors. The room was a cool relief from the heat outside. Inside there was a large central bar with a stage set in the middle. A girl clad in a black and white bikini danced lazily round a pole; her lack-lustre performance showed that her heart wasn't in it. All around the periphery there were high backed padded booths and tables. The walls and above the bar were littered with various bank notes from around the world and pictures of people having a good time. It was dark, lit only by coloured neon and the backdrop of music was not intrusive. Nikola recognised the tune straight away, it was 'The Prince' by Madness. His head nodded involuntarily along with the beat. This was a song he listened to when he was young. One of the main attractions of the Double Beat was its music. When custom was ramped up it was back-to-back two tone and ska.

There were even fewer people in the club than in the bars outside. Two men sat at the counter pretending not to notice the disinterested dancer. Ensconced in a booth, with a large pitcher of Margarita in front of them, sat a young woman and her boyfriend. Viktor and Nikola took stools at the bar. They were approached by a round middle-aged woman in a half black, half white one-piece dress. In her head she clung to the figure she had thirty years ago. The dress clung to the figure she had now. Both the dress and her self-image should have quit while they were ahead.

'Deutsch?' she enquired.

The general languages of currency seemed to be either German or English. It was probably futile to look for Croatian. Nikola's English was better than Viktor's, he answered,

'English,'

'I'm Joy, what can I get you?' she asked offering her hand over the bar.

Nikola gave her hand more of a tap than a shake and placed his order.

'Two orange.'

'There's a two for one offer on cocktails until seven, would you like to try?' she enquired going for the up sell.

Nikola was about to stick to his orange when Viktor cut in.

'Da, yes,'

'Ok then what would you like, I can give you Sex on the Beach, a Slippery Nipple, a Pornstar Martini, you choose I make it.'

She handed over a laminated list of drinks to Viktor. Viktor looked at it for two seconds then passed it back with the instruction,

'You choose,'

Nikola looked quizzically at him. Viktor replied to the look with,

'Like tourist,'

'Ok then, a gentleman who likes surprises and I am good at surprises,' Joy said as she dove behind the counter to seek out the various ingredients.

The two men sat looking round the bar. It didn't pay to dive in too quickly until they found out who and what they were dealing with. They needed to get a positive I.D. on Billy and what connection, if any, he had to Kiet. Billy, being the owner of this place, certainly made the job of tracking him down easier. Behind the bar Joy flitted from bottle to bottle like a bee gathering nectar. It looked as though every single drink in the house was being poured into a blender along with handfuls of ice and fruit. As the blender whirred, she carved up a pineapple with the skill of a master butcher. Soon there was an empty pineapple shell and a plate of chunks sitting on the bar. Joy poured the contents of the blender into the shell and topped it with two umbrellas, cherries, a couple of tinsel straws and a plastic parrot. She proudly offered it up like a first Prize trophy. Viktor didn't quite know what to make of this glorious sight.

'What this?' he asked quizzically.

'That is a Kit Kat Kaboom! One of my own, a big drink for big men,' said Joy with a twinkle.

They both took a sip. The alcohol content was through the roof, but the inclusion of fruits and coconut milk gave it a smooth refreshing edge. It was surprisingly good. While Joy was with them Nikola thought he would try for some information.

'My partner and me run security for bar, make sure everyone have happy time, make safe. We look for job. You have job here?'

'You'd need to see Billy about that,' said Joy.

Nikola ventured further.

'Billy manager?'

'Billy owns this place,' Joy answered, 'he does all the hiring and firing.'

Just then Viktor nudged Nikola's arm and nodded to a framed photograph above the bar. It was a picture taken at the backstage of a concert. On the left of the picture was a young David Hasselhoff with his arm around the shoulder of a slim Thai gentleman dressed all in black and wearing sunglasses.

The signature said, "To Billy, a man who knows how to party from The Hoff."

Nikola pointed to the photograph.

'This Billy?'

'It certainly is, but he's not in at the moment,' answered Joy.

'What time he back?'

'I don't know, but I do know you'll be wasting your time.'

'Why? Security good.'

Joy hoisted herself half over the counter on her tip toes in order to bring her face close to Nikola's.

'Honestly honey I'm the only security they need round here. But personally, those muscles of yours can 'pop in' anytime.'

She kissed her hand and tapped it lightly on his nose. With that she glided away to serve another customer.

Billy was out, but now they knew what he looked like. Once Viktor saw a face, he never forgot it. It could be years later, they could be fatter, thinner have lost their hair, grown a beard, be wearing sunglasses or a hat. He may only have seen them for a moment in a faded pixelated photo, it didn't matter, Viktor always remembered a face. He was, what was known as, a super-recogniser. It was an incredibly useful skill in his line of business.

Billy's face was locked in. Now all they had to do was to wait for him to return.

21

A $20 orange

It was late when Nok stepped down from the train, night had
fallen. The station was deserted. The journey had been long
but comfortable in her first-class compartment. The trip had
given her plenty of time to think, but what things were going
to look like beyond the next few hours was still vague. Only
the core of her original plan still remained, rescue her sister,
Gia, from the family home and start a new life.

After fleeing the abusive grip of her father, like many lost
souls before her, Nok had made for the capital. Bangkok took
her under its black wing. For a girl with no qualifications and
little experience, opportunities were not falling at her feet.
After weeks of trying to get a decent job, she chilled at the
prospect of having to return home defeated. Then a random
conversation with a girl at a street food stall opened the
possibility of making money from her natural gifts. With her
obvious beauty she was quickly able to find employment as a
bar girl serving drinks and providing 'company' for sad

frustrated men and unashamed sex tourists. The money was as good as how low you were prepared to stoop. Nok made a living, but the vast proportion of her earnings were devoured just surviving in the voracious city. Consequently, she was able to set aside very little. The promise she made to Gia, to save enough to start a new life with her, looked like it was forever going to be out of reach. Then came the pregnancy, who the father was who could tell. In the window of possibility, it could have been any one of a dozen men. With no means to support a child, termination was her only option. Without medical care she was forced to turn to a back-street provider. The procedure didn't go well, and she was left sick for many weeks. What little she had saved was quickly eaten away and if it weren't for the support of her fellow workers, dying could have been a real possibility. After she recovered, she decided to escape the grime of the city and try for a fresh start in Pattaya. With no initial grounding in the town, she had worked the streets independently and that's when she had met Kiet. The proposition he put to her was risky, but 100,000 baht was too good to turn down. This was enough to lift her from the street and kick start her plan. 100,000 baht wouldn't have kept her and Gia forever, but they would be able to travel anywhere in Thailand and, if they were careful, to keep them for at least a few months. This would have given Nok the breathing space to get a decent job to support them. Gia

201

had now turned thirteen, if they lied about her age, she too could find work. With both of them earning things would have been comfortable.

Initially it had seemed to her that with both the money she now had and the drugs it would not just be the country that had opened up to them, but the whole world. And it wouldn't be just the next few months that would be comfortable it would be the rest of their lives. The hours on the train, however, had given her time to think and it was not as easy as she first thought. The money was in U.S. dollars and around $200,000 was not the sort of money you could casually exchange at a TT counter or deposit in a bank without some awkward questions being asked. As for the drugs, every hour she had them on her person she could feel a death sentence hanging over her. She had zero connections and no knowledge of how to safely make connections to move this quantity of heroin. The irony was crippling. Here she was with the equivalent of around 6,000,000 baht in dollars and heroin with a probable value many times that and she had no easy opportunity to access it. Until things became clearer, she decided to filter through just a few dollars at a time and stick with the immediate plan for now. Getting Gia was her main objective.

It had been almost two years since the night she'd left with a vow to come back for Gia once she had the means to support them. Even if their future were uncertain, one thing that Nok did know for sure was, once free of her father, Gia would never have to go through the things she had been through, or do the things she had done, just to survive.

 Nok made her way out of the station and into the main street. Little had changed. Essentially the town was nothing more than a giant crossroads. One road ran north to south and followed the train line, the other bisected the town east to west and ran into the deep country. All streets spidered out from these two main roads. Although it was made up of no more than a couple of hundred buildings the town held all of the essentials to be self-contained.   Apothecaries, convenience stores, eateries and even a dentist all stood side by side. As she passed by the main junction, she saw on her left the town's market square. She remembered when she was young, getting up before the sun with her father to sell the fruits they had grown. This was when they had owned land to grow fruits. At this time of night most stores were closed. The only life echoed from bars dotted here and there. At one time the town had been more prosperous than it was now. The fall in the town's fortunes had correlated closely with the increase in the consumption of alcohol as men began to find themselves without the discipline and direction of work. Hurrying by one such drinking establishment she became aware that in all probability her father would be in one of

203

these bars, drinking away the money that could be used to buy food. She only hoped he was and that he would stay there until her and Gia were safely away.

It didn't take long for the main town to thin out. The low hum of overhead cables was overtaken by the chirping of cicadas and the dim pools of the sparse streetlights were now at her back. Electric light began to give way to oil lamps and the permanence of brick gave way to makeshift building materials such as wooden off-cuts and corrugated iron. Crippled shanties lined the road. Through the open doors and windows, the warm glow of habitation spilled yellow light into the darkness of the street. Here and there Nok caught the snatch of a conversation, the sight of movement from within or the flicker of a TV from the more affluent houses. Most of the dwellings doubled as stores and inside people squatted, sat or lay amongst the goods they peddled during the day, using rice sacks and beers crates as improvised pillows and seats. Here it was not like town. It was not so easy to tell what each individual 'household' sold. It seemed you could get everything from a haircut to a motorcycle repair under the same roof. The further she walked the more neglected the houses became. The few that were now left leaned against each other for mutual support, without which they would probably have collapsed into the road. She wandered to the end of shacks; this was the very edge of town. At the end of the row a thin young boy sat on some low wooden steps at the front of a dilapidated house. At his bare feet lay a large bowl of oranges. As Nok approached he called out in a plaintive voice.

'Orange lady? Very sweet, very tasty.' Nok looked down into his thin, dirty face.

'How much?' she asked.

The boy looked her up and down, he had never seen her before and judging from her clothes she wasn't from here.

Tentatively he said,

'50 baht,'

'50 baht!'

Nok raised her eyebrows in feigned shock.

'They're good oranges, very sweet,' said the boy, qualifying the price and holding one out for her to inspect.

Nok took the orange and examined it closely.

'This does look good; do you take U.S. dollar?' she asked.

The boy shook his head vigorously.

'No, not dollar, baht,'

Nok dipped her hand into her bag where she had already separated out some of the money into manageable chunks and pulled out a $20 note.

'I don't have much money in baht, what if I give you $20 for this orange and you can change that for baht later.'

The young boy stared at her incredulously $20 for a single orange. That was more than he'd made from oranges in a month.

'Do we have a deal?' said Nok offering him the note.

Cautiously he took it, half expecting it to be taken back at any moment. Then, quickly, he stuffed it in the pocket of his shorts.

'Thank you, pretty lady,' he beamed.

'Thank you,' said Nok bowing.

Pealing the orange, she plunged into the long shadows of the track ahead. As she walked away, she caught the excited cries of the boy as he ran into the house waiving his newfound fortune. There was a faint sound of footsteps on the porch as his parents came out to see who their son's benefactor was, but no one followed.

Her family home was about five kilometres outside of town, next to the river. It was part of a cluster of houses whose families tended the surrounding land and fished the waters. Her father had always been a drinker and an abusive man but at one time he had owned a plot of land which he'd inherited from his father. The land had given the family a base level of subsistence. This was until the alcohol took over full time and he sold it to a rival farmer for little more than a few months drinking money. Once the farm had gone her father lost all structure to his life. In the years that followed he made a living doing what he could when he could. Any money he made was primarily used to fuel his habit and secondly, if there was anything left over, to feed his family. In an attempt to feel control in a situation over which he had lost all control he turned his frustrations on the home.

Bullies always have a way of exploiting what they see as weakness. Her mother was a passive woman, with dull compliant eyes, almost ill-equipped to deal with life itself. Nok didn't understand psychology, but it was clear that by the time she was nine her mental faculties surpassed her mother's. In her most introspective moments Nok could acknowledge that her mother was probably the greater victim. She was a victim of her own limitations and a victim of her father. But a child looks to their mother for protection and after years of watching her standby that man knowing what he was like, making excuses for his behaviour any tattered shreds of potential love had been replaced by an uneasy resentment … 'Daddy does not do this because he loves me'. She could still feel his rum-soaked tongue in her mouth, the very thought of it made her wretch. Although he was mentally and physically abusive, in all that time he had never once touched Gia, in that way. Nok never understood why, but she thought perhaps even the biggest bastard needs to think that there is some part of them that can be pure. In the very darkest corners of her psyche, she sometimes resented being the sexual shield for her

207

sister. With clarity of thought she knew that to have Gia suffer in the same way she had would in no way have made her situation better. Secretly, through a friend in the village, she had communicated with Gia a handful of times since she left. In that time, her father's behaviour had degenerated largely into a pathetic tope. Thankfully, Gia had gone untouched, although she still lived in fear of his bursts of self-pitying violence.

The path ahead was lit only by the stars and a waxing moon but having walked this track a thousand times before she could have found her way in total darkness. As she made her way down the single-track side road which led to her village, she planned for her next move. This was the final hurdle. She had not had the time to get word to Gia that she was coming. If, however, her father's old habits were anything to go by he would not be back in the house until after midnight. This should give them enough time to get out before he returned. She knew her timing was bad as there was no train out until the following morning. But given the money she had she was certain she could secure them a bed for the night in town. They could then be out on the first train at dawn. As she stepped into the clearing that was her village, she could see the dancing flames of the oil lamps in the windows. There were only eight houses in the cluster, all in the traditional Thai style, built of wood, thatched with palm frond and all elevated

208

on short stilts. Those that could afford it kept a coup of chickens outside and those with even more means kept diminutive black pigs in the space beneath the house. Nok could hear the quiet clucking and soft snuffling of the animals.

The village was much the same as she had left it, some houses even looked better. Old fences had been replaced with new, the occasional wall had been painted and someone had even rigged up an outdoor shower consisting of a wooden enclosure with a suspended bag of water attached to a shower head. As always, the village spirit house stood out bright and pristine. Fresh fruit and sweet cakes lay on its platform and slow curls of smoke rose from dying incense. Spirit houses could be found throughout the country. A highly ornate mini dwelling mounted on a pillar or dais. The spirit house was a shrine that provided shelter for spirits that could turn malignant if not appeased by a comfortable place to live and daily offerings.

When she was young and when no one was looking Nok would often steal the tastiest offerings for herself. When her father's behaviour was bad Nok used to wonder if she had offended one of those spirits and it was her theft that had led a malign entity to take control of him. In an attempt to appease the spirits, she took to saving every sweet morsels that she came by and offered them up to try to atone for her transgression. But no matter how much she tried to make

209

amends nothing changed. Whether she left offerings or not, things never got any better and she quickly stopped believing in spirits. People were who they were and who really knows where evil in hearts of men comes from.

There in the small cluster of houses, standing on the banks of the narrow river, only her house had suffered the ravages of time. The balustrades on the porch were broken and missing. The thatched roof looked dishevelled and didn't even look like it was a match for a light shower never mind a tropical storm. There were shutters missing from the windows and the whole house had a distinct lean that was not there two years ago. As she approached, she could still see the remnants of the shells that she and Gia had stuck around the door in what felt like a lifetime ago. She remembered the day well, a day when they behaved like a real family.

She stood outside looking up. There were people inside, but who? Quietly she crept around the perimeter to the banks of the river, listening intently. No one was on the ramshackle balcony crumbling into the river. She could make out the occasional shuffle of movement, the strains of a radio show, but no one spoke. She needed to be sure her father wasn't there before she entered. Once again, she made her way to the front of the house and mounted the porch, placing each step as carefully as though she was walking on eggshells. The top stair creaked as she tentatively lowered her weight onto it.

She stopped for a moment, but no one came. She picked her way over to the flickering light in the window and risked a glimpse inside, just the same.

The house was one big room half divided towards the back by a pierced wooden screen. At the back, through the screen Nok could see the mattress on the floor. This was her parents' bedroom. The bedroom had a makeshift sliding door which opened on to the balcony overlooking the river. At the front of the house to the right was what passed for the kitchen, a two ringed hob fuelled by a gas bottle connected below. There was a chair, a low table and a storage trunk which stood next to a convertible sofa bed. This was the bed she had shared with Gia since she was a child. There was no bathroom; washing and toilet facilities were shared by the village. In the warm light Nok could see her mother sitting in the chair stitching a pair of trousers. She seemed unchanged except for her eyes, which were even more distant than before. Perhaps she had finally retreated fully into her own childlike world. On the sofa, reading a magazine, sat Gia. For an adult, two years of ageing makes little difference to their appearance. But for a child of eleven, two years can render them unrecognisable. Nok had left a skinny kid with a dirty face and short tomboy hair. She was now looking at the beginnings of a young woman. The gaunt face with a wide forehead and disproportionately large mournful eyes had filled

211

out and were now beautifully proportioned. Her previously short tufty hair was past her shoulders and had a lustrous sheen in the lamp light. The thin arms and gangly legs that were always uncoordinated, making her move like a young foal struggling to stand had grown strong and lithe. Many people had been captivated by Nok's looks, but she could see, even now, that she would only ever be a shadow of her sister. This made her even more determined that Gia would never be exploited, that she would never have to make a living peddling the gifts god had given her to the highest bidder. She had taken in the whole scene in less than a second and the one thing she had not seen was her father.

Nok walked over to the door and without knocking pushed it open. Gia looked up from her magazine, her eyes widened as it dropped to the floor. In the chair her mother stopped mid stitch, but her face remained expressionless. For a second no one moved, then with a shriek of joy Gia jumped up and flung herself at Nok. The two sisters held each other tight and Nok could feel Gia's chest heaving. Gia was beginning to cry, and this made Nok cry. Through her tears Nok looked over her sister's shoulder to where her mother sat. She never moved. Silently and without expression she watched the two girls in the doorway. Eventually Nok took her sisters head in her hands and looked into her eyes.

'Have you come home?' asked Gia her eyes puffy and red with tears.

'No, I've come to keep my promise,'

'Your promise?'

Nok wiped the tears from Gia's face.

'Remember the night I left? Remember I said when I had the money, I would come back for you, we would leave, you and me, find a better life.'

'Yes,' said Gia struggling to regain control of her breathing.

'Well, that time's now, tonight! Come with me and together we can make a better life.'

'What now?' said Gia wrestling with the suddenness of the proposition.

'Now,' said Nok 'it's a long story, just believe me that I can take care of us. We will never have to go without again.'

'What about mother, what about father?'

Gia wiped away the hair that clung to her tear-stained cheeks.

Nok's face hardened,

'The time of living in fear of that man is over,'

'He could find us,' interrupted Gia.

A smile played on Nok's lips.

'Gia believe me he wouldn't even know where to start looking, we have a world to choose from.'

There was a hesitation in Gia's voice, she cast her eyes down.

213

'What about mother?'

Nok looked at her mother in the chair. She had resumed stitching the trousers with the same faraway look in her eyes. There was no glimmer of acknowledgement that Nok had been away or that she had returned. Letting go of Gia's hands she knelt in front of her mother. Nok gently placed her hand over the stitching and looked into her blank face.

'Mother it's Nok, I'm home,' she said.

The glazed soulless eyes stared into a vague middle distance focusing on nothing in particular.

'Hello Nok,' was all she said.

Nok pressed on searching her mother's face for any trace of understanding about what was happening.

'Me and Gia are leaving mother, we're not coming back,'

There was no reply. Her mother just carried on sewing. Nok lifted her head and turned back to Gia.

'We need to think of us now, please pack,' she said in a low voice.

'But …' Gia was about to raise an objection.

Nok held up her hand.

'Leave with me now, once we are settled, I promise we can think about what to do about mother.'

Gia gave a momentary pause of indecision. Then at a snap pulled a bag from under the sofa bed and frantically started to stuff it with jeans and tee-shirts from the trunk. It didn't take long, there was not much to pack. Soon the bag was slung over her shoulder, and she was ready to leave. Nok held out her hand, Gia took it, and they turned to the door.

What they were faced with stopped them in their tracks.

22

He was looking at me 'funny'

Despite Chai Son's reassurance that he would be compensated for his losses and either his money or his merchandise would be restored, along with a consideration for inconvenience, Viv had insisted on travelling to Thailand to 'make sure right was done by him'. Chai Son understood the value of trust. It could be profitable to cultivate an ongoing relationship with Vivian Brownsword, so in the spirit of transparency he had agreed. Chai Son had no doubt that everything would be recovered soon, and this would be a good opportunity to show Mr Brownsword how he dealt with disruption. He had dispatched a car to the airport to pick up his guests and bring them to his office. Together they would apprehend this thieving farang.

Viv and Archie sat in the back of the midnight blue Jaguar iPace. The ride was smooth. The driver had been impeccably polite. He had provided them with the estimated travel time, bottles of water for the journey and enquired as to whether the temperature was to their liking. Viv had been less genteel, "Just fuckin' drive son." Archie believed this entire trip to be ill advised. They were without fire power, without back up and this Chai Son was an unknown quantity. Viv would often refer to Archie as his 'consigliere'. He told Archie everything and took his council on everything … well almost everything. It all depended on how bad he wanted to do something and how much against it he thought Archie would be. Viv was a man given to impulses and he sometimes found the colder, more analytical, approach of Archie stifling. So, when Viv thought Archie would think it a bad idea, but he really wanted to do it, he kept his mouth shut. This avoided any protracted discussion of relative pros and cons. This whole deal was one of Viv's impulses. For Viv, hard drugs had always been a minor income stream. His main line in this arena was hash and for years he had sourced his product entirely in the U.K. It was a solid, reasonably low risk, income. Profits were such that money was easy to filter through his lines of gambling machines, security firms and other business projects, not to mention the negligible percentage that filtered through his vanity project antique shop. Viv's various ventures had made him a lot of money in areas he knew a lot about. Money, however, was never his primary driving force. The real satisfaction for him was not the financial payoff, but how he got there. Viv was a classic 'thrill of the chase' man.

217

Viv had spent most of the flight sleeping and avoiding Archie's questions. Archie knew little other than things had not gone to plan with this deal. Right now, driving to meet someone he didn't know, in a potentially volatile situation Archie really needed to start filling out the gaps in his knowledge. He wanted a better idea of what they were about to walk into. Archie spoke.

'This Chai Son guy, you never said how you got in with him?'

Viv had been handing out information about this deal piecemeal even before this whole situation exploded. He knew Archie disapproved. Archie had been cautioning for years about growth being too rapid and expanding into foreign markets when there were safer profits on the doorstep. This was one of the questions Viv had been avoiding.

'Just a contact,' he said absently gazing out of the black tinted window.

Archie pressed on.

'Listen Viv, we are where we are now. We stand and fall together on both the good and the bad. So, who is this guy we're going to meet and how do you know him?'

Viv looked sheepish.

'He was passed on by Tony the Tongue.'

Now this was news.

'Fucking hell Vivian, what were you thinking of, taking tips of that mad Scottish psychopath,' blurted Archie incredulously.

Anywhere in Scotland if it went up your nose, in your arm or was dropped surreptitiously into someone's drink, chances were Tony the Tongue had a hand in it somewhere. He earned the nickname due to the fact that if you crossed him, he had a reputation of removing your tongue and keeping it as a trophy. In reality he had only done this twice. However, the impact of such an act was enough to create an enduring reputation. People liked the stuff of legend. Viv knew Tony's reputation but felt the need to defend his decision.

'Look Archie thanks to our little Chinese friend …'

'Thai,' Archie corrected.

Viv was unfazed.

'Whatever! Thanks to this Chai Son character, Tony's more than doubled his profits in the last eighteen months. He's got control from John o' Groats to Berwick. He's even bought himself a fuckin' castle. Archie, we've been playing in the kiddie pool for too long. International trade, bulk buying that's where it's at,'

'I know Vivian,' Archie replied, 'but seriously mate taking tips off Tony the Tongue. Didn't he shoot someone's horse because it was looking at him funny?'

This was one of those urban myths that surrounded Tony. To be fair he never actually shot the horse, he only hit it with a hammer, and it recovered later. Whether it ever looked at him 'funny' again is not known.

219

Viv was now in full justification mode.

'Listen I know Tony has issues with reality sometimes, but he knows business and we get on,'

For reasons only known to Tony he really did like Viv, or whatever passed for liking someone in his world. Viv pressed on,

'He's been dealing a lot with this Chai Son, and he says he's the best in the game. His gear's clean and the cheapest on the market and if Tony says he's reliable then he's reliable.'

'Reliable enough to lose your 200,000k?' Archie shot back.

Viv returned to looking out of the window.

Respect

Nok stood transfixed, her breath had been taken away and she felt a sickness grasp hold of her stomach. Silhouetted in the door stood her father, the oil lamps casting cruel shadows across his face. At one time he had been a big man, but years of alcohol abuse had taken its toll. A lot of what was formally muscle had run to fat and his face had become thread-veined and bloated. Even so he was still too big for two girls to handle and Nok knew he could be violent.

'You're back,' he said sneering, 'what have you come home for?'

Without dropping a stitch or looking up her mother answered from the chair.

'Nok is leaving with Gia and they're not coming back.'

'Is this right, were you going to sneak out in the night again, but this time take my daughter?' her father snorted.

Nok had no desire to acknowledge this man as her father, but against all sense she found herself saying.

'I'm your daughter as well!'

'You stopped being my daughter two years ago. In fact, I'm not sure you ever were my daughter … You're just a whore of a whore,' he hissed as he stepped into the room and closed the door behind him.

'Don't do this,' said Nok tightening her jaw 'we're leaving and there's nothing you can do.'

'We're leaving,' her father bounced back, 'you can leave, but she stays,' he said pointing a nicotine-stained finger at Gia.

Nok hardened her voice.

'Get out of our way old man,' she said pushing Gia protectively behind her, 'we're fucking leaving!'

Her father's face reddened, broken veins stood out livid purple on his cheeks and nose.

'You walk in here after two years and start to tell me how things are going to be in my house, my house! RESPECT,' he blasted, 'You need a lesson in respect!'

Nok saw his fists clench by his side, and he began to take a step forward. Over the years she had taken many forms of abuse from her father. In all that time she had always been the passive party. Although she had often fanaticised about it, Nok had never once retaliated; was it her not wanting to escalate the situation, the passive example set by her mother or the sense that she was absorbing the abuse to protect Gia? The reasons behind Nok's former inaction would take a lot of unpacking, but things had changed. One of the lessons she had learned watching drunken men vying to be the alpha male was that the person who lashes out first usually wins. This wreck of a man was not going to stand between her and Gia's new future.

Without warning and before her father had taken another step, she launched herself at him. With no weapon at hand, she aimed to cause the maximum amount of damage in the shortest possible time and attacked his eyes. His head instinctively dodged the onslaught and Nok's nails left three deep gouges down the side of his face. It was damage, but not enough to stop him. Realising she had missed her mark Nok went for his eyes a second time. The speed at which this shambles of a man moved took her completely by surprise. Before she had a chance to raise her hand a second time, she felt the jarring thud of a fist on the side of her jaw. The blow released a burst of stars and she crashed across the room. She lay stunned and semi-conscious on the floor. The world spun in and out of focus. In the distance she heard Gia scream. There was the sound of a sharp slap and the screaming abruptly stopped. Through her fluttering eyelids she looked up and could see her mother sitting in the chair, eyes wide, paralysed with fear.

The next thing she saw was her father's face, pushed close to hers, filling her whole world. His breath stank of cigarettes and cheap rum.

'I told you, respect, you will come to know respect.'

She felt herself being flipped over onto her front. His knee dug deep into the small of her back and his coarse hand ground her face into the floor. Roughly her backpack was torn from her and flung to the side. Her arms were pulled up high behind her. He started to unbuckle his belt. Nok screwed her eyes shut. Had he degenerated so far as to take her here and now, on the floor in front of her mother and sister. A second later she felt a thin leather strip bite into her wrists, tightly binding her. Then, still dazed, she was thrown onto her back. She lay looking up at her father standing astride her. He was breathing heavily. Large beads of sweat rolled down his face. He gathered himself for a moment, catching his breath.

'You need to learn lessons and respect,' he said between gasps.

He crossed the room to retrieve her backpack. Opening it up he said in a mocking tone,

'Let's see what you've brought your father as a present.'

As he looked inside his expression changed from one of contempt to shocked disbelief. Slowly he reached in and pulled out a fat bundle of dollar bills. His mouth hung loose; he had no words.   He dove in again and pulled out another bundle and then another.   He was almost starting to hyperventilate. His hand fished to the bottom of the bag. This time it was not a bundle of dollars that emerged, but a tightly wrapped package of caramel powder. As if in slow motion the bag dropped from his hand, and he knelt in front of Nok.

 Pushing the package in her face he whispered,

 'Where, where did you get this?'

 Nok looked hard into his wide eyes.

 'Fuck you!' she said and spat.

 Blood-filled saliva spattered across his dumfounded face.

 The last thing she saw was his expression flush with anger. The next instant, a fist made contact with the side of her head. She knew no more.

24

Dutch courage

Business never sleeps. Following his interrogation of Kiet, Chai Son had had a busy few hours attending to a number of financial issues. Now he was returning to his office apartment above his club to meet with Viv and Archie. Restitution for their inconvenience needed to be made. His extended network of eyes and ears had not let him down. Billy had located the potential partner of the man Alex and he had just received word from James McNulty to inform him that a man with Alex Whyte's passport and answering to his description had been arrested at Bangkok airport. He had been carrying a quantity of heroin. Picking up Alex's male accomplice should be easy. All Chai Son had to do was collect him from the hotel. Retrieving Alex would be a more difficult. James told him he had been taken to Bang Kwang, but not to worry as there was an ongoing 'understanding' with the governor.

Getting him out might take time and money, but James could do it.

Chai Son understood the impact of spectacle. With a swift and brutal show of power, this embarrassment could be used to his advantage. It could be made to act as an example of how he dealt with theft and so restore confidence. Stepping out of his car he looked at his watch, Vivian Brownsword would be arriving in about twenty minutes.

He pushed through the doors into the main bar and made his way to the private elevator that would take him to the third-floor apartment. The club was on the fringes of Pattaya away from the true centre of night life madness. Chai Son's target clientele was not sex tourist foreigners. He catered for the wealthier strata of young Thai society. It had a healthy, but subdued buzz, played out against a backdrop of light jazz. Passing by the bar he spotted an incongruity. Two western men stood in shorts and tee-shirts. They were somewhere in their late fifties. Although the club didn't have an official dress code, or any policies on age, it had a reputation for being the place where pretty young things went to be seen in their best finery. It was not usual to see foreigners, beach wear or older people. One of the men was chatting to, or what could more accurately be described as talking at, a stylish girl sitting at the bar. Despite her supreme indifference to his advances, he persisted with his one-sided conversation. Both men were

227

swaying, it was clear they'd had one too many. Chai Son decided to invest five minutes to observe. The larger of the two men propped himself on his elbow and invaded the girl's space with his round red head. He spoke with a heavy Dutch accent.

'Now what does it take for someone like you to come back to my hotel room?'

She made no reply. This didn't seem to faze him. He moved closer still, placing his arm on the back of her seat, closing down her exit.

'Come on, you might even enjoy yourself, you're in the driving seat. Tell me how much it would take?' he said in, what he thought was, a smooth voice.

She fully understood the content of the conversation but decided to feign ignorance in the hope that he wouldn't persist when there was a difficulty in communication.

'Chạn mị k̂hêācı,' she answered.

Unfortunately, this was one of the most basic phrases on page one of the Collins Learn to Speak Thai starter book. The Dutchman had progressed to page two. His accent was bad, though his intentions were clear.

'You don't understand. I was asking how much, Khuṇ thèā hị̀r, long time?'

This time the girl made no attempt at an answer and turning her back she attempted to leave the stool. The Dutchman was not to be deterred so easily. He had been in Pattaya for a week and given the establishments he had frequented so far, he believed that every girl in every bar had a price tag. It was just his job to negotiate. His arm closed tightly around her waist. His friend stood impassive, more interested in his drink than in the latest object of his companion's affections.

'Come on now, there is no need to be rude. Rākhā nān?' he said puling her close.

The girl struggled to leave but he held on. The smile on his face was starting to become strained. Chai Son had seen enough it was time to intervene. He spoke first to the girl.

'Don't worry you are safe,' then turning to the persistent Dutchman 'please take your arm from around the lady's waist.'

The request was firm, but polite. This was not something the man had encountered before. His first drunken reaction was confusion.

'What?'

Meeting the man's unsteady stare Chai Son's voice assumed a harder edge.

'I said please take your arm from around the lady's waist. I believe she wishes to leave.'

The Dutchman slackened his grip and the girl made good her escape. Although he had let go of the girl, he was not yet ready to let go of the situation.

'Who the fuck are you, her boyfriend or something?' he said with a drunken slur.

Chai Son decided it was time for the men to leave.

'Gentlemen I do not think you will find anything to buy in this bar, can I recommend you try somewhere more central.'

The Dutchman puffed out his chest and invaded Chai Son's space. The shift in dynamic had piqued his friend's interest and leaving his drink he moved over to box Chai Son in. Out numbering him two to one they believed their Dutch-courage to be well justified.

'You recommend what you like, I want to stay here and if I want to talk to anyone in here I will and you …'

He went to poke his finger in Chai Son's chest. The finger never met its target, he never finished his sentence. Without a further word Chai Son smashed the knuckle of his thumb into the side of the man's neck just below his ear. The man crumpled. Before he'd even hit the ground, Chai Son drove his elbow into the temple of the other man. They both fell to the floor within half a second of each other. The move was so quick and so quiet, it hardly caused a ripple of concern amongst the other patrons. Chai Son bent down and manoeuvred the two men into a sitting position with their backs against the bar. He beckoned the barman over.

'Pricha get Yut and drop these men in the street a suitable distance from here,' he instructed.

Pricha answered nervously.

'Yes boss.'

Pricha had witnessed the early stages of this situation. He knew he should've nipped it in the bud. It was his job to ensure there was order at the bar and he had failed in this duty.

'And Pricha,' said Chai Son.

'Yes boss.'

Pricha detected a slight break in his own voice. It sounded to him as though his words were spoken by another.

'This never happens again under your watch, do you understand?'

If there was going to be a consequence to what had just happened, Pricha knew it would be immediate. A wave of relief washed over him.

'Yes boss.'

The two men propped against the bar had still not stirred. Pricha decided to risk a question to see exactly what he had been charged with disposing of.

'Eh boss, will they be ok?'

Chai Son turned and straightening his waistcoat said,

'That depends,'

Pricha gave him a quizzical look.

'Medical science makes progress every day.'

Chai Son felt that this altercation had been a good warm up, a little something to sharpen the senses before his meeting with Mr Brownsword.

25

30 seconds

Viktor and Nikola had been watching the Double Beat for around an hour. Shortly after they had left the bar, they had done a reconnaissance of the perimeter. There was the main front door and round the back there was a service door secured with a chain and lock. To avoid any chance of missing Billy, they decided to split and position themselves at both entrances. A round of rock paper scissors decided who was to keep surveillance in the back ally and who was to watch from the relative comfort of the bar opposite. It was eventually over the top of an orange juice that Nikola saw Billy stroll into the Double Beat. It was showtime. He dropped fifty Baht on to the table and made his way to the back lane to find Viktor.

Viktor was nowhere to be seen. Then if he were to be seen he would not have been very good at surveillance. Nikola gave a short, two pitched, whistle and Viktor materialised from a pile of discarded packing boxes ten metres down the alley.

233

For a big man he could make himself invisible with some ease. The plan had been set that they would not risk making a full entrance through the bar. This time information would not be extracted so diplomatically, so they would enter through the back in order to leave less of a visual footprint. They approached the door; it was secured by a sturdy chain and with a 20mm shackle padlock. The padlock was the weak link.

Viktor nodded and Nikola took the lock in one hand and the chain in the other. He began to twist … and twist. His knuckles grew white, and a large blue vein throbbed on his temple, but he made no sound. After ten seconds a bead of sweat ran down his brow and his breathing became audible. After fifteen seconds he relaxed his grip and flexed his hands. He could see Viktor's face, there was a smile playing on his lips. Nikola knew he was being mocked. The reverse encouragement spurred him on.

Once more he took the lock and chain in his slab-like hands. This time the twists came in explosive bursts, punctuated by grunts. On the third twist there was a sharp crack and the chain fell away from the door. Nikola held the broken lock out to Viktor like a cat proudly presenting a dead bird. Viktor looked unimpressed. His only acknowledgement was,

'Thirty seconds,' followed by a disappointed shake of the head.

Before they'd left Double Beat earlier, Viktor had paid a visit to the bathroom. During which time he had taken the opportunity to discreetly appraise himself of the back-rooms layout. Luckily, everything appeared to be on the ground floor and very helpfully Billy had even labelled one of the doors 'Billies' office. Once inside the two men found themselves in an anti-room. The door on the left led to the cellars and the door to the right led them to the main back rooms. Taking the door on the right they silently made their way to Billy's office. They took up their positions on either side of the door. This routine was well rehearsed. Nikola gently knocked. A man's voice called out something in Thai. Nikola waited a few seconds and knocked again. The same voice answered, only this time louder. Again, he waited a few seconds and knocked again. He didn't understand what was being said but there was an agitated muttering followed by footsteps.

As the door opened both men moved like lighting. Viktor steamed in smashing the door into the face of the person behind it. Quickly he grabbed them spinning them round so he had a hold behind. A powerful arm wrapped around their body and gripped them by the throat, the other arm enveloped their head covering their nose and mouth. In the same instant Nikola entered the room kicking the door closed behind him. Instantly, he recognised Billy sitting at the desk. The whole situation had unfolded so fast there was no time for

Billy to react. Nikola was upon him before he could rise to his feet. His humungous frame pinned Billy to the chair. Nikola let loose with a piston punch to Billy's jaw. Despite this only being about a quarter of his power, it was enough to render Billy senseless.

When the mist cleared, Viktor was left holding Jade and Nikola was standing over the unconscious body of Billy.

26

A ladyboy show

Viv and Archie stepped out of the security elevator and into Chai Son's office. Archie took in the scene around him. There was only one entrance and one exit, the elevator behind them, this was operated by a security card held by the man who had acted as their chauffeur. This man was now standing between them and the only way out. It was a large open plan room, sparsely furnished. There were three other men apart from the chauffeur, all Thai. A tall, lean man immaculately dressed in a crisp white shirt and waistcoat, looked to be early thirties. A younger stocky man in a lightweight dark blue suit and a sharp hawk like man, whose eyes were constantly vigilant for threat. All in all, he and Viv were at a severe disadvantage. He could see the situation needed to be handled with diplomacy.

Viv strode forward and approached the man in the shirt and waistcoat. The man never moved, but Archie saw the two men that discreetly flanked him tense. Viv opened the conversation.

'It's taken me thirteen hours to get here on a very expensive flight, which, I might add, is a flight you'll be paying for. Now tell me, have you got my fuckin' gear, or my fuckin' money or both?'

Despite everything Archie knew about Viv he thought he would have been more tactful than this. When discussing how the situation would pan out, this was not what they had agreed as an effective opening gambit. The arms of the two flanking men moved to a semi defensive, easily launched attack, position. Archie heard the man behind him take a step forward. Chai Son alone registered no response. He lifted a hand in greeting and with a polite nod of the head said,

'Mr Brownsword it's a pleasure to meet you at last.'

His voice was calm and welcoming. Unfortunately, Viv was not to be pacified so easily and without taking the offered hand hit back.

'There's no fuckin' pleasure on my side son and there will be very little pleasure on your side if this isn't sorted.'

Chai Son made no obvious acknowledgement of the snub of his handshake. He beckoned Viv and Archie over to the couches in the middle of the room. As he did so he added,

'Mr Brownsword, it is considered very rude in my country to use foul language when you are a guest in another's house.'

238

When Viv was in a mood, he was not used to people being calm and answering back. Usually people said nothing, fidgeted, hung their heads, avoided eye contact or left the room to make tea and kept out of the way until he had blown himself out. Being told off was not in his repertoire of expected responses and it threw him for a moment.

'What! fuc …'

He was about to talk his way into something he wouldn't be able to behave his way out of when Archie grabbed his arm and gave it a squeeze.

'Please Vivian, remember what we agreed. When in Rome, when in Rome mate,'

Archie could see he was agitated. He sought to pacify Viv's impulses.

'calm and business-like Vivian, remember.'

He felt Viv's arm relax and the fire in his eyes dwindled. Chai Son had moved over to a well-stocked drinks cabinet.

'Please gentlemen take a seat, would you like refreshment after your long journey?'

Viv dropped himself into the couch and Archie sat opposite. This way he could keep a clear view of anything going on behind Viv's back.

'Bourbon,' said Viv.

Chai Son examined the range of bottles in front of him.

'I have Pappy Van Winkle, Kentucky Owl, Widow Jane …?'

Viv just wanted something wet with an alcoholic content.

'Whatever, and stick a splash of diet coke in.'

'I think a Woodford Reserve, it mixes better. And you?' asked Chai Son turning to Archie.

Archie was just happy that the situation seemed to be under control for now. 'Same as him will do thanks.'

Chai Son poured the drinks into to two crystal tumblers, added a splash of diet coke and a large cube of ice.

'I hope I did not kill the whiskey, with the coke,' he said handing them over.

Archie took a sip, it was good. He nodded his approval.

'It's very nice thanks.'

Viv made an incoherent grunt which at least sounded like a positive grunt. After a three second hiatus to enjoy his drink, Viv opened up the conversation.

'You keep a good bourbon, but I didn't fly six thousand miles for a drink. Right now, one of my men is lying in hospital and doesn't know New York form New Year and more importantly I've lost 200,000 dollars or nearly seven kilos of heroin depending on which side of the deal you're talking of. I've been screwed over and, if what you say is on the up, you've been screwed over as well. Now I don't know about you, but nobody screws me but my wife. So, tell me, what's happening here?' Viv said leaning forward cradling his drink.

Chai Son sat down, lent back in the chair and crossed his legs. He spread his arms in a gesture of openness.

'Mr Brownsword,' he began.

Viv cut him short. 'Look let's drop the Mr Brownsword. Nobody calls me that, I'm Viv, that's Archie and you're Cha Siu, how does that sound?'

Chai Son lifted a finger in correction.

'If I may Viv, it's Chai Son, Cha Siu is something very different.'

Viv had never been good with languages, he struggled with his native English at times. The rising falling inflections of Thai were lost on him. Wanting to keep things civil he tried for a compromise.

'How's about Viv, Archie and Chuck then. Would you be happy if I called you Chuck?'

Archie had read how Asians were big on respect. He prepared himself to step in and smooth over Viv's potential faux pas. As it was there was no need, Chai Son took it in his stride.

'Thai has five tonal values; it can be difficult for the western tongue. If it will help us move forward on a more intimate basis, you may call me Chuck,' he then moved on to appraise Viv and Archie of the current situation. 'Viv once again let me extend my apologies for this inconvenience. Let me assure you that this breach of security is an anomaly. We have not been passive in this matter. We have identified and located certain members of the offending party. We have one here now and we will have the others in our possession very soon. I intend to show you the example we make of these people. Their fate should reassure you that disruptive elements are rooted out and dealt with effectively.'

Viv looked unimpressed.

'And?'

Archie quickly interjected. Speaking to Chai Son rather than Viv he paraphrased what had been said, just for clarity.

'It sounds like you know who did it and we're going to get the stuff back.'

'Succinctly put Archie. Although we may not have all the people now, we thought you would like to be with us when we pick them up. You can see our business in action.'

Viv always liked to personally witness the people who crossed him suffer. The thought of moving in on these rats appealed to him.

'Now that Chuck, sounds like a plan, where do we start?'

Chai Son called over one of his men and whispered something in his ear. The man made his exit.

'We start, here and we start now,' said Chai Son.

As he spoke Kiet was led into the main room with his hands secured behind his back. He was brought to a halt in front of Viv and Archie. Chai Son did the introductions.

'Gentlemen this is Kiet. Kiet is a minor messenger who got ideas above his station. Although there are others involved, he was a key player. In terms of the information he can supply, he has outlived his usefulness. He must now pay for what he has done.'

Kiet stood his head hung low, his face cut and swollen from the beating he had taken. Viv looked the pathetic figure up and down.

'Looks like he's done some paying already,' he observed.

'Just an incentive to talk. Cut him loose,' instructed Chai Son.

The man who had brought him in produced a blade and severed the binds on Kiet's hands. Kiet rubbed his wrists to restore the circulation. Chai Son got to his feet and started to unbutton his waistcoat. Taking it off he dropped it to the chair. He then began to remove his shirt, all the time never taking his eyes off Kiet. Eventually Chai Son stood stripped to the waist. His body was chiselled, lean and lithe. Here and there could be seen a reminder of the cut of a knife or the sting of a bullet. The overwhelming feature was the tattoos. He was a patchwork of Sak Yan ink. Geometric shapes, animals and Thai script covered eighty percent of his torso.

Sak Yan, was an ancient tradition in many countries of Southeast Asia. The mystical symbols are believed to bestow power and protection on the wearer. Certain tattoos were even believed to invoke fear. If that was the case, they were now doing their work on Kiet, who was visibly shaking. Sak Yan ink was peddled to every Westerner in every tattoo shop, in every town in Thailand. With each reproduction they became further and further removed from their original philosophy. Chai Son knew the meaning of each one of his tattoos intimately and he had tested the extent of their power on many occasions.

Chai Son bent forward at the waist placing his head on his knees, he shook his head and rolled his shoulders, preparing his body for rapid movement. Beckoning Kiet to follow him, he moved over to the matted area of the room where he kept his gym equipment. Kiet followed mechanically as if knowing what to expect.

Archie positioned himself next to Viv to get a front row seat for what was to come. Viv leaned into Archie and with the quietest stage whisper he could muster said,

'What do you think we're in for here, a fuckin' ladyboy show.'

Archie kept his focus on the developing drama. Chai Son turned to the seated men.

'Gentlemen, when you pull the tail of a tiger, the tiger does not ask the bear to fight its battle,' then turning to Kiet he said, 'given your current condition the first move is yours.'

Kiet stood for what seemed an eternity.

244

He looked to Chai Son, he looked to the other men in the room, and he looked to elevator door. Whichever way he looked there was no escaping the situation. It ended here.

A lapse in Chai Son's security, however, had left him with one ace up his sleeve or, to be more precise, down his sock. Kiet always carried several knifes, weapons that were more often pulled for show than in earnest. Now, Kiet thought, might be the last time he drew a knife for any reason. If he was going to die, he at least wanted to inflict some damage before he did. He bent to his knee as if attending to a shoelace. A second later he was on his feet with the blade thrust in front of him. Immediately three guns were drawn, all of them pointing at Kiet.

This was the best show Viv had seen for a long time. His excitement was palpable. He let out a loud 'Ha!' followed by,

'Now this is interesting.'

Chai Son took a half step back in the face of the blade. He gestured to his men to put their weapons away. This was something he had to do twice before they complied.

Despite being armed Kiet was hesitant to go on the offensive. He stood shifting his weight from foot-to-foot tracking Chai Son with the point of the knife. Chai Son slowly circled Kiet forcing him to shuffle round to keep him in sight. After one full circle he began to move in, one half step at a time. All the time his head swayed from side to side like a hypnotic cobra.

245

When he was just within striking distance, Chai Son dropped his hands to his sides, almost inviting Kiet to attack. If it was going to be any time for Kiet, it had to be now. He lunged forward aiming the knife at the centre mass of Chai Son. Chai Son had anticipated this move, along with a dozen others. He swiftly turned to the side. The blade passed within millimetres of his chest. His movements were graceful and fluid. At the same time as turning he stepped in and caught hold of Kiet's weapon arm, trapping it in an excruciating elbow lock.

There was no time for Kiet to scream in pain as in the same second the palm of Chai Son's right hand struck upwards, smashing his nose. The blow jarred Kiet's head backwards, so violently, the snap of his neck was audible. His legs buckled.

He was held half standing supported only by Chai Son's arm lock. Chai Son loosened his hold and Kiet fell to the floor, dead. The whole fight had taken no more than a second.

Turing from the pathetic body Chai Son made his way over to Viv and Archie. One of his men handed him a handkerchief. He mopped Kiet's blood from his hand and wiped away the spatter that had caught him across the chest. He then proceeded to dress himself. Despite thinking Chai Son was 'up his own arse' as a fight fan Viv couldn't help but be impressed. Even though Viv's fighting style was rather more 'earthy', he appreciated the finer points of applied violence.

'Now that was efficient.'

246

This was as close as it got to praise from Viv.

'Perhaps he could have suffered more,' said Chai Son putting in his cufflinks.

'So, is this a regular thing with you?' Viv enquired.

'If there is an execution to be made, I do not shy from my responsibility. If there is a challenge to my authority, I meet it personally,' he answered putting on his waistcoat and taking a seat.

'I would have just shot him in the face myself,' said Viv, 'I mean what are you going to do when you get old and fat? You going to hop around then?'

Chai Son stared passively, but his answer was provocative.

'I suppose if I ever get old and fat then I too might consider shooting people in the face.'

Archie felt that familiar tension return. After the display he had just witnessed, it was clear the men in the room were armed and Chai Son had the infrastructure to dispose of bodies. How would Viv respond to this inferred slight? Slowly, Viv's face broke into a broad smile.

'Well, you can't get more deader than dead; does it matter how you get there,' he laughed, 'so that's one monkey out the way, but what about the rest and what about the gear.'

Chai Son gave them a full appraisal of what the next moves would be. He told them of the lead to the hotel where Richie was staying and how they would soon be on their way to pick

247

him up. He also explained the situation regarding Alex's arrest at the airport and how steps had been taken to retrieve him. Once they had secured Alex, he assured Viv and Archie that the drugs, or the money, or both would be close to being recovered. He strategically left references to Nok out of the briefing. He was still no further forward locating her. He was hoping that this whole affair could be resolved without having to try to hunt down one indistinct girl in a country of millions. After hearing the plan and with the excitement of being back on the front-line Viv was keen to get going. He was itching to see how Chai Son would deal with members of this 'gang'.

The time had come to pick up Richie.

27

Breaking the Cat

The throbbing pain in Billy's jaw slowly dragged him back to consciousness. His head pounded. He felt as though he'd been hit by a jack hammer. He went to raise his hand to try to rub away the thudding in his ears but found he couldn't move his arm. He tried to moan, but found his voice muffled and his breathing restricted. As the fog cleared his memory of what had happened began to return and as his eyes focused, he didn't like what he was seeing.

Looking down, he saw he was bound to his chair with tape. His legs, arms and neck were all secured in place and afforded him little motion. Thick duct tape covered his mouth. Lifting his eyes, he saw two enormous bald men, one standing over him and another, who could have been his twin, sitting on the sofa. Beside the one on the sofa lay Jade with her head resting in his lap. She too was trussed up with her arms taped behind her back. Her legs were drawn up behind her and there was a length of cord fastening her ankles to her neck with a slip knot. This meant that the more she kicked and struggled the more she choked herself. She was strung like a bow, and she too was gagged.

Billy was never a man that was lost for words, but if he could have spoken right then, he wouldn't have had anything to say. Shock and a dawning fear had stolen his voice. The enormous man standing over him noticed he was coming round and gently tapped his face to coax him back to consciousness. Billy thought his hand felt like a brick.

Nikola looked down on Billy. He needed to extract information from this man. Thinking that the whole situation spoke for itself he got straight to the crucial question.

'Where Kiet?' he demanded.

Even if Billy wanted to answer, with his mouth taped he couldn't. Nikola ignored this technicality and brought his imposing head close to Billy's ear and said again.

'Where Kiet?' his voice was quiet, intimate.

This time, as he spoke, he pulled the tape half from Billy's mouth. Billy may have been confused and frightened, but he was a man who, over the years, had become familiar with violence. He was definitely not a man who would break with a tap. He had learned that fear was something you felt, if you knew how to control your actions, it was not something others could see. Billy understood the power of image and the importance of loyalty. He knew exactly where Kiet was, but he was not going to surrender this information easily.

'Look man I don't know what this is about or who … who are you?' Billy started.

Nikola made no answer.

He replaced the tape over Billy's mouth only this time he nipped his nose so he couldn't breathe. From the periphery of his vision Billy saw Nikola produce a thin silver skewer from inside his jacket. The next thing he felt was a searing pain in the side of his knee cap. His whole body convulsed. His reflex action was to draw breath and scream, but neither of these actions were possible. He desperately fought for air; his vision started to close down. He was looking at the world down a long tunnel, once again he passed out.

Nikola and Viktor were well acquainted with interrogation techniques. They knew how to inflict suffering. Like a high-wire walker, they were skilled in treading the line between life and death. There were two main forms of interrogation, the one you used in the field, when the extraction of information was time critical, and the one you used when time was not a factor. When you had time, you could be subtle, build relationships, apply techniques of attrition, bargain for information. Building relationships and bargaining were never Nikola's and Viktor's strong points. In this class they were very much D grade. This deficiency, they made up for in the

251

art of field interrogation, the short brutal extraction of information. For this they were A+ students.

Nikola knew that Billy would have felt like he was dying and when he came round, he would be disoriented and confused. The one thing Billy would know was that things were not going to get any better unless he talked.

Billy's head lolled and his eyes fluttered. Again, he felt the concrete tap of Nikola's hand as he returned to the nightmare of the room. The heavily accented voice came again in the same flat tone.

'Where Kiet?'

Nikola removed the tape from Billy's mouth. He hungrily sucked in air through his clenched teeth. His words were punctuated between gasps of pain.

'Please man, please, what are you talking about, who's Kiet man?'

Mechanically Nikola replaced the tape over his mouth. Once again, Billy felt a burning pain boring its way into his knee. This time Nikola allowed him to breathe through his nose. There would be no escape from the agony through unconsciousness. The skewer went back in quickly. Billy could feel it scraping as Nikola slowly twisted it over his bone into the very joint itself, puncturing the synovial membrane. Nikola took a handful of Billy's hair and pulled his head back. He placed a thick finger

252

over Billy's taped mouth, waited for him to settle, then removing the tape asked again.

'Where Kiet?'

This time his voice was hard and there was an edge of frustration creeping in. Billy made one last attempt to hold out.

'Please man I don't know what the fuck you're on about. I don't ...'

His sentence was never finished. Nikola replaced the tape. Nikola looked down on Billy shaking in the chair. He had underestimated this man. Nikola had seen many men with a lot of front but no substance. There was more to this Billy than met the eye. He was scared but he was still holding out. This could indicate that there was a bigger incentive for Billy to stay quiet than the incentive to talk.

Nikola stepped back and looked over to Viktor who was sitting on the couch with Jade. He looked at Billy in the chair, the skewer still sticking out of his kneecap, his hair soaking with sweat. He saw Billy look to Jade and he saw the pleading look in her emerald-green eyes. Everyone had a weakness and Nikola knew relationships were the biggest weakness of the human species.

He nodded to Viktor. This was all that was needed to convey the next move.

Gently Viktor ran his fingers through Jade's hair. His hand seemed to cover the entire back of her head. After thirty years of pumping iron and living in a perpetual war zone his palms were thick with calluses. He barely felt the hair slip frictionless through his fingers. As he embedded his hand deeper in her mane it released the faint aroma of lotus blossom. The proximity of Jade's head to his crotch coupled with the sweet smell was faintly erotic. But there was no time to get turned on, there was work to be done. Viktor twisted Jade's hair around his fist several times and took a firm hold. He got sharply to his feet nearly ripping her hair out by the roots. He dragged her across the room until she knelt at the feet of Billy. Trussed up as she was there was no chance of resisting.

Nikola held Billy's head facing Jade and Viktor held Jade's head facing Billy. Slowly Nikola drew the skewer from Billy's kneecap and passed it to Viktor. Viktor brought the needle up to Jade's face. She screwed her eyes tight shut as she felt the cold steel touch her eye lid. She was catatonic with terror. A pearl drop of Billy's blood slipped from its tip and landed on her cheek. It was surprisingly cold. She flinched and the sharp point nicked her eye lid. She began to cry. Nikola once again addressed Billy.

'Where Kiet?'

254

Billy may have been on the cusp of talking as it was, but this move assured his co-operation.

Five minute later Nikola and Viktor left the room. This had been a productive interrogation. Not only had they been furnished with the current whereabouts of Kiet, but they also had Billy's phone with a picture of Nok and information on Alex and Richie. Behind them they left the lifeless bodies of Billy and Jade. Billy taped to his chair, Jade lying at his feet. As Viktor stepped back into the alley, he discreetly held his hand to his nose. The exquisite fragrance of lotus blossom still clung to his fingers. In his mind's senses he could still feel Jade's silken hair and her warm head on his lap.

28

Sawadee

The midnight blue Jaguar iPace pulled up outside the Nana Apartments hotel. Chai Son, two of his men, Viv and Archie stepped out. It was too mob handed for Chai Son's taste, but until he knew what he was dealing with, caution might be prudent.

The afternoon sun was at its strongest and Archie's shirt was starting to stick uncomfortably to his back. The men made their way to the main reception. The hotel was clean and simple with a friendly family atmosphere. The air-conditioning provided a welcome relief from the oppressive humidity outside.

Unlike Billy Chai Son generally didn't have to buy information or favours. He was widely known by sight and by reputation. And that reputation carried respect not just for the rumours of what he did to people who stood in his way, but also for the great deal of charitable work he did for the local community. When he asked for a key card to room 427, he met no resistance from the young man on reception.

Chai Son's two men took the stairs, while he, Viv and Archie crammed themselves uncomfortably into an undersized elevator. Chai Son pressed four and the doors closed. The silence lasted about three seconds before Viv broke it.

'Tell me again who this clown is we're picking up?' he said.

Chai Son spoke deliberately as if to a child.

'This man has been identified as a colleague of the man who is believed to have our goods.'

'I know that!' Viv knocked back, 'but who is he, is he a player, what do you know about him?'

Chai Son's reply was a little less patronising.

'We do not believe these people pose a significant threat, but we will proceed with caution until we know for sure.'

The elevator pinged and the doors slid open onto a T junction with a corridor off to each side. On the wall in front, it said rooms 400 – 415 on the left and 416 – 430 on the right. The three men turned right. The floor was tiled, the walls painted soft white and there was a pleasant smell of lavender. Halfway down the corridor Chai Son's men emerged from the staircase at the bottom and the two parties executed a pincer movement on room 427. As they approached, the door to room 425 opened and a tiny maid in bare feet backed out pulling a trolley laden with bed linen and miniature shampoos.

257

She was somewhere in her sixties. She jumped as she saw the men approaching. Archie quickly broke in.

'Sawadee,' he said in the best rising and falling inflections he could muster.

'Swạs̄dī kah,' she answered looking confused.

Viv looked at Archie.

'Sour cream what?'

'Not sour cream Viv, Sawadee, it means hello,' said Archie by way of an introduction to the Thai language.

Viv just shrugged his shoulders.

Chai Son stepped in and ignoring this lesson in linguistics spoke gently, almost affectionately to the woman. After a brief conversation, he placed his hand on her shoulder and gave her a thousand baht. The woman looked delighted, she pressed her palms together and bowed several times.

'K̄hx k̄hxbkhuṇ kah, K̄hx k̄hxbkhuṇ kah,' she repeated taking his hands and touching them to her forehead.

Chai Son bowed back. The tiny maid turned and disappeared down the corridor leaving the door to 425 still open. This afforded Chai Son the opportunity to look inside and get the general lay out of the rooms. Like all hotels of this design, the configuration would be mirrored in room 427. After inspecting the adjacent room, Chai Son gave a pre-task briefing.

'The room is entered by a narrow passage three metres long, the bathroom is to the left, the room then opens up about four and a half metres square. On the far wall, through double sliding doors, there is a balcony. There is only room enough for one person in the passage at a time.' He turned to his men. 'Wisit, you go first secure the bathroom, Prem you next cover the room, Mr Vivian, Mr Archie you follow me, please be aware to close the door behind you.'

He handed the swipe card to Wisit. Wisit held it in one hand and drew his gun with the other. Prem drew too and both men made a silent countdown. Wisit swiped the card, the door clicked then swiftly but silently they entered the room. Wisit covered the bathroom, it was clear. Prem moved into the main room, gun clamped in both hands securing the area. Chai Son walked calmly behind followed by Viv and Archie, who closed the door behind them.

The scene before them wasn't what they were expecting. A muscular woman was standing with her back to them stripped to the waist. Her rock hard, golden brown buttocks were thrusting backwards and forwards, she was moaning softly. A man was sitting on the bed in front of her. The woman's hands were grasping the side of his head, which was obscured by her gyrating ass. All that could be seen of the man was a hand clasping one of her cheeks and another pulling her legs towards him. The 'woman' spun round with a start revealing

259

an impressive seven inches of erection. The man fell back on the bed in total shock. They had found Pan and Richie.

Wisit backed Pan into a corner and Prem moved in on Richie, the gun giving a very clear message that he should remain on the bed. Richie lay on his back, hands raised in like a submissive dog. There was terror in his eyes. Chai Son approached the supine form. '

Mr Richard Chambers?' he said.

With his voice breaking Richie spluttered.

'I thought it was a woman, I swear she said she was a woman.'

29

Drawing moustaches on Kings

Alex woke in his cell after enduring a fitful night's sleep. Thankfully, he had remained unmolested. The first thing that hit him was the pungent smell of body odour and the mouldy dampness of the paper-thin pillow on which his head rested. The air conditioning was inconsequential, it was hot. He felt sticky and his mouth was dry.

There were six other inmates with him, five of them Thai and one pale, thin youth who looked no more that eighteen. With only the artificial light of the corridor and with no watch, he had no way of telling the time. Even though people were beginning to start their day, he got the impression it was still early.

His mind had been racing all night and despite his initial resistance to the idea it kept coming back to one thing, the girl, Nok. He could see her in his mind's eye standing in the bathroom with his backpack in her hand and saying *'I hope you don't mind I stole one of your tee-shirts, it smelled of you. I hope you don't mind.'* He didn't mind at the time, he thought it was sweet, but right there, that was the opportunity for her to have planted something in his bag. *'Could anyone have interfered with your luggage?'.* The honest answer to this question would have been yes, Nok could have. But why, this was the question that haunted him. What did she stand to gain from it? Surely the packet of drugs was not enough to warrant using him as an unsuspecting mule, there can't have been much profit in that. He didn't want to think this about her. But what did he really know about her, other than an affecting story of hardship?

Undoubtedly, a lot of poor girls had led a life of adversity, the scale of which he could never imagine. But he also knew that stories such as these were a very effective emotional lever to prise money out the wallets of lonely, naive tourists. But he had offered her money and she had refused it, so what did that mean? His thoughts were an intense, jumble of self-contradictory 'buts', all of which left him with a throbbing headache. The stench of shit caught his nose and lifting his head he saw a man squatting on a steel toilet in the corner performing his daily evacuation. Time to greet the day. Alex was rising from his cot when the pale young man jerked into view.

'You're English, aren't you?' he said.

262

His body twitched with nervous energy, and he mercilessly gnawed on his fingernails.

'Yes,' Alex replied, 'you too?'

'From Sheffield,' said the youth holding out his hand.

As he shook it Alex noticed that the nails had been bitten down past the quick and his fingers were red raw.

'What you in for?' he asked before stuffing his fingers back into his cadaverous face.

Not wanting to give too much away Alex replied,

'A mistake.'

The corners of the young man's mouth quivered into a smile. 'A mistake, we're all here because we made a mistake. Lachie made the mistake of killing someone.' He said pointing to a haunted man with long hair. 'And Pavo over there made the mistake of robbing a McDonald's and thinking he could get away with it. We all make mistakes; the biggest mistake was getting caught.' After this short introduction to the misdemeanours of his fellow inmates he resumed the feast on his fingers.

'What was your mistake?' Alex asked.

The words came out rapid, like machinegun fire.

'Desecration, desecration, desecration, very serious,'

'Desecration?' Alex asked puzzled.

263

'The King, Buddha bless him, never disrespect the King. Drink, that's what does it. I was drunk and thought it would be funny to draw a moustache on a banner of the King.'

As he spoke his eyes were cast down and he kicked his toes hard into the concrete.

'You drew a moustache on a picture of the king?' Alex said incredulously.

'Desecration, desecration, desecration, yes very serious. Never disrespect the King three years I got.'

'Three years!' Alex exclaimed.

Surely this could not be right.

'Lucky, lucky that was me though, it was going to be fifteen. Disrespect you see. But the British government stepped in. The Prime Minister himself sent a letter directly. It was on the telly didn't you see me?'

Alex shook his head, he had to admit this was the first he had heard of this young man's plight. He babbled on.

'It was a thing for a week or two, Thai courts backed down you see, said they never intended to give me fifteen years, that was just a maximum, a deterrent you see. It was cut to three, leniency you see. I was only seventeen, not fully responsible. Big victory for the Prime Minister then you see. Done two years now, might be out in six months. Lucky me, that's what I am lucky.'

The more the words spilled out the more it seemed he was trying to console himself that he had been let off lightly which, given the potential sentence of fifteen years, he probably had. As Alex listened to his pathetic story. As the young man babbled, his heart sank, and his stomach knotted. He knew this was a country of harsh sentencing and he knew the penalty for drugs was extreme. Up to this point, he had been comforting himself with the thought that this was just one huge mistake; something that could be cleared up once his government had stepped in, once he had a proper British lawyer. However, if this poor bastard was going to be left to rot for three years for simply scribbling on a banner, what hope did he have? He felt sick. He staggered to his feet and made his way over to the bars of the cell. Holding himself up he pushed his face against the bars and tried to suck up any fresh air he could to prevent himself from vomiting.

30

The price of freedom

James McNulty sat back in his chair; his long slender legs stretched out before him. Casually he raised a perfectly manicured hand to his lips and took a deep draw on his Treasurer's Aluminium Gold cigarette. Over the top of his Bvlgari tortoiseshell spectacles he met the eye of Nakia Ayutthaya, Governor of Bang Kwang prison.

It had taken a few phone calls and a modest financial outlay to get him here. It was now James' job to negotiate the release of Alex Whyte. The plan was simple, James would offer the right level of 'inducement' Alex would be surrendered into his custody. Desperate criminal that Alex was, at some point he would escape from James' care and either disappear or a day or two later be found dead in a ditch. The whole affair would be written off as a low-level drugs related killing. James would express his profound regrets regarding his lapse of judgement and the Thai authorities would look no further, as the state would have been spared the expense of housing one more prisoner in a system already under severe strain.

James McNulty had worked for Chai Son for six years. He was his representative in all matters of a legal nature. He ministered to all of Chai Son's legitimate businesses through which illegitimate finances were filtered. An ex-Etonian, with a master's in law from Cambridge, he had an acute legal mind with the ability to mould the law to his will, stretching it, but never breaking it.

Soon after graduation it was apparent that James was destined to take silk in record time. The conventional path, however, was never his to tread. James McNulty had been born with a thrill-seeking personality. The cut and thrust of the law excited him, but the conventions of court crushed the very life out of his soul. So, whilst on holiday in Thailand, James had a chance encounter with Chai Son, a new die was cast for his career. A career that would provide all the life affirming adrenalin James could wish for. As time progressed his affiliation with Chai Son grew deeper. An association which proved to be extremely profitable for both men.

Governor Ayutthaya spoke. His English was fragmented.

'Mr McNalt, it is not for prisoners to be leave the prison when like.'

James never expected that he would simply be able to walk out of the door with Alex on his arm. But he knew that parts of the Thai system were deeply corrupt and a facilitation payment or two to the right person could accomplish almost anything. He was never one to approach a situation blind, he liked to know who he was dealing with. Preparatory research on Mr Ayutthaya had been very informative. Everybody had a number to weigh their integrity against and James knew his. Taking another draw on his cigarette he leaned forward in his chair, a wry smile played on his thin lips. He left a long pause. Although he spoke Thai very well, he often preferred to use English as a tool of intimidation. He had the uncanny knack of making people feel inferior because they didn't speak his language.

'Mr Ayutthaya, I provide my services pro-bono in situations such as this when I fear there may be a gross miscarriage of justice. The young gentleman in question is of sound character and background with no previous convictions of any kind. I believe there has been a mistake, or at the very worst a momentary lapse of judgement.'

'Drugs, Mr Manut, very serious,' was the terse reply.

James stubbed out his cigarette, the dying smoke curled around his blond hair.

'Mr Ayutthaya I am not questioning the nature of the offence, however, what I would like to do is put into perspective the magnitude of the offence as weighed against the request which I am making. The quantity of drugs retrieved, although not insignificant, would not suggest a seasoned courier. The amount was more congruent with ... over enthusiastic personal use. All I am asking is for the young gentleman to be released into my custody for an afternoon in order that I can provide legal briefing in a convivial atmosphere conducive to establishing the facts. I will accept full responsibility for his security and safe return. This is a privilege for which I am willing to financially compensate you, personally, for any inconvenience.'

It was unclear how much of the conversation Governor Ayuttaya actually understood, but what he understood clearly was financial compensation.

'Compensation?' he probed.

James had spoken to a number of people who had dealt with this man in the past, and he had a good idea of what offer would tip the balance. Straightening the razor crisp crease in his trousers he posited.

'I think 120,000 baht should cover any essential administrative expenses.'

Mr Ayutthaya seemed insulted by the offer, his eyes rolled back, and he flung up his arms in an exaggerated manner.

'120,000 Mr McHanty, not cover, forms, records, people, 120,000 baht. No, no.'

269

James was expecting this. Everything was open to negotiation and everybody liked to think they were driving a hard bargain. This understanding was built into his first offer. The ritual, however, still had to honoured. James' face took on a puzzled countenance as if he couldn't understand why his offer had been rejected.

'Mr Ayutthaya under the circumstances, 120,000 baht should be more than adequate to cover costs, seen or unforeseen. I don't see how I could offer any more.'

Mr Ayutthaya was not to be put off.

'No, no Mr Manalt not enough, doing this put in difficult. Rules difficult, question asked, who pay answer.'

This was the dance of negotiation and James knew that this sort of thing could be a long-drawn-out process. He knew exactly how much it would take to blind the odd eye or to bend the odd rule. He wet his thin lips and furrowed his brow as if making an inner calculation. After a dramatic pause, he said,

'Mr Ayutthaya, I understand that there may be more than one person involved in this endeavour, I am, therefore, willing to increase the inconvenience fee to 200,000 baht.'

Mr Ayutthaya was not quite ready to give up the dance.

'200,000 difficult,' he said offering up the palms of his hands and shrugging his shoulders as if there was nothing he could do about the fixed costs of bribery.

It was time to draw the farce to an end. James rose slowly from his chair, buttoned up his jacket and smoothed out the folds. Adjusting his sleeves to show the regulation half inch of cuff, he offered out his hand.

'Well Mr Ayutthaya, thank you for your time. I'm sorry we could not come to a financial agreement.'

With that he turned for the door. He hadn't taken more than half a step when Mr Ayutthaya broke in.

'Mr Meknaly, 200,000, if perhaps say….'

James cut him short with a hard stare from his fathom deep blue eyes.

'I say 200,000 Mr Ayutthaya. Now you say either yes or no.'

The sentence hung in the air, James' eyes remained fixed on Governor Ayutthaya, believing the money was about to leave, he answered.

'I will prepare paper Mr McNanly. While do I get someone take you Mr Whyte who release as responsibility you.'

271

31

Sticky bun

Alex's face was still pressed to the bars of his cell when he saw a tall slender man being escorted down the corridor by two wardens. The man was impeccably dressed in a three-piece olive-green suit, his hand-crafted oxfords clicked on the tiled floor. Despite the heat he showed no signs of sweating. This didn't look like a man about to be incarcerated. To Alex's surprise the man came directly to him and offering his hand through the bars of the cage introduced himself. His manner was cheery.

'Mr Whyte, my name's James McNulty I'm here in the capacity of your legal representative in this unfortunate situation.'

The voice was vaguely reminiscent of a Pathé News presenter of the 1940's. Alex was confused. Ever since his arrest the previous evening he had not been offered, what he thought would be, his one obligatory phone call. As far as he knew, apart from the Thai authorities, nobody knew he was here.

'Legal representative? I don't understand, how did you know I was here? They've not let me speak to anyone, no phone call, nothing,' he said.

James shook his head as though this was a familiar story. 'Ah Mr Whyte I think you will find that the Thai judiciary system is not furnished with the same level of human rights you would be afforded at home.'

Alex was becoming painfully aware of this fact, and he still had no idea how this man came to be here.

'I can believe that, but how did you find me?' he asked.

James gave his best charming smile.

'Mr Whyte, brutal and inefficient as this system is, it still manages to cling to some basic procedures. When a British national is arrested, especially on a more serious offence, such as yours, the arresting body is duty bound to inform the British Consulate. The consulate then automatically appoints legal representation for the prisoner in order to establish the basic facts and potential ramifications. From there we are able to provide preliminary guidance as to the best course of action.'

It all sounded plausible, and it was the lifeline of hope Alex needed in this time of despair.

'Do you think you can clear all this up?' he said almost pleading for the answer to come back yes.

James placed a reassuring hand on his shoulder.

'Let's not get ahead of ourselves just yet Mr Whyte. It's not quite time for pudding, but as an entrée let's get you out of this dreadful cell. I've arranged for you to be released into my custody for the rest of the day. We'll go to my offices and there we may be able to decide what our options are going forward.'

Alex was released from his cell and led down the corridor. Behind him he could hear the echoing voice of his Sheffield cell mate repeating "Desecration, desecration, desecration". He was taken to the same room where he was shackled the previous evening. This time the shackles were removed. Alex was then presented with form after form to sign. As they were all in Thai, James directed him where to put his signature. James assured him that this was all a mere formality, more a requirement of James to ensure Alex's security, rather than any obligations that had to be fulfilled by Alex himself. When the paperwork was finished James turned to Alex and said,

'Mr Whyte you are now officially under my custody. I need you to understand the implications of this for both you and me. This is a risk I have undertaken, I am trusting, Mr Whyte, that you will make no attempts to do harm to my person or to abscond. Actions such as these would have very serious consequences indeed. Can I emphasise Mr Whyte that in a country that still holds the death penalty for drug related offences, if you break your custodial obligations, the law would afford you little mercy and you would be left without functioning legal representation. Do we have an understanding?'

His voice was grave as he held out his hand for Alex's bond of agreement. It was an easy decision to make, Alex shook it.

Alex sat in James' car. The forty-minute trip across town had been conducted in near silence. Alex had asked several times if he would be given an opportunity to call home to inform his parents of his situation. James had been polite, but parried the questions by saying that, if first they established some facts and explored some preliminary options, then when he did call his parents, he may be able to furnish them with a more positive picture of his situation than was currently available.

Alex didn't like the fact that, at this moment, no one he loved and really trusted knew where he was or what he was going through. He knew though that his options were limited so his best interests might be served by following James' guidance.

Eventually they pulled up outside James' private offices. The property was an ultra-modern beach front development. Inside the space was shared by several businesses, all of which rented varying degrees of square footage. They entered the elevator and James pushed for the fifth floor. At the top James led him to a glass and brushed aluminium security door. Etched into the glass were the words 'James McNulty, followed by the strap line 'Because it matters'. The same minimalist glass and aluminium theme was carried through to the main office. The reception area was manned by a woman who sat behind a milk green glass topped desk. She was Thai and about fifty. Her dark hair was lightly streaked with grey and gathered in a perfect chignon. She was dressed stylishly in a lilac skirt suit. As they entered, she greeted James.

'Morning Mr James. How are you this morning?'

Her English accent had echoes of James' anachronistic timbre. James answered politely.

'Good morning Ms Saeli, I trust you are well. Please let me introduce you. This is Alex Whyte. As you know I currently have him on release into my custody. He will be with us for the next few hours. Please could you log the time we have entered the office.'

'Of course, Mr James, will there be anything else?' she replied.

'If you could ensure that we are not disturbed that would be most helpful. Oh! and if you would be so sweet as to make a pot of coffee accompanied by an artistic assortment of sticky buns, I would be forever in your debt,' he said giving a low

276

bow. Then turning to Alex, 'I hope a pot of Java and a bun would not offend your pallet.'

It had been some time since Alex had eaten and the thought of a hot coffee and a sugar rush did not offend him at all. Ms Saeli nodded and swished through a side door while James escorted Alex through to his main office.

Alex had expected James to have been part of a larger law firm, but this didn't seem to be the case. Although the offices were undoubtedly of quality, this appeared to be a one-man operation.

Inside the office James forwent his seat behind the desk and gestured for Alex to sit in one of the comfortable red leather chairs around a low glass table in front of the window. The office commanded a tranquil view of a picturesque bay with a quiet promenade skirting the waterfront. James sat opposite and crossed his long slender legs. Taking a crocodile skin note pad and a Mont Blanc fountain pen from his inside pocket he flicked a glancing smile at Alex and said,

'Let's start at the beginning, shall we?'

32

A bit of a patsy

Sitting in the offices of James McNulty, who at this moment was probably the only hope he had, Alex thought it wise not to hold any information back, even if it was speculative and even if it was something he didn't want to admit to himself. James had been questioning him for the last hour. His questions had been open requests for information with long pauses for Alex to respond. Throughout the whole process James' style had been friendly and polite. It appeared his sole focus was to get the full story in order to best represent Alex's interests.

The first line of questioning had been background, personal details, home address, names of parents, travelling companions, full duration of his visit and itinerary. James then quickly homed in on how Alex had come to meet Nok. He wanted to know every detail, from Alex meeting her in the Shark Club, through to the last minute he waved goodbye to her from the taxi window. These were the events in which James had the keenest interest. He reflected and clarified each point, many times asking several questions around the same topic, framed in different ways. Sometimes he would repeat back what Alex had said, but with a deliberate mistake, which prompted Alex to correct him. It was obvious to Alex he was testing the veracity of his story to root out any inconsistencies. All the time James made subtle notes of the points he thought salient. Alex told him all he knew, which was actually very little. He told him all about the fight in the bar with the rat-like gangster. He told him about Nok, their night together and the conversations they had. He told him that apart from himself there was only Richie, Nok and someone he suspected of being a ladyboy who would have had probable access to his bag. He knew Richie would never plant anything on him and in all honesty, he couldn't see it being the ladyboy, she/he was still with Richie. This only left Nok. He had seen her with his bag in the bathroom, but he failed to see how she would profit from any of this.

James lent forward, placed his note pad and pen on the table and picked up one of the gold rimmed coffee cups. He relaxed back in his chair and took a sip.

'So just to clarify Alex, the only information you have on this girl is that she told you she is from Thung Na and that her name is Nok. Is that correct?' he said.

When it was put like this it was very shallow foundations on which Alex had based his feelings for her. Seen through the eyes of another there was no reason why this girl could not have set him up. But Alex still failed to see why. He nodded his head to confirm James' last statement. He still, however, felt the need to pour doubt on Nok's guilt for putting him in this position.

'She could have planted something, I suppose, she did have the chance. Why would she do that? What would she get from it? I offered her money, she wouldn't take it, it's not like she wanted anything from me. Why would she do this to me?'

It was like he was pleading with James to supply him with the answer for Nok's supposed duplicity. James replied strategically.

'Alex, ours is not to speculate on the motives of others, ours is to construct a credible alternative narrative to the one which will, undoubtedly, be presented by the prosecution.'

James took a deep breath and rose to his feet. Sliding his hands into his pockets he stood for a moment gazing absently at the view from the window. He looked deep in thought. Eventually he turned and without making specific eye contact appeared to address the room in general.

'Well, this is a pickle. I for one believe your story, but I'm not the one who it's crucial to convince,' then at a snap he turned to Alex, 'please excuse me for a moment, I need to make an important call.'

Alex thought this might be the time to raise the possibility of making a call of his own.

'If it's alright, could I ring home? I really need to let my parents know what's happening. They have no idea about any of this and Richie will still be expecting to meet me in Phuket.'

James carried on walking.

'All in good time dear boy, all in good time. Now I really need to make this call.'

With that he left the room leaving Alex alone. Back in reception James passed by Ms Saeli.

'Ms Saeli, as a precautionary measure please could you disconnect the phone line from my office and make sure Mr Whyte stays put for just a few minutes, if you could be so kind.'

James then took himself off to the documents room opposite reception. Inside he pulled out his mobile and called Chai Son to bring him up to date with his findings. The phone rang four times, Chai Son answered, James spoke.

'It seems like our man may have been taken for a patsy ... Not much really. His story concurs with the information you extracted from his travelling companion ... Over here to watch the Hard Bones competition and then sightseeing. A home background check shows no untoward connections ...

281

He corroborated the story we already know, meeting the girl in the night club and the ensuing altercation … Yes, he confirms the name she went by was Nok … That was about all really … It's very credible this young man is nothing more than a false scent trail … You know as well as I that nothing comes with an iron clad guarantee, but he appears to be genuine … So how would you like to proceed, we could just let the system deal with him … I agree closing down that avenue of enquiry would be a more prudent option … Ok I'll bring him over. Shall I meet you there in say, an hour … Such a pity really, he's quite attractive in a naive puppy dog way.'

With that he ended the call and made his way back into the office where Alex was sitting patiently waiting, his leg twitching nervously.

'Well Alex, I may be the bearer of good news,' said James entering the room.

Had James been able to supply the lifeline Alex had been looking for.

'What is it?' he said eagerly, good news was something he really needed.

James smiled.

'I have a friend who specialises in situations like this. I've just spoken with him. It looks like there will be an end to all your suffering soon.'

33

Cheesy maggots

The information they'd received from Billy had confirmed to Nikola and Viktor that Chai Son was now directly involved in the situation. This had become a lot more serious than cleaning up a back-street runner. Dealing with eventualities such as this, however, was exactly why they had been chosen for the job. Whenever Nikola and Viktor left a scene, all traces of their involvement and anything that could be related to their organisation were completely eliminated, regardless of what it took. Deep cleaning was their speciality. Now Chai Son was potentially in possession of information that could lead to war, the planning of their next move was crucial.

Nikola and Viktor were not afraid of anyone, that fact was in no doubt, but they were no fools. As the old Samurai adage went, 'a fool can die any day'. Formulating a plan of attack on someone of Chai Son's status required gathering information. They had learned from Billy the confused story surrounding

Kiet, the girl Nok and the two foreign men. A subsequent visit to the Nana Apartments Hotel had revealed that Chai Son and four men, two of them Westerners, had collected a man and a Thai 'lady' not long before they arrived. With gentle persuasion they had obtained copies of Richard Chambers and an Alex Whyte's passports, two more characters to add to this ever-increasing cast list. Not knowing what Chai Son's next move would be, they had decided to stakeout the office above his club. They knew this was where he conducted most of his business while in town.

They had been waiting bunched up in their compact hire car opposite his club for nearly two hours and there had been no sign of significant activity. Neither Chai Son, any of his known associates or any Western men had either entered or exited the club. Viktor and Nikola had no idea of the layout of Chai Son's office or the level of internal security. The safe assumption would be that, as a centre for business, this was not somewhere you could casually stroll into and start 'asking questions'. In a situation like this, all strategic advantage lay with the opposition; so, they waited.

Two hours was about the limit either man could go without eating and from experience they knew hunger led to mistakes. The smell of street food had been wafting through the window since they had parked up. Viktor could resist it no longer. He popped out to buy meal four of the day. He returned a few moments later with two halves of chicken, four pieces of sweet corn, two cartons of green curry, two bags of rice, two yogurt drinks, a bag of custard apples and four pancakes. He placed the large parcel of food on the central arm rest and offering Nikola a brown paper bag and said,

'Starter.'

Nikola opened the bag and looked inside. Taking a tentative sniff he said,

'What this?'

Viktor enlightened him.

'Maggot.'

'Maggot?' Nikola bounced back.

'Good protein,' Viktor answered.

Nikola took out a large pinch of the deep-fried larvae and popped them in his mouth. They were crispy with a delicate hint of cheese, all in all not unpleasant. He gave a nod of approval and went in for a second helping. Halfway through his third mouthful Viktor nudged his arm spilling a few maggots down his front.

'Sranje!' said Nikola brushing them off.

Viktor quickly drew his attention away from the spilt maggots and on to a large midnight blue Jaguar pulling up outside the club. The driver got out, walked round the car and opened the back door in readiness for his passengers. From where they were sitting, they could see three people get in, two

285

Western men one of them large, running a little heavy around the waist, the other shorter, leaner, square shouldered. Neither of these were the men on the passports from the hotel. The other passenger was Thai and they recognised him immediately, it was Chai Son. Throwing his packet of maggots on the back seat and dropping the parcel of food at his elbow into Viktor's lap, Nikola started the car and pulled out after the Jag. Keeping a discrete distance, he let the Jag get two cars ahead. Even though he liked the odds of only four men to deal with, there were still a lot of blanks to fill in. Who were these unknown westerners with Chai Son, who were the men staying at the hotel and where was this girl Nok of whom Billy talked?

There was no way of knowing how long this journey would be. Determined not to go any further on an empty stomach Nikola turned to Viktor and said,

'Pass me chicken.'

34

The stage is set

Alex sat in James' car as it drove through the suburbs of Pattaya. The radio played, what sounded like, a Thai quiz show. As he drove, James blurted out the odd answer in Thai just before or after the contestant buzzed on the radio. Judging by his reaction Alex was starting to get a pretty good idea whether he had gotten the answer right or wrong. When the quiz was over Alex decided to make some casual chat.

'You seem to speak Thai well, how long have you been here?' he asked.

James answered vaguely.

'Oh, long enough now.'

'What brought you here?' Alex was genuinely interested.

Momentarily James took his eyes from the road. He turned to Alex and in a cryptic tone said,

'Have you ever taken hallucinatory drugs Alex?'

The question was not what Alex was expecting. He immediately thought this might be a set up. He answered emphatically and actually truthfully.

'No, never, not my thing, no!'

Turning back to the road James licked his thin lips as though conjuring up tastes from the past.

'It's an experience I would highly recommend. Life should have as much intensity as it can possibly hold and from whatever source you can find it. When you drop this country on to your tongue it's like life on acid, it's vibrant, intoxicating. It's a kaleidoscope of experiences that can change in an instant. It confuses the senses; it frees the mind; it challenges boundaries and embraces the absurd. Thailand is life on acid and whether you have a good trip, or a bad trip is determined solely by your moral compass.'

James' revelation was a bit of a conversation stopper for Alex. He didn't rightly know how to respond, so with a non-committal "Err sounds like fun," he returned to looking out of the window. Initially Alex thought they would only be making a short journey across town. He had, however, been in the car for almost an hour now. This trip to see James' associate was taking longer than he had anticipated. After a while he began to feel strangely uneasy. It was a cliché of a question, but he had an increasing desire to know the answer. He asked,

288

'Are we nearly there yet?'

James replied in his usual easy manner.

'I believe my associate's input into this situation would be invaluable. As I officially have you until this evening, I believe it's worth us making the effort to meet with him.'

'Do you really think he can help?' said Alex.

James seemed confident.

'I am sure if anyone could help put an end to this he can.'

The whole business of releasing prisoners and driving all over the place with them was starting to seem somewhat suspect to Alex. He was acutely aware, however, that he had no idea about how the Thai law worked. All he really knew was, at this moment, sitting in an air-conditioned car was infinitely better than rotting in a Thai cell. With this in mind, he made no further enquiry as to how much further they had to go.

Pattaya was now far behind them. The road ahead had grown blank and featureless. After a further fifteen minutes of driving James turned down a narrow side-track, with no signpost to indicate a destination. The track was unsurfaced and littered with potholes. The car ploughed on, kicking up a billowing cloud of dust in its wake. As they bounced along Alex's unease began to return. Where was he being taken? Sensing the tension in his body language James reached over and gave Alex's knee a gentle squeeze.

'Please forgive the rough ride, a high percentage of roads in Thailand are not made up. My associate is semi-retired, he prefers to spend most of his time on his country estate rather than being embroiled in the madness of town,' he said in an effort to comfort.

His words were reassuring, but only went part way to quelling Alex's mounting anxiety.

After fifteen minutes of uncomfortable ride, they passed through an open gate in a chain fence perimeter and pulled up on a hardstanding area next to a single-story building. Waiting there already was a large midnight blue Jag with blacked out windows and a private number plate. The building itself was constructed of cinder block and painted white. It was unlike any country estate Alex had ever seen. It was more akin to an abandoned military compound.

Again, James seemed to have a plausible explanation for a situation that was becoming an increasing concern for Alex.

'My associate considers himself somewhat of a gentleman farmer. This is one of his indulgences. He spends a lot of time tending his nests.'

Alex had never heard of any animal or crop being referred to as a nest. Did this place house birds, or was this turn of phrase just one of James' eccentricities? James stepped out of the car and made his way to the battered green door in the gable of the building. Alex stayed put in the passenger seat.

After a few paces James stopped to brush the dust from his trouser leg. As he bent, he turned and beckoned Alex to follow. Alex exited the car to join him.

Inside the building they found themselves in a narrow corridor, only marginally cooler than the thirty-seven degrees outside. It was dark and dank. The floor had a thin coating of slime and blooms of mould clung to the walls. The worst thing of all was the smell. Alex felt as though he was wading through it. It was a rancid mix of decaying meat and ammonia. Despite the grimness of the surroundings James kept his upbeat facade.

'Uninviting is it not. I'm afraid animal welfare is not a top priority in Thailand,' he said with a chuckle in his voice, 'just through here.'

With that, he led Alex through two wide swing doors on his left. As he stepped through Alex felt as though he had entered an arena. He was faced with a cavernous room lit only by an oculus in the roof which opened directly on to the sky. The light from the aperture cut through the gloom like a sabre. Around this crepuscular beam was a narrow halo of twilight. It reminded Alex of a picture he had seen as a child whilst he was on a tour of a castle. The illustration showed a condemned man imprisoned in an oubliette. The pathetic figure sat in a single shaft of light. Just like that picture the very corners of this room were drenched in darkness. It could have been a stage dressed for drama.

Directly in front of him there was a viewing balcony comprising of a low wall topped by a makeshift scaffold railing. Standing in the gloom close to the wall stood five men, three Thai's and two westerners. One man was wearing a khaki shirt and shorts. He looked rather like a zookeeper. The other four men were dressed city smart. Alex started to feel a sickness wash over him. Was it the heady mixture of intense acrid smells or the surreal nature of the situation that was flipping his stomach? James brokered the introductions.

'Gentlemen, may I introduce Alex Whyte.' he said, gently placing his hand in the small of Alex's back and nudging him forward.

Without speaking, the taller of the three Thai men, who was dressed in a teal three-piece suit, beckoned him over. As he did, he spoke to James in Thai. Alex didn't understand what had been said, but he saw James give a graceful bow and go to leave. Alex felt a momentary dread and involuntarily shouted out.

'James?!'

It was a question and a cry not to be left alone all in one. James paused in the doorway. But the tall, well-dressed Thai waived the back of his hand to dismiss him. Without further word James left. Then the man called to Alex.

'Mr Whyte, come,'

His voice had no hint of menace.

It was only about four metres to where the men stood, but it seemed like a long walk. Alex felt the intensity of their eyes on him. As he approached it became possible to see over the low wall into the pit below. What he saw filled him with horror.

35

Riding the tail of the tiger

At first following Chai Son's car had been easy. The task had been helped by the fact that it was large, expensive and had a private number plate. It was distinct to all the other vehicles on the road. Identifying the target car and keeping it in sight, however, was not the real art of tailing. The real skill lay in not allowing yourself to be identified.

Going through the busy town this had not been a problem for Nikola and Viktor. The car they were driving was like every other car on the road. The traffic was heavy, which allowed them to blend in a few cars behind. It was also slow going in town, so Chai Son was never able to speed off or get too far ahead. The pace wasn't taxing, and the two men took advantage of the many traffic jams to demolish as much of their stockpile of food as they could. As the traffic thinned and they started to get on to the open road, following became more difficult. There were less cars to conceal them, and Chai

Son's Jaguar was considerably more powerful than their Fiat Cleo. This meant that when the Jag was cruising Nikola practically had his foot to the floor just to keep it in sight. The situation was made somewhat easier by the road being straight and flat. This afforded them the ability to see quite a distance ahead and they could follow keeping Chai Son's car just on the edge of their vision.

After nearly an hour of driving, they saw the car turn off onto an unmarked side road. They pulled up at the junction where the car had exited. In terms of tailing this was going to be tricky. They were certain they had not been spotted so far, but it would be hard to miss a tail on a road like this. It would be like driving down a blind alley then turning to see a car right behind you. They gazed up the track. The vegetation on both sides was just high enough to obscure a car. Above the top of the greenery, they could see a plume of dust kicked up. This was the wake of the Jag. This cloud would be their tracking beacon which would also obscure any trail they would make. The two men followed, watching the guiding cloud and marking the tyre tracks on the road ahead. After less than ten minutes they stopped the car. About 400 metres ahead they saw a clearing. It was surrounded by a chain fence with an open double gate at the front. Inside was a single-story compound. Viktor, who had the better eyesight of the two, could just make out the Jag parked in the clearing at the front of the building.

It was obvious they couldn't just drive in unnoticed. About 100 metres back there had been a side-track and they doubled back to it. Turning the car into it they scoured either side of the narrow road for a suitable place that would offer concealment for their vehicle. Eventually they found some relatively firm ground and reversed in. They would now approach on foot.

They got out of the cool car and into the heat of the day. Simultaneously, they drew their Makarov semi-automatic pistols and checked them over, a safety precaution in case they needed to engage. Viktor and Nikola liked the design of these weapons. They were stripped back to their functional essentials, offering reliability and simplicity of maintenance.

They had only been walking for a couple of minutes when they heard a car approach from behind. Quickly they darted into the side undergrowth as the car sped past. They had not been seen, but Viktor had caught a glimpse of someone he recognised sitting in the passenger seat. It was a face from one of the passports. He pointed to the receding vehicle and turning to Nikola and said,

'Alex Whyte.'

This was starting to get interesting.

Once they arrived within striking distance of the compound, they made a reconnoitre of the perimeter fence. The site was not large, about sixty or seventy metres each side. The low building occupied the space closest to the gates. At the back of the building there were a number of artificial outdoor pools. What occupied these pools proved to be intriguing. Crocodiles, dozens of them, gaping in the sun, lazily snaking their way through the water or lying semi submerged only visible by the scutes on their backs poking above the surface. Most of them were around three or four metres with an enclosure to one side housing the smaller crocs. Although Viktor and Nikola had never been to one, they recognised it as a crocodile farm, and it raised an eyebrow of interest. The preliminary surveillance revealed that there was only one point of access and that was the double gates through which the two cars had entered earlier. There were no visible CCTV cameras, so security didn't seem a priority. They supposed the owners believed a few dozen crocodiles would be a deterrent to even the most ardent of would-be-burglars. Back at the gate both men drew their weapons and Nikola took point. Holding his pistol low and keeping his eyes on the main door he ran to the side of the building and pressed himself close to the wall. He was swiftly followed by Viktor. Earlier they had noticed a service door to the side of the building and decided to make this their point of entry. Nikola gently

297

nudged the door with his shoulder, it opened a crack. After a tentative glance he slid inside, his weapon held high, his elbows tucked close to the body. He covered the left Viktor followed covering the right.

They found themselves in a narrow, dimly lit, corridor. Pipework ran along the floor and across the ceiling. Up ahead there were two doors on the left. A shaft of light from the window in the first door cut across the gloom. With Nikola facing forwards and Viktor looking back, they edged their way to the light. Nikola looked through the window. Inside it was an incubating room. There were a number of vivarium, some held eggs and some housed hatchlings. The tiny crocs pawed at the glass or lay motionless staring out with glazed eyes. Apart from that, the room was empty and there was no other way in or out. They passed it by.

The second door was open. Inside it was gloomy, there were lockers, low wooden benches and hooks on the wall, one of which held a solitary khaki jacket. It must have been a changing room. On the opposite wall was a staggered entrance with a shallow foot bath, much like those of a public pool. The two men could hear voices from the room on the far side, the indistinct murmurs echoing against the brutal concrete walls.

In total silence they edged their way round the staggered wall to get a view of the adjoining room. Viktor watched his back

298

and Nikola observed. From this vantage point Nikola could see all of the room beyond, whilst he remained concealed in the shadows.

Standing in a bright pool of light he saw Chai Son, his bodyguard and the two western men they followed here. There was also a third Thai man dressed in khaki shorts and shirt who had not been in the car. Standing in front of them was the man, Alex Whyte. The acoustics were bad, but Nikola was able make out what they were saying.

36

Cops and robbers

What Alex had saw as he approached the low wall behind the five men chilled him to the heart. The pit below was writhing with crocodiles. Alex's first inclination was to run, but the taller of the three Thai men, the one who had dismissed James McNulty, approached him and held out his hand. Alex instinctually took it. It was a slim hand, but it felt like a steel trap.

'My name is Chai Son Thawon, have you heard of me Mr Whyte?' he said in a smooth urbane manner.

It was hardly a conventional opening for an introduction and in his confused state Alex didn't really know how to respond to the question.

'Err sorry?' he replied with a look of puzzlement.

Still holding Alex's hand Chai Son rephrased the question with deliberate emphasis.

'I am asking, do you have any knowledge of me?'

Alex answered honestly, not knowing if it would offend Chai Son's ego if he admitted he'd never heard of him.

'No, sorry, should I have? All I know is that Mr McNulty brought me here and said that you, I think you, might be able to help me. That's all I know.'

He cut himself short as he could feel he might be about to babble. Chai Son paused a while then raised his hand to his chin.

'I think you need to help yourself. Now tell me how you met the girl Nok and everything you know about her,' he said.

Alex had just spent the last couple of hours relating that exact story. He thought James must have given this man some briefing or he wouldn't have known Nok's name. Alex didn't want to appear rude or ungrateful, but he was unsure what more he could add.

'I've been through all of this with James, I don't know what else to say.'

'Indulge me Mr Whyte,' came Chai Son's reply.

Again, Alex proceeded to tell his story for the second time that day. He tried to make sure he left out no detail. He told again of seeing Nok being assaulted in the bar, how he had stepped in, the meal they had shared afterwards. He told of her coming to his room. He told how, along with Richie and another 'woman', they had eaten breakfast and how he had left them all to go to the airport. He elaborated on how he had

301

seen Nok with his day bag, the one in which they had found the drugs and how she could have possibly set him up, though he couldn't think why. He even told how Nok said she was leaving to pick up her sister in her hometown of Thung Na near the river Ping. Nok's hometown being a detail he had forgotten to tell James. Throughout all of this Chai Son and the men remained silent. When he finished Chai Son stood staring at him. The silence was only broken by the soft lapping of the water around the moving reptiles below. Uncomfortably Alex filled the gap.

'That's all I know, there's nothing else,' he said.

Chai Son sighed heavily and half turning to the men behind him said,

'I believe him, I think we have all we need here.'

This conclusion, however, didn't seem to satisfy the large heavy-set western man. So far Viv had quietly stood back and watched Chai Son's line of questioning. To Viv this was going nowhere. He felt it was time to try his own, more direct, approach to interrogation, an approach which had never failed him in the past. Viv strode directly up to Alex and thrust his finger in his face. Alex's head jerked back to avoid his eye being poked out. Viv's tone was not as measured as Chai Son's.

'Now listen here you ginger bastard, don't fuck me around.'

Spittle flew from his lips as he spoke. It was a complete seventies cliché but before Alex could stop himself, he heard the words coming out of his mouth.

'What's this? Good cop, bad cop!'

This quip did not go down well with Viv.

'Good cop, bad cop, good fuckin' cop, bad cop. There are no cops here son, only fuckin' robbers.'

With that he took one step forward and with a remarkable speed for a man somewhat out of shape slammed a punch straight into Alex's diaphragm. The blow caught him by surprise and Alex fell to his knees, winded. Viv wanted Alex to know he meant business.

'I take it you don't know who I am either, so I'll tell you. Depending on how you look at it I'm the man who's fuckin' drugs or money you stole, and this, son, is your last fuckin' chance. Where are they?'

Alex made a motion to stand. As he did, Viv stood directly over him daring him to get up.

'You get to your feet son, and I swear I'll gut you.'

Alex looked to the other men beyond. They were passively watching. The Thai man in a suit, the one who had not spoken yet, had pulled a pistol. It was lowered, but Alex could see he was poised to engage in a nanosecond. There was to be no help from that quarter. Alex stayed on his knees. Even if he could take the man in front of him, there was no way he was going to be able to make an escape before being shot.

There was nothing Alex could say other than,

'I swear that's all I know. I've told you everything I know.'

Viv turned back to Chai Son.

'I think you're right he knows fuck all,' he said.

As he spoke Alex could see him fishing around in his pocket. In the next instant Alex saw a flash of metal and felt a sickening crack to the side of his head. He reeled backwards, automatically he put his hand to the injury. Blood oozed through his fingers and ran down the side of his neck. The next blow was perfectly aimed to the point of his jaw. It was like been hit with an iron bar. Alex was resilient, but this was too much for anyone. He fell forwards, unconscious, his head slammed onto the concrete.

Viv stood beside the senseless body of Alex. Slowly he removed the brass knuckles from his right fist. Taking a handkerchief from his inside his jacket he wiped the blood from them and put them back in his pocket. Along with his socks and briefs, his brass knuckles was the first thing he'd packed. They were his favourite toy. Archie had said it was a waste of time bringing them. Inside Viv gave himself a smug pat on the back. He had just proved him wrong.

'Well, that was a waste of fuckin' time. His mate told us all of that,' he said dropping his bloodied handkerchief on the floor.

'At least we have confirmed the story from two sources now. It would appear the only link left in this chain is the young lady who calls herself Nok and we did get more information on her,' said Chai Son reflecting on the certainty of facts.

'It wasn't much though, was it?' said Viv not seeing any possible use in what Alex had just told them.

'Something is better than nothing,' said Chai Son, 'my enquiries have turned up little on this girl, which means it is unlikely she has spent any amount of time in Pattaya. Now we have a possible lead on where she might be from.'

'And where might that be?' asked Viv.

'Before you put Mr Whyte in his present condition, he said that the girl told him she was from Thung Na. That could be significant.'

'What do you intend to do now then, knock on all the fuckin' doors in Kung Pa and ask if she's in?'

Viv's tone was sarcastic.

Chai Son made no acknowledgement of Viv's attempt at wit.

'I don't know Thung Na directly,' he said, 'but our friend here said it was by the Ping river. Towns in that area are not large. Even if we did have to 'knock on all the doors' this might not be such a big task.'

'And what if she's lying, she could be from anywhere if you ask me,' said Viv objecting to what he saw as blind optimism.

Chai Son tapped a finger to his temple. 'You may not know Thailand well, but I do. If I were to hide a tree, I would plant it in a forest. If this girl were trying to conceal where she was from it would have been better to say Bangkok, Nonthanburi, Nakhon Ratchasima or Chang Mai. These are large cities; it would be easy for her to hide and impractical for us to look for her. If she had said she was from any of these places our search would almost certainly end here. But Thung Na that is an unlikely place to say. In my opinion this information is specific enough to have the ring of truth.'

Viv mulled this over for a moment, even though he thought this was turning out to be a wild goose chase, Chai Son's logic seemed plausible.

'It's not much, but I suppose it's worth a shot,' he conceded.

Chai Son called over the man in khaki.

'Yaalon, prepare Mr Whyte for the crocodiles. Afterwards rotate the creatures to bring in the hungry ones, we may have another customer soon. Also please scour the enclosure and dispose of any …,' he searched for a suitable euphemism, 'left over's.'

Viv had once watched a film where someone disposed of bodies by feeding them to pigs. Personally, he had never actually known anyone to do this, but he had often wondered about its practicality. Crocodiles, however, were a whole new level of disposal and before they left, Viv really wanted to know more. He decided to ask a few questions to satisfy his curiosity.

'Tell me how did you get into this alligator lark then Chuck?'

Instead of being answered by Chai Son it was Archie that chipped in.

'They're crocodiles Viv not alligators,' he said correcting him.

Viv was not bothered about the exact taxonomy of the reptiles, he wanted to know important details like how long did it take them to finish a body, what did you do with the bones etc. He brushed off Archie's correction.

'Crocodiles, alligators all the fuckin' same.'

Archie was not ready to let this detail slip lightly.

'They're not the same though Viv, Crocodiles are from the crocodylidae family, while alligators and caiman are from the alligatoridae family. Alligators tend to be more fresh water, while crocodiles favour saltwater. Also, crocod …'

Viv could tell when Archie's habitual pedantry was about to get the better of him.

'Archie, leave it mate, who do you think you are Johnny fuckin' Morris?'

Even after all of these years Archie was surprised at Viv's lack of interest outside of anything that involved violence in one form or another. He hoped that this new use for crocodiles might be a stimulus for Viv to appreciate the natural world more.

307

'Johnny Morris, he's been dead for over twenty years mate, I'm more of an Attenborough man myself. Crocodiles or alligators these are interesting animals,' he said gazing into the pit below.

It was Chai Son who then took up the mantle of Viv's education.

'Mr Archie is right. Crocodiles are fascinating creatures; their basic design is so perfect it has remained virtually unchanged for ninety million years. These are Siamese crocodiles, not the largest of their species, although they can reach over ten feet. The ones we house here,' he said turning to Archie 'are actually freshwater crocodiles, even though they are typically smaller than their saltwater counterparts, they still have a bite force of over two-thousand pounds. Because of the encroachment of man and hunting, this species has now become endangered. Most crocodile farms in Thailand are for the entertainment of tourists. This farm helps reintroduce these animals to the wild.'

This was all very interesting, but it wasn't the crucial facts Viv wanted to know. 'What about the body disposal business?' he interrupted.

The wonder of nature was wasted on some people. Chai Son cut to salient facts that would grab Viv's attention.

'I do not own this farm I merely pay for its occasional 'services'. These animals are perfect for disposing of inconveniences.   Siamese crocodiles are not typically dangerous to humans, but, if presented as purely meat, six of these animals will get through a body in less than five minutes. They can crush bone to splinters and will devour a corpse in large chunks. A crocodile can secrete stomach acid ten times faster than any other creature alive. This acid is strong enough to dissolve nails, hair and bone, so there is no need for any post digestion processing. Full digestion of a human can take up to twenty-one days. Is that the type of information that interests you?' he said hoping this would sate Viv's appetite.

Viv was impressed.

'Can you ship these things? How much space do you need to keep say, just one or two? If you haven't always got bodies, what would you feed them on?'

The questions spilled out. Like a child Viv wanted one of these service machines for himself.

'Mr Viv, we have a saying in my country, *"kom na, kom ta,* bow down one's head and eyes", we must focus our attention on the task in hand,' he said placing his hand on Viv's shoulder and directing him away from the crocs, 'For now, let us retrieve this girl. Later I will make enquiries about the possibility of shipping a small batch of these animals back to England as my way of apologising for all this inconvenience.'

As he led Viv from the room Chai Son turned back to Archie and Archie could have sworn he saw him wink.

37

50 / 50

Back in the open entrance to the changing room Nikola had been silently watching from the shadows. He had been able to hear the full questioning of Alex. He had seen many people interrogated and had an instinct for when people were lying. It was clear to him that Alex knew nothing about what was going on. Like Chai Son he had concluded that the key player they needed to locate was the girl Nok. Could she be the last person who would be able to identify any link to the Croatian involvement? If so, it would be extremely beneficial to eliminate her before Chai Son and these men got to her. This wouldn't be easy; Nikola had never heard of Thung Na, but it appeared as though Chai Son had. This meant that he and Viktor would be playing catch up on this hunt. If Chai Son got there first, who knows what she might tell him and then it might be cause for a considerably deeper clean-up operation than expected.

It was never easy to eliminate the head of an organisation. If there was any indication who did it, it risked a situation of an all-out war. Both men knew that, in war, advantage went to those who fought on the home ground. This was Chai Son's country; this was his field of battle. In a situation of full-on conflict with Petar's organisation the odds were heavily in Chai Son's favour. What worked for them at the moment was that, so far, no one knew who they were. The full element of surprise was on their side. If no one knew they were involved, then no one would be making provisions to protect against them. It wasn't easy to protect against Nikola and Viktor, even if you were fully aware they were on your trail. If you didn't even know they were coming for you, then your chance of survival was zero.

Nikola had watched as Viv knocked Alex unconscious. The instructions that Chai Son gave to the khaki clad keeper had made it clear that, very shortly, Alex was going to have an appointment with the crocodiles. This was helpful as it was one less loose end for them to tidy up.

As Nikola saw the men about to leave, he turned and nudged Viktor, indicating they needed to retreat. They traced their steps back to the service entrance and then round to the front of the building, just in time to see Chai Son, his bodyguard and the two western men getting into the Jag. They watched as the car sped through the double gated entrance. They let it get far enough ahead so they wouldn't be seen, then ran back up the dirt track to their own modest car. Following Chai Son would be difficult. They couldn't get too close on the track and risk being spotted, but if he got onto the highway too far ahead of them, he might speed out of sight. Looking from a T-junction to an empty road there would only be a 50 / 50 chance of making the right choice.

They took off on the trail of the Jag. The car ahead must have been making good time, as by the time they were on its trail the dust cloud had already died down and they were unable to make visual contact. Testing the car's suspension to its limits they thundered down the track bouncing over and frequently into potholes. Fifteen minutes later, jolted, but still in one piece, the car arrived at the T junction to the main road. Viktor stopped the car and looked both ways. As feared, the Jag was out of sight. The two men climbed out of the car to consider the best course of action. Now that following no longer seemed a viable option they were in the territory of trying to locate this village on a map. Nikola had only ever heard the name of the village and although he had an excellent memory to recall it, he had no idea of the spelling, this would require an extra layer of enquiry.

As Nikola stood with his elbow on the roof of the car, thinking of how much time this would cost them, his train of thought was distracted by the clicking of Viktor's fingers. He looked up and Viktor beckoned him over. As he rounded the car Viktor pointed at the road. There, leading off to the left for about five metres, were fresh dust tracks from a wide base vehicle with sports tires. Nikola checked the right side of the road, it was clean. There was only one vehicle which could have made these tracks. This was all the clue they needed. They clambered back into the car and Viktor floored the accelerator. As long as Chai Son didn't leave the main road, if they maintained top speed, they might be able to catch up.

38

Mushin

Alex felt a sharp pain dart across his left eye jolting him back to consciousness. This was followed by a dull thudding in his head. The pain from the rest of his body began to flood over him. It felt as though his arms were being pulled out of their sockets, the tension this placed upon his chest left him struggling for breath. He seemed disconnected from the world, as if he were floating above it. The only thing that was anchoring him to his body was the pain. He scrunched up his eyes willing them to focus and concentrated on regulating his forced breaths.

Slowly, the grainy images of the world became sharper. He looked up to where he felt the greatest pain. As his head cleared, he saw his hands above his head bound to a hook, which was attached to a steel cable that disappeared up into the darkness of the ceiling. He could feel he was dangling in mid-air. The nylon rope cut deep into his wrists. He had no idea how long he'd been hanging, but his hands had turned a livid purple. Struggling to make sense of the situation, he looked down. What he saw only made him more confused. He was completely naked. His bare chest was spattered with blood. Probably from the blow he'd taken to the head, he thought. As his depth of vision improved, he began to make out the scene beneath him. The shock at the sight below hit him like a truck. He was trussed up on a winch above the crocodile pit.

About ten feet below the creatures were starting to make their way across the enclosure and through the shallow pools to gather beneath him. As they milled around, one particularly large creature climbed up on the back of another and lunged up. As it strained to catch its prize, Alex saw deep into its gaping maw lined with countless yellow dagger teeth. It was so close he could almost feel its fetid breath. The jaws snapped shut inches away from his feet and the animal fell back into, what was fast becoming, a writhing mass of bodies. The creatures were starting to get excited at the prospect of a meal.

Alex instinctually lifted his feet as the huge animal attempted the manoeuvre again. SNAP! This time, even with his feet raised the crocodile got closer. He heard a low rumble and a hiss as it fell back into the shallow pool below. Was this the

315

sound of frustration or the cry of victory as it knew next time it would get its prey. Wracked with pain, his head pounding he couldn't tear his eyes away from the horrors of the pit. Just as he thought it couldn't get any worse, he saw something that filled his body with such emotional pain, for a moment it blocked out all physical feelings.

Close to the wall of the enclosure, away from the growing mass below him, was a smaller crocodile lying motionless with its mouth agape. Alex could see that its snout was stained a deep mahogany red. Wedged between its teeth were shreds of torn meat and hanging over one tooth was something he recognised. It was a yellow and orange platted string bracelet, the very same bracelet he had given to Richie in the temple only two days and a lifetime ago. He had given it to remind Richie he had a soul. At the time Alex could never have imagined this token would bear witness to Richie's soul leaving his body. All this time, he had been thinking Richie was waiting for him in Phuket, blissfully unaware of what was going on. He fought back the tears. The cocktail of emotions was in danger of overwhelming him. Grief and anger fought for dominance. One thing was certain, there was now no doubt what his fate would be if he didn't act and act fast.

There was never going to be a time as important as this to put all of his physical and mental training as a fighter into practice. Emotions had the potential to be the greatest enemy a fighter could face. If they were not harnessed in the right way, they strangled you. Being a slave to emotions closed down thought processes, narrowed the field of perception and took away the ability to react to the changing landscape of a fight. Alex knew many good fighters in theory, became very bad fighters in practice, simply because they didn't know how to control their emotions. A racing mind made for an inefficient mind.

In his early years of martial arts, he had held a romantic notion of becoming a warrior monk, wandering the land at peace with himself and the world around him; only using his powers to defend the weak and defeat injustice. Because of this, he had joined a school that dealt more with the spiritual aspect of martial arts rather than the physical. His Shifu was the grandly named Master Li Qiang. Li Qiang introduced Alex to the power of mushin, the state of mind without mind. He taught him how, through deep meditation, he could free himself from anger, fear and emotion. By removing the ego, he showed Alex how the body became free to act without disturbance. By being tethered to nothing, you were open to everything. You occupied space with the same qualities as water, possessing the ability to mould yourself to every environment. In this state it is not the man who strikes, it is the fist that finds its own target. This is the state of flow, the mind working at such a high level its actions are unconscious.

317

He may have been a deep thinker, but unfortunately, Master Li Qiang wasn't particularly accomplished as a martial artist. It didn't take long for Alex to learn all he had to offer in terms of combat. To progress his overall fighting skills Alex had to seek tutors anew and this was how he'd found Graham. From Master Li Qiang, however, Alex had absorbed an abiding philosophy which had served him every day since. Faced with death, as he was now, it was time to bring the physical and mental training together in decisive action.

Centring his breathing he brought his focus to bear on this exact moment in time. Closing his eyes, he shut out the distractions of the creatures below him. The sounds and the smells faded away. He didn't even hear the snap of the big croc as it made yet another bid to catch his leg. Stepping outside his body he looked at it as a dispassionate observer would. The pain was not really gone in the conventional sense, but Alex was able to acknowledge it as an experience of being, without becoming absorbed by it. In this state anything that could be interpreted as fear was nothing but an abstract energy which could be used as a fuel to feed the muscles.

In this state of mindfulness, the sequence of events necessary to free himself fell into place in his mind's eye. First things first; he looked up to his hands and examined the rope. Whoever had tied him had not been expecting an attempted escape; his hands were merely straddling the hook. He

318

examined the knot holding the ropes in place. It was nothing but a reef knot. Alex knew that if he could take the tension out of the rope this type of knot could easily be pulled apart. But how to take the tension out? An image of himself kicking down in order to provide some upward momentum flashed across his mind, then quickly faded away. He knew that this would only jolt his arms and end up cutting the rope further into his wrists. Worse still he could be bumped from the hook and end up plummeting into the pit below.

Slowing his thoughts, inspiration presented itself to him. He had always had excellent core strength; this was a good time to make it pay. Grabbing hold of the hook with both hands, slowly he lifted his legs into the pike position. He then went further raising his legs and feet above his head until his entire body was inverted. He took his right leg and wrapped it around the cable above him, then, with his left leg, trapped it tightly behind his knee. He was now supporting almost all his weight only with his legs. The next move was harder and more dangerous. Holding himself in place he inched his bound hands over the hook until they were free. He could feel the strain on his legs instantly increase as they took up his full weight. He slipped several inches down the cable. Tightening his legs until they burnt, he arrested his fall. He needed to act fast as he didn't know how long he could hold himself like this. If his legs failed, he would plunge headfirst into the jaws of the

319

waiting reptiles. He quickly brought the rope to his teeth and started working on the knot. Once the tension was off, it was easy to pull the knot apart. It came loose and the rope fell free. With his hands unbound once again he was able to grab the hook and lower himself to alleviate the strain on his legs. As the blood began to flow back into his fingers the former numbness gave way to searing pain and he feared he was going to lose his grip.

Instead of the pain he focused his attention only on the shape his hands made. What does a grip look like, hold that shape, the pain is merely a feeling to be observed, hold the grip! Now Alex needed to widen his field of vision for the next part of the plan. He was no longer bound, but he was still dangling on a hook above a pit of crocodiles. He could see that the low wall overlooking the pit was only about six feet away. If he could get some momentum going, he might just stand a chance of reaching it. Alex began to throw his legs backwards and forwards until he started to swing. It only took him three hard kicks to get the height he needed. At the apex of the swing, he let go. It was only a fraction of a second, but the time he spent in the air was the longest moment of his life.

Alex hit the ground with a thud. Feeling the concrete beneath his feet he took a moment to reassure himself he was on the right side of the wall and not, through some accident of mistiming, in the melee of crocodiles. Reassured he was where he wanted to be Alex stood up and looked around.

The room was shrouded in shadows and empty. Apart from the occasional splash of water and low rumble from the pit below, it was silent. Just because there was no one to be seen it didn't necessarily follow that there was no one around. Before he was knocked unconscious Alex had seen at least five men. Were they still here, or had they left? The fact that he had been left dangling and hadn't been finished off would infer there was at least one person left to supervise the 'feeding'.

Cautiously he made his way over to the double doors through which he had entered god knows how long ago now. As he was approaching one of the doors swung open and he recognised the figure of the khaki-clad keeper entering. The man had his head down looking over a sheet of paper on a clipboard. Before he was seen, Alex swiftly jumped to the side of the door. The man took a few steps into the room and lifted his head. Immediately he saw that Alex was no longer suspended above the pit. Dropping his clip board, he ran to the low wall to look for Alex's body. Alex could see him from behind, his head darting around in the bright shaft of light looking for traces of a corpse. Alex thought about bolting through the door to make good his escape. There was no time for this though. Undoubtedly, the man would hear him and raise the alarm. If the others were still around, they

321

would search for him. Alex had no idea where he was, and he knew these men had guns. He would probably be caught before he even got out of the compound. He could then end up being shot first and then fed to crocodiles.

How far was it to the man, fifteen, sixteen feet? The decision was made. He took off sprinting. The keeper was just turning around when Alex was upon him. Alex aimed a blow to the point of his jaw, but it glanced off as he flinched and cried out in shock. The man launched into a frenzied defence, wildly flailing his arms. Alex covered up and felt several punches land on his head and shoulders. This man was obviously no fighter. Alex could feel straight away that none of these hits would cause him damage. The more pressing problem was the screaming, which carried the danger of attracting help. Alex had to shut him up and quickly. He attempted to cover his mouth to stifle the cries, but after being bitten, hard Alex was forced to pull his hand away. The screaming continued.

Driving from his back foot, right up through his shoulder Alex caught the keeper with a powerful uppercut. Alex heard a crack of bone as the jaw broke. As he looked up, he saw a momentary look of shock and horror in the man's eyes as he reeled backwards and toppled over the wall.

Alex heard a wet slap on the floor below, swiftly followed by the sound of large bodies splashing through shallow pools. Alex leaned forward and looked into the pit. The man lay unconscious blood pooling round his head, his arms and legs splayed out at unnatural angles. A large crocodile made a lunge at the left arm taking it into its mouth up to the shoulder. A smaller croc seized hold of the right leg. There was going to be fight over this fare. Under the tension of the vying animals the body lifted from the floor. Alex turned his head, the last thing he saw before he looked away was the larger of the two crocs go into a death spin, tearing the entire arm from its socket. There were no screams of pain, the man was unconscious. Would that have been a concession afforded to Richie. Although it was unintentional, he had just killed a man. For a brief moment, he reflected on how he felt about this. His answer surprised him … Nothing!

A sense of the immediate danger returned to him. The keeper had made a lot of noise. Alex was expecting people to run in at any moment, but no one came. Apart from the crunching sounds from the pit below all was silent. No sound of people coming to the rescue.

Cautiously he made his way out of the arena and down long, dank corridor. The slime of the floor oozing through his toes. Tentatively he pushed open the door at the end. He was once more looking out on to the car standing area at the front of the building. He could see straight away that James McNulty's car was gone, as too was the Jag that was here when he'd arrived.

Now what? Run out naked into the surrounding countryside without any idea what he was running into? The main thing was that he was free and, for now at least, it appeared like there was no one else here but him. He made his way back into the building. If he were going to make an effective get away, there may be things that would be of use to him.

Retracing his steps, he came to a door immediately opposite the crocodile arena. Stepping through he found himself in, what was likely, the central office. There were two desks with computers, a couple of filing cabinets, a narrow locker and a coffee making area. A white board hung on the wall with a map of the compound sketched out. In various areas there were photographs of crocodiles stuck up with, what could have been, a short biography beneath. On the right of the board was something that was immediately recognisable, an orange first aid box. Alex opened it. It was the usual contents, an assortment of bandages, plasters and a bottle of antiseptic, suitable for minor injuries. He ripped open a packet of surgical wadding and doused it with the antiseptic. Tentatively he dabbed the wound on his head, mopping away the dried blood. The sting made him wince. Apart from a large lump, he could feel his wound was merely superficial, one small blessing. He cleaned himself up with the wadding and spirit as best he could and then turned his attention to the desk behind him.

The first drawer contained nothing more than stationery, but the second made him stop. There, nestled at the bottom, was a revolver. He went to grab it but stopped himself. Suppose he took it, what would he do with it? Could he use it for protection? Could he use it to intimidate, could these people be intimidated? The big question was, would he be prepared to use it? Alex had never fired a handgun and he wasn't sure that, if the time came, he could use one with deadly intent. Besides what if he was caught by the police with a weapon. Surely this would destroy any shred of defence that might be left in his favour.

Next to the handgun, however, was something he was sure he could use, a set of car keys. If there was a set of car keys, there was going to be a car. He snatched them up and turned his attention to the locker. Wrenching open the door he found something he really did need a set of clothes, shirt, three quarter shorts and a pair of trainers. He quickly pulled on the shorts and reached for the shirt, then he stopped, his stomach churned. These were the clothes Richie had worn on their last fateful night out. A light green, Ted Baker, shirt with subtle flamingo print, the white Superdry cargo shorts and, just in case there was any doubt in his mind, at the bottom of the locker, a pair of Nike VaporMax trainers. Alex had always ribbed Richie about paying so much for 'trainers' when he never trained. Grief welled up inside him. Breathing hard

Alex pushed it down inside. Even though he felt physically sick, he threw on the shirt and slipped on the trainers. Right at this moment he could not afford the luxury of grief.

After a cursory search of the rest of the office the only other thing of use was 2,000 Baht locked inside a petty cash box which he smashed open on the side of the filing cabinet.

Exiting the office, he made his way outside. Stepping into the bright sunlight made his eyes smart. If there was a car, he needed to find it and leave. Every moment he spent here ran the risk of someone turning up and he could be right back where he started. He knew there were no vehicles in the hard-standing area to the front, so he scouted round the side of the building. He didn't have to look far. No more than twenty metres to the left was a recessed area with a covered pergola. Inside, dirty, battered, but still looking serviceable was just what he was hoping for, a 4x4 Toyota Hilux. A perfect match for the keys. He climbed into the cab and fired up the engine. It made a satisfying rumble as it burst into life.

Pulling out of the pergola he swung it onto the narrow path running parallel to the building. In seconds he was out through the double gates and back out onto the dirt track. He made note that when he was brought here by James, they made no turns to the right or the left so, bar the twists and turns, it was a straight route back to the main road. The Hilux was infinitely more suited to this sort of terrain than James' car had been. It was still a bumpy ride, but the suspension evened out the worst of the potholes. He roared along through the low forest encountering neither man nor beast. Eventually he arrived at the open road and stopped. So far, he had been operating on pure adrenaline, fight and flight working in perfect harmony. Now looking up and down an empty road gave him pause for thought. In that moment it suddenly hit him, he had no plan of where he was going or what he was going to do next. Up until this point his primary goal was to get as far away from the crocodile farm as possible, but to what end?

He pulled out onto the main road and after five minutes driving, he found a lay-by and pulled over. He switched off the engine and turned on the radio. Flicking through the channels he found what he was looking for, relaxing classical music. Alex knew little of classical music, it could have been Mozart, Handle, Brahms or any one of a dozen composers for all he knew. All he knew was the effect the music had on him; it was an excellent facilitator of thoughts. He turned the music down low and closed his eyes. A wave of physical and mental exhaustion crashed over him.

As his body slowed down, his mind started to sift through possibilities. His first impulse was to return to the authorities, hand himself over and tell them exactly what had happened. Surely after what he had been through it would be obvious to them that there were much larger forces at play. They had to understand that he had been set up and just happened to be the wrong man in the wrong place at the wrong time. The trouble with this plan was that he had no idea what or who these 'larger forces' were. For all he knew they could be from the prison or the police. They could have control over any number of people. He only had one name, James McNulty, but who was James McNulty really? For James to have orchestrated his release he must have connections within the prison; for him to have brought him to the farm he definitely had connections that were willing to commit murder. James didn't even seem to be the top man. When Alex had first entered the arena, it was apparent that James was not the man in charge. It was the tall Thai man who did all the questioning. He was the one who looked to be in control and Alex couldn't recall his name. Besides, who knows what the hierarchy might be above him. If Alex chose to hand himself in, he could have escaped one death sentence, only to find himself facing another. That was if he ever made it to sentencing. It would be extremely unlikely these people would let him reappear after they thought he was dead. If they put a contract on his head, he doubted his chances of ever reaching a Thai court, never mind being convicted. The probability was he would be found stabbed to death in a filthy prison cell. Death in a Thai prison might not be so grizzly as death in the jaws of a

328

crocodile, but either way he played it, the result was exactly the same, one dead Alex.

In the interests of self-preservation handing himself in was not a viable option. If not that, then what?

Given James' and the Thai Man's preoccupation with his encounter with Nok Alex deduced that she must be a key element to this whole affair. It was now beyond all reasonable doubt that it was her that had planted the drugs on him, and she was no friend of his captors. If he could find her, make her talk, drag her to the authorities, she could clear his name. Her guilt in this would prove his innocence.

Back at the crocodile farm his Thai interrogator had asked a lot of questions about Nok, how Alex met her, who she was, where he thought she had gone. The impression Alex got was that these men were very keen to find Nok and not in a good way. At this point he thought the best thing to do was to assume that they would be looking for her as well. If he were to find her, he needed to do so before they did. This meant there was now some urgency to this plan. If they found her first, the only person who could clear his name may very well end up dead and Alex had little doubt that his death would follow hard upon.

But where to start looking? His mind peeled back the experiences of the last couple of days. He started with his interrogation. What had he told the men at the crocodile farm and what had he told James earlier? All he could make at this stage was assumptions. Alex assumed the only knowledge they had about her was what he had told them. He had told them about that skinny punk in the bar and the fight he'd had with him. He'd told them of his walk through Pattaya, of her stopping off at her apartment, the trip back to the hotel, their night together and the departure when he had left for the airport. What else had he told them, what were the details? He had told them about the town of Thung Na. Now what was the name of the nearby river? Ping, that was it. The last time they had spoken that's where she said she was heading. But could he believe this? If she had lied about other things, why wouldn't she lie about this?

 Alex cast his mind back to them walking through the streets hand in hand, Nok chatting about her childhood. He pictured her face; he recalled the sincere affection in her voice when she spoke of her sister and her desire to create a new life with her. Was this true? It seemed at this point he was faced with a choice, return to town to look for her, or believe her story and search for this town Thung Na. Alex really didn't relish the thought of going anywhere near Pattaya, especially when now there was undoubtedly a warrant out on him. Besides would she really be stupid enough to return to the scene of the crime? His assumption now, was that his interrogators would be faced with the same decision of where to look. He further ventured that if they chose to go to Thung Na, they were probably on their way now. But supposing he also headed there, what then? He needed more. All he had was a name, he didn't even have a picture of her to show to anyone. So how was this hunt really going to work for him? Was he going to walk up to random people in the street and ask, *'do you know Nok?'* … *'Nok who?'* … *'I don't know just Nok'*. It seemed a strategy that was unlikely to yield success. He didn't even know if Nok was her real name, he could end up chasing a ghost.

Was there anything else he could remember that he didn't tell these gangsters, anything that would give him an edge? His mind entered a semi dream like state as he revivified his conversations with her. What more did he know? As his thoughts relaxed, it presented itself to him. He remembered her saying that she didn't actually live in the centre of Thung Na she lived in a tiny village about five kilometres outside, what else, now what else? The sounds and images of that night came flooding back. There were only about eight houses in her village. Her house was by a river. It had a balcony overlooking the river and there were shells, shells around the door. This was information he hadn't revealed to anyone. It was not much, but it was these details that might be the advantage he needed.

Just then he was jolted back to reality by a loud banging on the window. He jerked his head to the side to come face to face with a Thai police officer, with a helmet tucked under one arm. Alex glanced in the rear-view mirror to see that a patrol motorcycle had pulled up behind him. The officer was indicating that Alex should roll down the window. For what seemed like an eternity Alex sat motionless in his seat just staring, each heartbeat pounding against his chest. The officer tapped again, this time with his baton which he had removed from his belt. Alex rolled down the window. He felt momentarily unable to speak. He didn't need to; the officer spoke first.

'You illegal!' he said.

Alex didn't know how to respond to this. His voice waivered and cracked, all he said was,

'Sorry,'

'You illegal,' repeated the officer, 'sleeping on road illegal, you arrested.'

Oh god no, thought Alex, after all this to be taken down for shutting his eyes by the side of the road, it was too much. It was pathetic he knew but feebly he found himself saying.

'Please don't arrest me.'

The man poked his finger into the car.

'I could arrest you now, you not want to be arrest?'

It seemed an obvious answer, but Alex gave it anyway.

'No,'

'Then you pay fine, you can pay fine now, yes?' demanded the officer with a knowing smile.

So, that's all this was, a thinly veiled attempt to solicit a bribe. Alex had heard of this sort of thing happening. Some of the advice was to call their bluff. What you were doing probably wasn't illegal and even if it was, the paperwork involved in bringing you in was most likely not worth the effort of the arresting officer. Under the circumstances, however, Alex didn't feel he was in a position to call anyone's bluff.

'How much?' he asked hoping that he would have enough to cover it.

'2,000 baht,' said the cop weighing him up.

'2,000 baht!'

This was all he had managed to find at the farm. If he handed that over he would be penniless.

'Ok, ok, you pay now, money now, 1,000 baht,' came back the demand.

It was the quickest negotiation ever and one which Alex was not going to argue with. Pulling a 1,000 baht note from his pocket he handed it through the window. Briefly the officer looked at it before folding it into his shirt pocket. He stared hard at Alex and then poking his baton through the window tapped him on the shoulder.

'Now you go,' he said, 'no more sleep.'

With that he walked back to his bike put on his helmet and sped off down the road looking for another easy target to supplement his meagre wages.

Alex breathed a long sigh of relief. He had lost half his money, but he was still free. With a rudimentary plan formulated he needed to move. He turned on the engine and checked the clock. It was hard to believe it was less than an hour since he had walked into the crocodile farm. If these other men were ahead of him, in a car like this, he might be able to make up the time. He turned on the sat nav. Damn it, it was in Thai. Working through the settings, using only the symbols as a guide, he managed to change it to English. He was not sure of the exact spelling of the town name, but he was sure he had the first three letters right. Typing them in he let the computer do its work and it presented him with a short list. Scrolling down it was not too difficult to find what he was looking for as nothing came close in terms of phonetic pronunciation. He clicked on Thung Na, and the computer presented him with the route, 514 kilometres from where he was now. He checked the fuel gauge, the display read 623k range, more than enough for the job. With his foot to the floor, he should be able to make it before dark. With the wheel on full lock, he spun the pickup a 180 degrees back onto the road, happily noting to himself that this was the opposite direction in which his corrupt cop had gone.

39

Fish and ice-cream

Nikola and Viktor had been on the road for nearly twenty minutes and had yet to catch up with Chai Son's car. Even with Nikola's foot flat to the floor, the engine of their Cleo was no match for the 394hp of the Jag. Up until about five minutes ago there had been no turn offs from the main highway. Unless it had crashed off the road and into the surrounding countryside, the car they were following could only have been heading in one direction. Now, however, they were starting to encounter a number of side roads, any one of which Chai Son could have taken. No amount of searching for tyre tracks could now help them follow their quarry. It was dawning on them that to carry on ploughing down the main road hoping to spot the car was going to be an exercise in futility. Nikola checked the fuel gauge. They had less than a quarter of a tank. Even, if by a fluke of luck, they did spot the Jag they would still have no idea if they would have enough fuel to follow it all the way to its final destination. They needed to formulate a new strategy.

 In terms of tactics Nikola's and Viktor's minds were nearly always in perfect agreement, so much so that very often they moved as one with no need for verbal communication. When Nikola turned to Viktor and said, "fuel station" he knew what they needed to do. It was another twenty minutes before a fuel station presented itself and it was not quite the substantial stop they had hoped for. Nikola pulled into the forecourt.

 There were only two old pumps and a battered building that was masquerading as shop. It was one of those rare independent stations with no affiliation to a large oil company. The two men got out of the car. Nikola started to fill up while Viktor took himself inside to search for the other thing they needed. The little building was a makeshift structure, a mishmash of brick, wood, concrete and glass all painted in peeling white. Outside the main door was a pile of kindling, several sacks of rice, a sack of yams and a rack of faded newspapers, the most recent of which was several days old.

 Inside the building it was more like a junk shop come grocery store rather than a garage. The place was a complete disarray of disparate goods. There were shelves full of books, stacks of magazines, there was a section for CD's, DVD's and videos, there were units with various food stuffs, tins, bread, biscuits and fruit juice. There was a cooling fridge with milk and beer and a chest freezer where glassy eyed fish lay in their final repose, incongruously stacked next to mint choc-chip ice-cream. Despite the beach being many miles away there was even a rack with swimming trunks, beach balls and a snorkelling set slowly perishing in the sun.

Viktor picked his way curiously through the Aladdin's Cave of flotsam and jetsam scanning for what he needed. Considering that it was located in the middle of nowhere he wondered who bought this stuff. Judging from the layer of dust that covered almost everything, the answer was probably no one since 1985. Outside Nikola had finished filling up the car and came in to join him. The two men stood looking for anything that would resemble a service attendant. It was as still as the grave. Nikola shuffled through to the back of the shop where there was a cramped storeroom. Several times knocking a book or a dusty tin of soup off a shelf, the aisles were not made for a man of his size.

The backroom was dark, oppressively hot and even more cluttered than the front of the 'store'. Not wanting to venture in, lest he should get stuck, he stood at the doorway and shouted. 'service!' There was a rustling of paper and the squeak of a spring. In the semi-darkness the fragile figure of an old man rose from a low folding cot and stepped, squinting, into the light. He could have been anywhere between 70 and 170. Wispy white hair danced around a head dappled with

337

liver spots. Heavy folds covered his eyes to the point where Nikola wondered if he could see at all and with no teeth for support, his cheeks were sunken and heavily lined. He wore only a loose vest and oversized shorts to cover his emaciated body. Bare footed the old man shuffled right up to Nikola until he was almost touching him. He was less than chest height. He looked up at the large man blinking rapidly then graciously bowing said,

'Swạ̄sdī.'

Nikola hardly ever spoke more than half a dozen words in a day at the best of times, so it was difficult to tell if anything left him speechless. But the other worldliness of this man and the surreal shop definitely gave him pause. The little man pushed passed him and tottered up to a bench which served as a counter. In a cracked voice he asked,

'You petrol?'

Yes,' Nikola replied. '

'How much take?'

The old man smiled retrieving a tin security box from below the counter.

'1,350 baht,' said Nikola taking 1,500 baht from his wallet and handing it over.

The old man took the money. Placing it in the tin, he began raking around for change. Taking out various notes, in turn, he held each one up to the light and examined it closely. He

338

pulled out several twenties and tens until he found the hundred and fifty baht notes he was looking for. He handed the money over to Nikola and with a warm smile and a nod said,

'Khx k͞hxbkhuṇ krup.'

The sale had obviously been an interruption to his afternoon nap, and he began to make his way back to his cot to mop up another couple of hours sleep. As he shuffled his way to the back of the shop Viktor gently tapped him on the shoulder.

'You have map?' he said.

The little man looked up at the giant with his rheumy eyes and said,

'Yk thos̄' h̄ī c̄haṇ, krup?'

Viktor had no Thai at all, but by the tone of the old man's voice indicated he might have to repeat himself. This time he rephrased the question hoping it would be clearer what he was asking for.

'We buy map. A map of road.'

The old man listened intently, processing his limited English. His lips twitched as he thought. Eventually he raised a bony finger and said,

'You look map?'

Viktor was pleased, he had made himself understood, a rare smile flicked across his face.

'Da, da, yes map you have map?'

339

The old man looked around the shop slowly nodding.

'Map have, map have, map have.'

He set off on his hunting mission. He scuffed from shelf to shelf and from one pile of papers to another, looking on, under and behind them, all the time chuntering to himself.

'Have map, have map, have map …'

Each time he disturbed a new stack of papers, motes of dust rose up into the air which made him sneeze. Eventually he found what he was looking for on a shelf behind several tins of carrots. It was an old fold out road map. He knocked off the dust against his leg and proudly handed it to Viktor.

'Map,'

It looked worn and discoloured, but it would probably do.

'What price?' Viktor asked.

The old man waived his hand.

'No price, you keep, be happy.'

Viktor looked down on the tiny figure in front of him. Kindness was an alien concept to him. Most of the things he received for free were given out of fear rather than generosity. As small a gesture as it was this was new. In Viktor's experience free things ultimately ended up costing more than things you paid for. He took the old man's tiny fragile hand in his massive iron hand and shook it as delicately as he could.

'Thank you,' he said.

The little gentleman patted him on the chest as light as a bird and smiling benignly said,

'Friend, you be safe.'

With that he withdrew to the back room and the comfort of his cot.

Outside Viktor unfolded the map onto the bonnet of the car. Back at the crocodile farm Nikola had heard the name of the town Chai Son was heading to Thung Na. Providing there weren't two towns with the same name and the spelling was as it sounded, finding it wouldn't be too much of a problem. With this map, however, it would be, it was entirely in Thai script, with no English key. Nikola was about to go back inside the shop to question the old man further, but Viktor stopped him.

'Let sleep,' he said.

Nikola looked at him quizzically.

'Ask next car, old man no English.'

It actually took three cars and nearly thirty minutes to get the information they were looking for. One car pulled in and when Nikola tried to approach the driver, he quickly wound up the window and sped off. Nikola waited until the second driver was filling up his car before he approached him, so this time he couldn't immediately run away. The man was hesitant to speak and never made eye contact. He mumbled a few words of mixed Thai and English and made it very clear he couldn't help. Viktor noticed that after he had filled up his car, he never woke the old man in the back room. He simply placed his money on the counter and left. There must have been something about the old man that solicited this level of honesty amongst his patrons. After these two attempts to get help Viktor and Nikola were beginning to think there was something about them that made people uneasy. Asking for information without brutalising it out of people was proving difficult.

The third driver was about fifty-five with glasses and a smart shirt. He looked like a middle management executive. Nikola presented the man with the map and said,

'You show where Thung Na please?'

After the first two attempts it was Viktor's idea to add the please. He was pleasantly surprised. The man's English was perfect. He asked Nikola to repeat the name of the town several times, even venturing to correct his pronunciation to make sure he fully understood. He then circled the town on the map, wrote the English script translation below it and traced out the optimum route. When he'd finished, he bowed politely before entering the shop and leaving his money on the counter.

Although they had lost a lot of time, at least they now knew their destination. With Nikola in the navigation seat, they got back on the road. Given the lead Chai Son had it was almost a given that he would find Nok first. This would mean that they would probably have to take out more people than first anticipated. Still, there were only three men with Chai Son and Nikola and Viktor could assess any potential danger from this girl when they arrived.

40

Robin Hood

Viv, Chai Son and Archie had been in the car for almost four hours. Archie sat up front next to the driver, Tan, while Viv and Chai Son chatted in the back. It was actually a very generous assessment of the interaction between the two men to describe it as a 'chat'. Viv had become rather obsessed with the idea of owning crocodiles. He had taken the journey as a chance to find out as much as he could about them and interrogated Chai Son incessantly. "How long do they live? How big do they grow? How easy are they to breed? Can you train them?" All the while he kept consulting with Archie about the possibility of *'setting something up'* back home. For his part, Archie made the occasional, strategic, non-committal, mumble.

Chai Son, for his contribution, played the part of genial host fairly convincingly, answering Viv's questions honestly and with only the tiniest hint of strained patience. Archie knew only too well Viv's, almost childlike, obsession with dangerous animals.

He remembered them all, including, but not exclusively, the *"Mike Tyson's got a tiger, we could build a pen in the back garden"* phase, the *"We need to get a hawk, Tony said we could hunt on his land"* phase and, not to forget, the *"What about getting Carl a snake for debt collecting and we could write it off as tax deductible"* phase.

None of these infatuations ever amounted to much. Viv would never have the patience or commitment to look after anything more exotic than a dog, of which he had four, two Rottweilers, an English Bull Terrier and a Deerhound. Viv treated the animals both as his employees and his children depending on his mood at the time.

Eventually, and with great relief, the conversation surrounding crocodiles died down. Not knowing what he didn't know prevented Viv digging too deep into the subject and Chai Son volunteered only the most concise answers, never expanding on the subject. Eventually the talk turned to business. With Chai Son's assurance that this whole situation was an exception which would be cleared up very soon Viv was interested to know just how his operation worked in Thailand. Chai Son may have indulged Viv's curiosity surrounding crocodiles, but it became quickly apparent that he

345

was not going to extend the same courtesy in relation to his business.

All of Viv's questions regarding the scale of his interests, the sourcing of product, dealing with the authorities and shipment infrastructure, were all met with a combination of fogging and stonewalling. The most exhaustive answer Chai Son gave was *"We are efficient and will be able to adequately meet your needs in all departments."* Archie was beginning to sense Viv's frustration at the lack of information. Viv tried another avenue to explore.

'You have an interest in clubs, the one below your office, I take it that's yours?' he probed.

'Yes, I have an interest in night clubs Mr Brownsword.'

Since the conversation had veered into business Chai Son had dropped the informality of his first name.

'In places like that, how does the set-up work with the girls?' Viv enquired.

'How do you mean?' said Chai Son genuinely puzzled.

Viv pressed on clarifying his question.

'Well, this is the first time I've been over here, but I've got some mates who come every year. They were saying that you pay a bar fine if you want to take girls away from work and then you pay the girls direct. Do you make your cut from the bar fine, or do you also get a cut of what the punters pay the girls, or do you have some sort of set up where the girls pay

346

you for space to work at the bar or something? One of the lads back home runs a lap dancing place and he charges the girls a couple of hundred a night to work there and then anything they make off the punters is theirs. Is it the same stamp here?'

During most of Viv's lines of enquiry since the car journey started Chai Son had stared passively ahead. He now turned to him direct.

'I do not peddle in flesh Mr Brownsword,' he said in an absolute voice.

Viv was surprised.

'Really Chuck I thought that was the backbone of the economy round here. There seems to be an endless supply of willing girls and it must turn a healthy profit,' he offered helpfully.

'Others make their profit how they see fit; I make mine in ways fitting to me.'

It was clear by his tone that Chai Son wanted to close down the conversation. Viv, however, had never been one to pick up on social subtleties.

'If you don't mind me saying Chuck, I think you might be missing a trick. A bit of diversity in income never hurts. We all take a hit in some areas, it's always good to have a bit to fall back on.'

At this point Viv actually believed he was dispensing sound business advice. Chai Son's voice became hard.

'And what would we be falling back on Mr Brownsword? My country is becoming a cesspit, a playground for the depravities of morally redundant Western men. And, unfortunately, there are those who would profit from this toxic relationship. You talk of "willing girls" but how many of those young girls are really 'willing'. How many act out of desperation and sell the only thing they have as a way to survive. People like you Mr Brownsword take a girl for a short time, people like me see the long-time damage it causes.'

Viv had never minded a 'wrong'un' as he called them. He had always seen honesty in people's open dishonesty. One thing he couldn't stand, however, was a hypocrite, especially one who lectured him on morality.

'Now back up Chuck. Let me put you straight on something, I've never taken anyone for a short time or any other time and it's a bit rich getting a moral lecture from you. If I'm not mistaken, I'm sitting next to a man who trades in heroin and feeds people to crocodiles. Where does that sit on your moral compass?'

There was now some heat in Viv's voice.

'All of the goods I produce, Mr Brownsword, leave my country. While other countries degenerate, we grow strong on their weakness. You ask me the size of my operation Mr

348

Brownsword, I directly employ over four-hundred people to produce my product, all of them clean, healthy, well paid and protected. Families can afford to have their children educated in order that they go on to be valuable members of society. No one in my employ would ever have to see their children sell themselves cheap. And as for feeding people to crocodiles … the world will not miss one less perverted farang.'

Chai Son never raised his voice to match Viv's. He delivered his rebuttal in the same measured tone as before.

'Well now, who's the proper fuckin' Robin Hood then!' sniffed Viv sarcastically.

Chai Son didn't get the reference, was it an insult?

'Robin Hood?' he asked.

Archie had been listening from the front and felt he really must step in to smooth things over before they got out of hand. Leaning over the back of the seat he spoke to Chai Son.

'Robin Hood is a folk hero in our country. He used to steal from the rich to give to the poor who needed it. There's Hollywood films and songs about him. He was a good guy.'

Archie knew that this was not how Viv had sarcastically meant it, at least his spin was historically accurate, if not intentionally accurate. Chai Son dredged his memory and remembering something he had seen on TV many years ago, he sat forward, raised a finger and said,

'Ah Hollywood, Robin Hood, this was Errol Flynn, am I right?'

349

He lent back in his seat pleased at his recall.

Archie was relieved that the parallel had met with approval.

'Yes, that's right Errol Flynn, he played Robin Hood,' he smiled.

Archie heard Viv take a draw of breath as if he were going to add to the conversation. At the point they were at now anything Viv was going to say was unlikely to be helpful. Archie shot him a look and discretely shook his head to shut him down before he started up again. Fortunately, his efforts of distraction were backed up by Tan, the driver, who interjected.

'Meūxng xyū k̂ĥāng ĥn̄ã.'

Chai Son instantly translated.

"Tan said we are nearly there.'

'Thank Christ for that,' said Viv, 'now what?'

Chai Son offered his opinion for consideration.

'If I may make a suggestion. In these minor towns, English will not be as common as it is in Pattaya. Archie, I know you have tried with our language, but I think you have to admit that it would not be adequate to question people.'

Archie was forced to nod his head in agreement. The total extent of what he had picked up only covered him for hello, thank you and how much?

Chai Son continued.

'Western men asking questions about Thai girls may not be met with a favourable response. If you and Viv would be content to occupy yourselves, Tan and I will split up and make enquiries.'

Although Viv didn't want to be left out of the action, what Chai Son said seemed to make sense.

'Sounds good to me Chuck. So where are you going to start?'

Chai Son laid out the first part of the plan. 'As far as we know this girl worked the streets independently in Pattaya. She may have learned her trade in her hometown if this is her hometown. I think we will start with the bars. In places like this everyone knows everyone in bars. If we uncover nothing there, we will extend our search to local stores and markets. We will cover any centre where people gather.'

As Chai Son spoke Archie looked out of the window. The car was making its way past a row of dilapidated wooden houses. Almost every shack had a makeshift stall set up outside selling various wares, from fish to bananas to motorbike parts. There were baskets of live chickens and the occasional goat tied to a post, all looking like inmates on death row. Shabbily dressed and largely barefooted people milled around in the late afternoon heat buying from and selling to their next-door neighbours. It was a level of poverty Archie had never seen before, even in the poorest areas of Newcastle

351

where, in some cases, not having a 50inch flat screen TV was seen as depravation. Despite what looked like subsistence living, people seemed genuinely happy.

Children laughed and shrieked as they kicked balls in the street and people smiled as they chatted. Archie couldn't help wondering if these smiles masked deeper worries of where the next meal would come from. Or were they a testimony to the freedom of a simpler life? Freedom from the constant pressure to amass huge quantities of material goods, goods which only brought with them their own burden of worries. Who knows until you've walked in another's shoes? The scene brought back something his father had said to him when he was a young man. It had not meant much to him then, but over the years it had given him many a moment for reflection, *"The reason the grass is always greener on the other side of the fence son is because from your side of the fence, you can't see the cowpats!*

As always Viv had his own unique social commentary to add to Archie's thoughts.

'Bit of a shithole isn't it?' he observed.

'Yes, it is mate,' said Archie still staring out of the window.

Soon the ramshackle homes were behind them, and they were heading into something recognisable as a town. A short drive around afforded them the layout of the place. It was not large, so if they split up it would not take Chai Son and Tan long to cover a good percentage of the major establishments. Tan found a convenient parking place on the main street running East to West and pulled up outside a chemist. Chai Son turned to Viv and Archie to outline what he saw as happing next.

'It is difficult to tell how long this will take. We may find out something straight away or we may find nothing at all. Either way we will see you back here, at the car, in a maximum of one hour. We can then review what to do next. We may, with luck, be a lot sooner, so if you are going to move around it would be wise not to let the car out of your sight. We do not want to have to search for you as well.'

'Yes dad,' said Viv sarcastically.

'Pardon?' Chai Son looked genuinely confused.

Viv was starting to get tired of Chai Son running the show. He was not a man used to taking instructions.

'Look Chuck, you just worry about finding that fuckin' girl, me and him can take care of ourselves. We'll be ready when the time comes, son.'

Chai Son and Tan took out their phones and both checked they had the picture of Nok, then they exited the car. Through the smoked glass Viv could see them chatting. Tan crossed the road. Chai Son carried on past the chemists and ducked into a side door. Viv and Archie were alone.

'What do you make of him?' asked Viv.

Archie had been lost in thought and the question blindsided him.

'Who?'

'Who do you fuckin' think,' Viv snapped back, 'Fu Man Chew there, Chuck. What do you think of him?'

Archie thought for a moment. Three days ago, he had not expected to be in a remote town in Thailand chasing 200,000k and a few kilos of heroin with a Thai drug baron. It was a lot to take in.

'So far, he's been courteous, and this seems as much of a surprise to him as it has been to us. The fact that he's included us in this hunt indicates he's not trying to hide anything. If what Tony the Tongue told you about him is anything to go by, generally he seems like a reliable supplier with a pretty secure system. This whole situation could just be an unfortunate anomaly. On a personal level though I find him a little pretentious, but that might just be a cultural thing.'

'Well, I think he's a cunt!' said Viv.

41

Pancake answers

Alex had been driving for over three hours. All this time he had thrown caution to the wind and floored the accelerator. Luck had been on his side and apart from his initial encounter at the start of his journey, he had seen no further police. He knew if Chai Son and the other men were on the road too, he had to make up the time. Keeping the speed up to between 140 and 150kpm he was sure he would have closed the gap. The sat-nav was telling him he was now about to enter the town of Thung Na. With nowhere specific to go, this was the end of its usefulness for guidance. Alex could see the built-up area approaching, but this far out, it was sparce shanties.

He pulled the Hilux over to the side of the road about a couple of kilometres from the centre. He needed to think. He had assumed that the men would head straight into town, as the name of the town was the only information he had given them. The one thing he didn't want to do now was to charge in and risk meeting them. Although his skills had played a big part in his escape from the crocodile farm, he knew overall, he had been very lucky, and he was not keen to tempt fate further. He needed to try and capitalise on the extra knowledge he had in order to get ahead. This was the information that might lead him to Nok before them.

Alex got out of the car and looked up and down the bleached road. After being so long in the air-conditioned environment of the car the heat made him gasp. It was far more humid inland, a marked difference to the coast in Pattaya. He could feel himself becoming clammy as beads of sweat formed on his back and chest. It was just over an hour to sun set and for some unknown reason he felt that, as the sun went down, so did his chances of success. Perhaps it was some primal fear that darkness holds no promise other than danger. There were very few people milling around at this time. Those that were, carried water, fruit and bags of rice from one house to another. It looked as though the daily shop was done and now people were returning home to prepare meals. About ten metres to his left, he saw an old woman squatting near a flat metal plate which was heating over coals. She was mixing batter to make pancakes. The smell suddenly made him realise that, except for a cup of coffee and a pastry in James McNulty's office, it had been over 24 hours since he last ate. If there was anything for him to face going forward, he would be better equipped to handle it if he were not faint with hunger. Besides, he needed guidance, and this was as good a place to start as any. He made his way over to the old woman.

'How much?' he asked pointing at the hotplate and the various cooking ingredients scattered around.

She looked at him blankly. Alex's Thai was poor, but he knew some tourist basics.

'Tao-rai pancake?'

'Yîsíb baht,' answered the old woman.

Yîsíb Alex took a second to process and then said,

'Yee-sip, twenty baht?'

Silently the old woman nodded. Alex held up three fingers.

'Sorng please,'

The old woman smiled and held up two fingers and said,

'Sxng,' she then put up another one and said, 'Sãm, Sãm.'

Alex nodded in agreement, and she proceeded to pour the thick batter on to the plate. Almost instantly it began to solidify and turn a rich golden brown.

'Kîwy?' she asked.

Alex shrugged his shoulders; he had never heard this word before.

'Kîwy?' she repeated.

As she did, she picked a banana from a paper bag of fruit and held it up to Alex.

'Kîwy?'

He nodded and peeling it open she sliced it on to the pancake and folded it over. Flipping it expertly into a folded paper napkin. She handed it to Alex and started on the next one. He bit into it, it was hot, sweet and delicious. As she cooked, he thought he would try and get some information.

'You know where river is?' he asked in the pidgin English British people adopt when abroad.

The old woman shook her head. It was clear to him she was not answering the question, just indicating she didn't understand. Alex's Thai didn't extend to this sort of conversation. He tried a different angle. He knew the word for water.

'Nahm, village nahm,' he said, 'close here, Nahm village.'

His pronunciation was only good enough for a partial understanding and in response she held up a plastic bottle of mineral water.

'No, no you don't understand. I look for nahm village, close here.'

With this he pointed up the road.

'Nahm,' repeated the old woman and held out the bottle again.

Alex rubbed his face and the woman seemed to sense his frustration at not being understood. She turned round and called out into the crumbling house behind her.

'Lawana,' she shouted, 'Mā nī̀ sī̆.'

Out of the gloom of the doorway appeared a small girl in dirty shorts and tee-shirt. She was about seven.

'Yay,' said the girl stretching, it looked as though she had just woken up.

The woman pointed at Alex 'Kheā phūd phās'ā xạngkvs',' she said gesturing for the girl to come over.

The girl walked up to Alex and in a confident voice said,

'Can I help you please?'

'Yes, I look for a water village.'

The girl looked very confused.

'Sorry, what you mean, I don't understand, what is water village? You speak English yes or you Yexrmạn … err … German?'

Alex had assumed that her English would have been no better than the old woman's. His underestimation of her made him feel embarrassed. He started again.

'Sorry, I'm looking for a village just outside of the town here.'

'There many village outside of town, do you know what called?' said the girl.

'No, I don't have a name,' said Alex, 'but I do know it is not far from town, five kilometres, close enough to walk and it is next to a river.'

The girl didn't have to think much.

'There are two village next to river outside town, one this side town and one on other. You know more?'

359

This was excellent news for Alex, now he had some confirmation of Nok's story, Thung Na did exist and there was a village next to a river on its outskirts. Still two villages, could he narrow it down further.

'This village is very small, no more than eight houses,' he said, 'people they fish and farm.'

'All people next to river fish and farm,' said the girl smiling 'but village on other side of town many house. Village this side of town little number of house, seven, eight, nine maybe.'

Alex felt his heart jump. He was on the right side of town.

'Where's the village on this side of town?' he asked excitedly.

The young girl pointed down the road on which he had just come.

'You go up, three, four kilometre, turn down path on left. You see easy, then village two minute in car.

'And that's the only village like that here?' Alex clarified.

'There other village,' said the girl waving into the distance, 'but many more kilometre and not next to river.'

He felt as though there was no time to waste. He snatched up the remaining two pancakes the old woman had just finished making and rummaging in his pocket pulled out five-hundred baht and handed it to the young girl.

'For you and for the pancakes,' he said dashing for the car.

'But it only sixty baht!' shouted the girl after him.

'Keep the change,' said Alex as he fired up the car and swung it round in the road.

42

SangSom

Chai Son and Tan had been searching for about forty-five minutes. In this time, they had only covered about five bars each. Chai Son knew that to walk into a bar and pull out a photograph of a young girl and start asking where he could find her was unlikely to yield much information. People tended not to be very forthcoming if they didn't know who they were talking to or what they were getting in to.

To help put people at ease, he and Tan had agreed to buy one drink in each bar and to pose as the girl's cousin. The back story being that their mother, her aunt, had passed away and left a monetary consideration for her. The family, not being in touch for some time, had lost her exact address. Chai Son knew the strong cultural bind of family and that in a poor town like this people were going to be far more likely to help him if they thought he was there to help others. Unfortunately, this strategy was time consuming. Although the town was compact there were more places to chase up than Chai Son had anticipated. Given his deadline to rendezvous back at the car in no more than an hour, he decided to try one more call before returning to reassess plans.

With no other criteria than it was the closest, he walked into the next bar 'The Teak Door'. The name promised something traditional with an air of sophistication. Although the name may have promised it, the interior definitely did not deliver. His initial impression was not good. The establishment obviously catered for the seasoned drinker who cared little for the surroundings and focused more for the price of the liquid in their glass. The few tables were of battered Formica and the chairs were cheap tube steel and vinyl. The floor tiles were cracked and sticky under foot and the walls were painted in, what he could only describe as, bile yellow. The whole interior looked like it had been designed to be hosed down at the end of the night, though by the appearance no one had done so in many years. There were only four other people in the place. Even at this early hour they were in a state of inebriation more associated with closing time. In the corner a television was mounted on the wall silently playing bouts of cockfighting to an indifferent audience.

Chai Son's initial reaction was to turn around and try somewhere else. This girl may have been a thief and a whore, but objectively, he had to concede she was very beautiful, and it would be unlikely that any of these men would be her target client base. Then he reconsidered. Drunks rarely have anything better to do than gossip, they tend to stay put and they tend to know people. He'd had no luck elsewhere, so what was there to lose here?

He approached the counter. The barman was in his late fifties clad in a sweat stained short sleeved shirt. He was greasy and fat. In his 2,000-dollar city suit, Chai Son was aware of how out of place he looked. Could this work in his favour as a stranger in town he thought? He sat at the bar next to a man with thinning hair, dressed in brown corduroys, sandals and a Maneki Neko tee-shirt. Chai Son couldn't help observing that the golden cat didn't seem to have brought him the fortune it promised. Perhaps the man might have been better sticking with a good luck symbol from his own culture. The man nodded; Chai Son returned the polite gesture.

'What can I get you sir?'

The barman was unexpectedly polite.

Chai Son didn't think he would build many bridges in a place like this with a soft drink, so he scanned behind the bar to see what was on offer. There was nothing to his taste, so he decided to stick with something that was at least a reliable brand, if not quality.

'SangSom please,' he said.

The barman pulled down the bottle, placed a tumbler in front of him and poured straight into the glass. There didn't seem to be much regard for conventional measures, this was at least a treble. The barman returned the bottle without stating a price. Chai Son took a sip, it had not been watered down. It had been a long time since he had tasted SangSom, and the sweet dark rum was more pleasant than he remembered. Over the years his palate had become educated to more 'select' drinks. The syrupy taste brought back memories of a time when he and Aat were working the street hustles and living on the edge. He made a mental note to buy a bottle later as an act of sheer nostalgia. After a couple of sips, he decided to break the ice with the barman.

'Is this your place?' he asked casually.

'Has been for over thirty years.' said the man, cleaning the pump of the only draft beer on offer.

'Thirty years that's impressive,' said Chai Son, making sure to get in a complement.

'It's a long time, I'm not sure it's impressive,' he replied with a resigned smile.

'You must see a lot of people?' Chai Son went on.

'My fair share,' he said as he continued the cleaning.

'You might be able to help me?'

'Helping is part of the job description my friend. We all need a helping hand at some time.'

'I'm trying to find someone,' continued Chai Son.

'We are all looking for someone, the question we need to ask ourselves is who and why.'

Chai Son had not expected his line of questioning to be philosophically dissected in a backstreet dive. It was an uncomfortable realisation that his assumptions were becoming tainted by his current social status. Chai Son knew that in his trade, where he had to deal with the full spectrum of society, underestimating somebody could be fatal.

Chai Son fished his telephone from his inside pocked and opened up the picture of Nok.

'This is who I am trying to find.'

As he opened the picture the man on the barstool next to him took an interest in the conversation and sneaked a look. The barman took the phone and studied the picture.

'Why do you need to find her?' he asked not committing himself.

'She's my cousin. My mother, her aunt, died a few days ago and left her a few things in her will, I said I would get them to her,' Chai Son explained.

The barman wanted a little more.

'Sorry to hear about your mother. Do you have the girl's address?'

'No, I'm afraid not. There was a disagreement and our families parted. Mother loved Nok though and kept in touch.

I found the letters. There was no address only the town name and a zip code, that's what brought me here.'

Chai Son left it there, he knew that if he overly elaborated it might sound too contrived.

'Is this a recent photograph?'

He had now stopped cleaning the pump and was taking an interest.

Chai Son knew it had only been taken a few days ago but decided to plead ignorance in order that his story might sound more genuine.

'I'm not really sure,' he said, 'the last time I met her was many years ago, before family unpleasantries.'

The barman carefully looked over the picture once more and then handed the phone back to Chai Son.

'Can't be sure my friend, I don't think I know her.'

Chai Son knew it had been a long shot in a place like this but in this search, they were dealing with longer odds.

'Thank you,' he said and went to slip the phone back in his pocket.

Before it was comfortably tucked inside, the man in the Lucky Cat tee-shirt spoke.

'I might be able to help. Show me that picture again,' he slurred.

Chai Son took out the phone and handed it to the man. He studied the face.

'You know who this is don't you?' he said calling the barman over again, 'it's Ritthirong's daughter.'

He held the phone up for him to inspect the picture. The barman tilted his head.

'But she's clean and her hair's tidy,' he smiled.

'Still the same girl, you said her name was Nok?' he asked Chai Son.

'Yes Nok,' Chai Son replied.

'Then that's her alright,' said the man handing the phone back, 'was it Ritthirong's sister who died or his wife's.'

Chai Son was on the verge of finding this girl and he didn't want to blow it. He had never expected to be on the end of a line of questioning himself and had not prepared a back story to this degree. He thought on his feet. This man knew the father, so he might know something of his family background. If Chai Son said it was the father's sister this might prompt further questioning. He decided to take a risk.

'No, not his sister, his wife's,' he ventured.

The drunk slowly shook his head.

'Don't really know Mayuree. She's quiet, never speaks.'

This was good, it was unlikely there would be further questions about family connections. Chai Son pushed for a location.

'So do you know where I can find her, it would be good to try and heal old wounds between our families.'

At this point the barman interjected to lend his help to the situation. 'That's easy my friend, head off out of town on the road going south. Past the outskirts, maybe five, six kilometres, you'll come to a turning on the left, it's the first one you'll come to on that road. About two minutes down that track, you'll find their village.'

'Do you know which house it is?' said Chai Son.

'It's not verry big my friend, once you're there you won't have any problem finding her.'

Chai Son knocked back the rest of his drink. He had the information he needed it was time to move.

'Thank you,' he said, 'you have been most helpful, I know passing on the inheritance and making amends would mean a lot to my mother.'

He rose from the bar and indicated he wished to settle the bill.

'Seventy baht,' replied the barman.

Seventy-baht, Chai Son reflected that patrons of his club wouldn't even get an orange juice for that price. He could clearly see why the bar had been an attraction for serious drinkers for the past thirty years. The owner knew his audience. Pulling out his wallet he dropped 300 on the bar.

'You have been most helpful. I am grateful, please take one for yourself and one for this gentleman.' he said patting the man with the Lucky cat tee-shirt on the back.

369

With that he made his exit.

When he got back to the car Tan was just arriving. Viv and Archie were still patiently waiting. Chai Son indicated to Tan to take the wheel and he jumped in the back with Viv.

Jet lag had caught up with Viv and he was napping when Chai Son climbed in. The slam of the car door startled him into life.

'So?' he said trying to pretend he was fully alert.

'Tan, drive south,' was all Chai Son said.

43

"Leik bã!"

Alex found the turn off without a problem. He drove the 4x4 down the track to the village. It didn't take long until he came to the clearing by the river. He pulled to the side just before the few houses and made his way on foot into the dusty square. It was quiet save for a woman sitting on a veranda bathing a child while a scruffy dog took the opportunity to drink the bath water. The woman shooshed the dog and looked up. She watched Alex curiously, saying nothing. He took in his surroundings.

  The village was the right size and by a river which ran at the back of the three houses to his right. Nok said her house backed on to the river, so it had to be one of those. The sun was low in the sky and the diffused light set the houses and surrounding forest alight with tips of golden flame. It was wonderfully still, the silence broken only by the rasp of cicadas and the high pitch chirrup of frogs. He wandered over for a closer look. If she was in one of these houses, then which one?

Two of the houses were remarkably neat and tidy, but the third had signs of long-term neglect. Walking up to the base of the porch, he saw something that confirmed he was standing in front of the right house. Around the door, just as Nok had described it, were freshwater shells, some of which still had flecks of red and green paint clinging to them. He took a deep breath.

Alex knew Nok was probably the only person who could clear his name, but he doubted she was going to put her own neck in a noose for the sake of his. Still, what were his options, try to force this girl into the open or face the Thai authorities and these mad, crocodile feeding, gangsters alone. How he would get her to talk Alex didn't know. It would be one step at a time from here. He mounted the porch, walked up to the door and gave it three sharp raps. There was low scuffling from inside. The door opened a crack, he was met with the partial view of a large puffy faced man in his mid-forties. The bloodshot yellow eyes glared at him under heavy lids.

The man looked him up and down.

'Khuṇ khūx khır?' he said in a suspicious tone.

Alex reverted to his pidgin English in a hope of making himself understood.

'Nok, I look for …' he searched his limited vocabulary, 'girl name Nok, ying cheu Nok.'

He was not sure of the word for woman or girl, however, he assured himself he got at least 'name' and 'Nok' right. The man pulled down the corners of his mouth piling up the flabby skin of his jowls.

'Leik bā!' he said shaking his head and went to close the door.

This was Alex's last chance. He was not about to be fobbed off so easily. Before the door slammed shut, Alex's foot was in the gap.

'Sorry, please, one minute 'Yah poot Thai," Alex was trying to say he didn't speak Thai, but as he could not really speak Thai, he wasn't sure if he was succeeding. 'Nok, listen Nok, I'm looking for a girl named Nok, she lives here, yes.'

The bloated man redoubled his efforts to close the door.

'Xxk pị cāk pratū k̄hxng c̄hạn, Leik bā!' he bellowed, and he banged the door hard against Alex's foot.

Just then from inside Alex heard a muffled yell. The words were severely dampened, but he was certain he heard someone call his name. With no idea what he was barging into, Alex put his shoulder to the door and crashed in with all his weight. The door smashed open. The force sent the man reeling backwards.

Alex took a second to process what he saw. There, trussed up and gagged on a threadbare sofa bed was Nok. Beside her

373

was another girl bound only by her wrists and with no gag. The girl was the double of Nok but several years younger.

Any animosity Alex harboured towards Nok vanished in the heat of the situation. In that instant all he saw was a girl who was being held captive and was in distress, instinct took over. He forced his way past the stunned man and ripped the gag from her mouth. The corners of her lips were red raw, her voice was dry and hoarse. The belt binding her had cut welts into her wrists and her face contorted with pain as he wrenched at the leather restraining her.

'I'm sorry, I'm sorry, please get me out of here,' she sobbed.

She had been crying so much the tears had gouged vivid white lines down her cheeks.

Behind him the man, now blue with rage was screaming, what Alex could only imagine were, profanities. The second Nok was free she turned to the girl by her side and began to untie her hands.

Alex turned to face their captor. The man's lips were dripping wet, and his face lathered in sweat. Enraged he was shouting.

'Khuṇ xxk pị cāk b̄ān k̄hxng c̄hạn!'

He had inflated his chest and thrust out his chin. His arms remained by his side, his fists clenching and unclenching. This was the posture of a man who was hoping that a display of aggression would negate the need for real violence. Ritthirong

374

may have been big enough to get the better of slight young girls, but he was no match for Alex, and he knew it.

Nok and Gia were now free and standing behind Alex.

'Mị̀ klā txn nî̂ khuṇ. Ħemāa sǎ̄ħrạb tī p̄hǔ̄hỹing thèānận,' Nok threw from over Alex's shoulder.

He had no idea what she said, all he knew was that they had to leave and fast. Alex's words cut her short before she could launch into another tirade.

'Get what you need we're going … NOW!'

He fixed his attention on the man, whilst at the same time trying to keep the girls in his periphery vision. In this tangle of lies and deceit, he couldn't be certain if the danger were in front of him or at his back. Nok and the girl grabbed two back packs and re-joined him. Alex put himself between the two girls and the man and edged towards the door shielding them with his body.

'Back away,' he said.

The man seemed to understand and shuffled backwards as Alex and the girls made their way forward. He didn't step aside, however, and was still barring their exit. Ritthirong's eyes were darting from Alex to the girls and around the room. He was desperately searching for options. If he had of been twenty years younger Ritthirong might have considered going in with his fists, but now he needed something to even up the odds. As he came level with the improvised kitchen area, his hand shot out and snatched a large boning knife from the bench. As a young man Ritthirong had known knives, he knew Alex was not going to get past him without being cut. Gia screamed and Alex took a step backwards to escape the arc of attack. This was the second time in as many days he had been faced with an edged weapon. Alex weighed him up. Ritthirong may have been fat and out of shape, but, unlike Kiet at the club, he looked like he knew knife craft.

The knife was held in a reverse grip tucked behind his forearm, concealing the blade from Alex. It was a perfect grip to launch both an attack and to defend from an attack. He didn't wave his arm around in front of him, which would have given Alex something to grab. Instead, he held his arm close by his waist. This meant that in order to take the blade, Alex had to enter into Ritthirong's space and leave himself open to be stabbed. Alex had always been told that the best way to defend against a knife was to run away. He had been lucky the last time defending himself from Kiet, a second time might be over playing the odds. Unfortunately, in a confined space like this, running was not an option. Ritthirong slowly advanced.

'Txn nî čhạn ca tạd khuṇ.' he sneered.

His lip curled exposing stumpy yellow teeth.

Alex backed away the girls bunching up behind him. He considered his next move. In a street fight, kicks to the head were risky, but here it would give him the range he needed. In

376

the space available it was impractical for a roundhouse, so Alex decided on a front kick, straight to the face. If Ritthirong wasn't knocked out, hopefully it would disable him enough for Alex to grab his arm. With the blade neutralised Alex felt he could easily overpower him. He elbowed the girls back to get the space he needed and adjusted his stance. He was just about to launch the kick when he saw a large shape loom up behind his attacker. There was a sound of metal coming into sharp contact with skull and Ritthirong fell to the floor in a heap. As he dropped away, standing behind him, rubbing the blood from his brass knuckles, was Viv.

'Knock, knock,' he grinned.

44

Every dog has its day

The hire car was only ever meant to be used within the confines of Pattaya, short journeys of convenience. As ever, with an eye on frugality, Viktor and Nikola never spent more than necessary, so they'd opted for a budget model Renault Cleo. Now after almost five hours on the road they were regretting their choice. The car had little in the way of performance and even less in the way of comfort for men of their size. The going had been frustratingly slow and several times they'd had to change who was driving just to get out and stretch. Still their journey was coming to an end, and they were entering the town of Thung Na.

As expected, they had not been able to catch up with Chai Son. This had put them at a severe disadvantage. Now they would have to hit the streets again and start to gather information. They had a picture of the girl; they had a picture of Chai Son and his associates, so they weren't starting with a totally blank canvas. They were sure that if any of these people were here, they would find them. As they drove down the main road Nikola was looking out of the window to get an impression of the town's size and layout when all of a sudden something caught his attention.

'Turn, turn!' he said, sharply elbowing Viktor in the arm.

The blow was hard enough to jolt the car over to the curb. His voice was as close to surprised as Nikola ever got, which on a normal spectrum of emotion, was only one step up from apathy. Viktor knew that Nikola never requested anything without good reason, so he never asked why.

'Where?'

'Back the way we came,' answered Nikola.

Viktor put the wheel on full lock and spun the car around in the street.

'Fast!' instructed Nikola.

Viktor put his foot down and, in a few seconds, saw what had arrested Nikola's attention. There, ahead, was Chai Son's car. Viktor permitted himself a rare wide smile. After losing someone finding them again was seldom this easy. They had been blessed with extremely good fortune. This lucky encounter had eliminated a lot of tedious leg work. Now they had Chai Son in sight Viktor pulled back and followed the discrete protocols of tailing. Even though they had found Chai Son's car the two men were still left with an uncertainty. Had he already located what he was looking for and was now leaving, or was he still searching? Either way they knew the best strategy was to keep the prime target in view until they had further intelligence.

They followed the car out of town on the South road. This might not be a good sign. The car was heading back out on the same road they had come in on. This could indicate that Chai Son had found the girl and was now returning to Pattaya. However, they'd not been following the car long when it took an unexpected deviation and left the road down a side-track. Not another stinking crocodile farm hoped Viktor.

The two men stopped the car at the turn off and gave it a minute, to cut down the chances of being spotted. Once moving again, it didn't take long before they reached a cluster of houses around a central clearing. Standing on the far side of the clearing was Chai Son's car. The only thing they'd passed on the way in, was a Toyota Hilux parked incongruously in a passing place by the side of the track. The forest on either side was dense and there was no place to conceal the car, so they parked up next to the Hilux. As always, they carried out a pre-engagement check on their weapons before setting off.

Dusk was starting to fall as they entered the village. Light could be seen in a couple of the windows, all was still, save for a couple of stray puppies play fighting in the dust. As the men passed, one of the little dogs jumped up and wagged its tail.

Viktor bent down and tickled it behind the ear. The puppy licked his hand. Despite his indifference to the human race, Viktor liked dogs. For him dogs had proven useful in the arena of war. He admired their unquestionable loyally and ability to be fearless. Keen noses could sniff out everything from insurgents to I.E.D's. He knew from experience if you wanted to clear a house, break up a crowd or loosen a stubborn tongue, letting slip the dogs of war would do it every time. Dogs were useful.

The two men skirted the village keeping to the encroaching shadows of the surrounding trees to avoid exposure. The houses all looked similar and at first glance it was difficult to tell which one Chai Son and his men were in. Then approaching one of the houses, which was considerably shabbier than the rest, they noticed the door was open. Even though the light was dingy they could make out the unmistakable figure of the tall, lean, well dressed, Chai Son. Nikola signalled to Viktor to reconnoitre before engaging. As they drew closer the scene became clearer. In addition to the men who were with Chai Son when he'd left the crocodile farm there were several other people in the house.

There was an unconscious man on the floor, two girls, one of them they recognised as Nok and, to both their surprise, the man they last saw knocked unconscious at the crocodile farm, Alex Whyte. Both men thought Alex would die at the farm.

381

How he'd escaped and managed to get here before they had was a mystery they couldn't afford to ponder at this moment? This wasn't the time to speculate 'how', this was time to deal with what was. And having all the key players close together in one room had its benefits. If Viktor and Nikola could thoroughly clean this scene, in one fell swoop, they would have eliminated all connections to a Croatian involvement. Their work would be done.

Viktor signalled to Nikola to approach the house in a pincer movement. This avoided any chance of being seen on approach. Holding their weapons low, they closed in from the left and the right. They came to the edge of the three steps that led to the crooked veranda. The dying sun was now deepening the shadows and the escaping lamp light painted the steps yellow. Even in this dim light it made it easier for the two men to see in, but harder for the people inside to see out.

Nikola eased his foot on the bottom step. It bowed significantly under his weight and let out a low painful groan. He eased off the load fearing the step might fail and let out a crack that would alert the men inside. The rest of the steps and the fundamental structure of the veranda was in no better shape. Any chance of covering this short distance stealthily was out of the question. Surprise must now come through speed. Nikola held up his hand for Viktor to stop.

Both men readied their weapons and then Nikola raised three fingers. Viktor understood, a synchronised assault. Three finger became two, two became one and then at the fall of the last finger both men launched themselves into the house.

45

Show me

Viv stepped over the heap on the floor that was Ritthirong. He was closely followed by Chai Son, Archie, then Tan. It was hard to tell who was most surprised Alex or them. A stunned silence hung in the air. As always it was Viv who broke the verbal stalemate and asked the obvious question.

'How the fuck did you get here?' he said looking Alex up and down.

Alex thought it was best to avoid that question considering the cost of his escape. The death of the crocodile keeper wasn't going to be the good way to start their reacquaintance. All he could do was to reiterate his innocence.

'I know how this might look, but I'm just here to clear my name. I really have nothing to do with drugs, money or anything.'

Chai Son stepped forward. Slowly he bent and took the boning knife from the lifeless hand of Ritthirong. He weighed up the scene in front of him. Alex stood hands up in surrender with Nok and another girl sheltering behind him. Both girls had full back packs as though they were about to leave. None of this situation spoke of innocence to him.

'I am tired of this chase, return what is mine now or I will peel the skin from your bodies,' he said holding the knife casually by his side.

This was not hyperbole. There was an absolute conviction in his words. The whole situation was too much for Gia and she began to sob and convulse uncontrollably. She was the only person in the room who had absolutely no idea what was going on. Nok held her tightly to stop her shaking and kissed her forehead.

Chai Son's eyes had now taken on a cold dead look, his voice was almost a whisper.

'I will not ask a second time, return what is mine.'

Even though Chai Son didn't move, Alex found himself edging backwards. He could feel the girls pressing hard against him. Nok was clinging to his arm.

'Please,' said Alex, 'I...We don't know anything.'

This was a desperate situation; he could see no way out. Chai Son honed the boning knife on the palm of his hand.

'Tan,' he called.

Tan drew his weapon from inside his jacket.

'Anyone moves, shoot them, but keep them alive. I will start with the little girl you, Mr Whyte, will watch.'

Viv was no stranger to violence. His entire life had been steeped in it, however, skinning girls alive was a whole new level he wasn't sure he was ready for. He felt he had to say something.

'Woah, come on let's slow down here, that's rough. I mean, feeding that streak of piss to alligators is one thing but …'

'Crocodiles!' Archie interrupted.

Viv couldn't believe Archie's timing.

'Archie shut the fuck up for Christ's sake.'

It didn't take much to put Viv off his train of thought, but he made his feelings as clear as he could.

'Skinning little girls Chuck, really?'

Chai Son felt it was time to give Viv a lesson in management.

'Mr Brownsword you wanted to know how I run my business; well, this is it. I take care of the people who work for me, I provide for them, and their families and I protect them when they are in need. This breeds loyalty and most importantly respect. For those who are not loyal or show disrespect, for all those who try to take what is mine there is only fear. Fear Mr Brownsword is the greatest weapon in our business. You want to know how I do business, then see how I create fear.'

Archie could see that Viv was not entirely happy with the situation. But they had come this far and as Tan was standing at their backs with a gun, the time for an intervention had long passed. Then just as Chai Son took a step forward Nok screamed out.

'Stop!'

She tore the backpack from her shoulders and flung it at his feet.

'Take it, take it, but don't touch her, leave her, she has nothing to do with this,' she pleaded, pushing Gia behind her.

Chai Son kicked the backpack over to Tan.

'Open it,' he ordered.

Tan picked up the bag and opened it up. Inside, most of the money was still wrapped. Digging beneath that, Tan came to the film clad heroin. By the quantity and weight of the packages and the denomination of the bills in the bundles, it appeared that, give or take a nominal amount, it was all there. Tan held up a sample of the notes and the heroin.

'It's here,' he said.

Chai Son turned back to Alex and the two girls. Surrendering the package had bought them a few moments reprise. Chai Son had what he was looking for, now he needed to know who he was dealing with. Pointing to Nok he said,

'You were a whore of Kiet, but you.' he said turning to Alex. 'Who are you? Nobody walks out my farm. Whose man are you because you didn't come here only to watch the Kradūkkhæ̌ng?'

'I didn't come to watch the tournament,' said Alex.

This seemed to confirm Chai Son's suspicions.

Then what did you come for?'

'I came to fight in it,' Alex clarified.

Chai Son's interest had been piqued. He had been led to believe by James McNulty that Alex was a mere spectator of the event. Given that a lot of western people came to watch, this was a fair expectation. Even during Chai Son's interrogation of Alex, he had said nothing to contradict this assumption.

'You came to fight?' Chai Son said with an air of surprise.

He knew many westerners aspired to fight in the tournament, nearly all were rejected before ever setting foot in the ring. Only a handful made it to a fight and ninety-nine percent of those who did were knocked out in the early bouts. Chai Son had followed the Kradūkkhæ̌ng in its earlier days. Over time, his interest had faded as a foreign commercial element began to creep in. Even for Alex to be accepted was an achievement. Chai Son wanted to know more.

'So where did you place?'

If Alex were lying, a simple line of questioning would expose him.

'I got to the final,' said Alex.

Chai Son didn't believe this could be true. He knew that only one Western man, the infamous Jeroen Jansen 'The Beast of Amsterdam' had ever won the tournament and only two westerners had ever made it to the finals. The schedule was always stacked heavily against farang. Chai Son found Alex's story doubtful. Chai Son dug further.

'And who did you fight in your final match?'

Alex was happy to furnish him with the information. Perhaps this was what Chai Son needed to finally convince him that he had nothing to do with all of this.

'I knocked out Decha Puntasrims in the second round of the semi and I was stopped by Yod Rak Sakda in the third round of the final.'

Chai Son had heard of Puntasrims and Rak Sakda, both men were prestigious fighters. He also knew both bouts would have followed hard upon each other. And after fighting Puntasrims, to last three rounds with Rak Sakda was remarkable, as he had a fearful reputation as a vicious fighter. Chai Son paused. Alex had to die for what he now knew, but Chai Son had respect for a fighter. As well as respect, if what Alex had just said was true, he now had a burning desire to test Alex and to test himself. Chai Son had always kept

389

discipline in the ranks with his bare hands. He knew this maintained the legend and increased his authority. This form of regulation, however, was never extended to transgressors outside of his organisation. He'd had many fights over the years and ended many lives. In that time, all but a handful of people had come anywhere close to challenging his skills. Could a challenge be standing in front of him now? He had to find out.

Chai Son studied Alex carefully from head to toe. Alex was about his weight, though maybe two or three inches taller. He had long arms and legs; Alex was not broad, his physique was sinewy, athletic. Chai Son marked his hands carefully, the knuckles were distended with calluses and flecked with scars. One of his ears showed signs of cartilage damage, there was a thin cut below his right eye and the skin was thickened around his prominent cheekbones. Chai Son turned his attention to Alex's elbows, they were hard with ossified bone spurs, a result of constant striking, those elbows could cut. Chai Son had not been looking for it before, but, on closer inspection, Alex was every inch a fighter.

After long consideration Chai Son said,

'Show me.'

Alex didn't understand what was being asked of him.

'Show you what?'

Chai Son threw the boning knife to the floor. It buried itself in the wood with a shudder.

'Show me your fight Mr Whyte, fight me now.'

'You want me to fight you,' said Alex, 'you want me to fight you and then you'll either shoot me or skin me. That's not much of a choice.'

'No Mr Whyte the choice simple you win, you walk. You lose you earn a quick death,' said Chai Son laying down the wager.

Alex considered the offer. If Chai Son were as good as his word, winning a fight against him would seem to be the only way he was going to walk out of here alive. Then he felt Nok's grip tighten on his arm. He also felt the damp of Gia's tears soak through his shirt as she pressed her head against his back. Alex may not have known what drove Nok to do what she did or how her sister was involved, if she was involved at all, but whatever they did, whatever the motives, they didn't deserve to die at the hands of Chai Son.

'What about the girls?' Alex asked looking to make a bargain.

'What do you care of these women, they must answer for their own actions,' said Chai Son.

'Let them go too or I won't fight,' said Alex.

He tried to sound like he was giving an ultimatum, even though he knew he didn't have any cards to play. Chai Son considered the proposition, would Alex fight harder if he thought he was fighting for more than his own life?

'If you want a larger prize, the stake must be higher Mr Whyte.'

Chai Son paused as though calculating fair odds. Then he spoke.

'You kill me, you and the girls leave unharmed, you lose, both you and the girls suffer a long and painful death.'

As he said this Chai Son could feel a rush of adrenalin through his body. It was a real high that he hadn't felt for some time.

It seemed to Alex the ultimate stake, was the manner of his death. Was this something he was willing to gamble in order to save virtual strangers? He could still feel Gia shivering behind him, whatever Nok was, Gia was only a child. Even if she was involved in this, she was certainly not old enough to understand the consequence of her actions.

'Agreed,' he said holding out his hand.

Chai Son took it, and they shook. Just then Tan burst in.

'Xỳā thả xỳāng nỉ Chai Son.'

Chai Son turned and answered in English.

'Do not worry my friend. I cannot die.'

Tan wasn't happy with this dismissal of his concerns. He had, of course, heard of Chai Son's belief in his own immortality. Some who heard it thought it an eccentricity, while others believed it. Tan was of the opinion, whatever the reality, it was probably best not to put it to the test. He knew that when Chai Son had made up his mind nothing could shift him, but he tried one more time to appeal to Chai Son's logical brain.

'Chai Son D̄wy khwām kheārph xỳāng s̄ūd s̄ūng c̄han mị khid ẁā nī̀ ca c̄hlād,' he said with a deep sincerity.

Chai Son was now firm in his commitment.

'I value your opinion and respect it, but I will do this.'

For the past five minutes Viv felt like he had been side-lined whilst Chai Son played out his Bruce Lee fantasy. Whether Chai Son died or not was of little consequence to Viv. What he wanted to know was how this cookie was going to crumble for him.

'Hold on Chuck if you want to dance with this ginger beanpole that's your affair. What's in that bag your man's holding over there is my affair. What happens if lover-boy here turns out better than you think?'

Chai Son was determined to go through with what he had started.

'Mr Brownsword let me assure you, I will not lose. But to put your mind at ease Tan is here for you. He will ensure that you have safe passage with both your goods and your money, and my organisation will continue to supply any amount of product you want in the future, regardless of what happens here.'

Viv nodded to Archie, If Chai Son was as good as his word this was a win, win situation for him. Tan still had the gun and no matter how good Alex was, he couldn't fight bullets. So even if he did beat Chai Son, he was hardly likely to try to turn on them. With a reassurance of both his goods and his money Viv could sit back, relax and enjoy the show.

46

To the death

For the second time that day Alex found himself in a position where he would have to fight for his life. The fight at the crocodile farm was in the heat of the moment. He had never intended the man would be killed. His death was an accident. This situation was very different. He was not just fighting for his life, but he was also fighting for the lives of Nok and Gia. The only chance they had of surviving was for him to beat another human being to death with his bare hands. Alex was no stranger to fighting, but he knew that fighting on the street was very different to fighting in the controlled environment of the ring. Many good fighters in the ring were thrown by the chaos of street fighting. He had no idea who this Chai Son was or what sort of fighter he was. Before he had entered the Kradūkkhǽng he'd spent many months with Graham reviewing all the film he could find of all the fighters he might face. They had studied their game closely to find any weaknesses in their

395

style, to look for anything Alex could exploit, anything that would give him an advantage. Here, with Chai Son, he had nothing, nothing but the prospect of kill or be killed. He had agreed to the fight, but he had no idea how this was going to start or how it would end.

'Where do you want to do this?' he said to Chai Son.

Chai Son considered this for a moment. Alex had a longer reach than him, which would give him an advantage at distance. It would be best for Chai Son to restrict the space available. He felt himself to be physically stronger than Alex. To keep the conflict close would be advantageous to his strength and on the inside fight make Alex's long limbs work against him. He pointed to the back of the house overlooking the river.

'Outside on the balcony,' Chai Son then turned to Tan, 'Tan, give Mr Brownsword the goods and the money to hold. Train your weapon on these girls if they move shoot them. If Mr Whyte makes any attempt to run, shoot him and then shoot them,' he then turned to Viv and Archie. 'would you gentlemen care to come through to the back, you might find this interesting.'

Tan sat Nok and Gia down, covering them with his gun. Gia's face was still buried deep in Nok's breast, she couldn't bear to look. The whole situation was overwhelming her senses. Nok stared hard at Tan, whether Alex won or lost this fight, she was not sure if he would honour his boss's wishes. Chai Son led Alex to the back balcony followed by Viv and Archie. Outside the sun was dipping below the horizon, its dying rays burnt the sky blood orange red. Fireflies danced their chemical light show in the dusk, water lapped gently against the shore. A cool breeze swept up the black river bringing a welcome relief to the oppressive humidity. The balcony was only about three metres by two metres and was in bad shape. As he stepped on to it Alex thought there might just be a chance it would collapse putting all of them into the river. Alex stood with his hands by his side, his senses were on alert, but he was still not sure how all of this would start. In front of him Chai Son casually removed his jacket, he unfastened his shoulder holster and waistcoat. Folding his clothes neatly, he hung them over the handrail, placing his gun and holster on top. Then he removed his shirt. As Chai Son flexed in readiness, the dying light of the sun chiselled out each muscle in razor shadows and the faint ripples of the reflected light from the river animated each of his many tattoos until they took on a writhing life of their own. All of the fights in the Kradūkkhǽng had been fought bare chested. Alex was used to fighting men with good physiques, but faced with Chai Son, Alex couldn't help feeling intimidated.

Even Viv felt compelled to acknowledge the drama of the scene.

'Fuck me this is good,' he said nudging Archie.

397

Chai Son was the first to test the fight. He feigned a leg lift while shooting out an exploratory back hand. Alex parried it easily. Chai Son could see that he had decisively responded to where the attack came from not where he had been sold it. It had started. Alex knew that those who were constantly forced to defend rarely won. He needed to take the offensive and launched a straight left jab to Chai Son's face followed by a tight right hook. Alex knew he was fast but unfortunately Chai Son was faster. Chai Son stepped in, his head slipped to the right and Alex's jab went clean over his shoulder. Ducking under Alex's hook Chai Son came in with a slicing elbow to the temple. Alex barely had time to react. The fraction of an inch he managed to move was just enough to turn a knockout shot into a glancing blow. It was nearly over before it had started. Alex had to make distance. He covered his head and thrust out his knee. It connected well with Chai Son's midriff and knocked him back a few feet. Alex could feel a warm trickle of blood run down the side of his face from the slash of the elbow.

Chai Son stood in front of him, he was actually smiling. Alex was not afforded any time to compose himself before Chai Son launched a second offensive. This time he came in low, Alex thought this a mistake and swung an arching kick to the back of his neck. His foot hit nothing but the boards of the balcony. Like a spring Chai Son loaded himself for a flying knee to the

398

head. Alex brought up his forearms just in time to take the full impact of the attack. Chai Son's knee struck him like a freight train, it lifted his whole body. Even though he managed to get his arms up in time to cushion the blow, the impact thundered into him jolting his head backwards and smashing several teeth.

Alex had no time to mourn their loss, he needed to keep up the offensive against this onslaught. He knew that if he could take control of Chai Son's head his body would follow. Pulling Chai Son close, Alex clasped his fingers tightly round the back of his neck and tried to wrench him down to deliver a knee strike of his own. However, Chai Son was too strong and was able to resist. Fighting Alex's strength, Chai Son reared his head and the two men stood eye to eye. Chai Son was now close, very close.

Alex met his cold calculating gaze and could feel his breath on his face, it was slow and even. This was no time for an intimate moment. Alex seized the opportunity, and, in rapid succession, he placed two head butts on the bridge of Chai Son's nose. He felt the sting of the impact on his forehead and there was a crunch of bone as Chai Son's nose broke. Alex was just about to go for a third when Chai Son dropped his head and unleashed a flurry of punches to his body. Alex felt as though his insides were being mashed up. Each strike reverberated like a sonic shock wave cracking ribs in its wake. Then one well-placed punch caught him on the right side under the ninth and tenth rib. It came in upwards and backwards driving towards his spine, it was a liver shot. Alex's entire body was flooded with excruciating pain, and he felt his system about to lapse into debilitating shock. He had to do something fast.

Quickly he brought the point of his elbow down on the top of Chai Son's head and thrust him away as hard as he could, both he and Chai Son stumbled backwards. The pain was so great Alex could do nothing but fall to his knee. Alex looked up at Chai Son standing in front of him. The head-butt and elbow combination had clearly stunned him, his eyes were dull with a vacant look. Blood was streaming from his nose and ran in rivers down his chest. If ever there was a time for Alex to finish this, it was now. Unfortunately, he had pain of his own to deal with.

He tried to rise but fell to his knee again. He held up his arm in a futile attempt at defence. Slowly Alex watched as full consciousness crept back into Chai Son's eyes. Chai Son reached up and touched his nose, which was now bent at a remarkable angle. His face grimaced. His former blank expression was replaced with one of unrestrained rage. Alex needed to shake off the pain and fast or he had no doubt he had but moments to live.

Chai Son spat. Bloody spittle spattered Alex's outstretched arm and the side of his face. Chai Son readied himself for the final assault. Charging forward he swung his leg to deliver a brutal axe. It was perfectly aimed at the back of Alex's hanging head. This kick would not miss and when it made contact the force would be enough to snap Alex's neck instantly. Just as the kick was reaching its zenith in readiness for its deadly descent, with one last effort of sheer will, Alex sprang up into a squat and executed a perfect sweep on Chai Son's back leg. The leg gave way. The force of Chai Son's kick was still on the rise and its momentum sent him tumbling backwards, crashing down on the handrail of the balcony. Alex knew that a sweep was not enough to put Chai Son out of action. Still in great pain he staggered to his feet. He had no idea what his next move was going to be. All he knew was that if he were going to die, it would be standing up. He braced himself for another onslaught … but it didn't come.

It took him several seconds to fully comprehend what he was looking at. Chai Son had fallen backwards and broken through the handrail of the balcony. The full impact of his body weight had driven a rotten shard of a spindle clean through his neck. With each dying heartbeat, blood pumped from the wound several feet across the balcony. There was a look of pure shock in his eyes. Fighting to the last Chai Son reached up to his throat to try and snap himself free, but his hands couldn't make the journey. He grasped feebly at the air. Alex could hear his spluttered breathing. As well as bleeding out, he was choking on his own blood. It was a strangely still moment. Chai Son's eyes flickered, rolled back and glazed over; his arms fell limp. The whole scene seemed to unfold over an eternity, but in reality, had only taken seconds. Someone had to say something and as usual it was Viv. He called back into the house.

'Err Tan!'

Despite his reservations, Tan had expected Chai Son to finish this farang off like he had done every other challenger to his authority. He turned his attention from Nok and Gia to face the balcony. He saw the blood-soaked body of Chai Son lying dead, a shard of wood thrust through his throat. Next to the body stood Alex, still very much alive.

The gun he had trained on the girls slowly lowered to his side, his mouth hung open, his eyes wide. Then his jaw clenched, and his face hardened. He raised up his weapon bringing his other hand up to meet it in order to steady his trembling. He levelled the gun for a shot straight to Alex's head. It was clear Chai Son's bargain had died with him. Tan had no intention of honouring his master's wishes. Alex screwed up his eyes and prepared himself for the shot.

47

How many people have I killed?

Just as Tan had raised his gun to Alex, Viktor and Nikola ploughed into the room. In point of fact, it was only Viktor who had made it across the threshold. The rotten wood of the porch was no match for the additional charge of Nikola's weight and had given way on his thundering approach. The splintering wood caught his foot, he was trapped just outside.

Tan reacted instantly. He swung the gun from Alex to meet the new threat. Viktor opened fire on the first armed target he saw, but Tan was already ducking for cover. Viktor's shot narrowly missed him and passed through to the back of the house where it caught Archie's shoulder. Archie cried out in shock. Seeing that Viv had not recognised the immediate danger, he grabbed his arm and pulled him to the floor.

'Jesus Viv, get down!' he shouted.

Almost instantly Tan returned the fire. He hadn't had time to aim, and the shots were wide of Viktor, but Nikola, snared as he was, was not so lucky. Both rounds caught him in the stomach. He toppled backwards dropping his gun into the dirt. Viktor took not one second to acknowledge his fallen partner; he advanced into the room firing on Tan. Tan was able to fire three more shots, one lodged harmlessly in the wall, while one caught Viktor in the shin and the other glanced his hip. Viktor didn't even register the hits and his next four rounds clustered into Tan's head.

Outside, on the balcony, Viv was not going to be a passive observer in this fight. He dived for Chai Son's gun, which was still hung over the handrail, and started unloading into the room. It was nine rounds in rapid succession, a full clip. Six of them missed Viktor altogether and Viktor was still able to return fire. Viv heard two rounds whistle passed his ear and a third shattered the panelling next to his head. A shard of flying wood cut his cheek.

Although six of Viv's shots missed their target, the seventh didn't. It caught Viktor clean between the eyes. There was an abrupt end to the gunfire and Viktor crashed to the floor, the impact of his fall shook the little house to its foundations.

Smoke swirled languidly in the still air, lending a dream like quality to the horrific tableau. Beside the kitchen area Ritthirong lay dead from the blow to the back of the head administered by Viv. Taking up the entire centre of the room was the huge body of Viktor, with an ever-expanding halo of blood. Sprawled in a corner was Tan, crimson spatter on the wall behind him. Huddled in the opposite corner were the intertwined bodies of Nok and Gia. They'd dived for cover when the shooting had started. Nok had tried to cover her sister as best as she could. They clung to each other not daring to open their eyes. On the back-porch Archie lay flat on the ground where he had dropped, Viv crouched next to him checking his friend's injury. Alex had taken refuge in the only place available to him, behind the lifeless body of Chai Son. Viv slowly rose. His body was afire with adrenaline. He couldn't contain his excitement.

'Fuck, me, fuck me, that was intense, did you see the size of that fucker. Right between the eyes. I got him right between the fuckin' eyes. Archie did you see it.'

Like a child, Viv needed an audience to appreciate how clever he'd been. Archie rose unsteadily to his feet, clutching what he hoped was just a graze.

'Who the hell is that?' he said nodding towards the mass of Viktor.

'Who *was* that mate, how many people is that I've killed now?' said Viv still in his own world of questionable achievements.

Archie looked confused, Viv had badly hurt many people, but he had never, to his knowledge, actually killed anyone. He was sure that fundamentally Viv wasn't opposed to killing people, it was just that killing people was messy and on the whole bad for business.

'Err, one Vivian,' he replied.

If he had known Ritthirong's current condition he could have answered with a more accurate two.

'Well, that was fuckin' entertaining. I don't know about you, but the best night I've had for a long time,' said Viv nudging Archie in his recently shot shoulder. Archie sucked in air through his teeth. 'But I think it's about time we got out of here.'

With that he slung the backpack with the drugs and money over his shoulder and made for the door. Archie stopped him halfway.

'What about them?' he said gesturing in the direction of Alex, sheltering behind the body of Chai Son and the two girls huddled together in the corner.

Viv paused and shook his head.

'Nothing personal son,' he said swinging his gun towards Alex.

Just then there was a sound behind them. A huge shape filled the entire doorway blocking out any of the remaining twilight. At first, they thought it was Viktor, but his humungous body still lay on the floor. It was Nikola, he had been shot, but he was not down. He stood bolt upright glaring in at them. His face was impassive and ashen white. He clutched his hand to his belly and blood oozed between his fingers. Ignoring the two girls he advanced on Viv and Archie. Vivian raised his gun and pulled the trigger. There was no bang, merely several soft clicks, EMPTY!

Viv threw the gun. It hit Nikola square in the chest and bounced harmlessly off and clattered to the floor. Viv couldn't help thinking that it wasn't like this in the movies when a thrown a gun was a major distraction. As Nikola silently advanced, Viv and Archie backed away. There was something possessed about this man he emanated an inhuman aura. As Nikola stepped over the body of Viktor he bent and snapped the gun from his stiff fingers. It had always been hard to tell whether Nikola and Viktor really cared for each other, but caring or not, one thing was for sure, Nikola was going to make these men suffer just on principle.

Nikola raised his weapon, first it would be kneecaps and then he would go in with his hands. If Viv was going to go down, he was going to go down with venom in his mouth.

'Come on then, you fuckin' gorilla, what you fuckin' waitin' for?' he bellowed.

Archie was not as verbal as Viv, but there was no less courage and no less fight in him. He readied himself. This monster was at least twice his size. Archie may not have been able to win this fight, but he was determined to come the best second this man had ever seen.

407

Nikola took a moment to gather himself; loss of blood was starting to take its toll. He put out his hand to steady himself. Viv and Archie were undoubtedly hard men, but they were not trained fighters, Alex was. Instantly Alex sensed a moment of weakness. Charging between Viv and Archie, he launched himself at Nikola. He caught hold of Nikola's wrist, deflecting the line of the gun and simultaneously delivered several pinpoint punches to the underside of his arm. The blows were aimed at a pressure point that should have paralysed the whole of his arm. Unfortunately, Nikola's body did not comply with the pressure point chart. His arm remained as ridged as a girder, the gun still firmly in his grip. Alex needed a change of tactic. Turning his head, he sunk his broken, jagged teeth into Nikola's forearm and started to tear at the flesh. Nikola let out a low grunt, which was the closest he ever came to a cry of pain. Alex's move may not have been in the 'teach yourself martial arts manual', but it was effective.

Nikola dropped the weapon. It was now hand to hand combat.

Ripping his blood-soaked hand from his stomach Nikola grabbed Alex by the throat. Alex felt his steel fingers bite in, crushing his windpipe. He only had seconds before he either passed out or his neck snapped. Wildly he pounded his fist into Nikola's stomach. It was like hitting a brick wall, it had no effect on the giant. Alex tore at Nikola's tee-shirt, his hand sliding over his gore drenched abs. Frantically searching he found what he was looking for, two bullet holes. They were close together. Alex stabbed his fingers into wounds pushing them in as far as they would go.

Nikola dropped his grip instantly and doubled in pain. The big man staggered back, as he did, he stumbled over the body of Ritthirong and fell to the floor. Alex was on him in an instant, raining blows on his head like a piston. Nikola reached up and took hold of Alex's arm. Alex tried to wrench away, but Nikola was too strong. With one arm disabled, the punches he was able to deliver were not enough and he didn't have the weight or the strength to pin this colossus down. Nikola rolled on top of him. His huge bulk hammered the wind from Alex's lungs. Nikola's iron hand pinned Alex's arm to the floor. The other hand, dripping with blood, covered Alex's face. The fingers probed for his eyes. Alex's free arm struck out erratically, inflicting no damage at all upon the granite body of Nikola. Nikola's thumb pressed down on his eyelid. He was going to take this slowly. Alex felt an immense pressure building, orange flashes cut through his head. He could feel his eyeball being slowly pushed into his brain. Blindly, Alex's hand scrabbled around. By chance it came into contact with something hard and sharp. It was the boning knife, the same one Ritthirong had threatened him with and the very one Chai Son had thrown to the ground earlier.

He took hold of the handle, pulled it from the floorboards and thrust. It hit Nikola centre chest, cutting through his breastbone. Nikola sat bolt upright looking down at the hilt of the knife, the blade buried inside him. He gave Alex a curious look, a look that could have said, 'YOU did this?'

Alex gave the knife a twist and pulled it out. The blade had sunk deep into Nikola's heart. His dead bulk slumped forward.

48

A lovely cup of tea

Alex lay under the immense weight of Nikola. He could feel the last of the man's life blood pouring over his body, gathering in a sticky pool around him. His throat felt like it was on fire, and he fought for breath. With his last vestiges of strength, he wriggled out from under the enormous corpse, only to be met with the sight of Viv picking up Nikola's dropped weapon from the floor. Viv sat himself down on the corner of the table and looked at Alex with curiosity.

'That's the third time today you've surprised me son. You just saved my life,' he said.

'Your life wasn't my main priority,' Alex said with a hoarse rasp.

After staring death in the face so many times over the last forty-eight hours, he had reached the point where he no longer cared. If it was going to happen then let it happen now.

'None the less son, taking down that horror show,' Viv said waiving his gun at the lifeless body of Nikola, 'did me a big favour and …'

Viv's sentence trailed away as a middle-aged woman wandered into the room carrying a bag of rice. She stopped in the doorway looking confused, more than distressed, at the carnage before her. It was Mayuree, Ritthirong's wife, Nok's and Gia's mother. Viv couldn't believe that this day could get any more surreal.

'Fuck me, who's this?' addressing no one in particular, 'this place is getting busier than Clapham Junction.'

The tiny woman approached him with no fear and spoke in staccato English.

'Who, you? What you do in my home? You break many thing, this much mess need be tidy.'

It was obvious to Viv that she had a bit of a problem with reality. She didn't even acknowledge the five corpses. All she seemed to see was the mess. Viv had seen this sort of confused detachment before. In her later years, his mother had suffered from dementia. Viv had found the best way to deal with her condition was to play along in her world rather than to try to impose his own. It was a kindness to indulge rather than to contradict.

'Hello love, my name's Viv, sorry about the mess. We'll make sure it gets cleaned up,' he said with a remarkable softness.

'You make many mess in my lovely home.'

She continued pathetically placing cups back on the table and cushions on the chair.

Viv reached into the bag containing the money and the drugs and pulled out a large bundle of dollars. He beckoned the little woman over.

'Look darlin' this should cover for any cleaning bills,' he said placing the wad in her hand.

'This much money,' she said with wide eyes.

'That should get you some nice new things,' he gave her forearm a gentle squeeze. Then he called to Archie.

'Why don't you put the kettle on mate, make a nice cup of tea for this lovely lady while I finish business with our friend here.'

Archie couldn't believe how casual Viv and this unexpected woman were being about this whole bizarre situation. All he wanted to do was get as far away from this place as possible.

'Seriously Viv, you think there's time for a cup of tea?'

'Archie, there's no situation that can't be made better by a lovely cup of tea. Am I right?' he said looking for confirmation from Alex. Then he said more earnestly, 'Just make her something to drink Archie, sit her down out back. Keep her

413

out the away for a bit, I need to clean up in here. We'll be away in less than two minutes, I promise.'

Archie led Mayuree to the sleeping area at the back of the house and sat her on the bed. This was the only space that didn't have a body in it. He left her with a few gentle words then picked his way over the corpses to the tiny kitchen to make a hot drink.

Alex had heard the words "clean up" from Viv and had come to the conclusion that the woman had been removed as Viv didn't want a direct witness to the murder he was about to commit. Alex was now sitting on the floor in front of him. He cast his eyes around the room amongst all this devastation there was no sign of Nok and Gia.

'Where are the girls?' Alex's tone was almost demanding.

Viv smiled.

'Those girls have got a fuck more common sense than you son. The second you started to wrestle with lurch there they took the opportunity and fucked off.'

Alex was in no mood for talk. Death was imminent and he had found himself strangely calm.

'Look if you're going to shoot me then fucking do it!' he said with defiance.

After the rush of the fight a strange reflectiveness had descended on Viv.

414

'I'm not going to kill you son. Whether it was your intention or not, you saved my life and that is something I won't forget.'

He paused and rubbed his chin with the barrel of the gun.

'Can I ask you a personal question son?' he said examining Alex closely.

This was not something Alex was expecting and there didn't seem to be an awful lot of options for answering other than,

'Yes,'

'How do you feel?'

'Scared,'

It was the first word Alex blurted out, based on the fact that the last few days of his life had been spent in the scariest situations he could imagine.

'No, I don't think so,' said Viv shaking his head, 'you see I've spent most of my life putting the frighteners on people. I know fear son. I know what it looks like in people's eyes. I know how it makes them behave. You've heard of flight or fight, when people are scared, they either run away or stand and fight. In my experience fighters are rare. What I usually see is flight or nothing. People either run away or just stand there, shaking like a shitting dog, begging for mercy. Now people who fight usually feel something other than fear. You've just put up one spectacular fight son. Let me ask you again … How do you feel?'

Alex considered the question. In the past few days, he'd been in many frightening situations. It's true his heart had been pumping, his senses had been buzzing and his hands twitched. He had displayed a lot of the outward signs of being scared, but when he really thought about it, was this actual fear? There was only one other emotion that solicited all these responses that was not fear. Truth was, being on the very brink of death had never made Alex feel so alive. He paused and then answered honestly.

'Excited, I feel excited.'

Viv's smile stretched from ear to ear.

'Feels good, doesn't it?' he said, 'you remind me of how I was twenty-five years ago. These last few days chasing round this shithole and watching you has brought all it all back for me,' he said with almost gratitude in his voice at being able to vicariously live the past through the experiences of Alex. 'Most of what I do now is manage business, tell others what to do. Drink and get fat. But this is what I got into business for, that feeling, the feeling you have now,'

He paused, almost sad at the passing of time, then continued.

'Do you know what the art of management is son?'

Alex shook his head. Viv enlightened his ignorance.

'A good manager spots talent and surrounds themselves with it.'

'Is that right?' said Alex not quite knowing where the conversation was going.

'Yer, that's right, I read it in a book once. What do you do for a living son?'

'I'm a carpenter,' replied Alex.

'And how much do carpenters make each year?' Viv enquired further.

'I work in my father's business, I take about 20k a year.'

'20k a year … do you like it?'

Viv sounded like he was taking a genuine interest in him. Alex pondered on the question. Did he really like it? He liked working with wood, however, it had been, no pun intended, a career carved out for him by his father. It had always been understood that he would follow him into the business. Alex considered the path of his father's life, could he see himself doing the same thing in thirty years' time, becoming his father.

'It's a good skill,' Alex said diplomatically.

'A skill you sell for 20k a year. What if I were to tell you that I could pay you 20k a month for another skill you have, the one I've seen here tonight?'

Maybe it was the adrenalin fuelled rush of the moment, the madness that a hyped-up system brings, but the proposition didn't sound as crazy as it might in the cold light of day.

'Sounds interesting,' said Alex, not ready to make a commitment just yet.

'Ok then, we might have something to work with here,' said Viv 'let's just get some basics in place. If you're caught, I know who you are and where you live, so if you want to keep yourself and the people you love above ground, when me and him leave you never saw us, right!' Alex nodded his head. 'Secondly, you probably already gathered my name is Vivian, I live in Newcastle, you know where Newcastle is don't you son?'

'Newcastle upon Tyne?' Alex clarified.

'That's the one son. Now if I'm not mistaken all you have in the world right now is the clothes you stand in am I right?'

Alex nodded.

'Ok the border's that way somewhere,' said Viv gesturing vaguely into the distance, 'if you can turn up at my door in one month's time, I can guarantee you a job that will make you a very rich man and the feeling you have now, that feeling of life, that fuckin' buzz, will just be part of the working day. What do you say son?'

Viv held out his hand. Alex looked down at his own hand, smeared with the mingled blood of Chai Son and Nikola. Slowly he wiped it clean on his shirt, took hold of Viv's hand and shook it!

The beginning

About the author

Shaun lives in the Northeast of England with his partner Audrey, two lanky teenagers James and Archie, their two whippets Arthur and Spike and the most vicious cat in the world Sheldon (DO NOT STROKE!).

He is an avid traveller, and the far east is one of his favourite parts of the world. He peppers his writing with the intoxicating sights, sounds and smells of the vibrant streets of Thailand. A beautiful country with warm friendly people and a rich culture, but as with anywhere there are dark corners if you dare to look.

In his spare time, he likes to pay his gym membership so he can put in lots of effort for very little gain. He also likes to buy various musical instruments to abandon around the house when learning how to play them becomes too difficult.

Contact author on:

talk2shaunc@gmail.com

follow on twitter @shaunwcurry

Printed in Great Britain
by Amazon